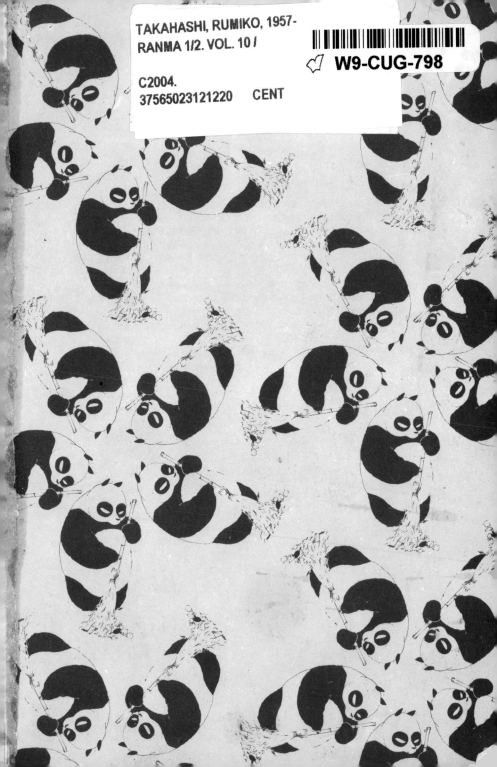

"**Rumiko Takahashi** doesn't miss a single farcical opportunity as every volume is crammed with raging hormones, romantic entanglements, gender-swapping, and martial-art silliness. Boy changes to girl, man to panda, girl to cat -- and everybody's kung fu fighting."

Anodyne Magazine

"If you've never watched any of the videos, or read the comic books they are based on, you're missing out on some of the funniest, wackiest, and most character-driven cartoons around."

Tony Isabella, comics critic

"**Ranma 1/2** is a must for anyone who likes a wicked sense of humor."

Gamers' Republic

OTHER TITLES BY RUMIKO TAKAHASHI

RANMA 1/2
MAISON IKKOKU
LUM*URUSEI YATSURA
INU-YASHA
RUMIC WORLD TRILOGY
RUMIC THEATER
ONE-POUND GOSPEL
MERMAID SAGA

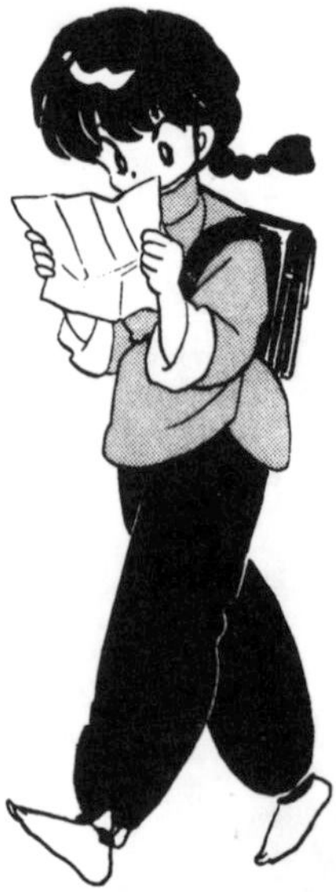

VIZ GRAPHIC NOVEL
RANMA 1/2™

10

This volume contains
RANMA 1/2 PART SIX #1 through #6 (first half) in their entirety.

Story & Art by Rumiko Takahashi

English Adaptation by Gerard Jones & Toshifumi Yoshida

*

Touch-Up Art & Lettering/Wayne Truman
Cover Design/Hidemi Sahara
Editor/Trish Ledoux
Managing Editor/Annette Roman

*

V.P. of Editorial/Hyoe Narita
V.P. of Sales & Marketing/Rick Bauer
Publisher/Seiji Horibuchi

*

First published by Shogakukan, Inc. in Japan

*

Printed in Canada
*

Published by Viz Communications, Inc.
P.O. Box 77010
San Francisco, CA 94107

*

10 9 8 7 6
Fifth printing, February 2002
Sixth printing, November 2002

VIZ GRAPHIC NOVEL

RANMA 1/2™

STORY & ART BY
RUMIKO TAKAHASHI

CONTENTS

PART 1
EMBRACEABLE YOU

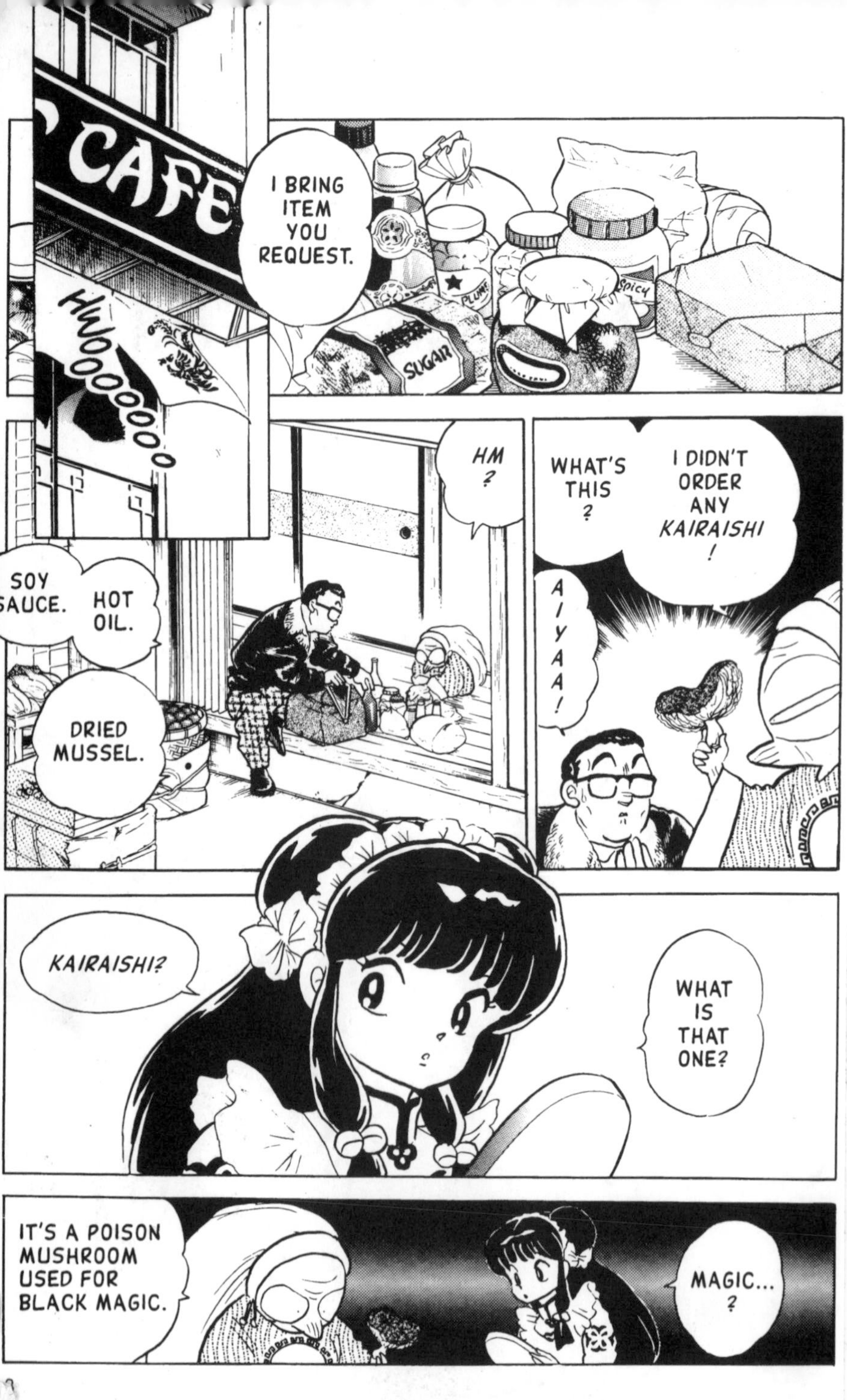
CAFE
HWOOOOOOOOO
I BRING ITEM YOU REQUEST.
PLUM
SPICY
SUGAR
SOY SAUCE.
HOT OIL.
DRIED MUSSEL.
HM?
WHAT'S THIS?
I DIDN'T ORDER ANY *KAIRAISHI*!
AIYAA!
KAIRAISHI?
WHAT IS THAT ONE?
IT'S A POISON MUSHROOM USED FOR BLACK MAGIC.
MAGIC...?

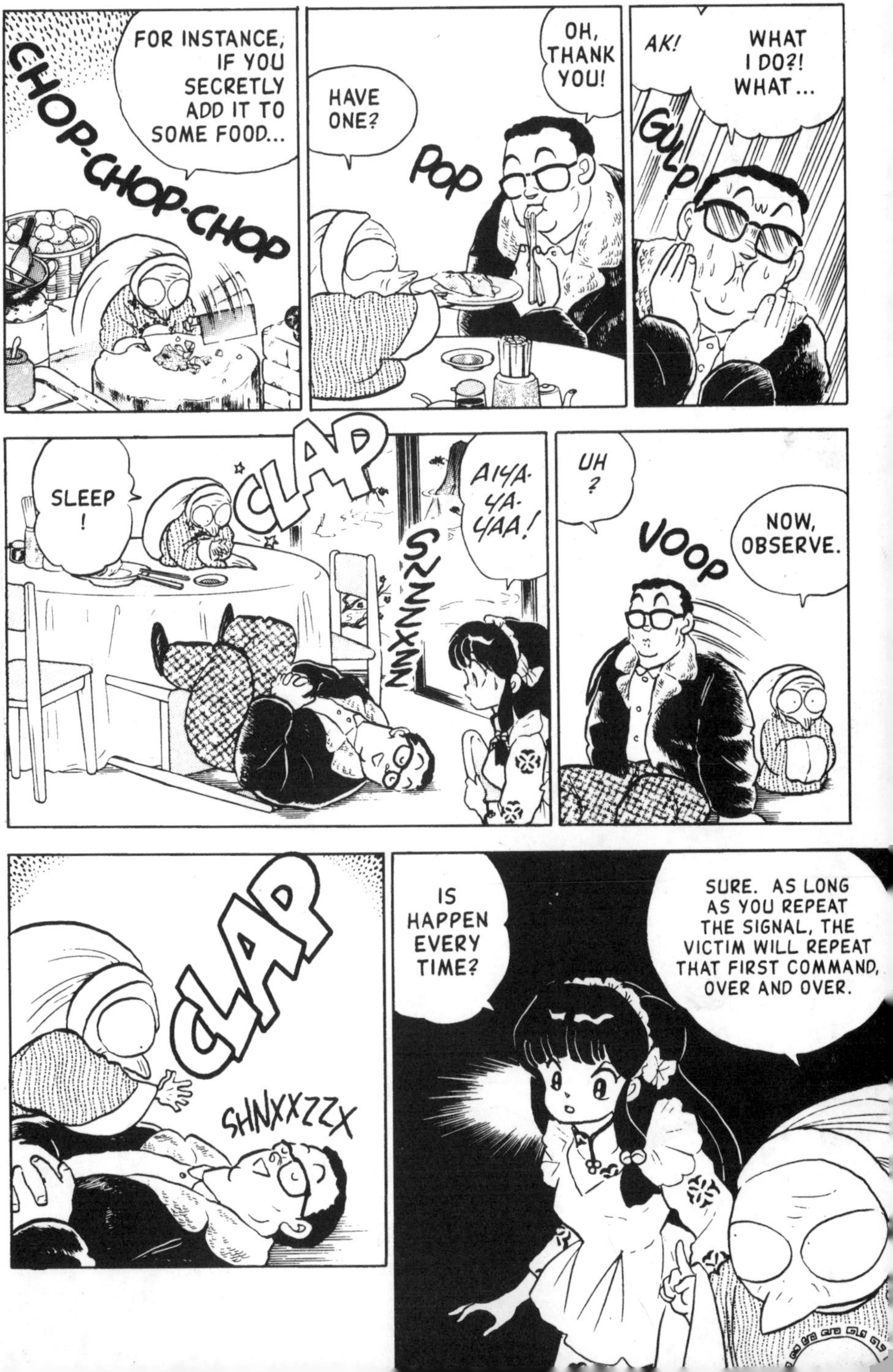
FOR INSTANCE, IF YOU SECRETLY ADD IT TO SOME FOOD...
CHOP-CHOP-CHOP-CHOP
HAVE ONE?
OH, THANK YOU!
POP
AK!
WHAT I DO?! WHAT...
GULP
SLEEP !
CLAP
SNZZZXXX
AIYA-YA-YAA!
UH ?
VOOP
NOW, OBSERVE.
CLAP
SHNXXZZX
IS HAPPEN EVERY TIME?
SURE. AS LONG AS YOU REPEAT THE SIGNAL, THE VICTIM WILL REPEAT THAT FIRST COMMAND, OVER AND OVER.

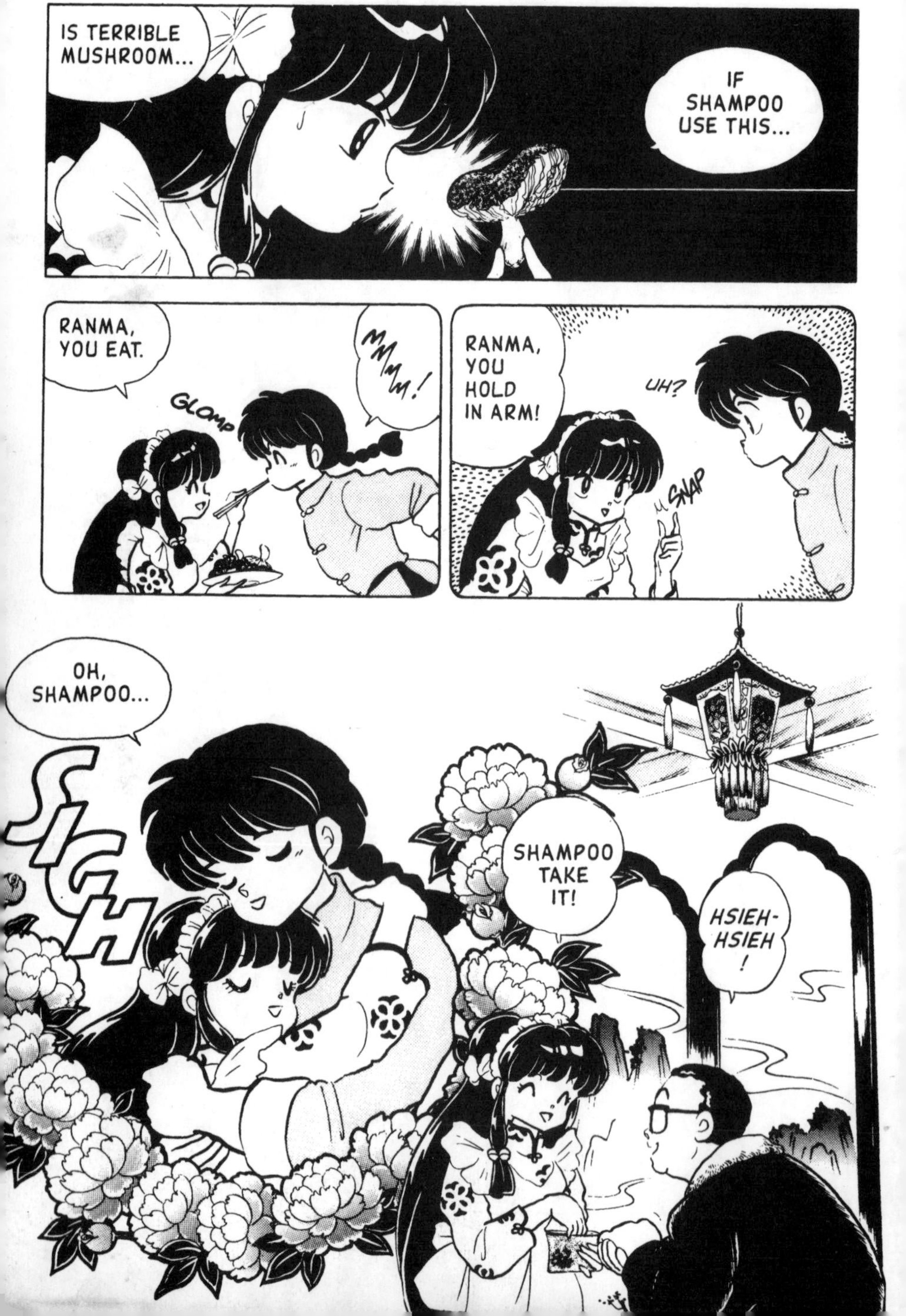
IS TERRIBLE MUSHROOM...
IF SHAMPOO USE THIS...
RANMA, YOU EAT.
GLOMP
MMMM!
RANMA, YOU HOLD IN ARM!
UH?
SNAP
OH, SHAMPOO...
SIGH
SHAMPOO TAKE IT!
HSIEH-HSIEH!

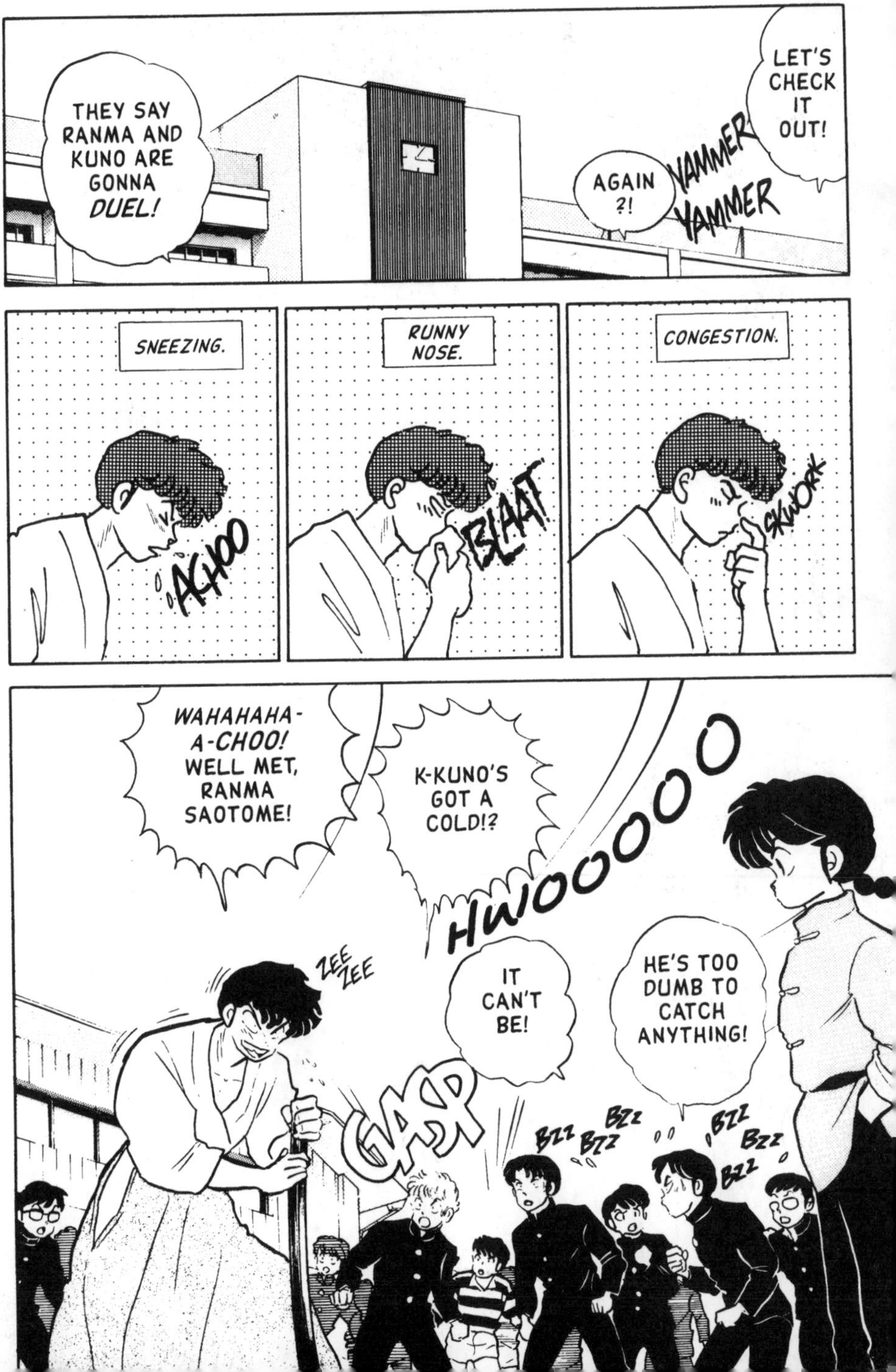
THEY SAY RANMA AND KUNO ARE GONNA DUEL!
AGAIN ?!
YAMMER YAMMER
LET'S CHECK IT OUT!
SNEEZING.
ACHOO
RUNNY NOSE.
BLAAT
CONGESTION.
SKWORK
WAHAHAHA-A-CHOO! WELL MET, RANMA SAOTOME!
K-KUNO'S GOT A COLD!?
HWOOOOOO
ZEE ZEE
GASP
IT CAN'T BE!
HE'S TOO DUMB TO CATCH ANYTHING!
BZZ BZZ BZZ
BZZ BZZ BZZ

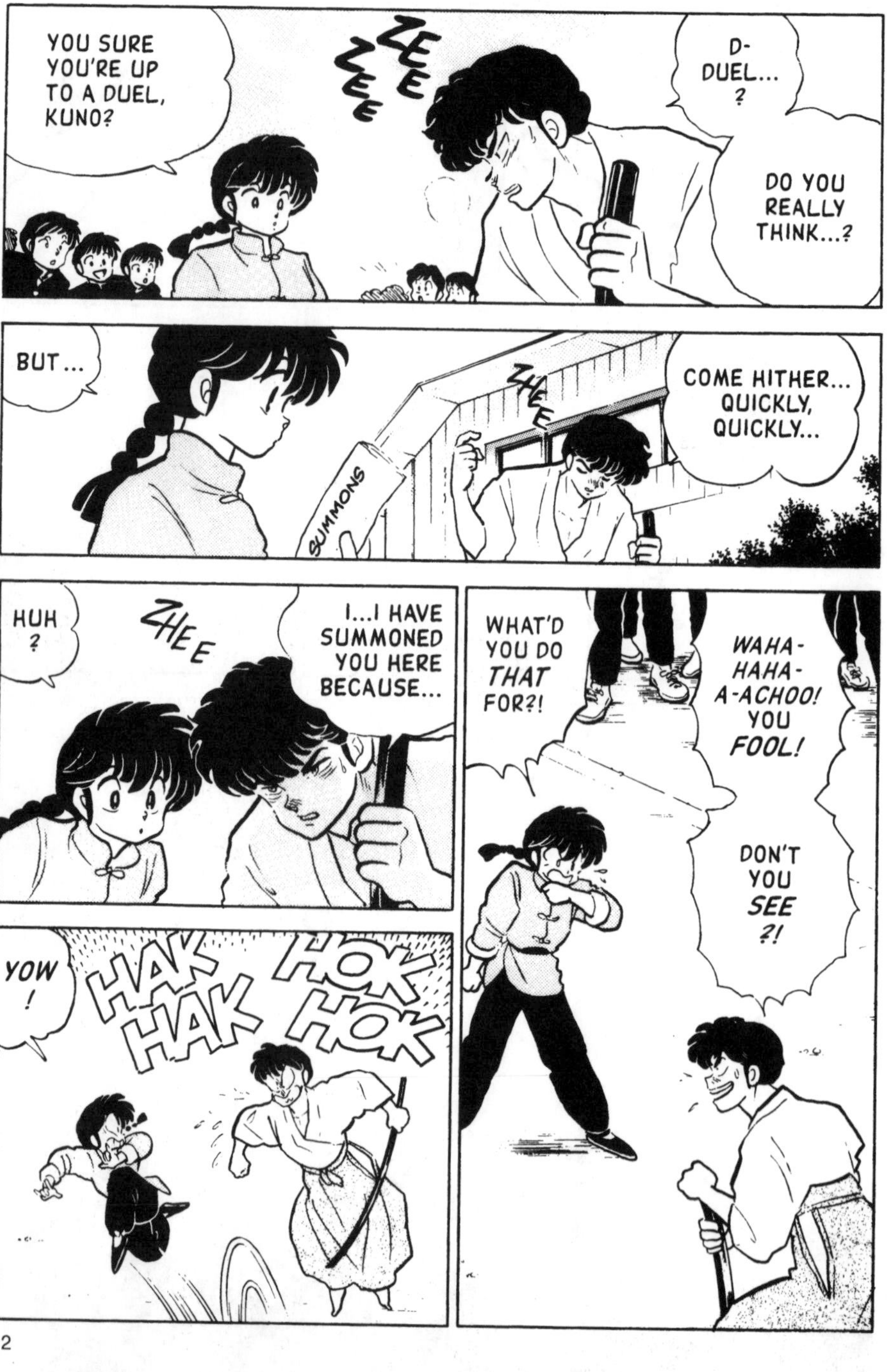
YOU SURE YOU'RE UP TO A DUEL, KUNO?
ZE ZE ZE ZE
D-DUEL...?
DO YOU REALLY THINK...?
BUT...
ZHEE
SUMMONS
COME HITHER... QUICKLY, QUICKLY...
HUH?
ZHEE
I...I HAVE SUMMONED YOU HERE BECAUSE...
YOW!
HAK HOK HAK HOK
WHAT'D YOU DO THAT FOR?!
WAHA-HAHA-A-ACHOO! YOU FOOL!
DON'T YOU SEE?!

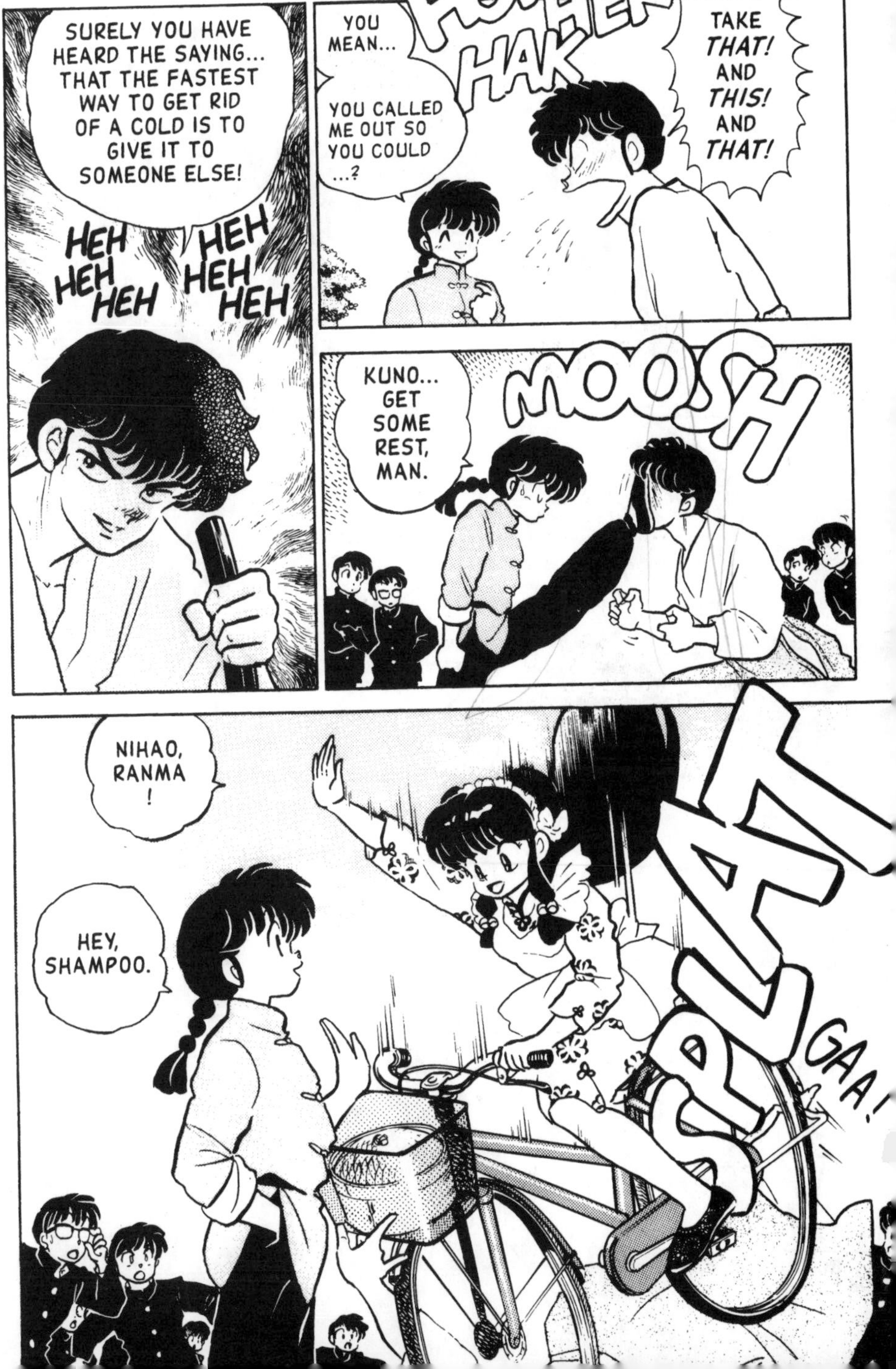
SURELY YOU HAVE HEARD THE SAYING... THAT THE FASTEST WAY TO GET RID OF A COLD IS TO GIVE IT TO SOMEONE ELSE!
HEH HEH HEH
HEH HEH HEH
YOU MEAN...
HOK HEK HAK
YOU CALLED ME OUT SO YOU COULD ...?
TAKE *THAT!* AND *THIS!* AND *THAT!*
KUNO... GET SOME REST, MAN.
MOOSH
NIHAO, RANMA!
HEY, SHAMPOO.
SPLAT
GAA!

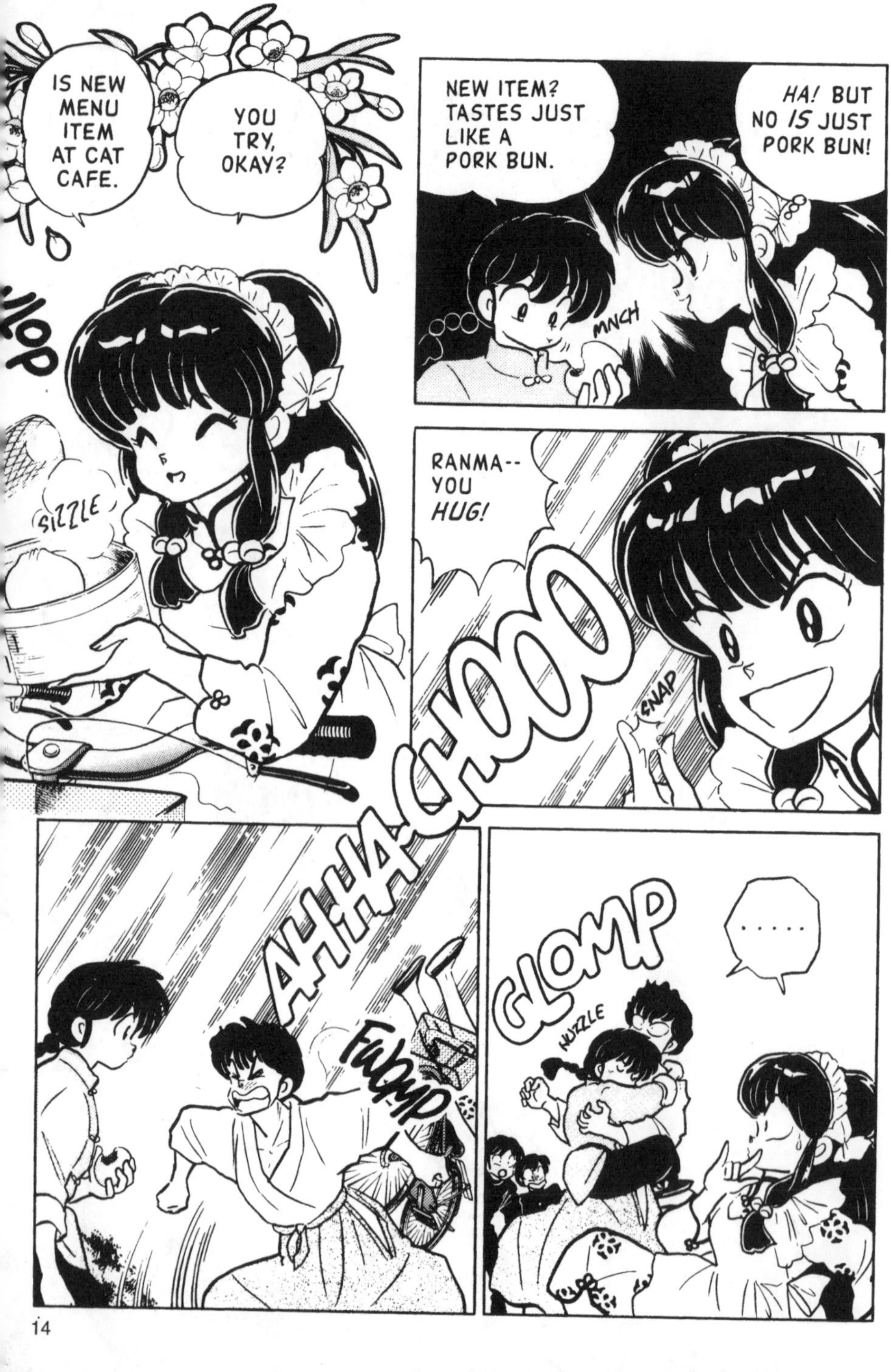
IS NEW MENU ITEM AT CAT CAFE.
YOU TRY, OKAY?
FLOP
SIZZLE
NEW ITEM? TASTES JUST LIKE A PORK BUN.
MNCH
HA! BUT NO IS JUST PORK BUN!
RANMA-- YOU HUG!
SNAP
AHHACHOOO
FWOMP
GLOMP
NUZZLE
......

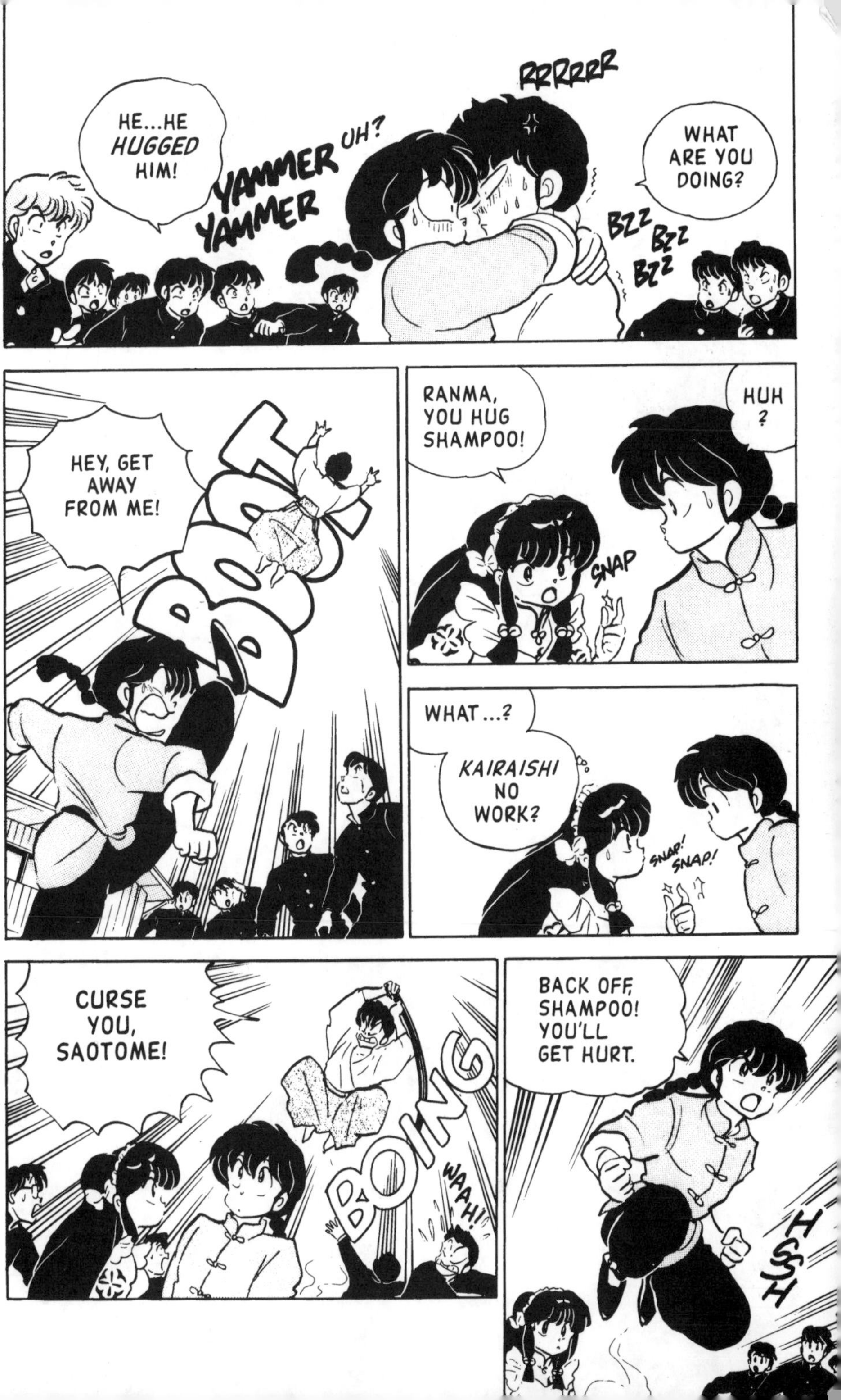
HE...HE HUGGED HIM!
YAMMER YAMMER
UH?
RRRRRR
WHAT ARE YOU DOING?
BZZ BZZ BZZ
HEY, GET AWAY FROM ME!
BOOT
RANMA, YOU HUG SHAMPOO!
HUH ?
SNAP
WHAT ...?
KAIRAISHI NO WORK?
SNAP! SNAP!
CURSE YOU, SAOTOME!
BOING
WAAAH!
BACK OFF, SHAMPOO! YOU'LL GET HURT.
HSSH

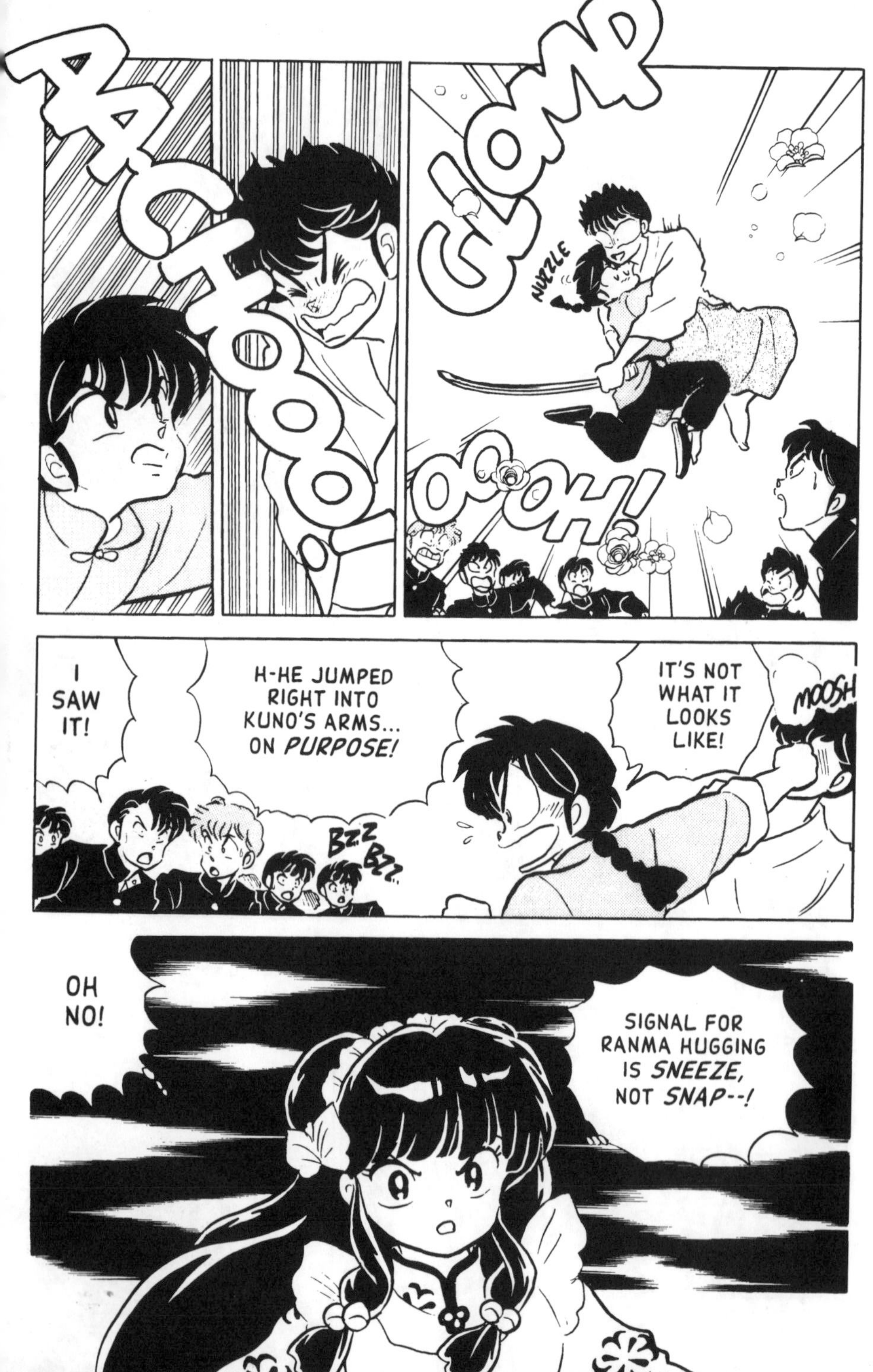
AACHOOO!
CLOMP
NUZZLE
OOOH!
I SAW IT!
H-HE JUMPED RIGHT INTO KUNO'S ARMS... ON *PURPOSE!*
BZZ BZZ
IT'S NOT WHAT IT LOOKS LIKE!
MOOSH
OH NO!
SIGNAL FOR RANMA HUGGING IS *SNEEZE,* NOT *SNAP*--!

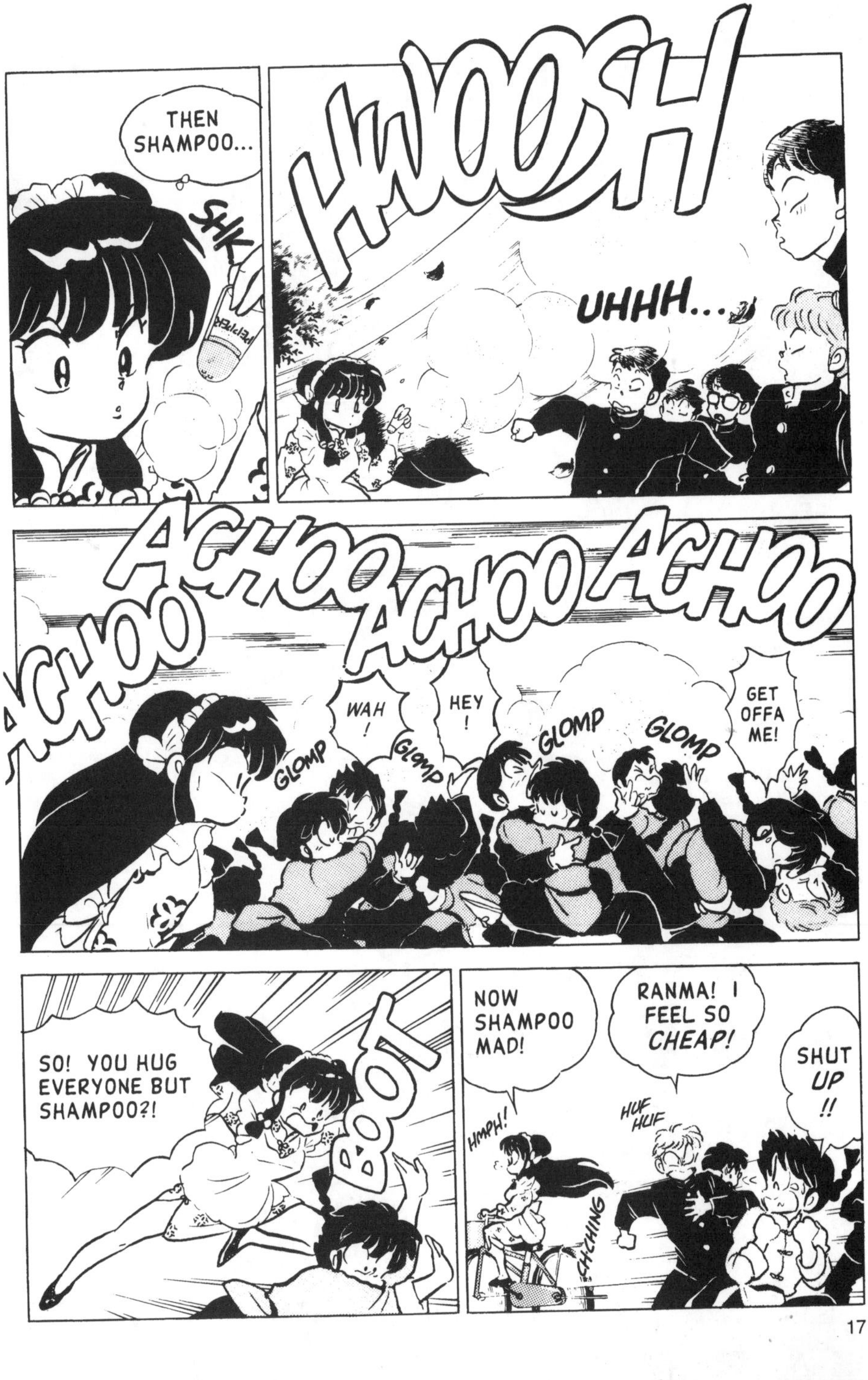
THEN SHAMPOO...
SHK
PEPPER
HWOOSH
UHHH...
ACHOO ACHOO ACHOO ACHOO
WAH!
HEY!
GET OFFA ME!
GLOMP
GLOMP
GLOMP
GLOMP
SO! YOU HUG EVERYONE BUT SHAMPOO?!
BOOT
NOW SHAMPOO MAD!
RANMA! I FEEL SO CHEAP!
SHUT UP!!
HMPH!
HUF HUF
CH-CHING

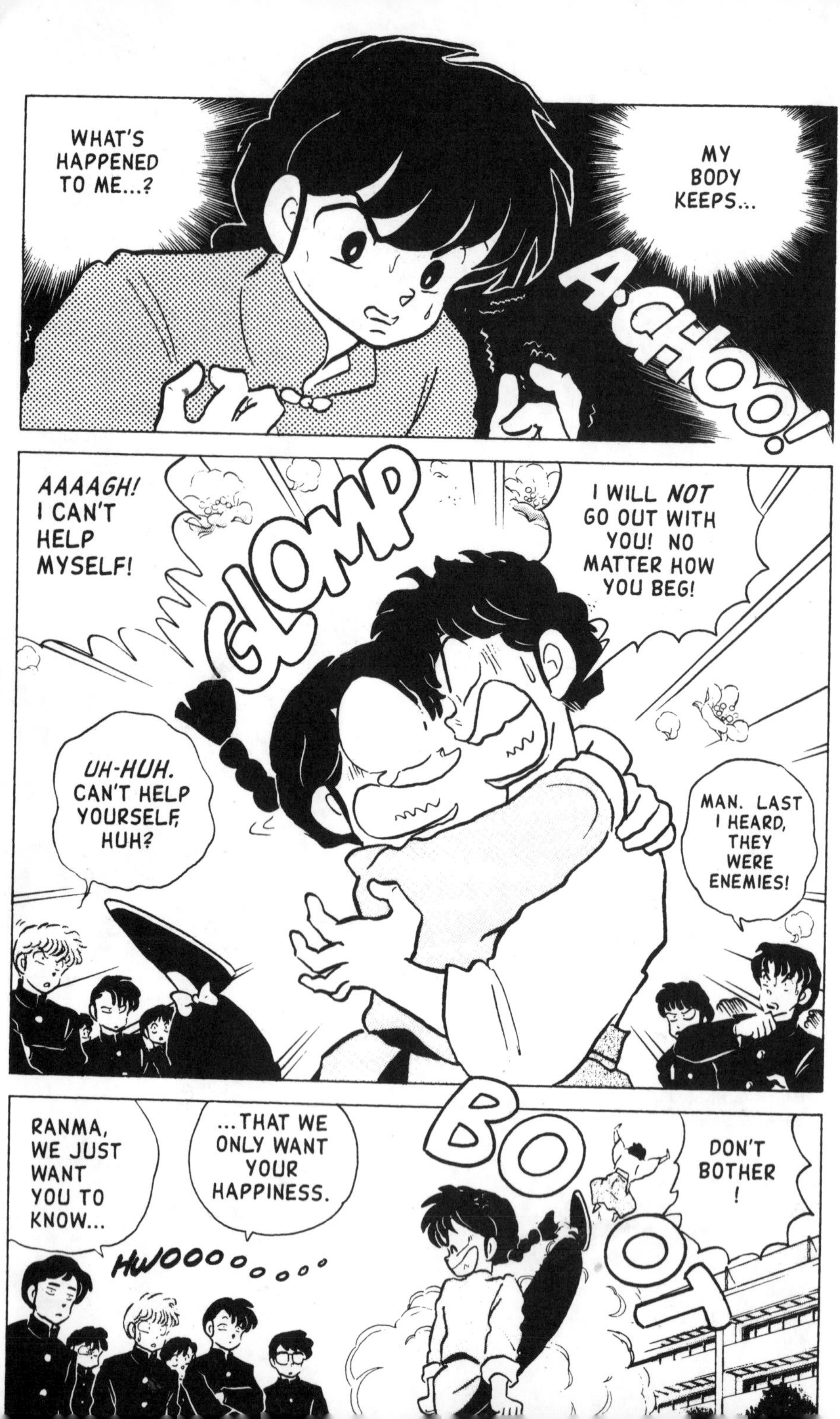
WHAT'S HAPPENED TO ME...?
MY BODY KEEPS...
A-CHOO!
AAAAGH! I CAN'T HELP MYSELF!
CLOMP
I WILL *NOT* GO OUT WITH YOU! NO MATTER HOW YOU BEG!
UH-HUH. CAN'T HELP YOURSELF, HUH?
MAN. LAST I HEARD, THEY WERE ENEMIES!
RANMA, WE JUST WANT YOU TO KNOW...
...THAT WE ONLY WANT YOUR HAPPINESS.
BOOT
DON'T BOTHER!
HWOOOOOOOO

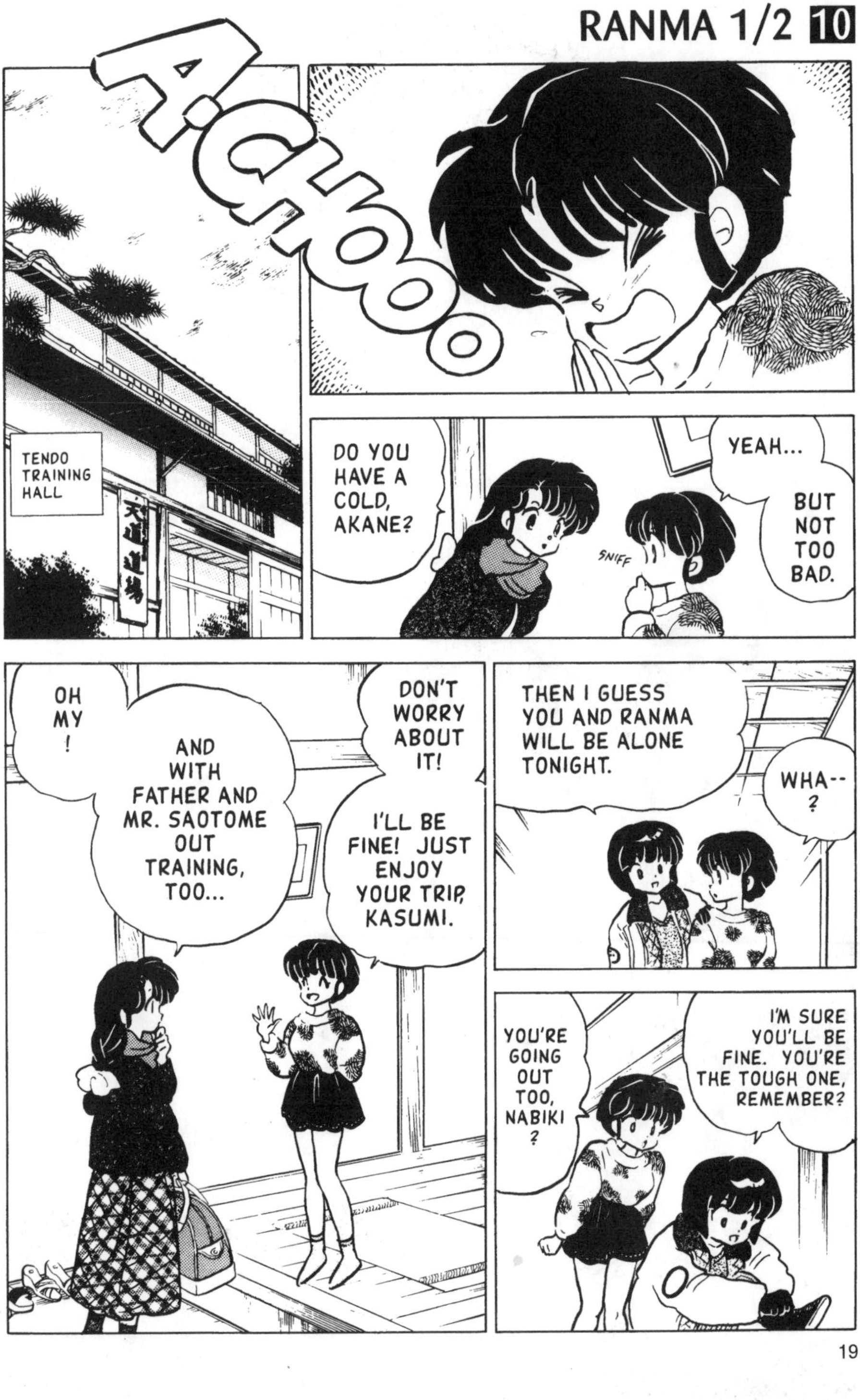
TENDO TRAINING HALL
ACHOOO
DO YOU HAVE A COLD, AKANE?
YEAH...
BUT NOT TOO BAD.
SNIFF
OH MY!
AND WITH FATHER AND MR. SAOTOME OUT TRAINING, TOO...
DON'T WORRY ABOUT IT!
I'LL BE FINE! JUST ENJOY YOUR TRIP, KASUMI.
THEN I GUESS YOU AND RANMA WILL BE ALONE TONIGHT.
WHA--?
YOU'RE GOING OUT TOO, NABIKI?
I'M SURE YOU'LL BE FINE. YOU'RE THE TOUGH ONE, REMEMBER?

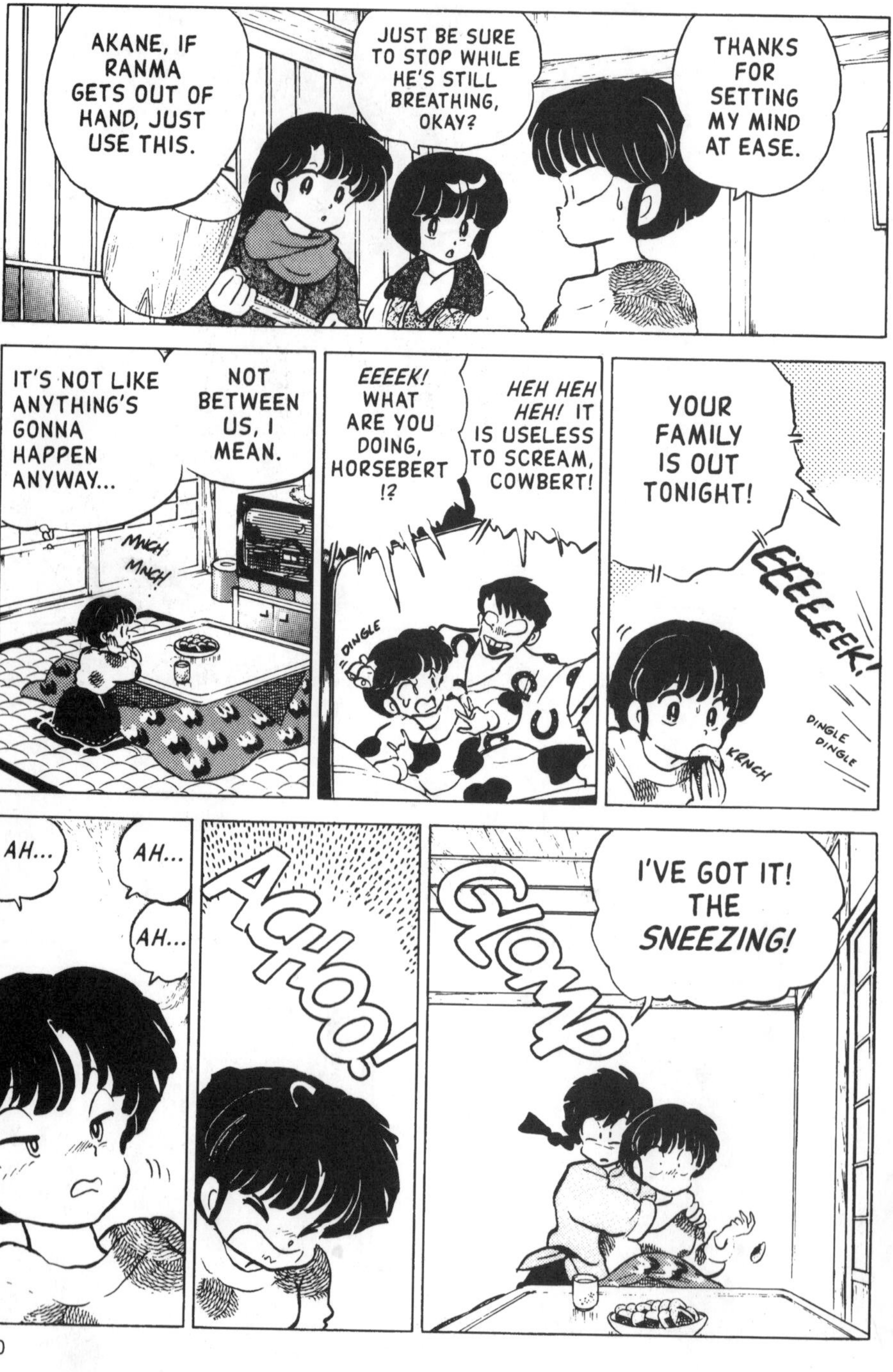

AKANE, IF RANMA GETS OUT OF HAND, JUST USE THIS.
JUST BE SURE TO STOP WHILE HE'S STILL BREATHING, OKAY?
THANKS FOR SETTING MY MIND AT EASE.
IT'S NOT LIKE ANYTHING'S GONNA HAPPEN ANYWAY...
NOT BETWEEN US, I MEAN.
MNCH MNCH
EEEEK! WHAT ARE YOU DOING, HORSEBERT !?
HEH HEH HEH! IT IS USELESS TO SCREAM, COWBERT!
DINGLE
YOUR FAMILY IS OUT TONIGHT!
EEEEEEK!
KRNCH
DINGLE DINGLE
AH...
AH...
AH...
ACHOO!
GLOMP
I'VE GOT IT! THE SNEEZING!

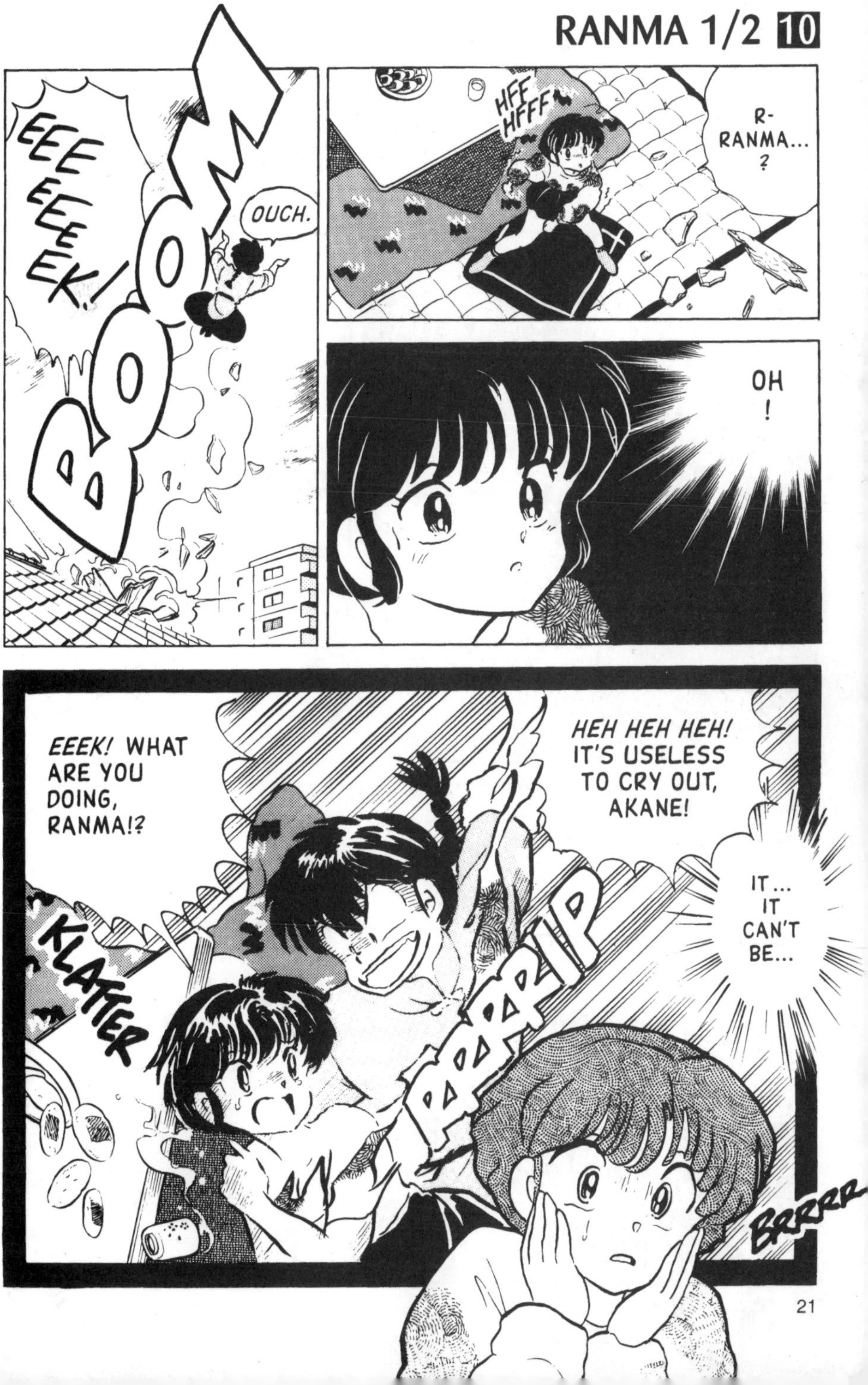
EEEEEEEEK!
BOOM
OUCH.
HFF HFFF
R- RANMA... ?
OH !
EEEK! WHAT ARE YOU DOING, RANMA!?
HEH HEH HEH! IT'S USELESS TO CRY OUT, AKANE!
KLATTER
RRRRRIP
IT... IT CAN'T BE...
BRRRR

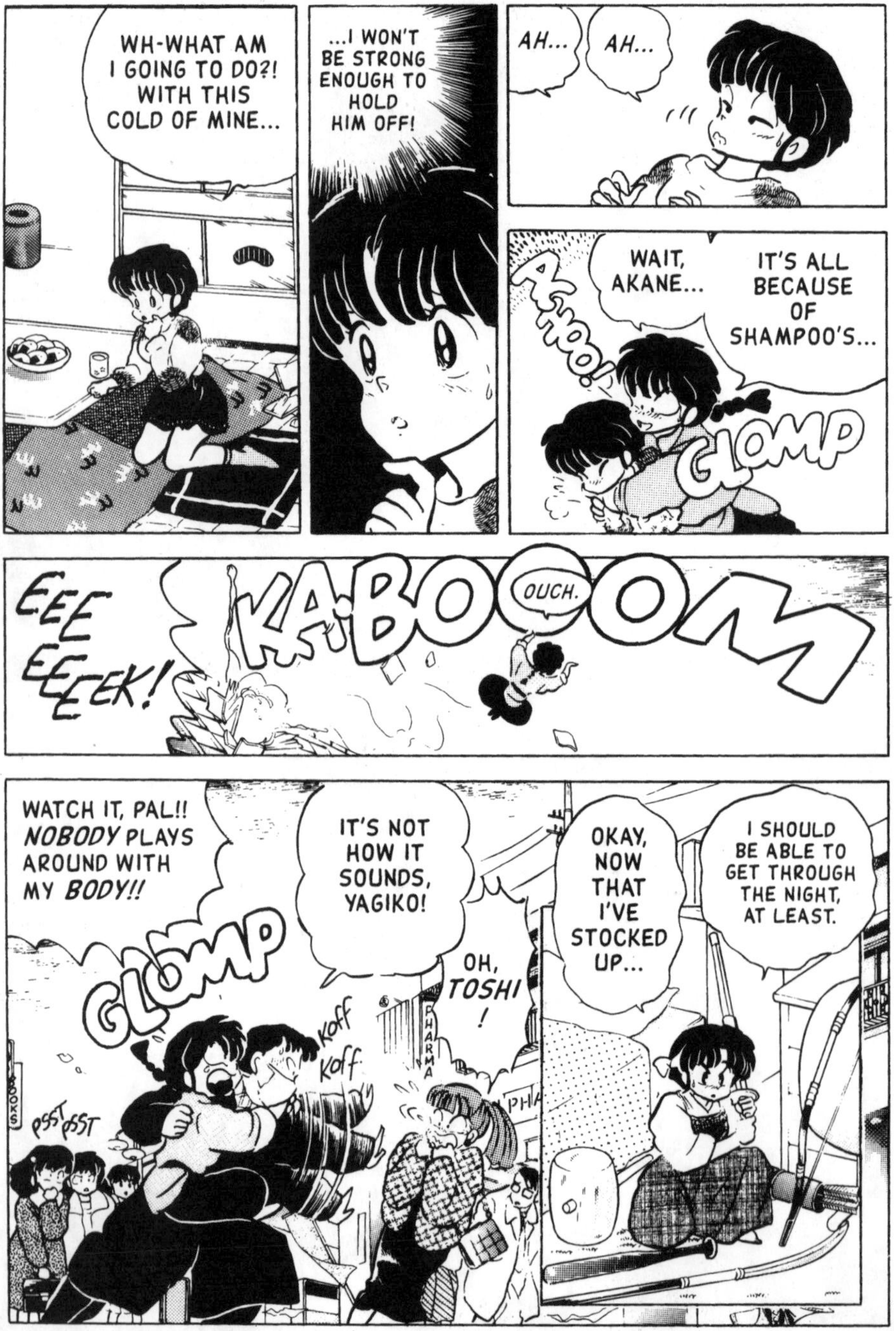
WH-WHAT AM I GOING TO DO?! WITH THIS COLD OF MINE...
...I WON'T BE STRONG ENOUGH TO HOLD HIM OFF!
AH...
AH...
WAIT, AKANE...
IT'S ALL BECAUSE OF SHAMPOO'S...
A-CHOO!
GLOMP
EEEEEEEK!
KA-BOOOOM
OUCH.
WATCH IT, PAL!! NOBODY PLAYS AROUND WITH MY BODY!!
GLOMP
IT'S NOT HOW IT SOUNDS, YAGIKO!
KOFF KOFF
OH, TOSHI!
PSST PSST
BOOKS
PHARMA
OKAY, NOW THAT I'VE STOCKED UP...
I SHOULD BE ABLE TO GET THROUGH THE NIGHT, AT LEAST.

PART 2
HOLD ME CLOSE

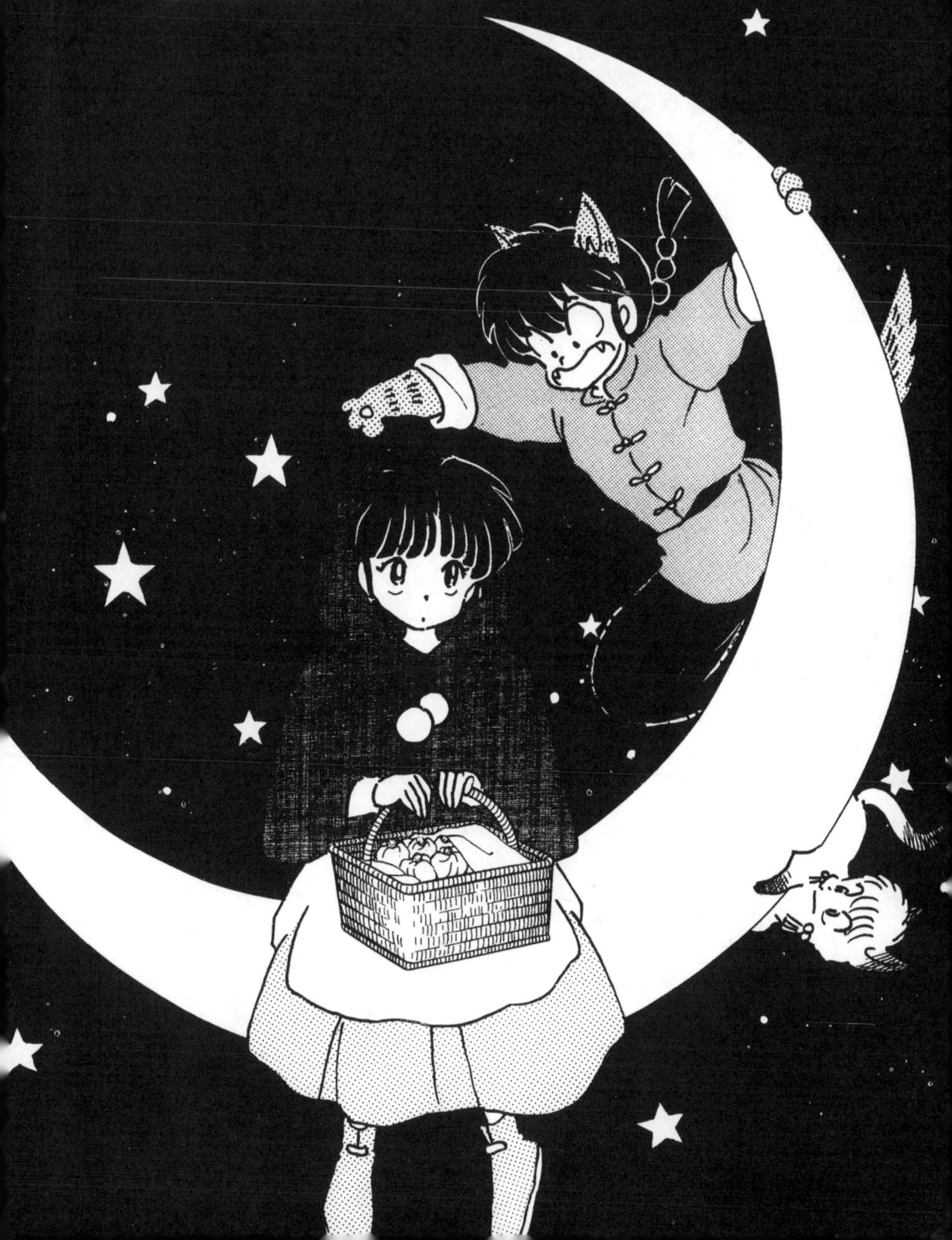

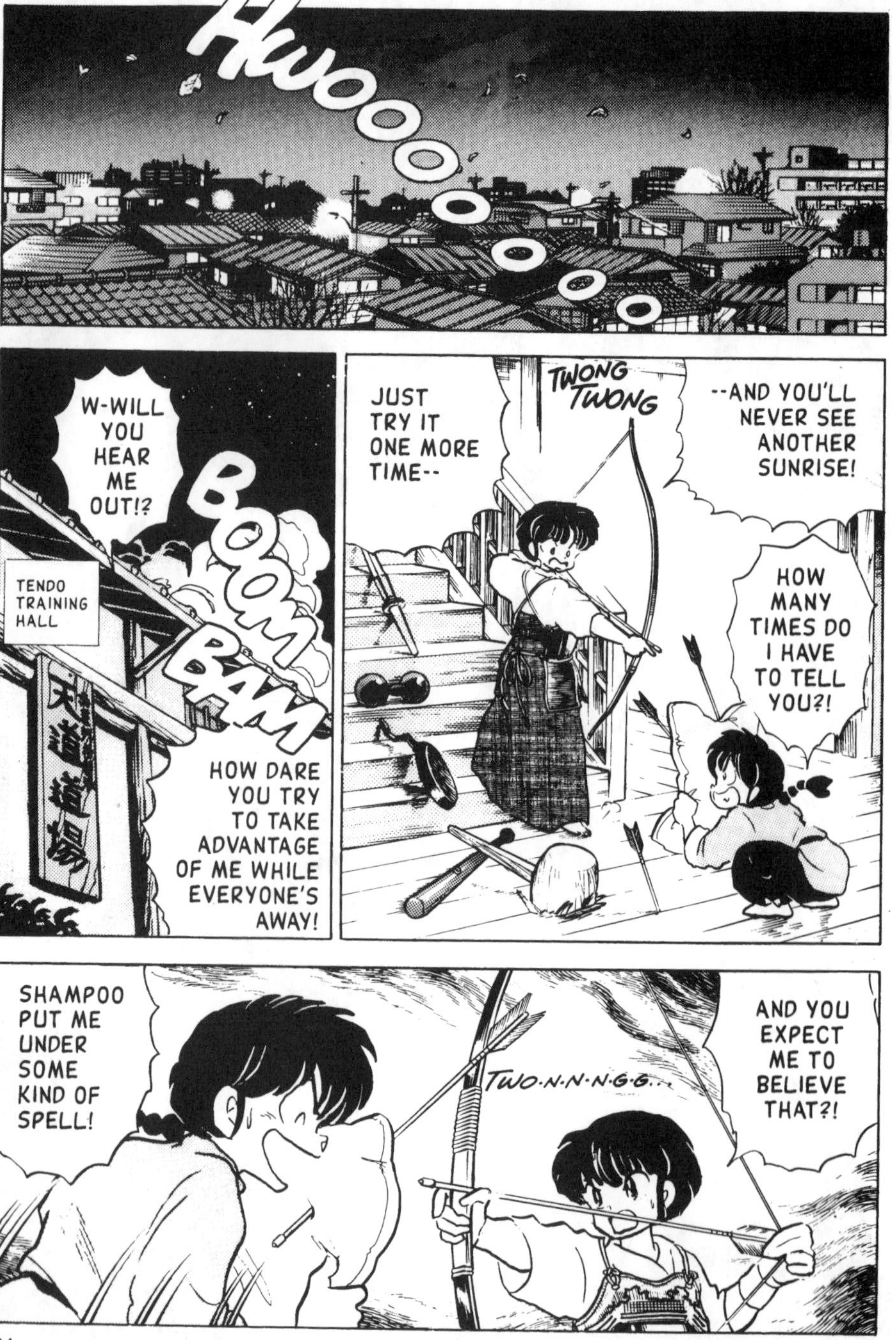
HWOOOOOOOOO
W-WILL YOU HEAR ME OUT!?
BOOM BOOM BAM
TENDO TRAINING HALL
天道道場
HOW DARE YOU TRY TO TAKE ADVANTAGE OF ME WHILE EVERYONE'S AWAY!
JUST TRY IT ONE MORE TIME--
TWONG TWONG
--AND YOU'LL NEVER SEE ANOTHER SUNRISE!
HOW MANY TIMES DO I HAVE TO TELL YOU?!
SHAMPOO PUT ME UNDER SOME KIND OF SPELL!
TWO·N·N·N·G·G...
AND YOU EXPECT ME TO BELIEVE THAT?!

AH... AH...

NO! DON'T! IF YOU SNEEZE...

ACHOO

PING

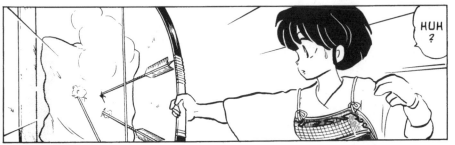

HUH?

IT MUST BE MY LUCKY DAY...

OF ALL THE UNCUTENESS IN THE WORLD, WHY DO *I* HAVE TO END UP HUGGING *YOU*!?

EEEEEEEEK!

GLOMP

NUZZLE

SO, YOU NOT ONLY ATTACK ME...

SIZZLE

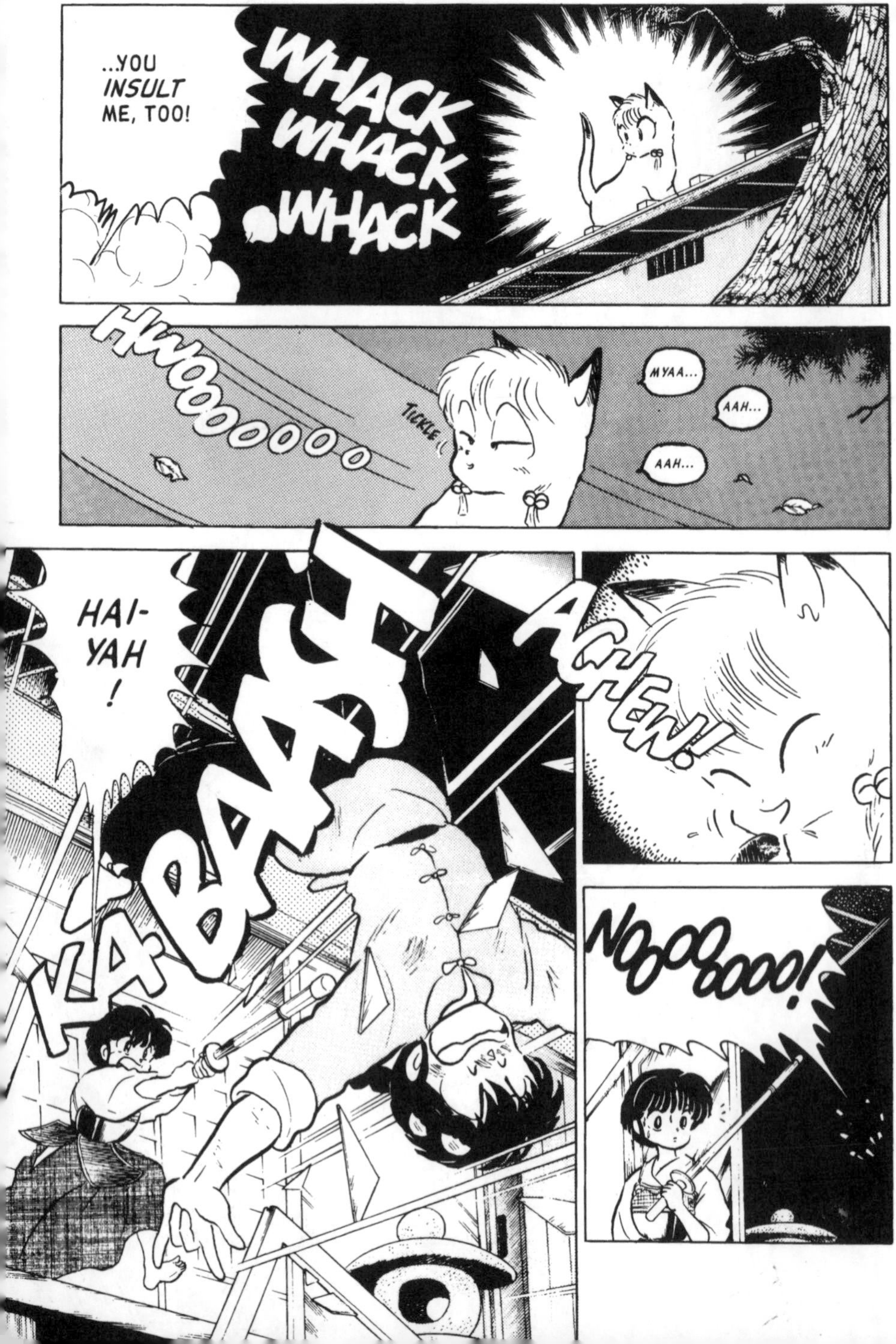
...YOU INSULT ME, TOO!
WHACK WHACK WHACK
HWOOOOOOOOO
TICKLE
MYAA...
AAH...
AAH...
HAI-YAH!
KABAAH
ACHEW!
NOOOOOOOO!

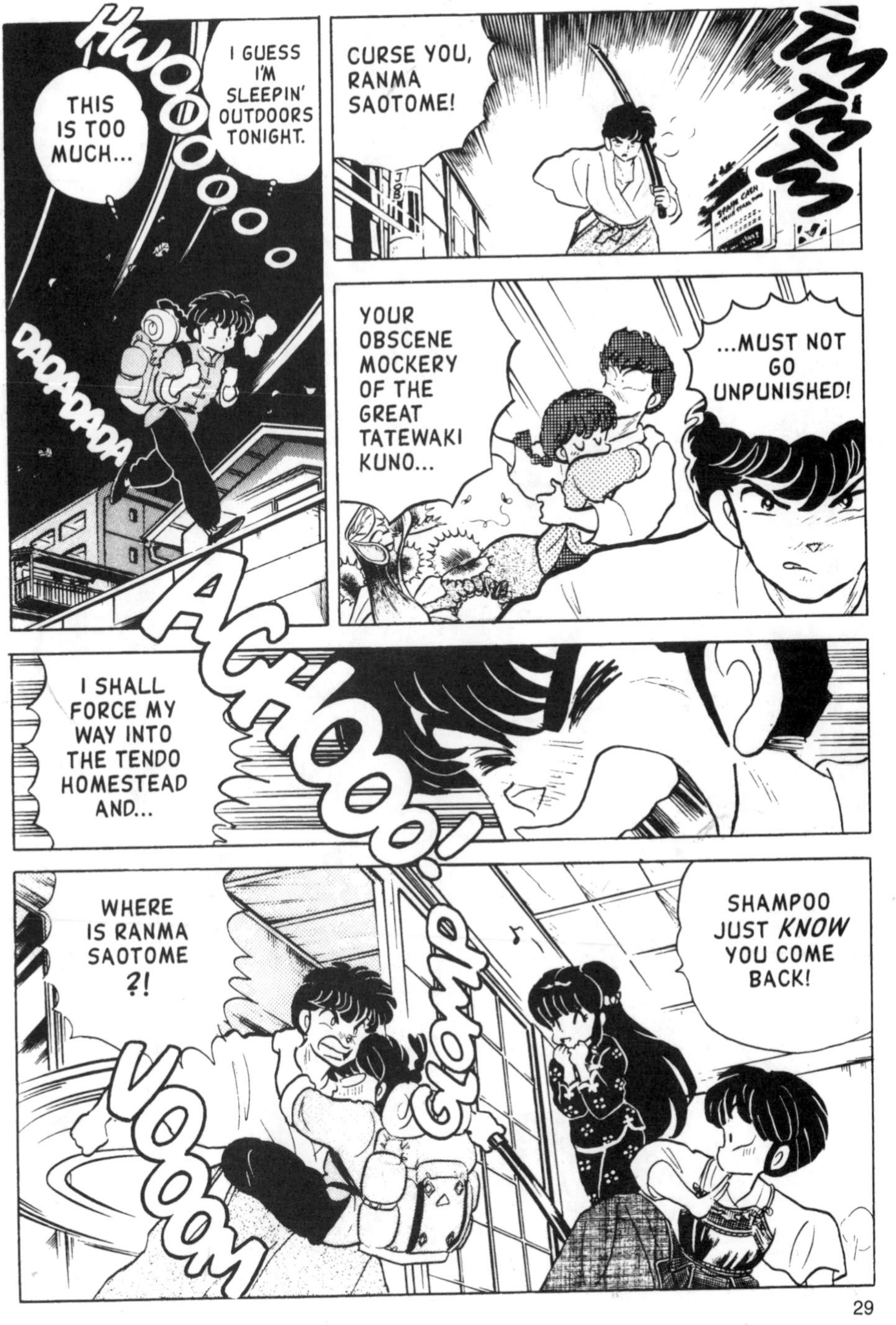
HWOOOOOOOOO
THIS IS TOO MUCH...
I GUESS I'M SLEEPIN' OUTDOORS TONIGHT.
DADADADADA
CURSE YOU, RANMA SAOTOME!
TM TM TM
YOUR OBSCENE MOCKERY OF THE GREAT TATEWAKI KUNO...
...MUST NOT GO UNPUNISHED!
I SHALL FORCE MY WAY INTO THE TENDO HOMESTEAD AND...
ACHOOO!
WHERE IS RANMA SAOTOME ?!
GLOMP
VOOOM
SHAMPOO JUST *KNOW* YOU COME BACK!

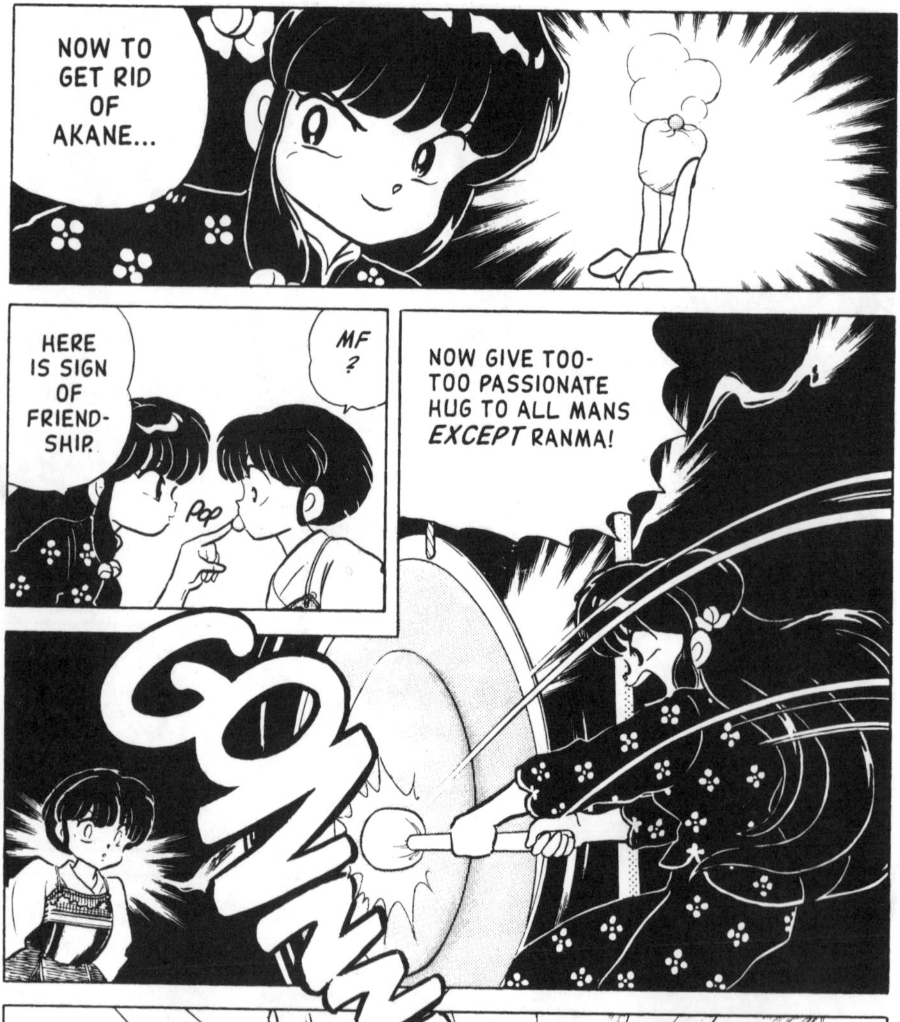
NOW TO GET RID OF AKANE...
HERE IS SIGN OF FRIEND-SHIP.
POP
MF?
NOW GIVE TOO-TOO PASSIONATE HUG TO ALL MANS *EXCEPT* RANMA!
GONNNNNNNNNG
NN GWAA!
KRAK KRAK KRAK
SQUISH
FEH.

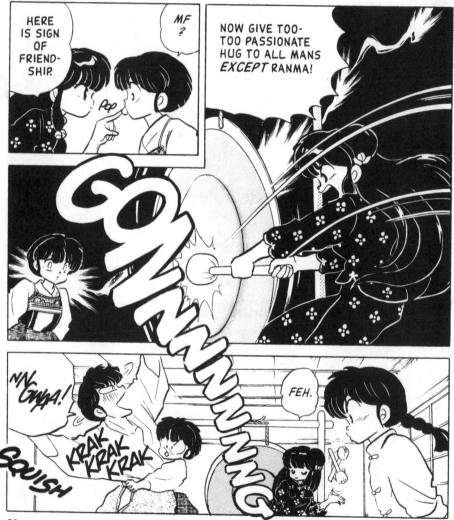

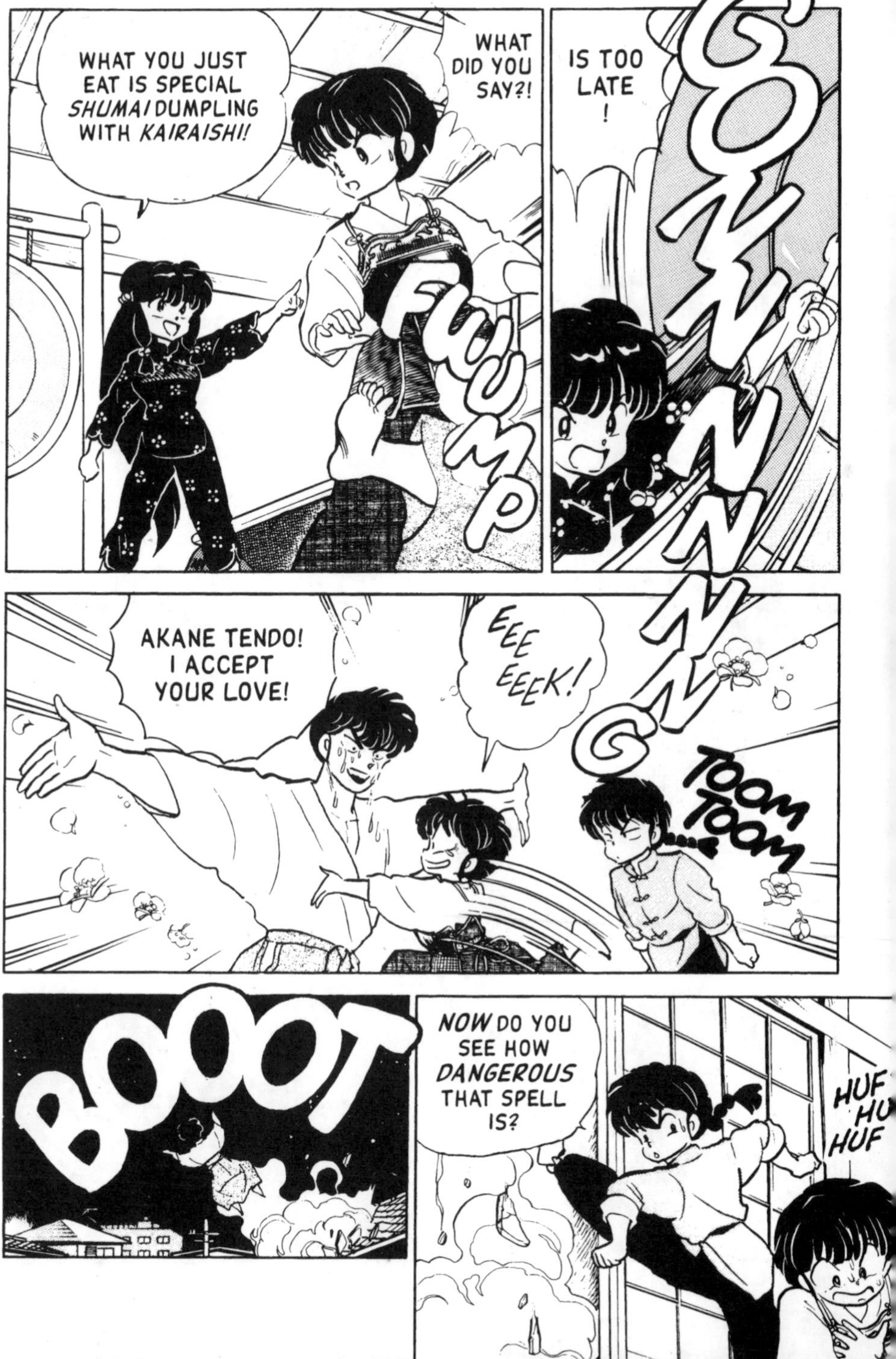
WHAT YOU JUST EAT IS SPECIAL *SHUMAI* DUMPLING WITH *KAIRAISHI*!!
WHAT DID YOU SAY?!
FUUUMP
IS TOO LATE !
GONNNNNG
AKANE TENDO! I ACCEPT YOUR LOVE!
EEEEEEK!
TOOM TOOM
BOOOT
NOW DO YOU SEE HOW *DANGEROUS* THAT SPELL IS?
HUF HU HUF

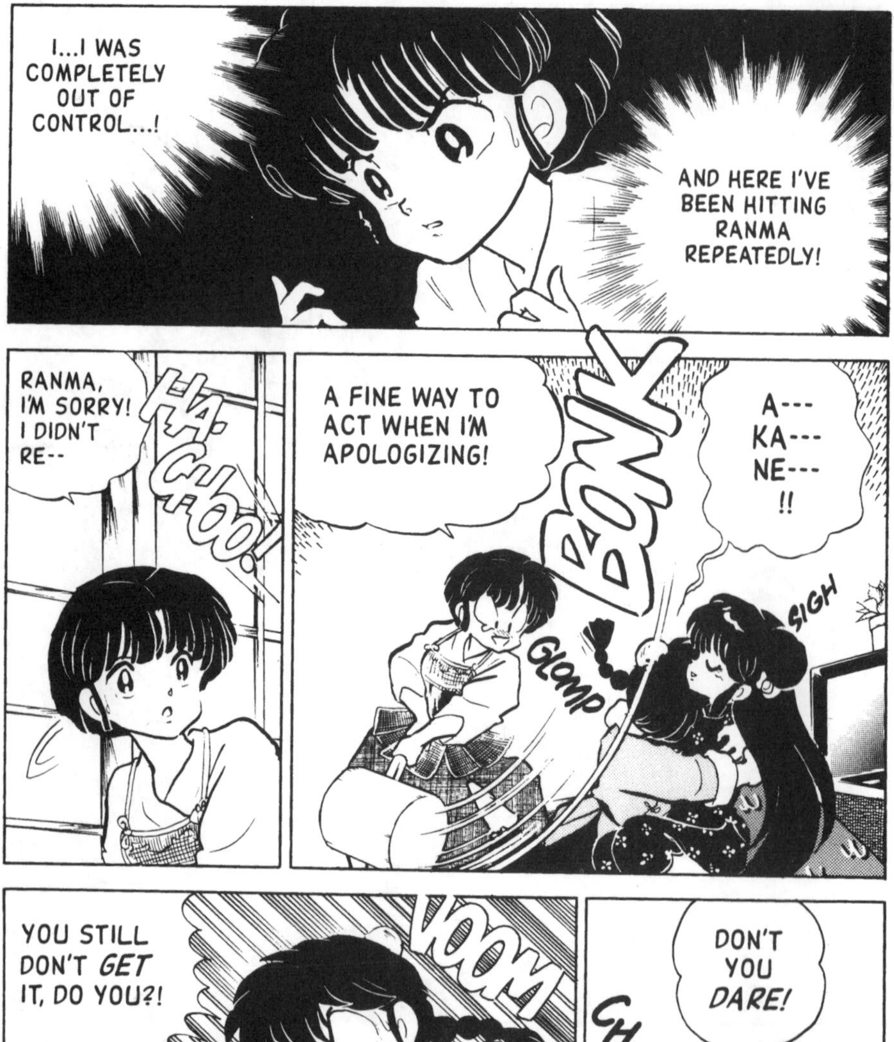
I...I WAS COMPLETELY OUT OF CONTROL...!
AND HERE I'VE BEEN HITTING RANMA REPEATEDLY!
RANMA, I'M SORRY! I DIDN'T RE--
HA-CHOO!
A FINE WAY TO ACT WHEN I'M APOLOGIZING!
BONK
A--- KA--- NE--- !!
GLOMP
SIGH
YOU STILL DON'T *GET* IT, DO YOU?!
VOOM
THAT'S WHY I WAS APOLG--
AH...
AH...
DON'T YOU *DARE!*
CHNNK
SQUINCH
POP

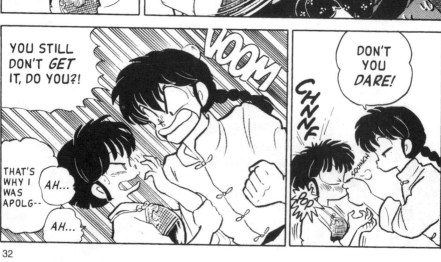

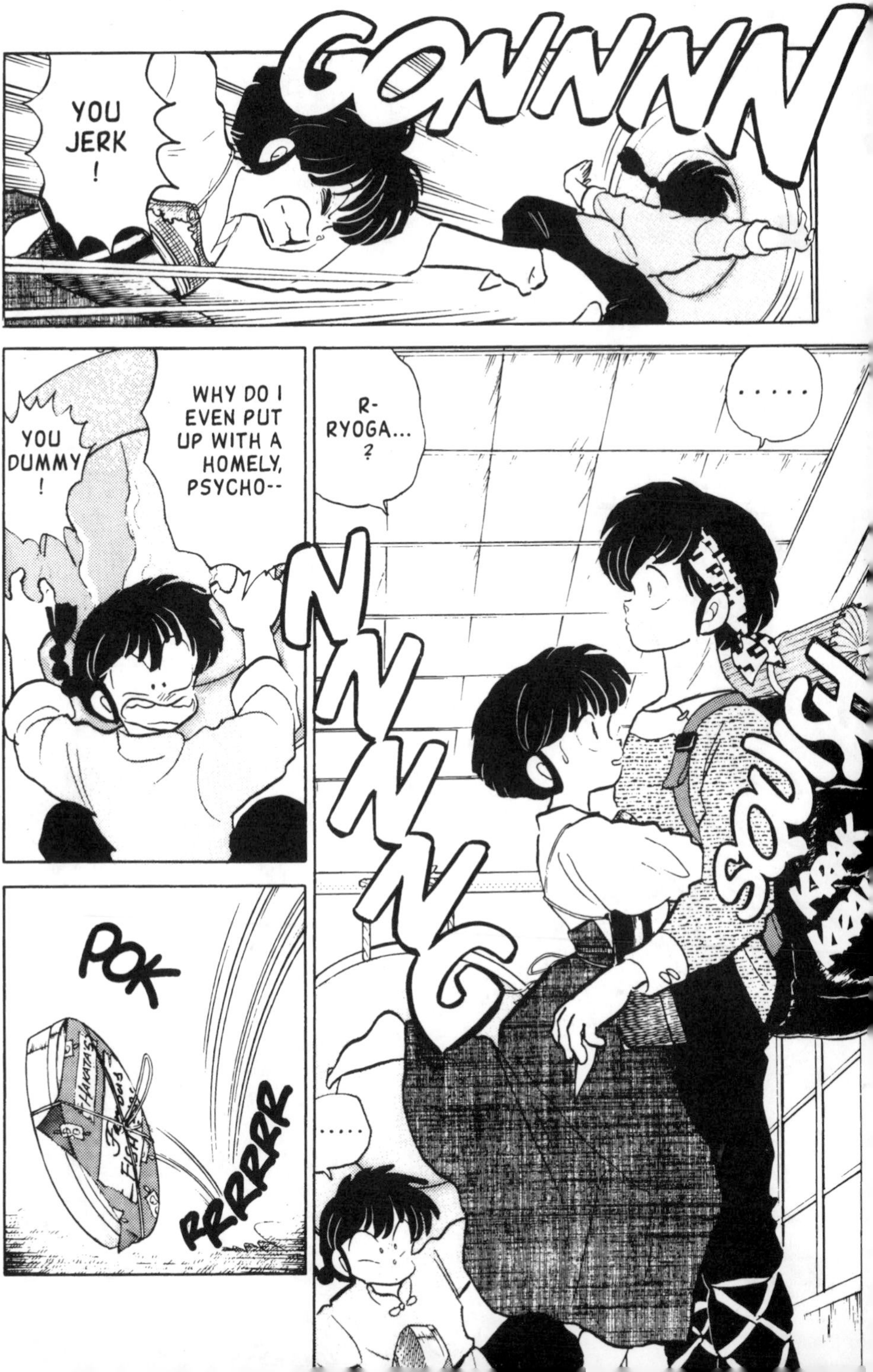
YOU JERK !
GONNNN
YOU DUMMY !
WHY DO I EVEN PUT UP WITH A HOMELY, PSYCHO--
POK
HAKATA'S
Famous FISH
RRRRRR
R- RYOGA... ?
.....
NNNNG
SQUISH
KRAK KRAK
.....

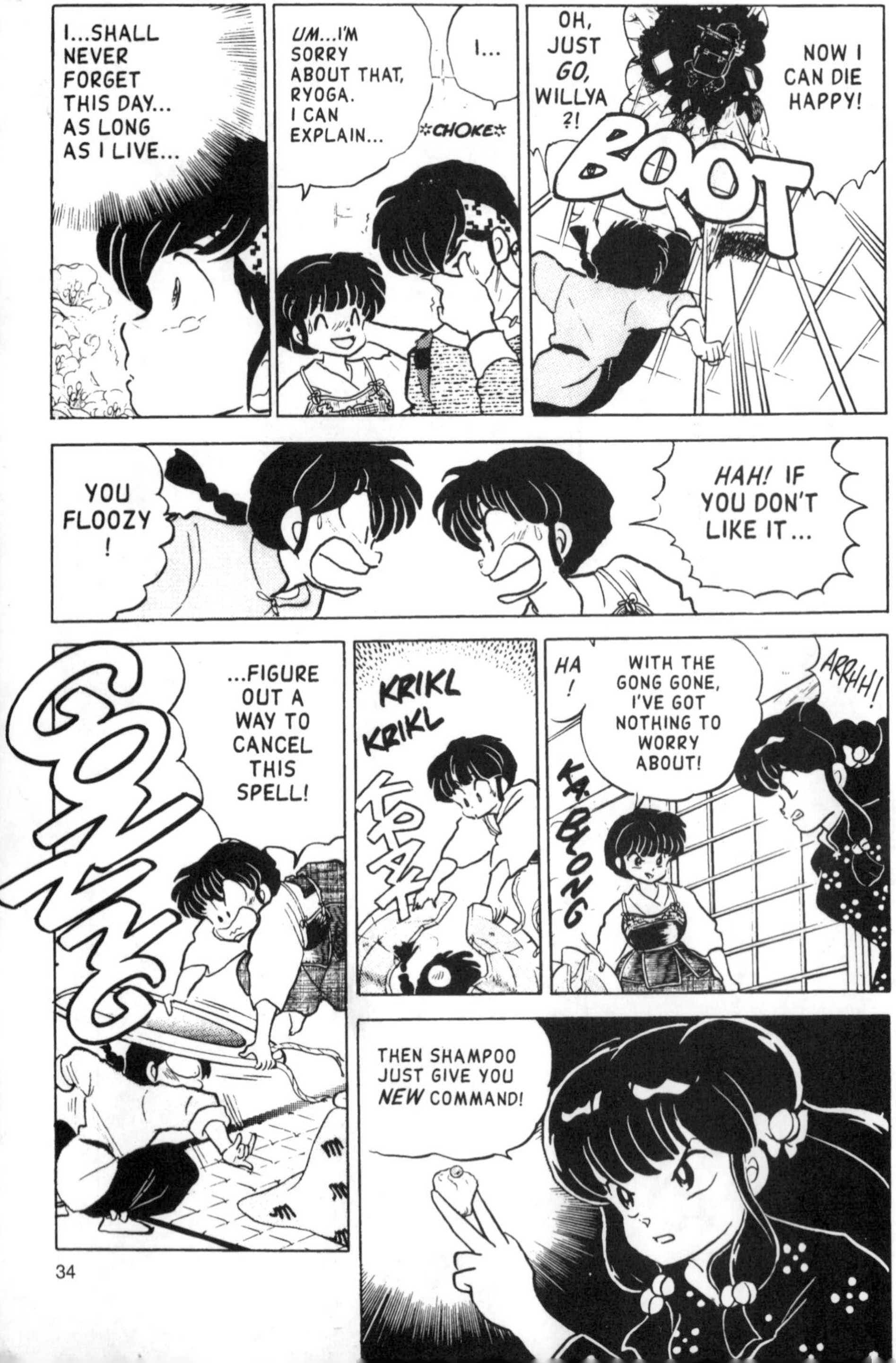
I...SHALL NEVER FORGET THIS DAY... AS LONG AS I LIVE...
UM...I'M SORRY ABOUT THAT, RYOGA. I CAN EXPLAIN...
I...
CHOKE
OH, JUST *GO*, WILLYA ?!
NOW I CAN DIE HAPPY!
BOOT
YOU FLOOZY !
HAH! IF YOU DON'T LIKE IT...
GONNNG
...FIGURE OUT A WAY TO CANCEL THIS SPELL!
KRIKL KRIKL
KRAK
HA !
WITH THE GONG GONE, I'VE GOT NOTHING TO WORRY ABOUT!
KA-BLONG
ARRHH!
THEN SHAMPOO JUST GIVE YOU *NEW* COMMAND!

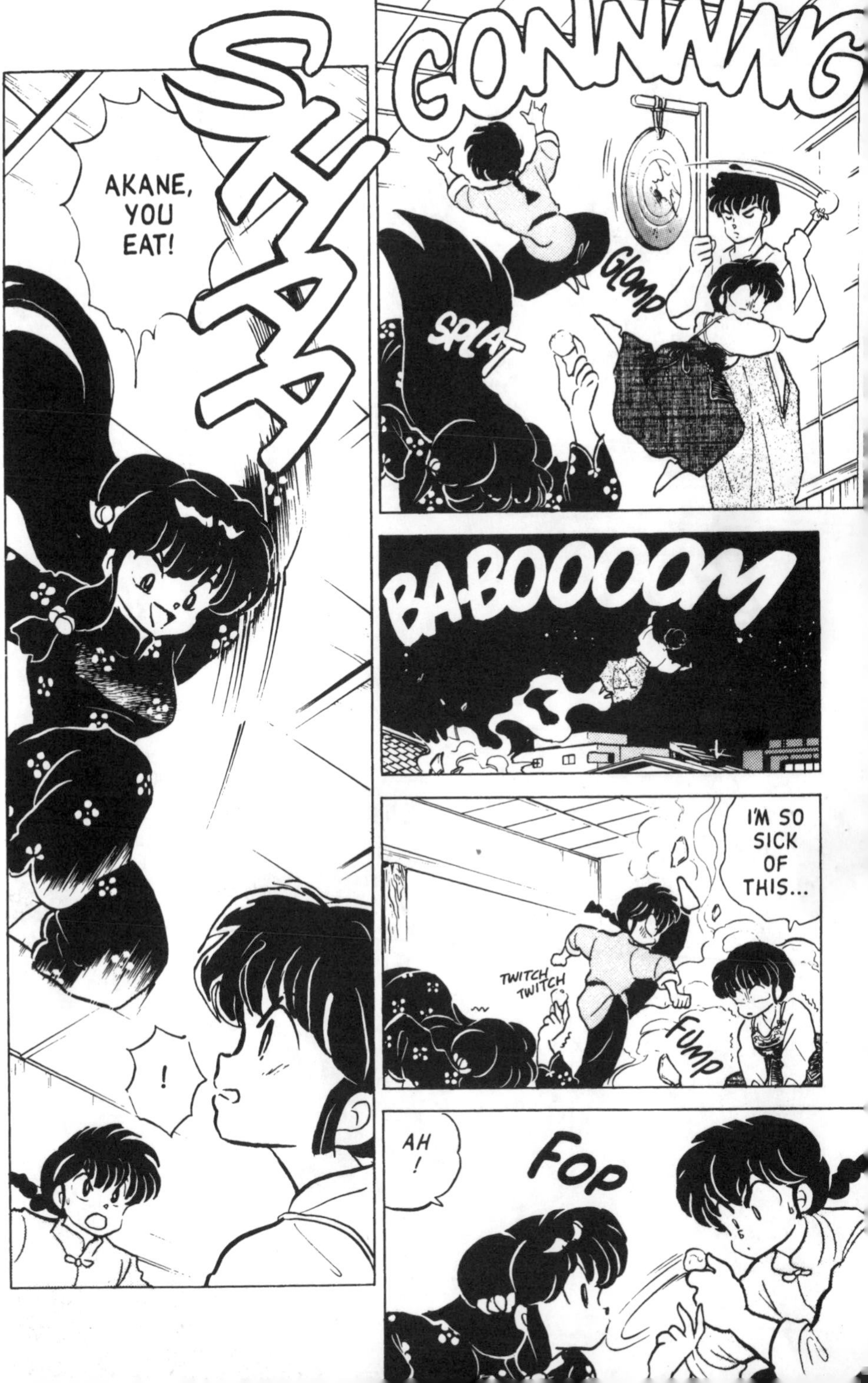
SHAA
AKANE, YOU EAT!
!
GONNNNNG
GLOMP
SPLAT
BA-BOOOOM
I'M SO SICK OF THIS...
TWITCH TWITCH
FUMP
AH!
FOP

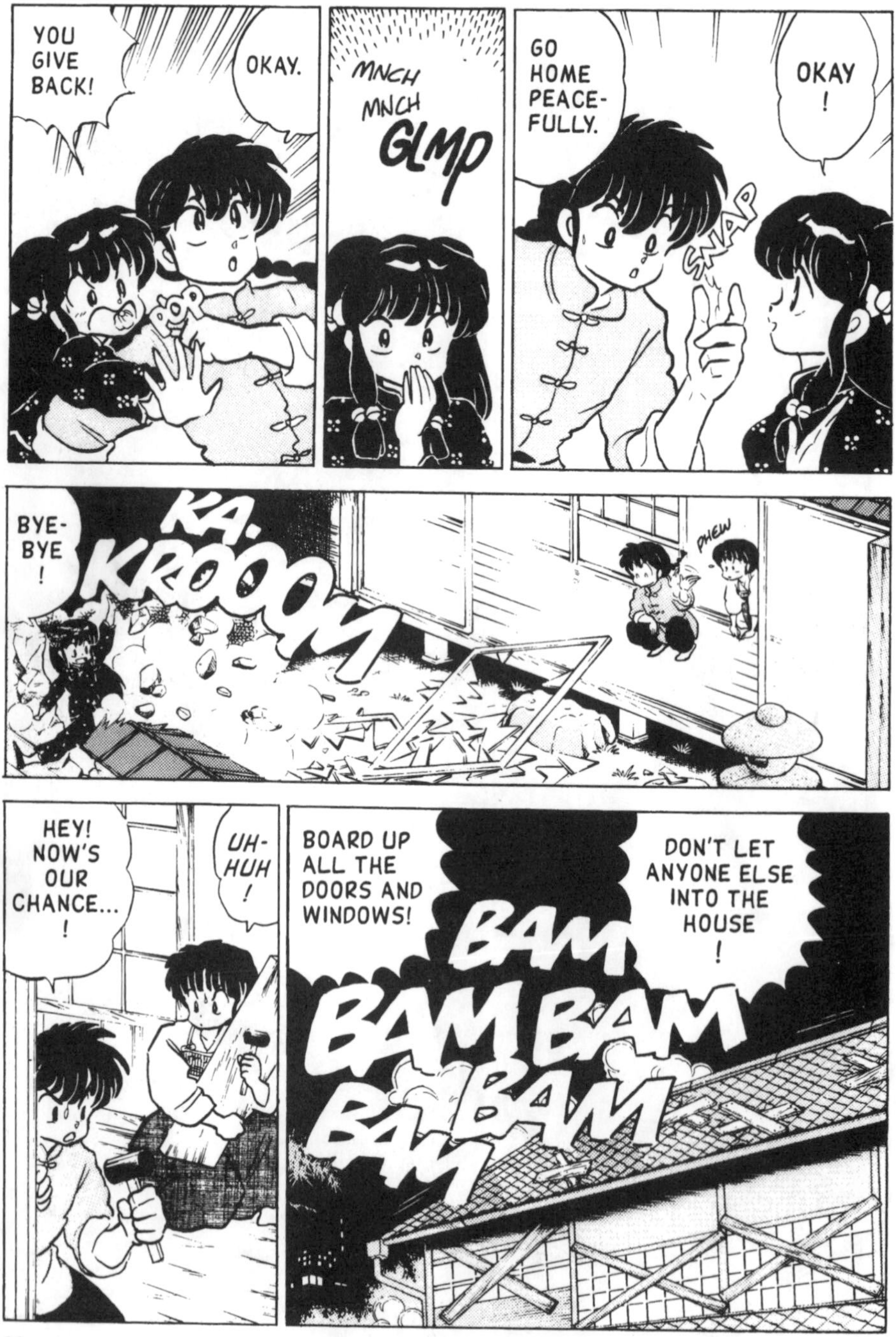
YOU GIVE BACK!
OKAY.
MNCH
MNCH
GLMP
GO HOME PEACE-FULLY.
OKAY !
SNAP
BYE-BYE !
KA-KROOOM
PHEW
HEY! NOW'S OUR CHANCE... !
UH-HUH !
BOARD UP ALL THE DOORS AND WINDOWS!
DON'T LET ANYONE ELSE INTO THE HOUSE !
BAM
BAM BAM
BAM
BAM BAM

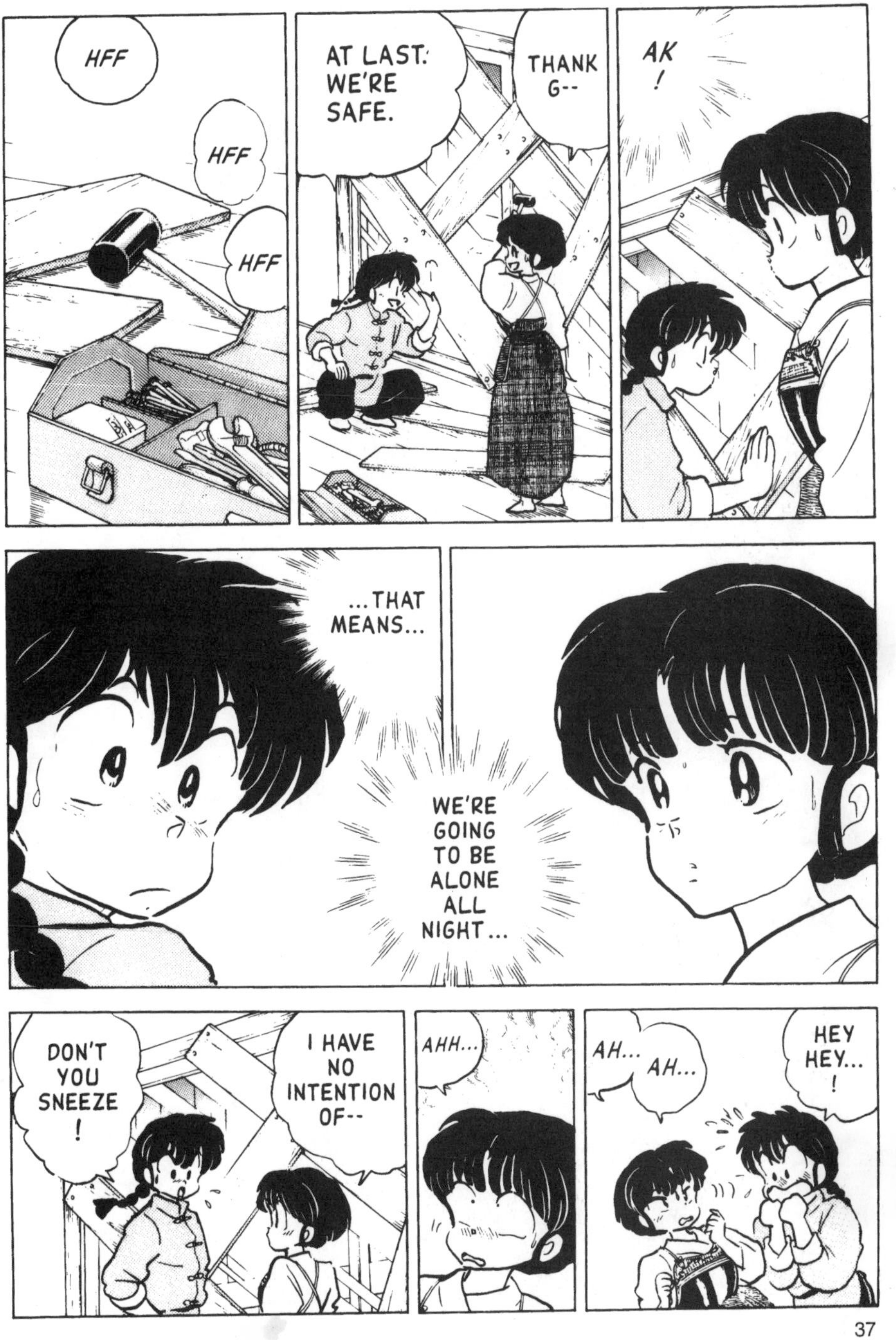
HFF
HFF
HFF
AT LAST: WE'RE SAFE.
THANK G--
AK !
...THAT MEANS...
WE'RE GOING TO BE ALONE ALL NIGHT...
DON'T YOU SNEEZE !
I HAVE NO INTENTION OF--
AHH...
AH...
AH...
HEY HEY... !

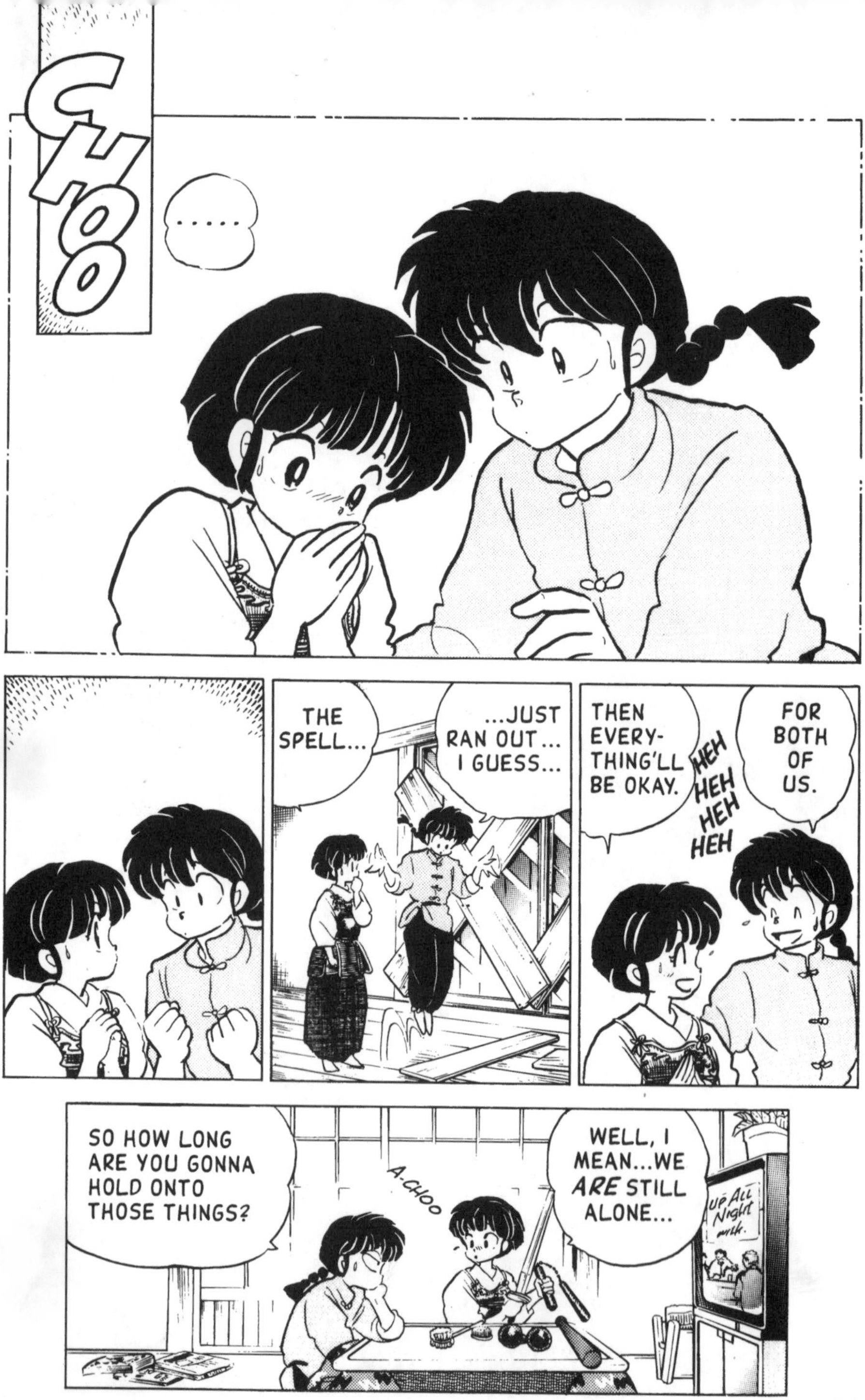
CHOO
......
THE SPELL...
...JUST RAN OUT... I GUESS...
THEN EVERY-THING'LL BE OKAY.
HEH HEH HEH HEH
FOR BOTH OF US.
SO HOW LONG ARE YOU GONNA HOLD ONTO THOSE THINGS?
A-CHOO
WELL, I MEAN...WE *ARE* STILL ALONE...
UP ALL Night

PART 3
AKANE'S POWER-UP!

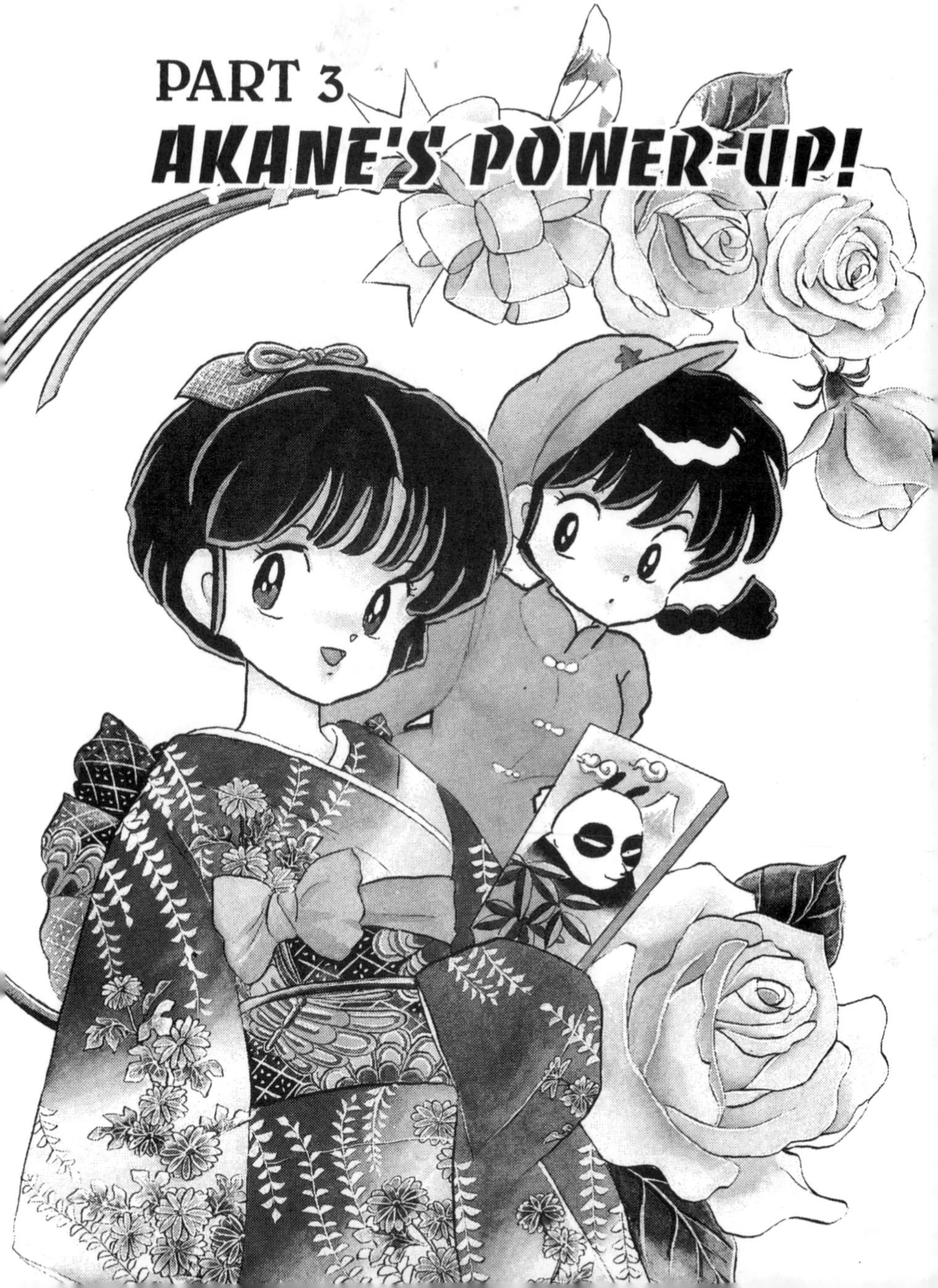

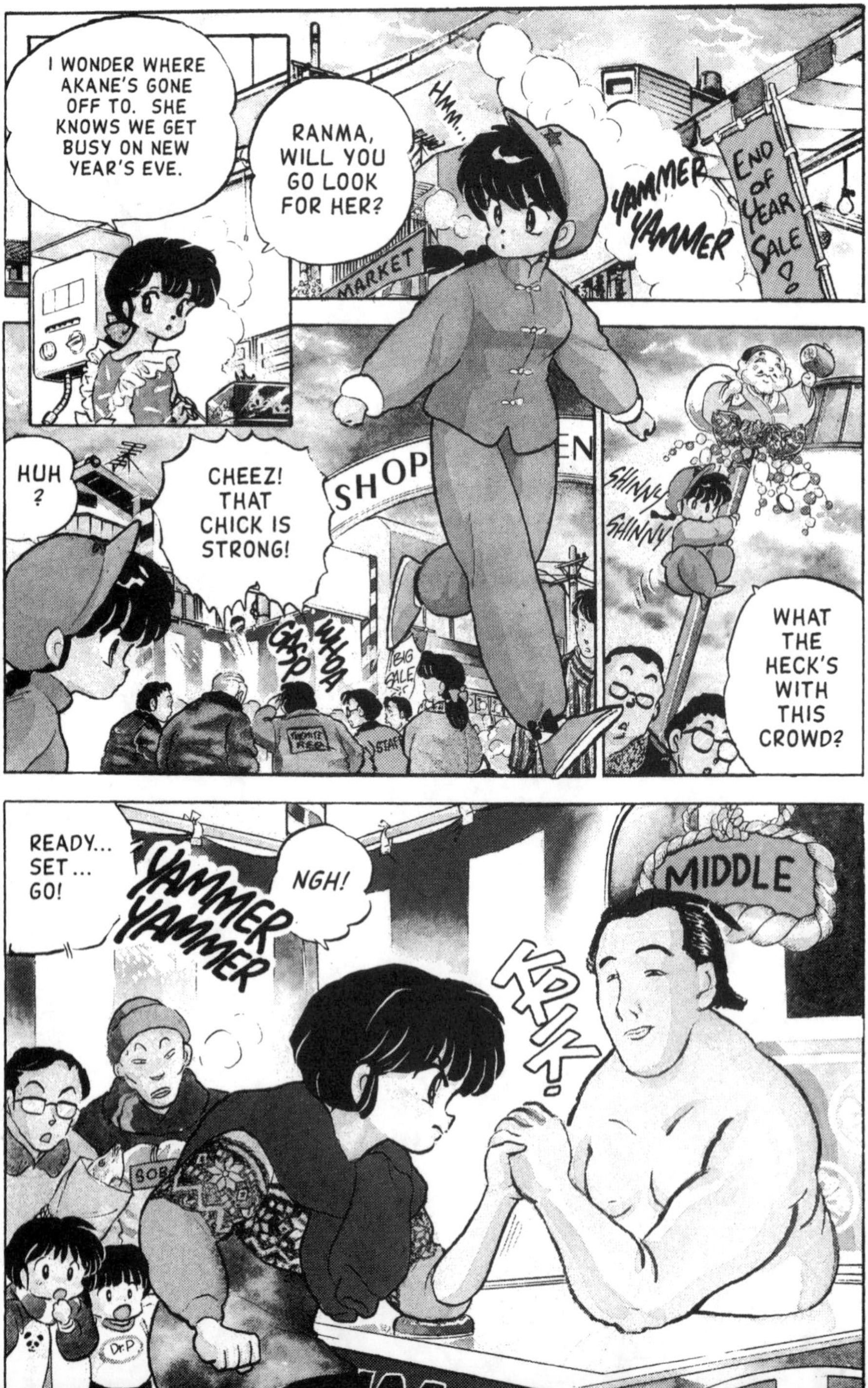
I WONDER WHERE AKANE'S GONE OFF TO. SHE KNOWS WE GET BUSY ON NEW YEAR'S EVE.
RANMA, WILL YOU GO LOOK FOR HER?
HMM...
MARKET
YAMMER YAMMER
END OF YEAR SALE!
HUH ?
CHEEZ! THAT CHICK IS STRONG!
SHOP
WHOA
GASP
BIG SALE
SHINNY SHINNY
WHAT THE HECK'S WITH THIS CROWD?
READY... SET... GO!
YAMMER YAMMER
NGH!
MIDDLE
Dr.P

NNNNNN~

KKKK...

-NGHAA AH!

BLONG

WHOA! SHE BEAT THE MIDDLEWEIGHT!

INCREDIBLE!

MAN, TALK ABOUT WASTING YOUR TIME...

HWOOOOOOO

O-KAY! NOW LET'S SEE IF YOU CAN BEAT THE HEAVYWEIGHT!

GARARARARA

HEAVY

SAKE

SAKE SAKE

BRING HIM ON!

VRR VRR

READY... SET... GO!

GLOMP

GCH

HM?

A TOUGH ONE, EH?

G'G'G.

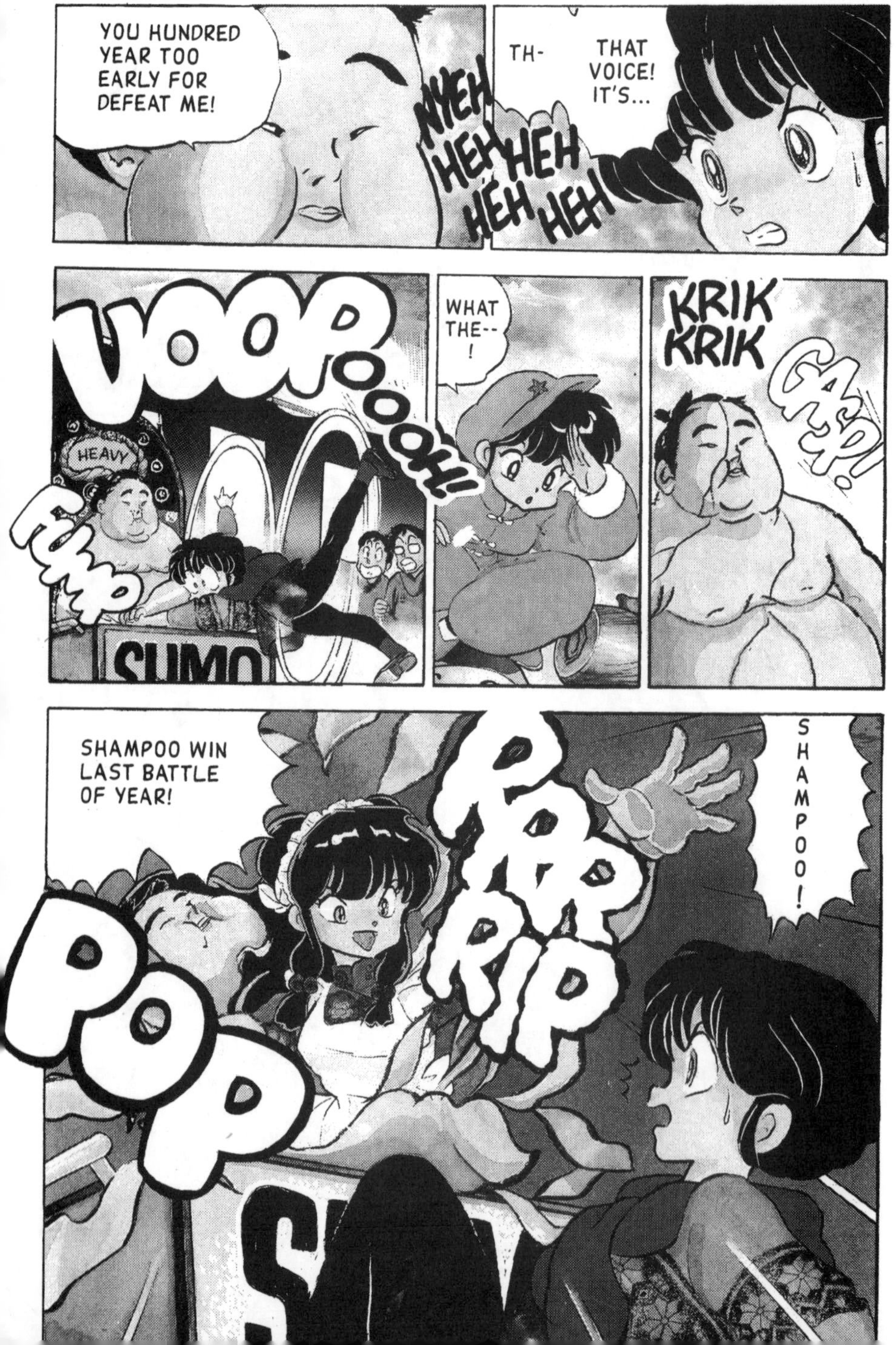
YOU HUNDRED YEAR TOO EARLY FOR DEFEAT ME!
NYEH HEH HEH HEH HEH HEH
TH-
THAT VOICE! IT'S...
VOOPOOOOH!!
FUMP
HEAVY
SUMO
WHAT THE-- !
KRIK KRIK
GASP!
SHAMPOO WIN LAST BATTLE OF YEAR!
RRRIP
POP
SHAMPOO!

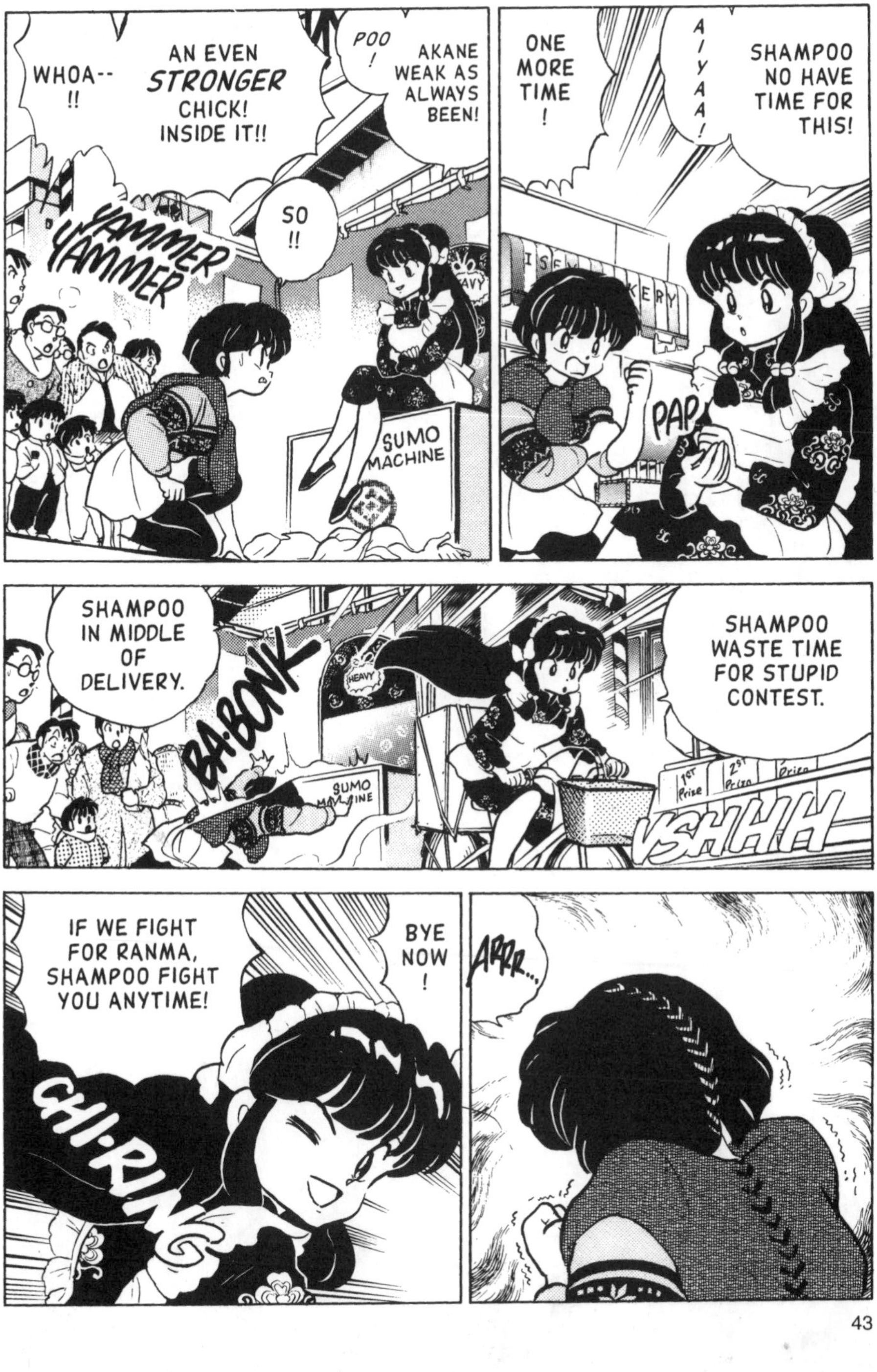
WHOA-- !!
AN EVEN STRONGER CHICK! INSIDE IT!!
POO !
AKANE WEAK AS ALWAYS BEEN!
YAMMER YAMMER
SO !!
HEAVY
SUMO MACHINE
ONE MORE TIME !
AIYAAA!
SHAMPOO NO HAVE TIME FOR THIS!
PAP
SHAMPOO IN MIDDLE OF DELIVERY.
BA-BONK
HEAVY
SHAMPOO WASTE TIME FOR STUPID CONTEST.
1st Prize
2nd Prize
Prize
VSHHHH
IF WE FIGHT FOR RANMA, SHAMPOO FIGHT YOU ANYTIME!
BYE NOW !
ARRR...
CHI-RING

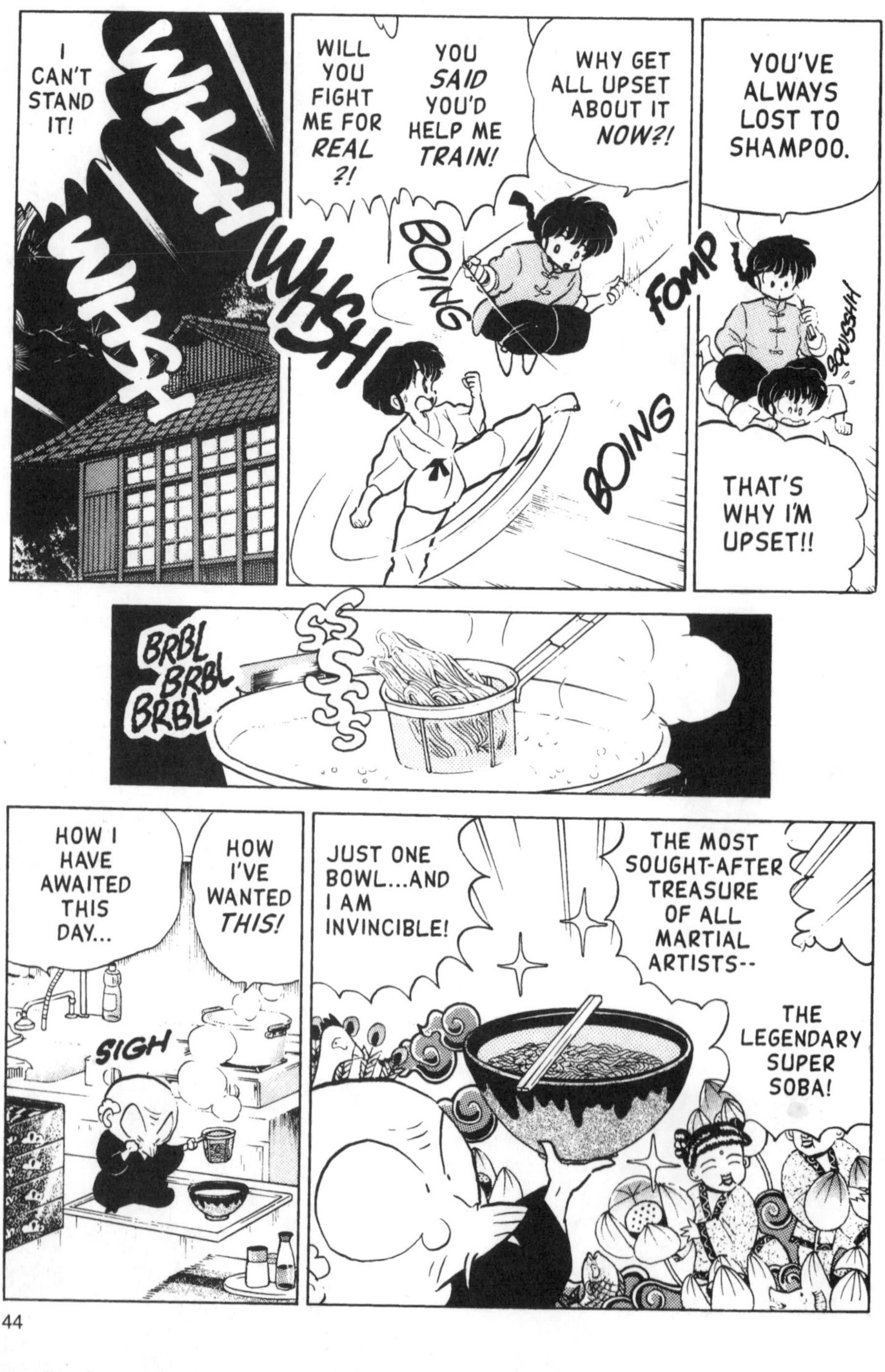
I CAN'T STAND IT!
WHSH
WHSH
WILL YOU FIGHT ME FOR REAL?!
YOU SAID YOU'D HELP ME TRAIN!
WHY GET ALL UPSET ABOUT IT NOW?!
BOING
WHSH
BOING
YOU'VE ALWAYS LOST TO SHAMPOO.
FOMP
SQUISSHH
THAT'S WHY I'M UPSET!!
BRBL BRBL BRBL
HOW I HAVE AWAITED THIS DAY...
HOW I'VE WANTED THIS!
SIGH
JUST ONE BOWL...AND I AM INVINCIBLE!
THE MOST SOUGHT-AFTER TREASURE OF ALL MARTIAL ARTISTS--
THE LEGENDARY SUPER SOBA!

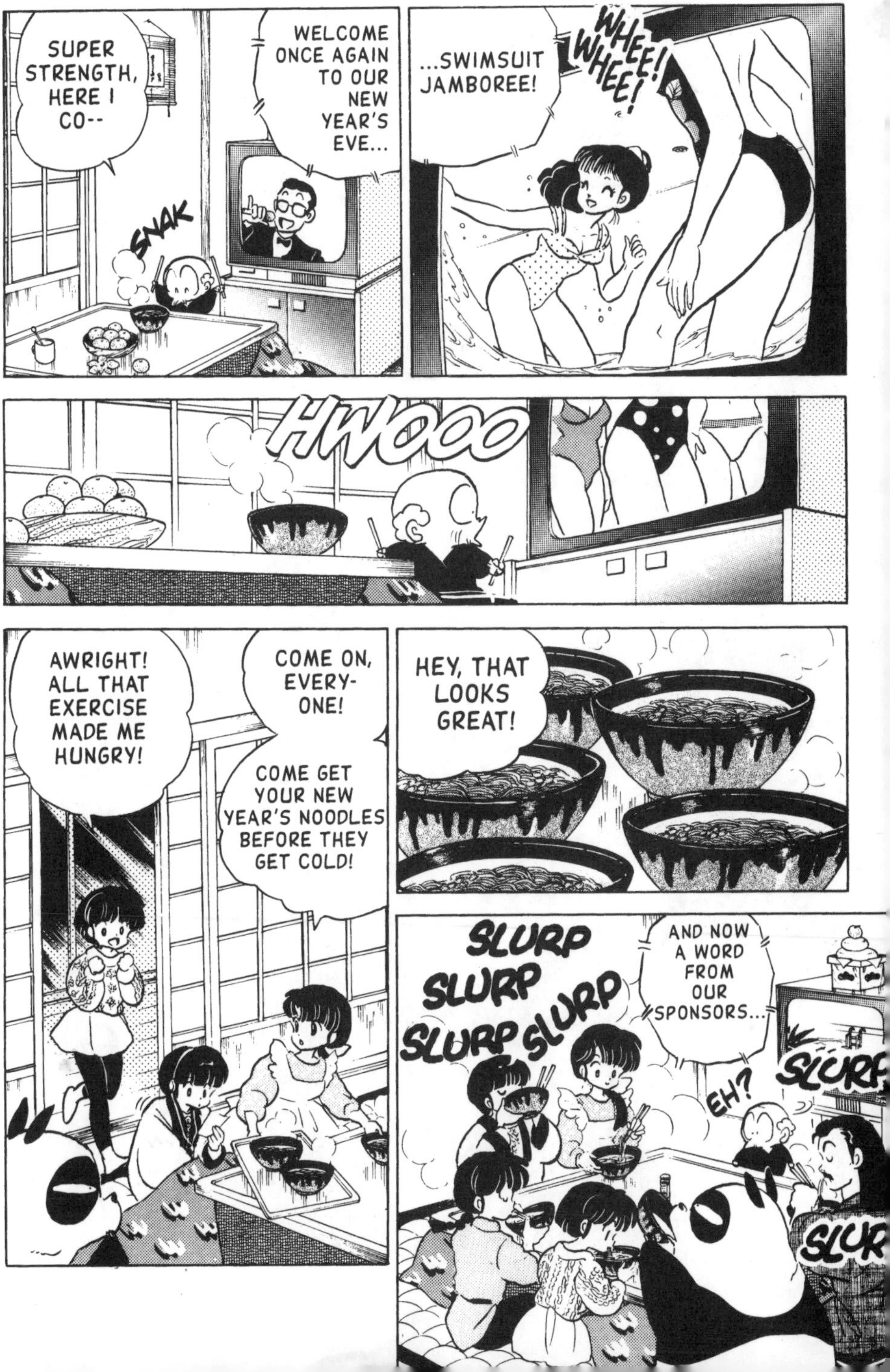
SUPER STRENGTH, HERE I CO--
SNAK
WELCOME ONCE AGAIN TO OUR NEW YEAR'S EVE...
...SWIMSUIT JAMBOREE!
WHEE! WHEE!
HWOOO
AWRIGHT! ALL THAT EXERCISE MADE ME HUNGRY!
COME ON, EVERY-ONE!
COME GET YOUR NEW YEAR'S NOODLES BEFORE THEY GET COLD!
HEY, THAT LOOKS GREAT!
SLURP
SLURP
SLURP SLURP
AND NOW A WORD FROM OUR SPONSORS...
EH?

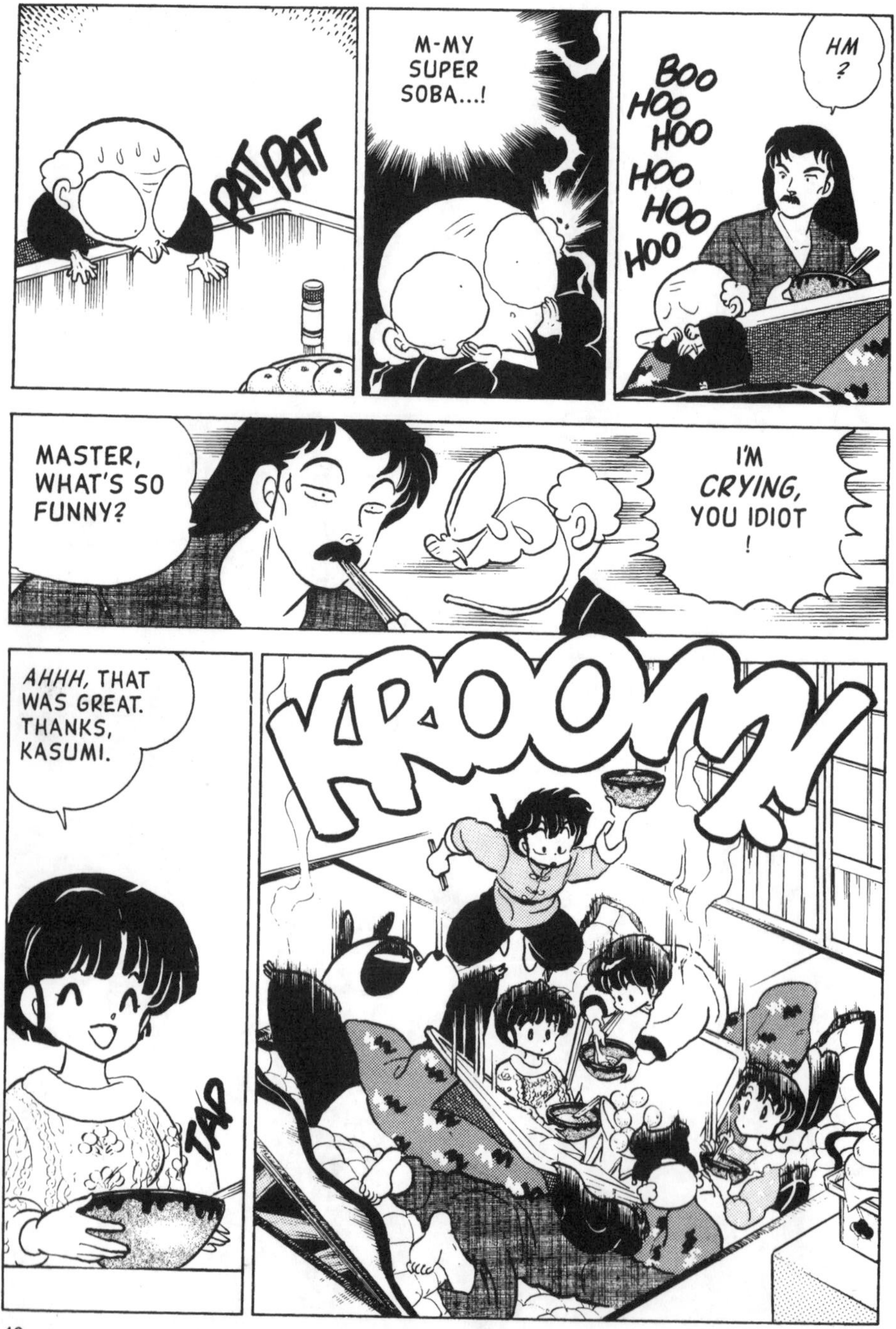
PAT PAT
M-MY SUPER SOBA...!
BOO HOO HOO HOO HOO HOO
HM ?
MASTER, WHAT'S SO FUNNY?
I'M *CRYING,* YOU IDIOT !
AHHH, THAT WAS GREAT. THANKS, KASUMI.
TAP
KROOM

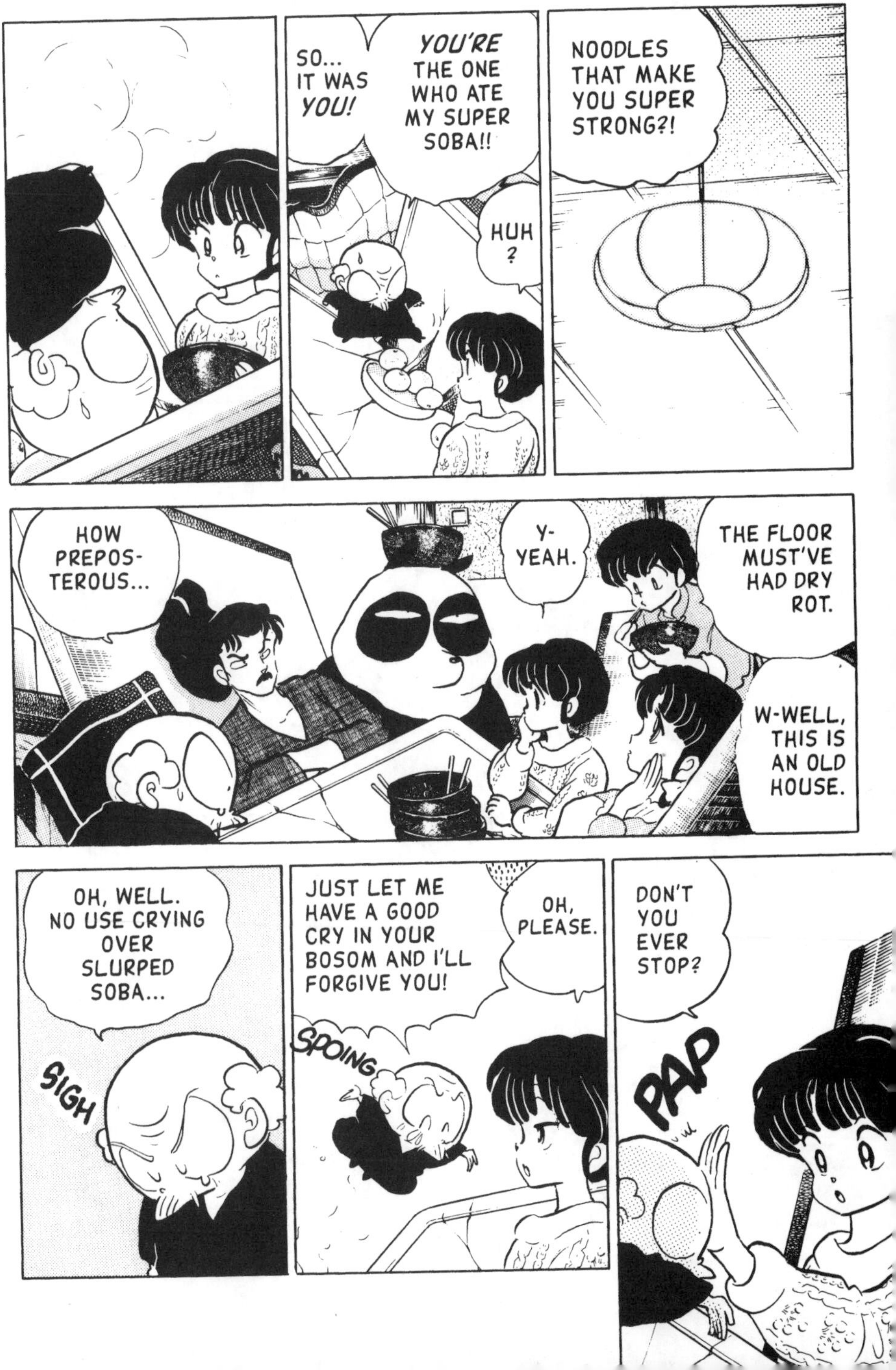
SO... IT WAS YOU!
YOU'RE THE ONE WHO ATE MY SUPER SOBA!!
HUH ?
NOODLES THAT MAKE YOU SUPER STRONG?!
HOW PREPOS-TEROUS...
Y-YEAH.
THE FLOOR MUST'VE HAD DRY ROT.
W-WELL, THIS IS AN OLD HOUSE.
OH, WELL. NO USE CRYING OVER SLURPED SOBA...
SIGH
JUST LET ME HAVE A GOOD CRY IN YOUR BOSOM AND I'LL FORGIVE YOU!
OH, PLEASE.
SPOING
DON'T YOU EVER STOP?
PAP

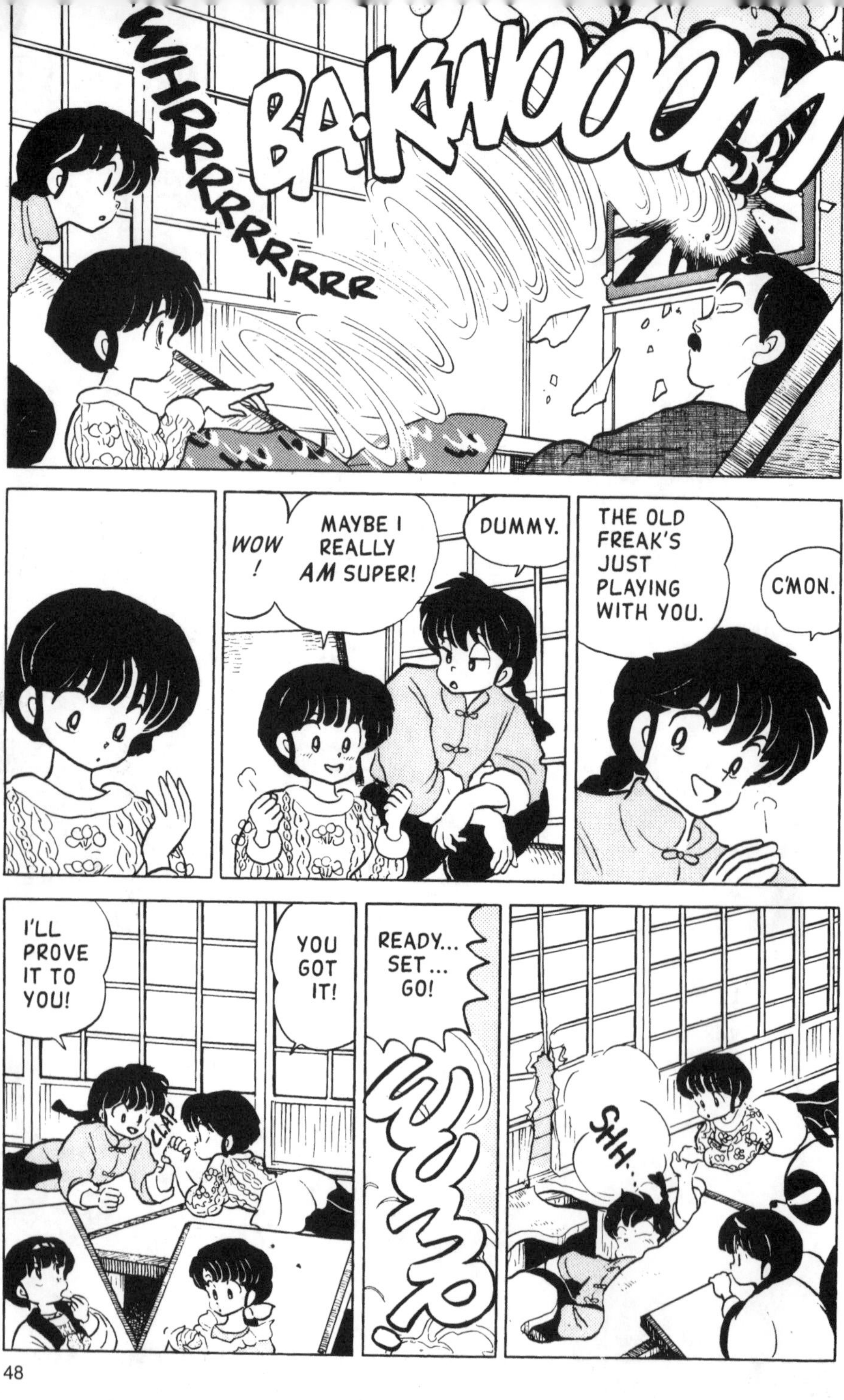
WHIRRRRRRRRRRR
BA-KWOOOM
WOW!
MAYBE I REALLY AM SUPER!
DUMMY.
THE OLD FREAK'S JUST PLAYING WITH YOU.
C'MON.
I'LL PROVE IT TO YOU!
YOU GOT IT!
CLAP
READY... SET... GO!
SHH...

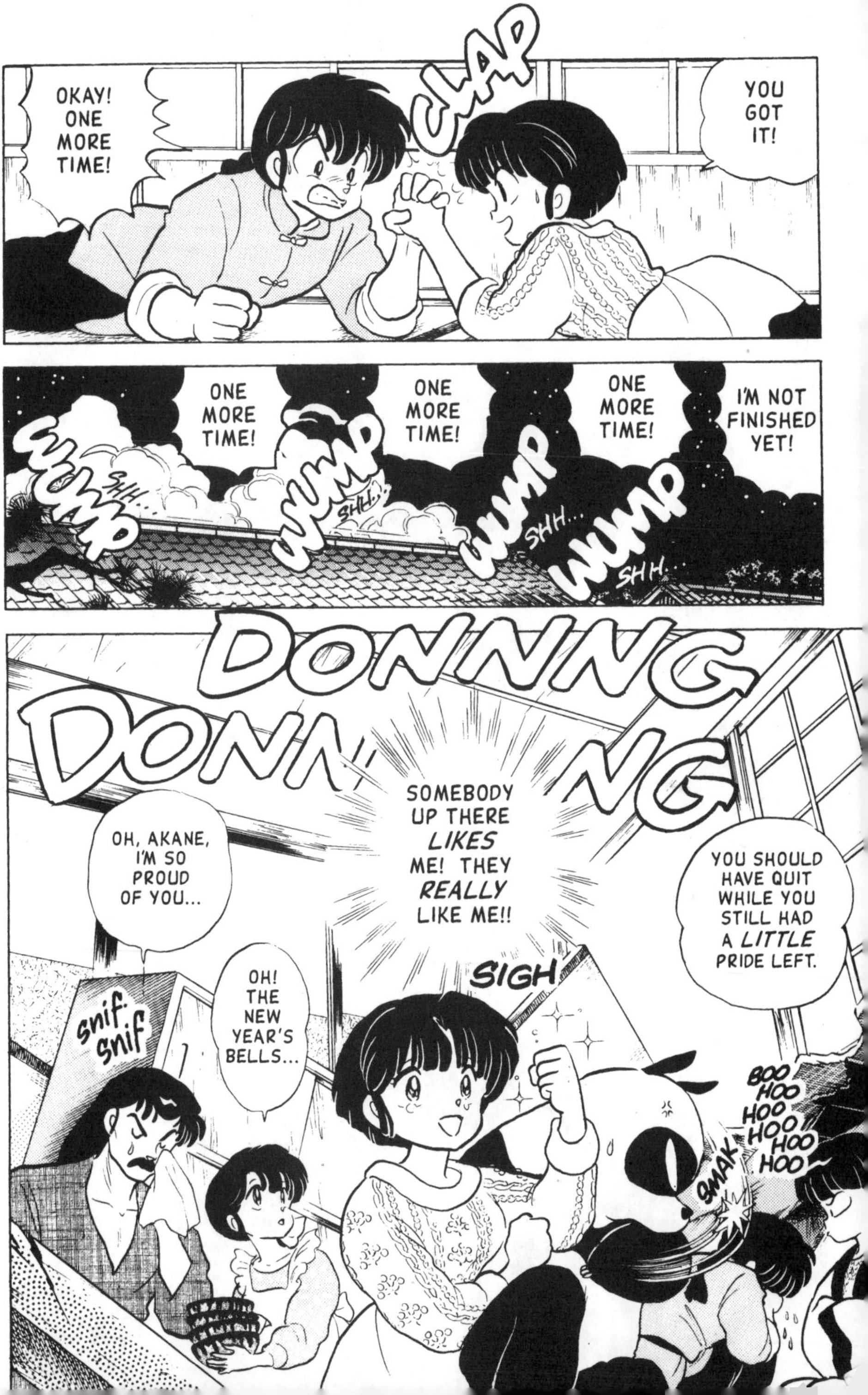
OKAY! ONE MORE TIME!
CLAP
YOU GOT IT!
ONE MORE TIME!
WUMP
SHH...
ONE MORE TIME!
WUMP
SHH...
ONE MORE TIME!
WUMP
SHH...
I'M NOT FINISHED YET!
WUMP
SHH
DONNNG
DONNNNG
OH, AKANE, I'M SO PROUD OF YOU...
SOMEBODY UP THERE *LIKES* ME! THEY *REALLY* LIKE ME!!
YOU SHOULD HAVE QUIT WHILE YOU STILL HAD A *LITTLE* PRIDE LEFT.
snif. snif
OH! THE NEW YEAR'S BELLS...
SIGH
SMAK
BOO HOO HOO HOO!! HOO HOO HOO

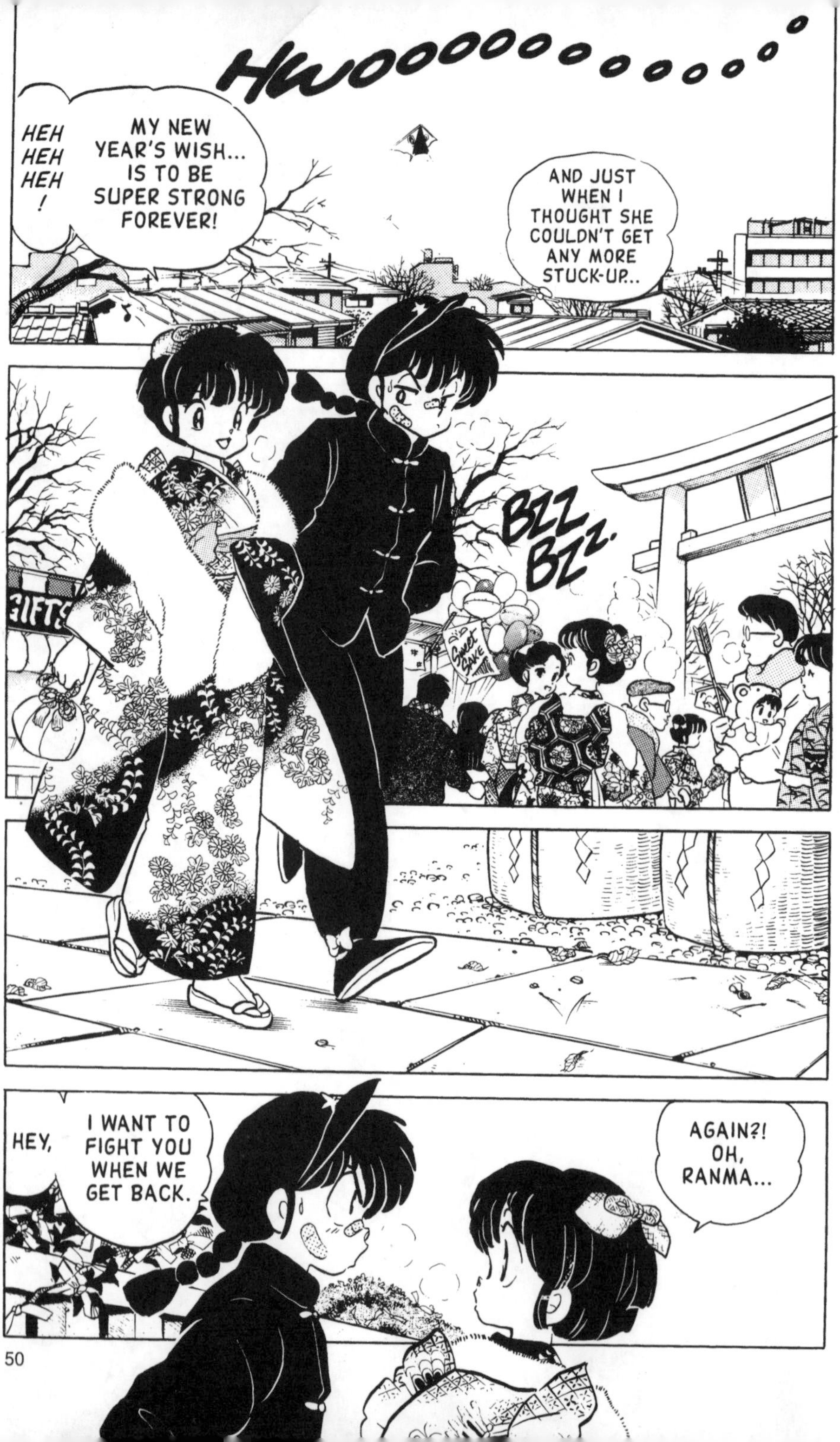

HWOOOOOOOOOOOOOOO
HEH HEH HEH!
MY NEW YEAR'S WISH... IS TO BE SUPER STRONG FOREVER!
AND JUST WHEN I THOUGHT SHE COULDN'T GET ANY MORE STUCK-UP..
GIFTS
BZZ BZZ.
SWEET SAKE
HEY,
I WANT TO FIGHT YOU WHEN WE GET BACK.
AGAIN?! OH, RANMA...

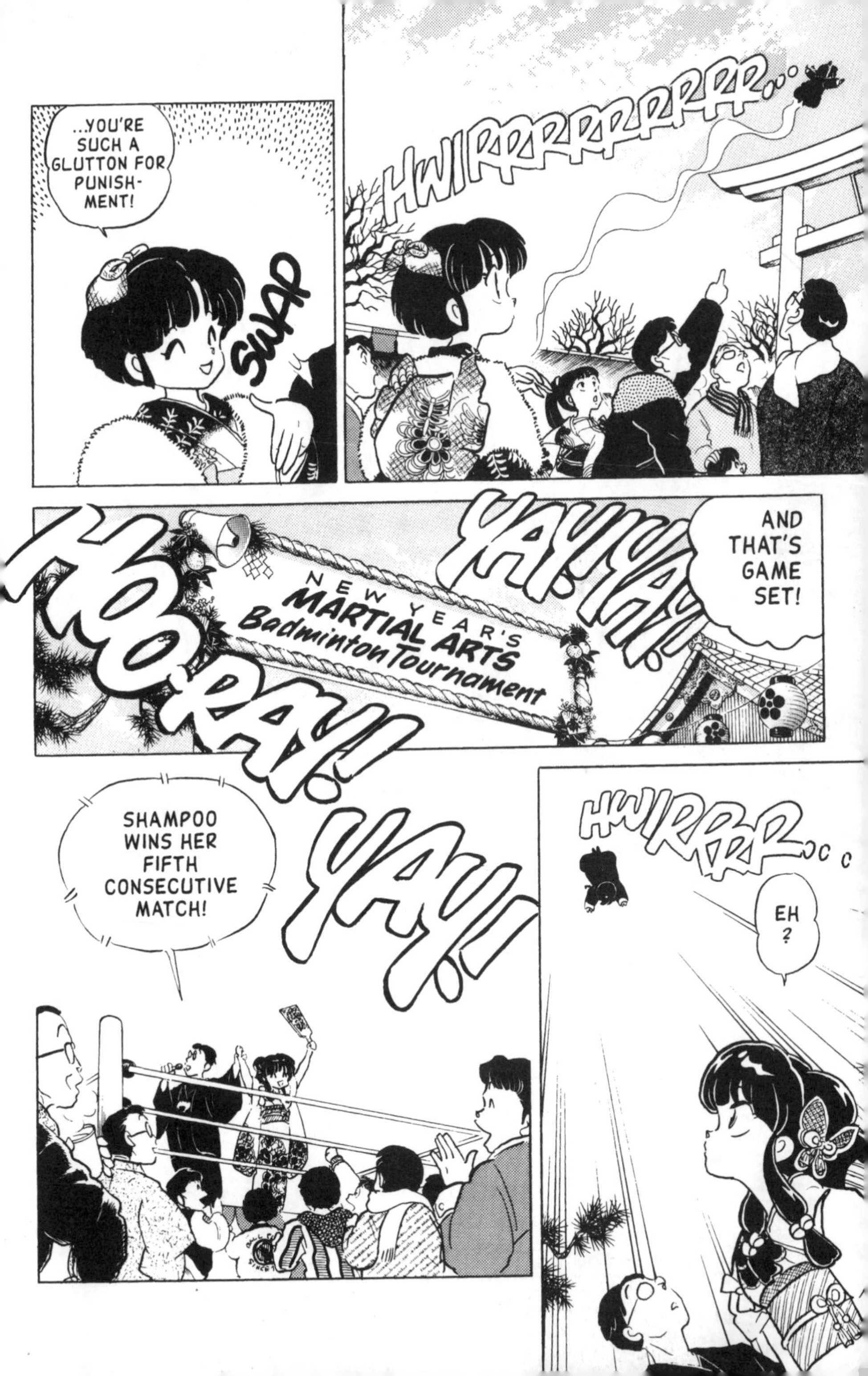

...YOU'RE SUCH A GLUTTON FOR PUNISH-MENT!
SWAP
HWIRRRRRRRRRR...
HOORAY!
NEW YEAR'S MARTIAL ARTS Badminton Tournament
YAY! YAY!
AND THAT'S GAME SET!
SHAMPOO WINS HER FIFTH CONSECUTIVE MATCH!
YAY!
HWIRRRR...
EH?

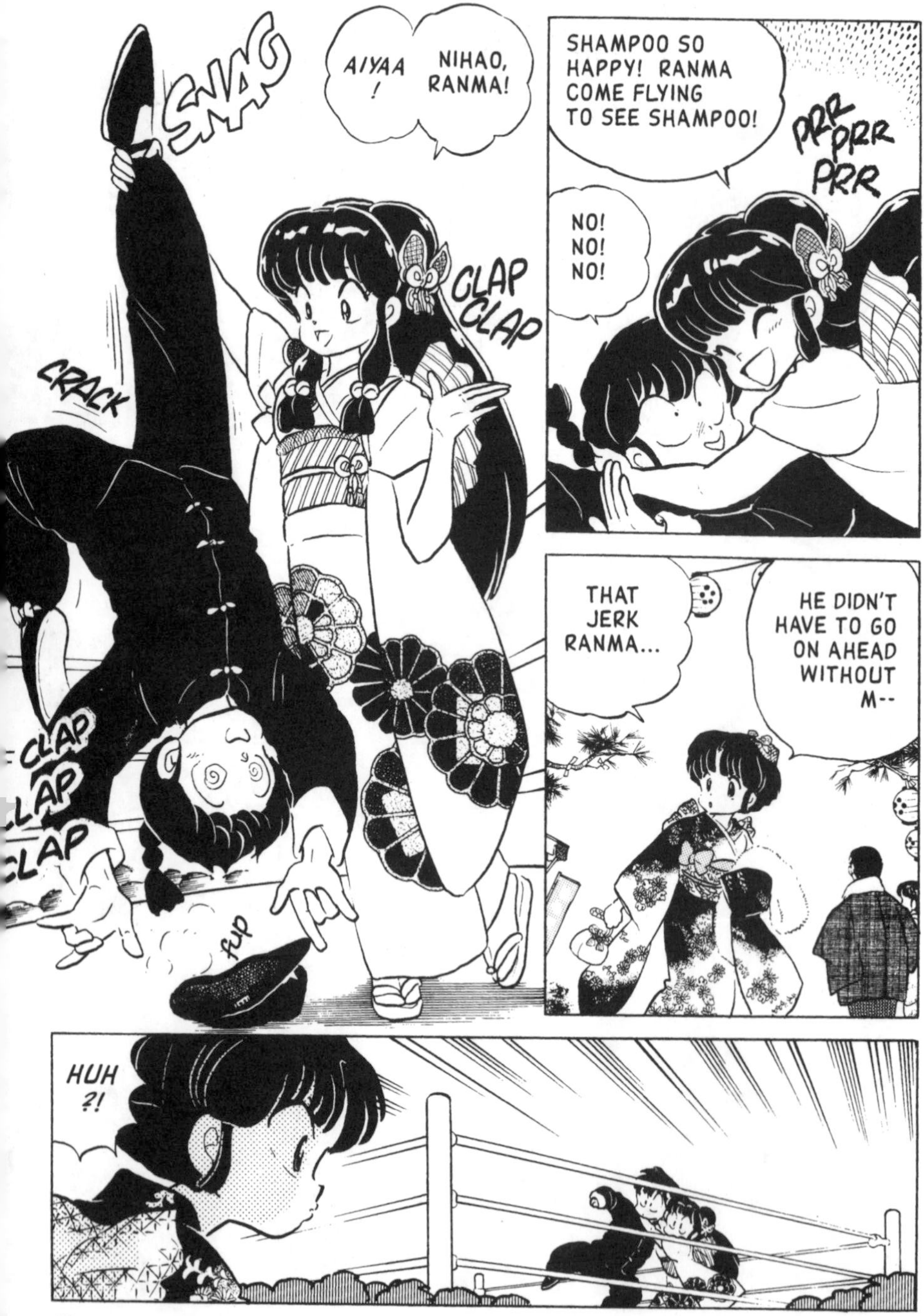
SNAG
AIYAA!
NIHAO, RANMA!
CLAP CLAP
CRACK
CLAP CLAP CLAP
FLIP
SHAMPOO SO HAPPY! RANMA COME FLYING TO SEE SHAMPOO!
PRR PRR PRR
NO! NO! NO!
THAT JERK RANMA...
HE DIDN'T HAVE TO GO ON AHEAD WITHOUT M--
HUH?!

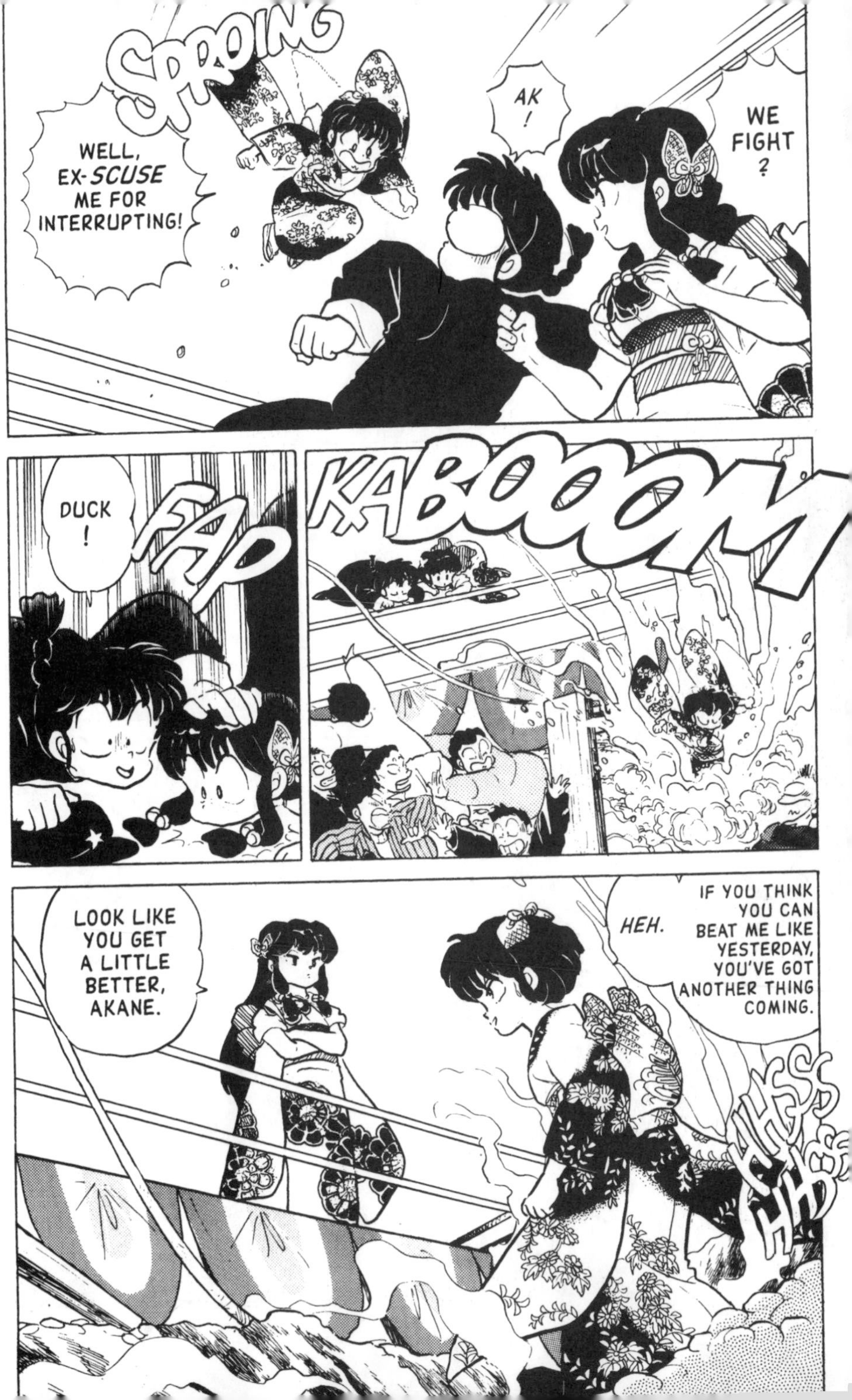
SPROING
WELL, EX-SCUSE ME FOR INTERRUPTING!
AK!
WE FIGHT?
DUCK!
FAP
KABOOOM
LOOK LIKE YOU GET A LITTLE BETTER, AKANE.
HEH.
IF YOU THINK YOU CAN BEAT ME LIKE YESTERDAY, YOU'VE GOT ANOTHER THING COMING.

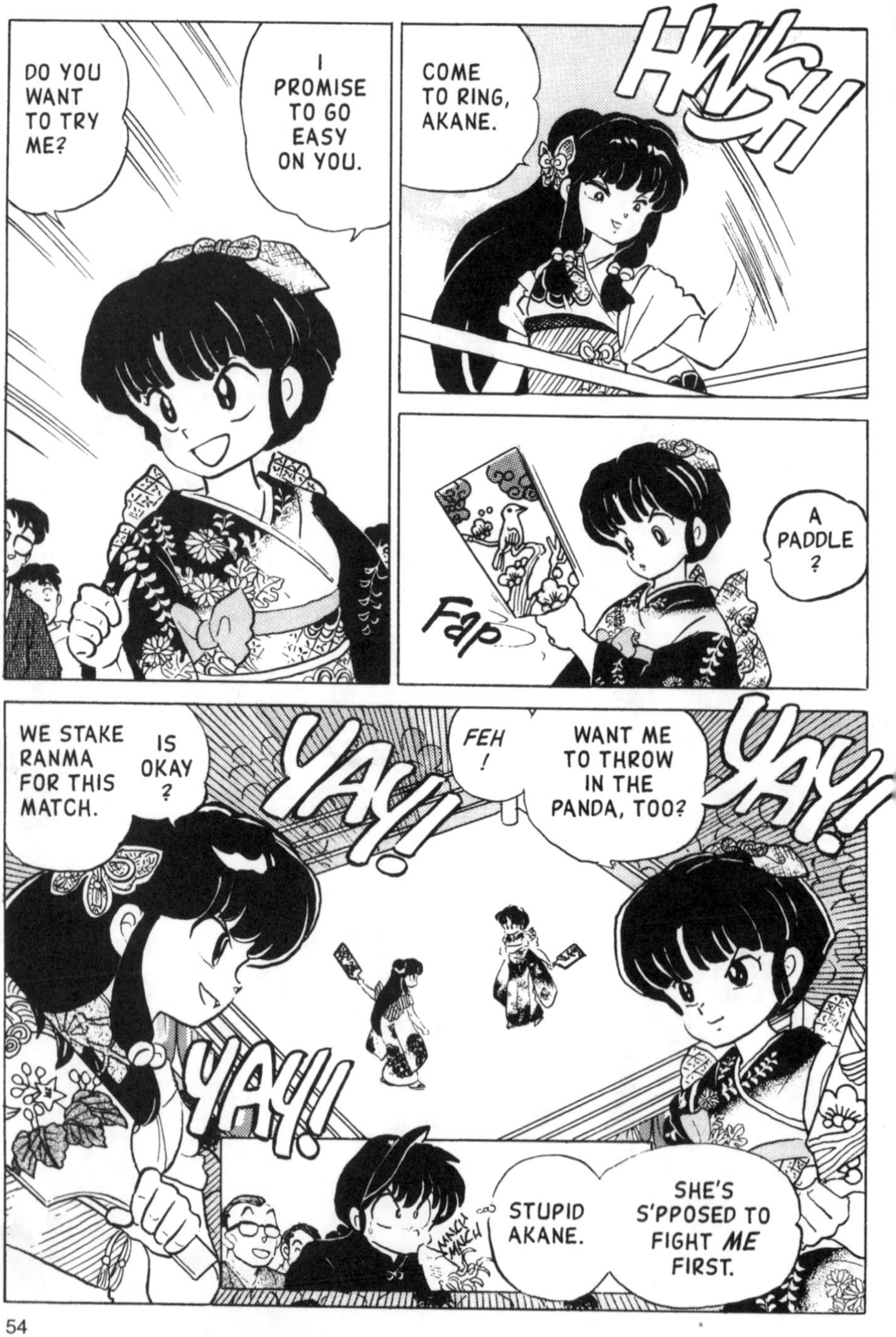
DO YOU WANT TO TRY ME?
I PROMISE TO GO EASY ON YOU.
COME TO RING, AKANE.
HWSH
Fap
A PADDLE?
WE STAKE RANMA FOR THIS MATCH.
IS OKAY?
YAY!
FEH!
WANT ME TO THROW IN THE PANDA, TOO?
YAY!
YAY!
STUPID AKANE.
SHE'S S'PPOSED TO FIGHT *ME* FIRST.

PART 4
SUPER BADMINTON

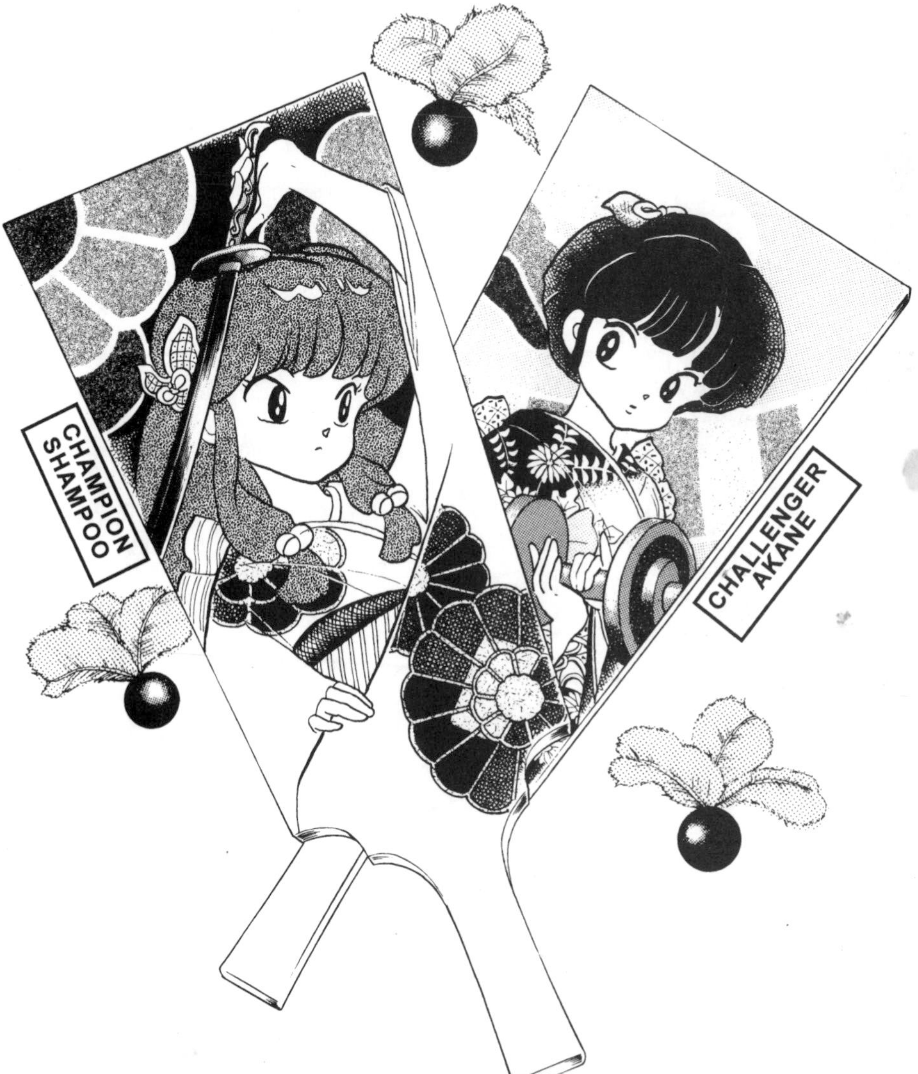
CHAMPION SHAMPOO
CHALLENGER AKANE

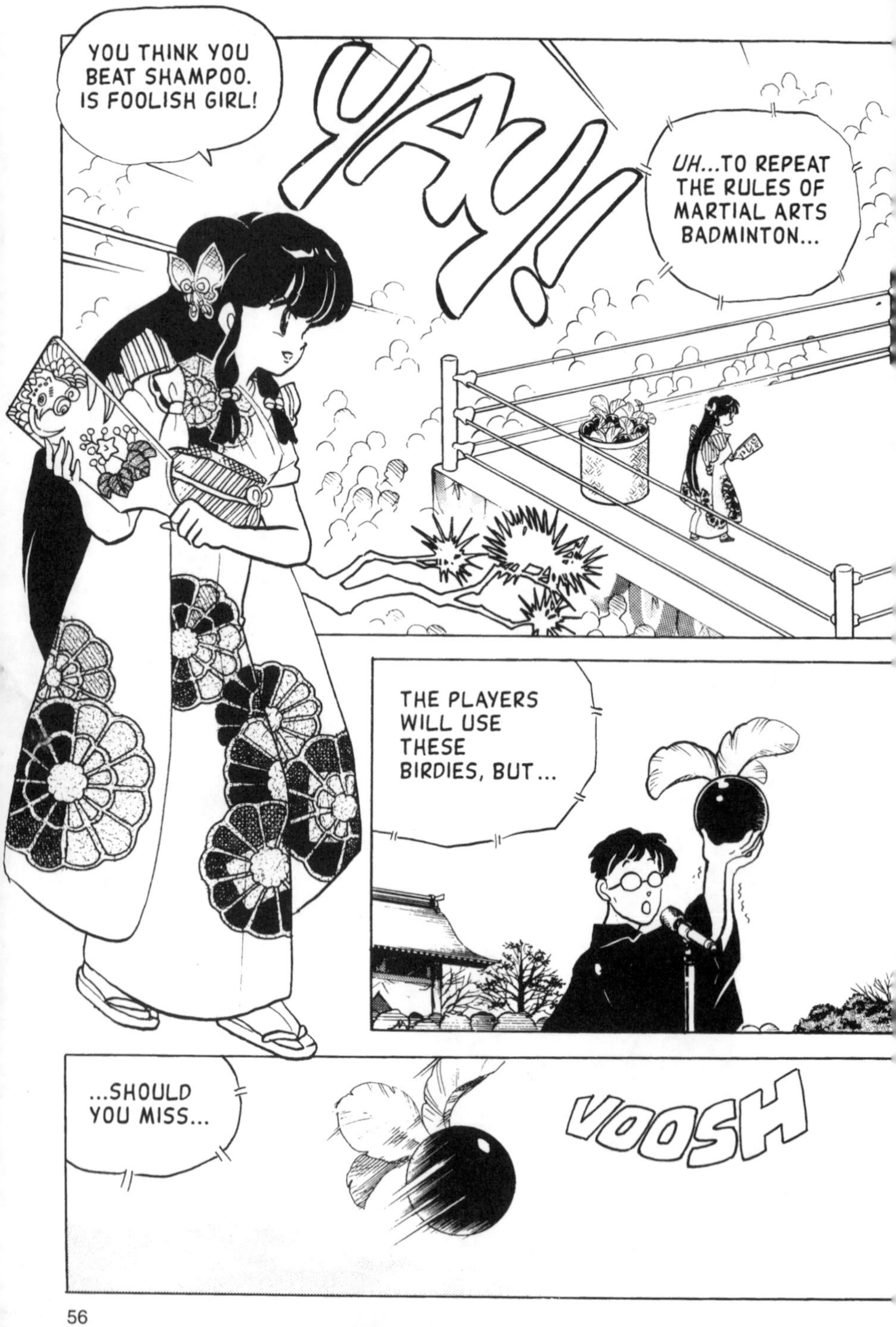
YOU THINK YOU BEAT SHAMPOO. IS FOOLISH GIRL!
YAY!!
UH...TO REPEAT THE RULES OF MARTIAL ARTS BADMINTON...
THE PLAYERS WILL USE THESE BIRDIES, BUT...
...SHOULD YOU MISS...
VOOSH

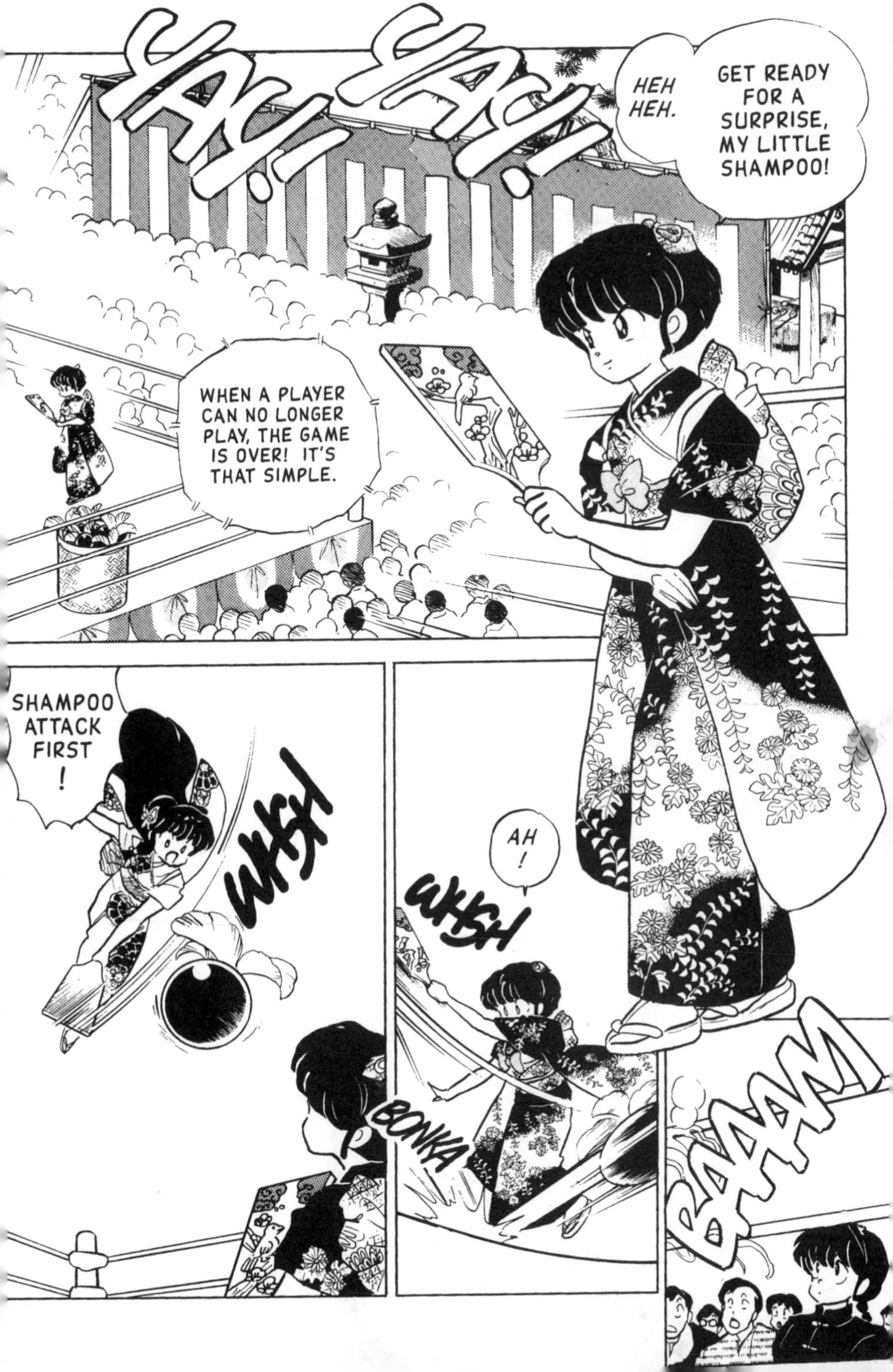
YAY! YAY!
HEH HEH.
GET READY FOR A SURPRISE, MY LITTLE SHAMPOO!
WHEN A PLAYER CAN NO LONGER PLAY, THE GAME IS OVER! IT'S THAT SIMPLE.
SHAMPOO ATTACK FIRST !
WHSH
AH !
WHSH
BONKA
BAAAM

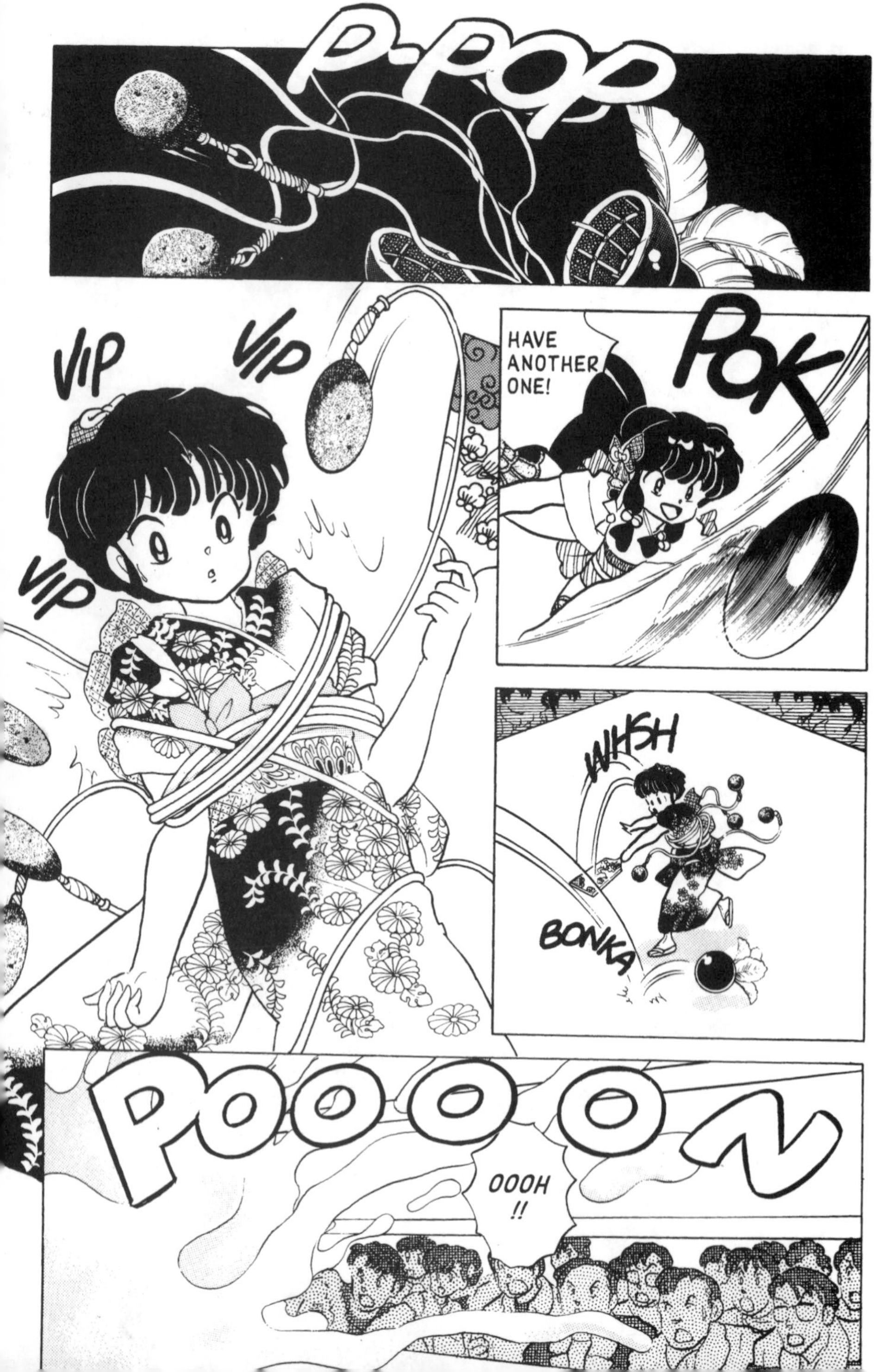
P-POP
VIP
VIP
VIP
HAVE ANOTHER ONE!
POK
WHSH
BONKA
POOOON
OOOH !!

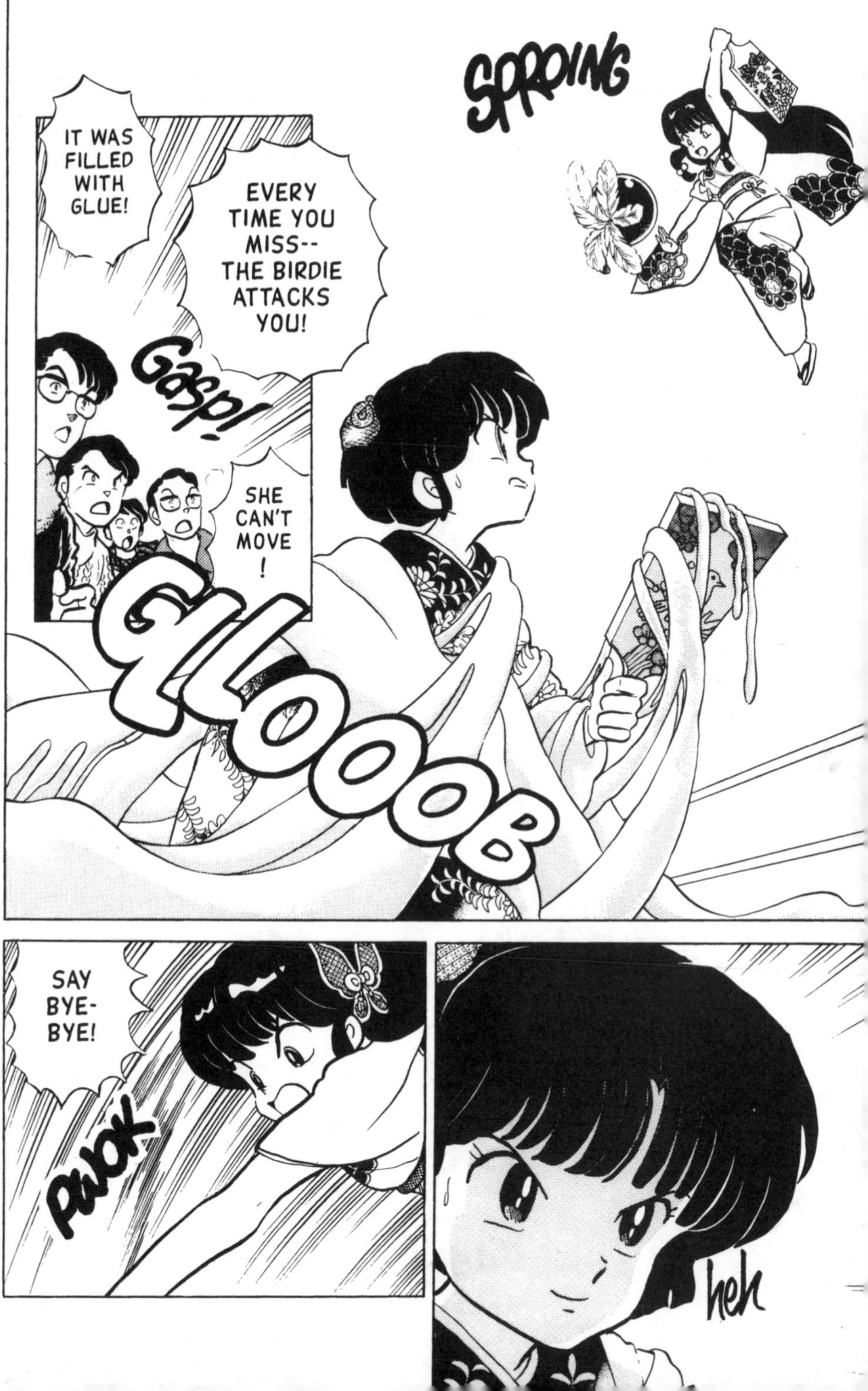
IT WAS FILLED WITH GLUE!
EVERY TIME YOU MISS-- THE BIRDIE ATTACKS YOU!
SPROING
Gasp!
SHE CAN'T MOVE!
GLOOOOB
SAY BYE-BYE!
PWOK
heh

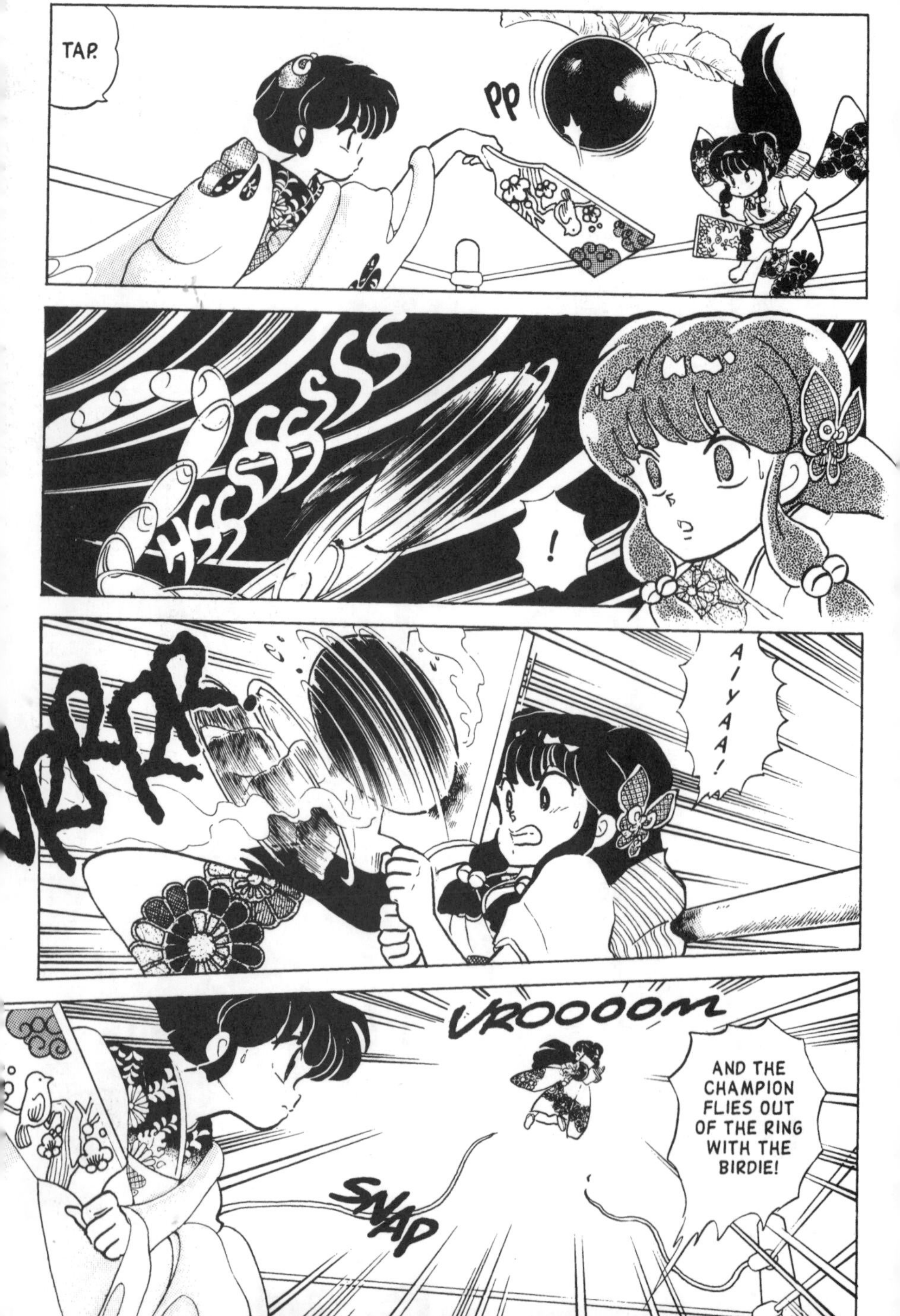
TAP.
PP
HSSSSSSSS
!
AIYAA!
VROOOOM
AND THE CHAMPION FLIES OUT OF THE RING WITH THE BIRDIE!
SNAP

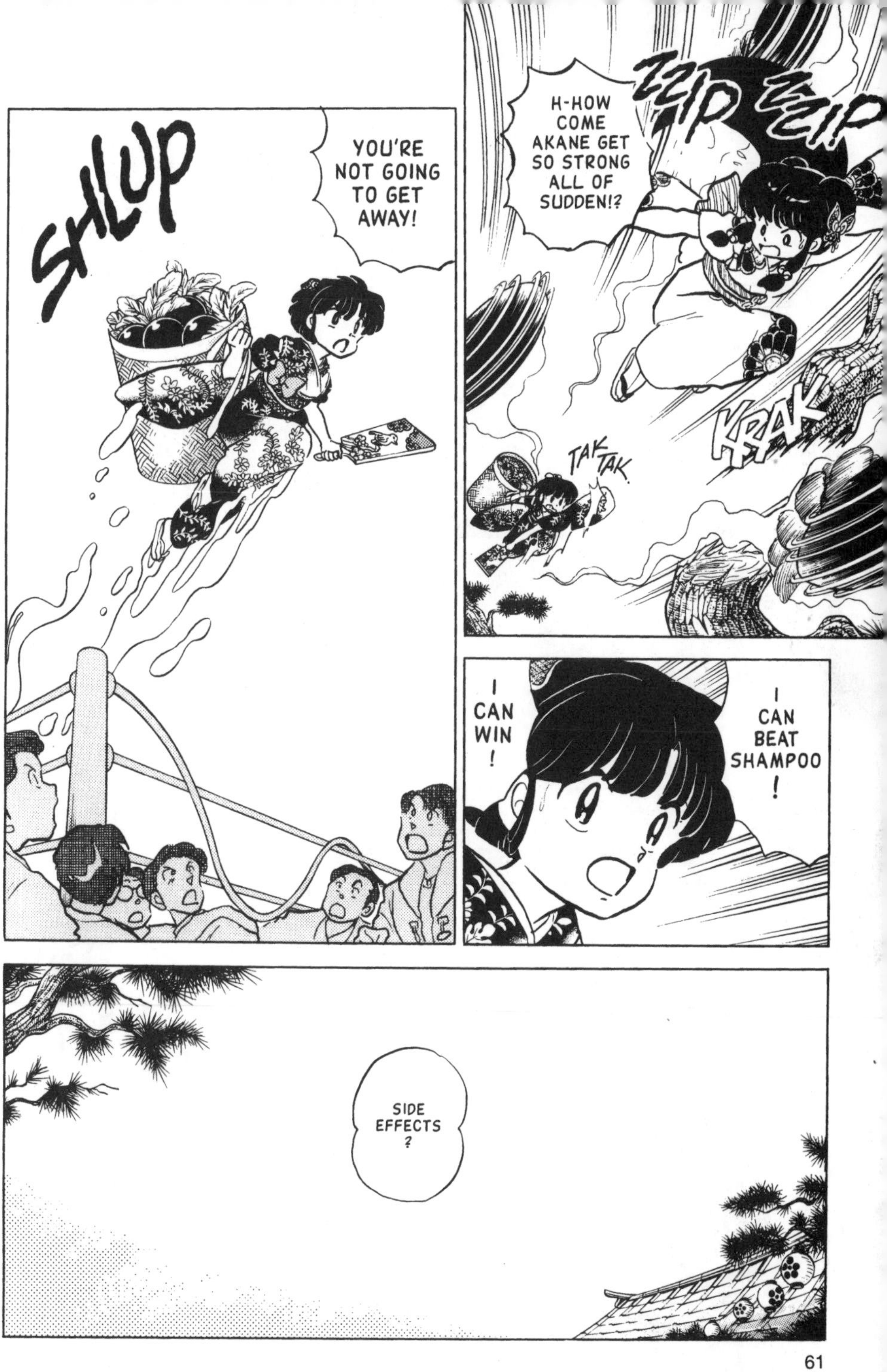
SHLUP
YOU'RE NOT GOING TO GET AWAY!
H-HOW COME AKANE GET SO STRONG ALL OF SUDDEN!?
ZZIP ZZIP
KRAK
TAK TAK
I CAN WIN!
I CAN BEAT SHAMPOO!
SIDE EFFECTS?

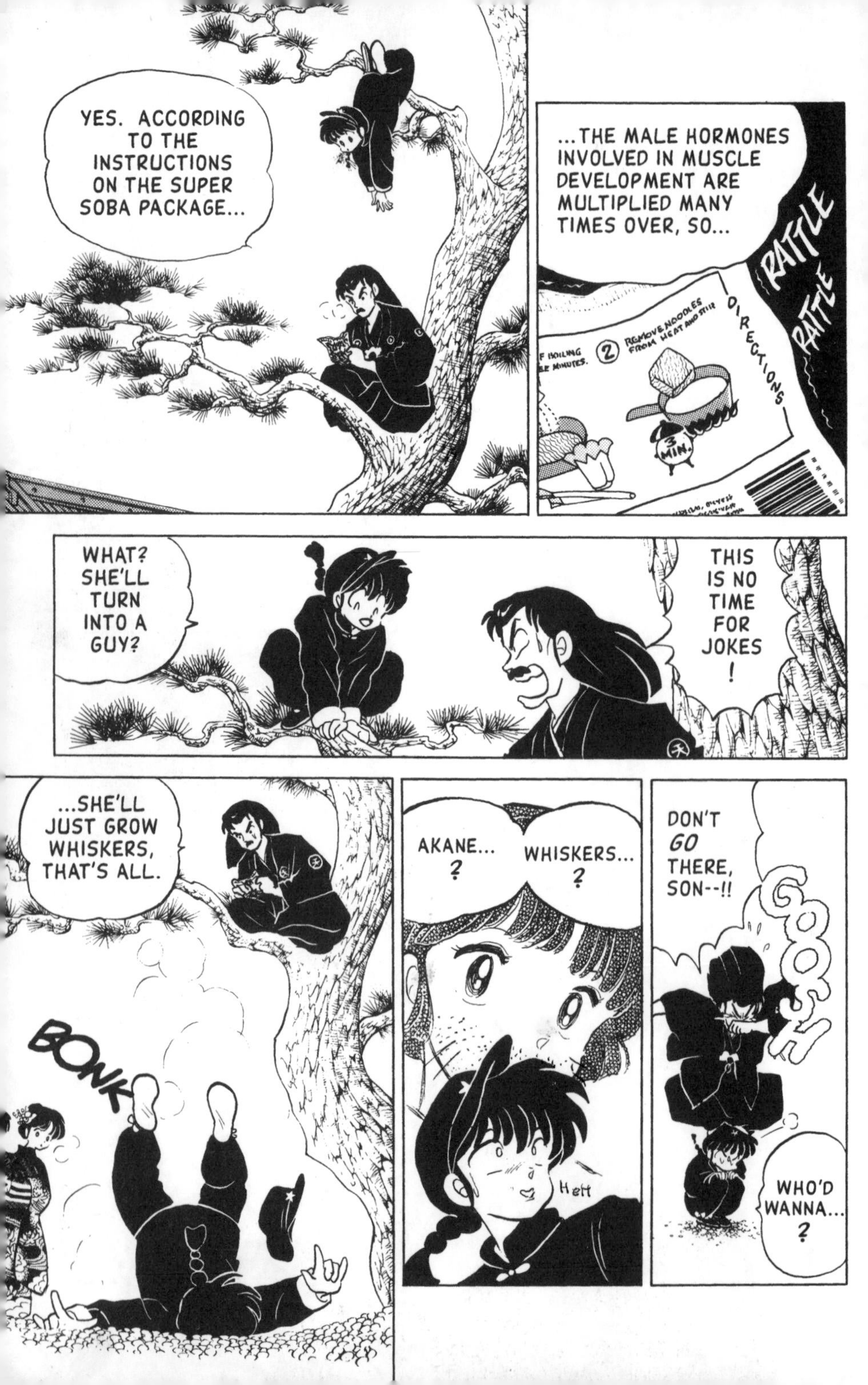
YES. ACCORDING TO THE INSTRUCTIONS ON THE SUPER SOBA PACKAGE...
...THE MALE HORMONES INVOLVED IN MUSCLE DEVELOPMENT ARE MULTIPLIED MANY TIMES OVER, SO...
RATTLE RATTLE
DIRECTIONS
2 REMOVE NOODLES FROM HEAT AND STIR
3 MIN.
WHAT? SHE'LL TURN INTO A GUY?
THIS IS NO TIME FOR JOKES!
...SHE'LL JUST GROW WHISKERS, THAT'S ALL.
BONK
AKANE...?
WHISKERS...?
Heh
DON'T GO THERE, SON--!!
GOOSH
WHO'D WANNA...?

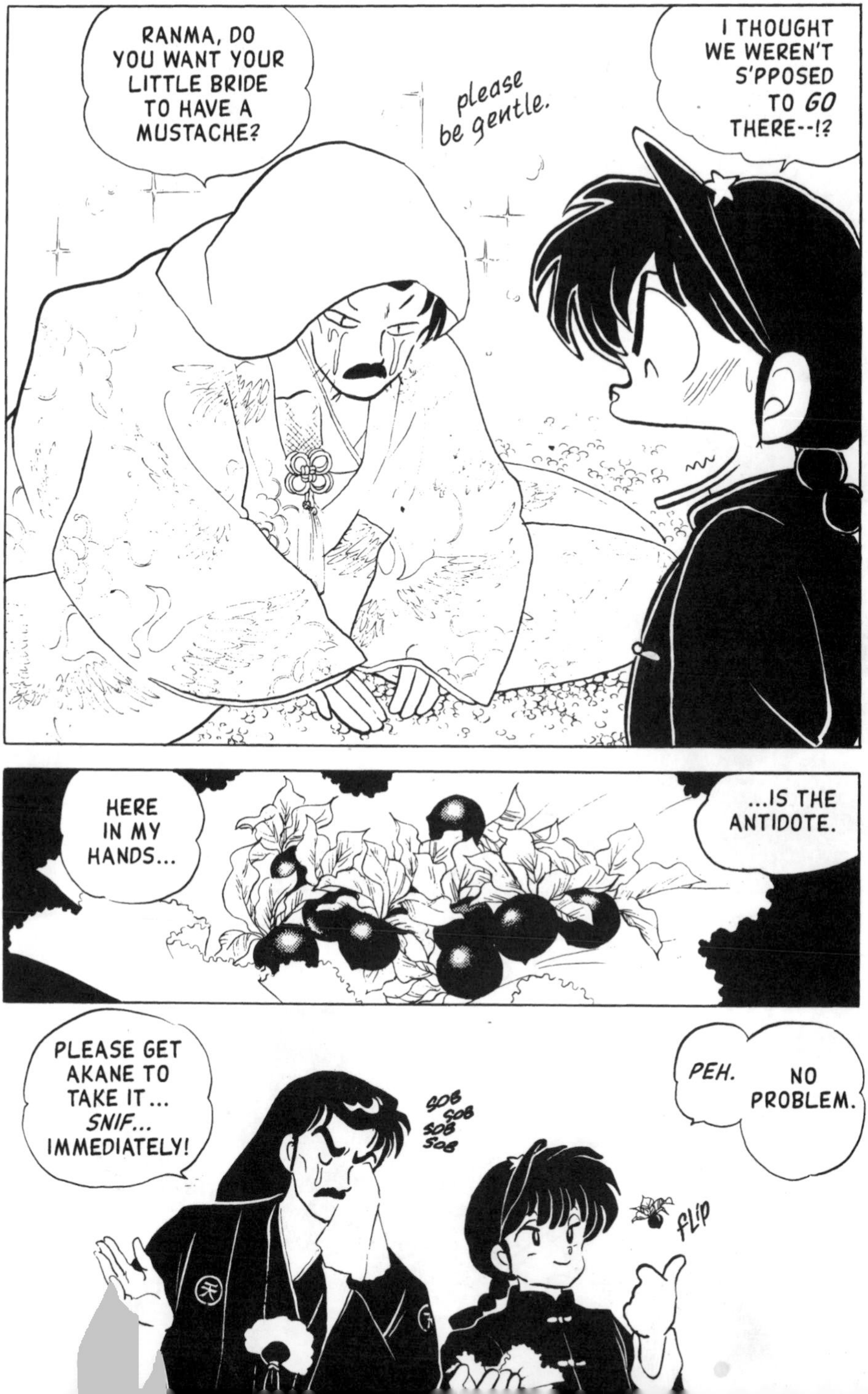
RANMA, DO YOU WANT YOUR LITTLE BRIDE TO HAVE A MUSTACHE?
please be gentle.
I THOUGHT WE WEREN'T S'PPOSED TO *GO* THERE--!?
HERE IN MY HANDS...
...IS THE ANTIDOTE.
PLEASE GET AKANE TO TAKE IT... *SNIF*... IMMEDIATELY!
SOB SOB SOB SOB
PEH.
NO PROBLEM.
flip

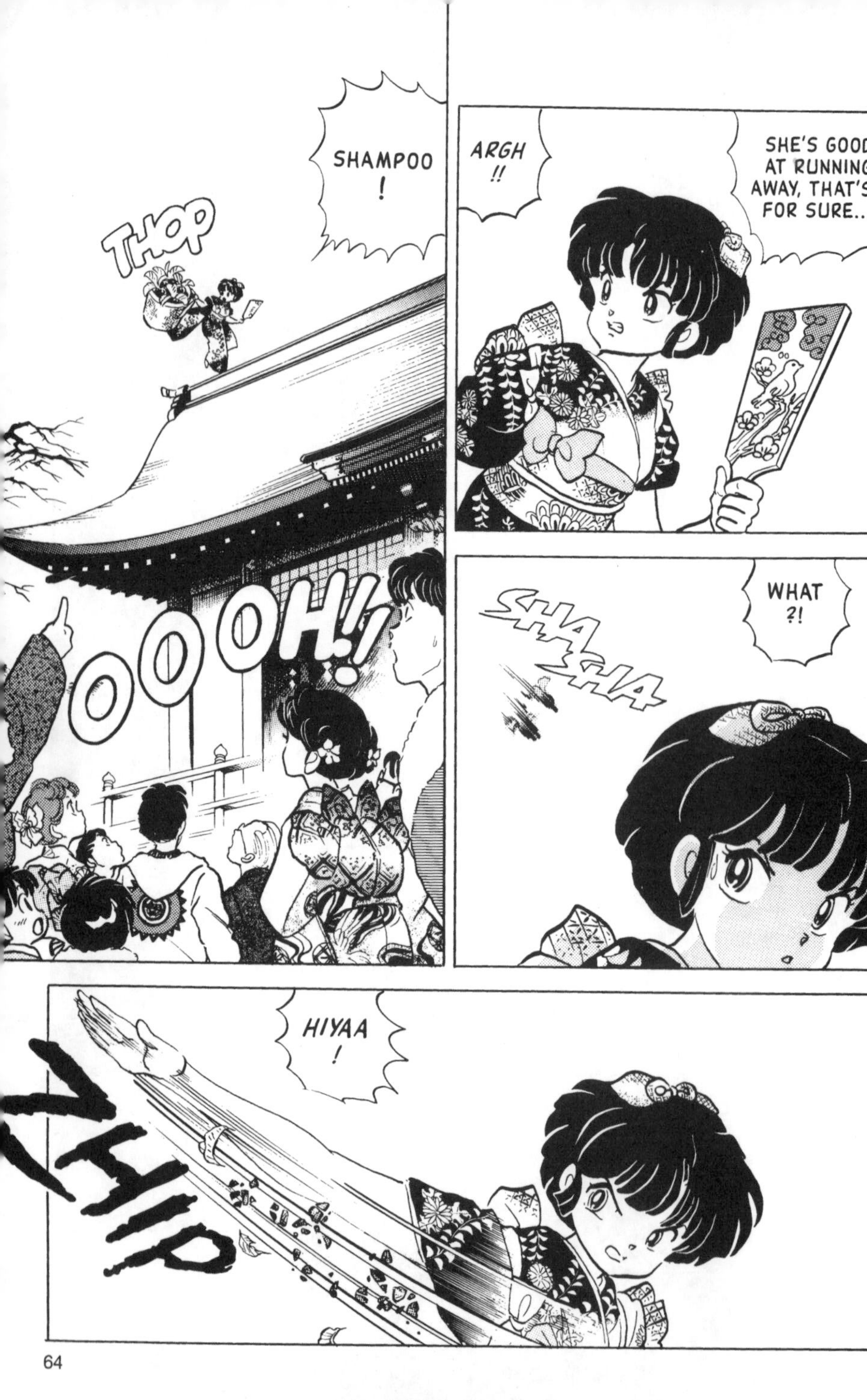
SHAMPOO !
THOP
OOOH!!
ARGH !!
SHE'S GOOD AT RUNNING AWAY, THAT'S FOR SURE...
SHA SHA
WHAT ?!
HIYAA !
WHIP

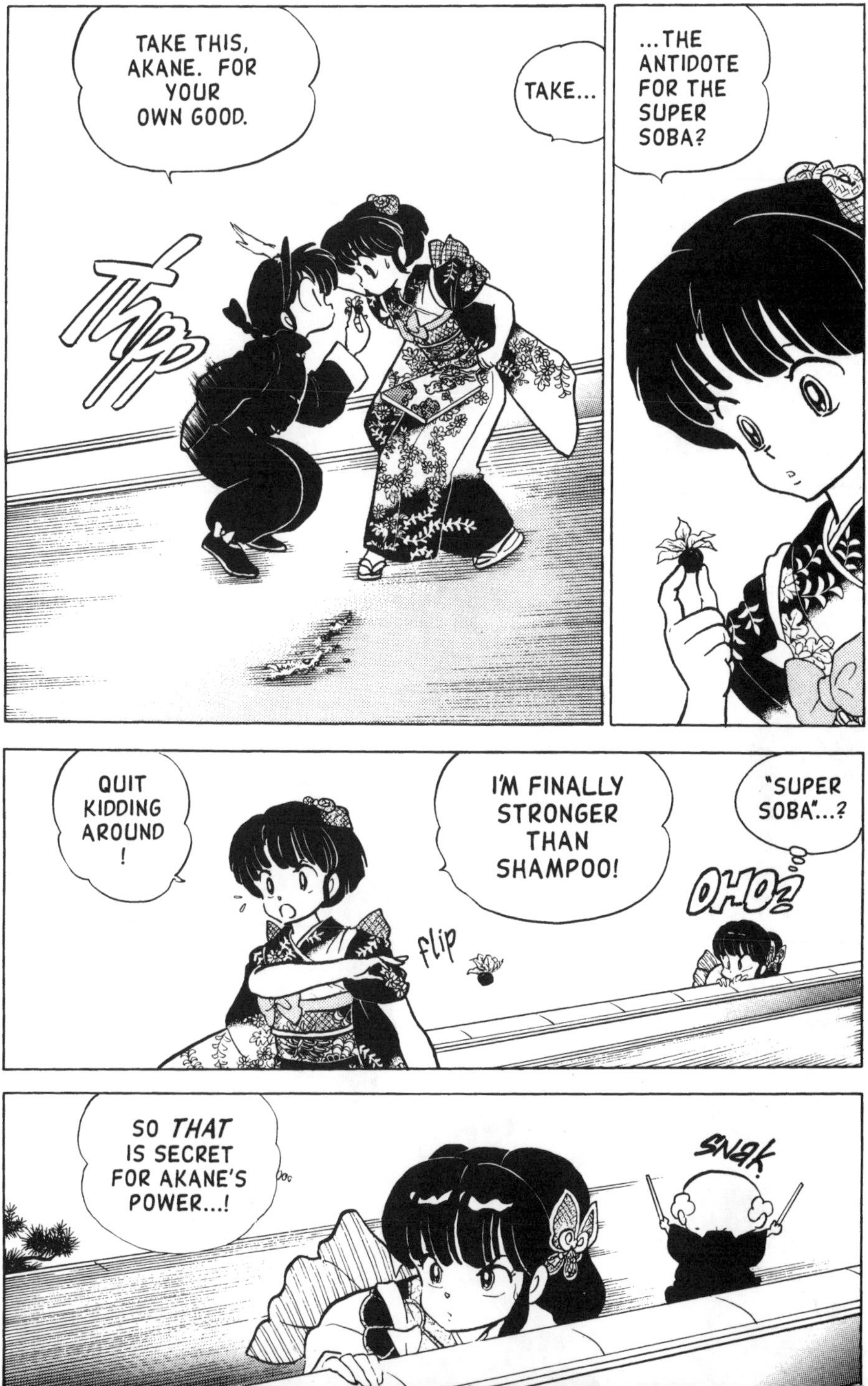
TAKE THIS, AKANE. FOR YOUR OWN GOOD.
TAKE...
THPP
...THE ANTIDOTE FOR THE SUPER SOBA?
QUIT KIDDING AROUND!
I'M FINALLY STRONGER THAN SHAMPOO!
flip
"SUPER SOBA"...?
OHO?
SO THAT IS SECRET FOR AKANE'S POWER...!
SNAK

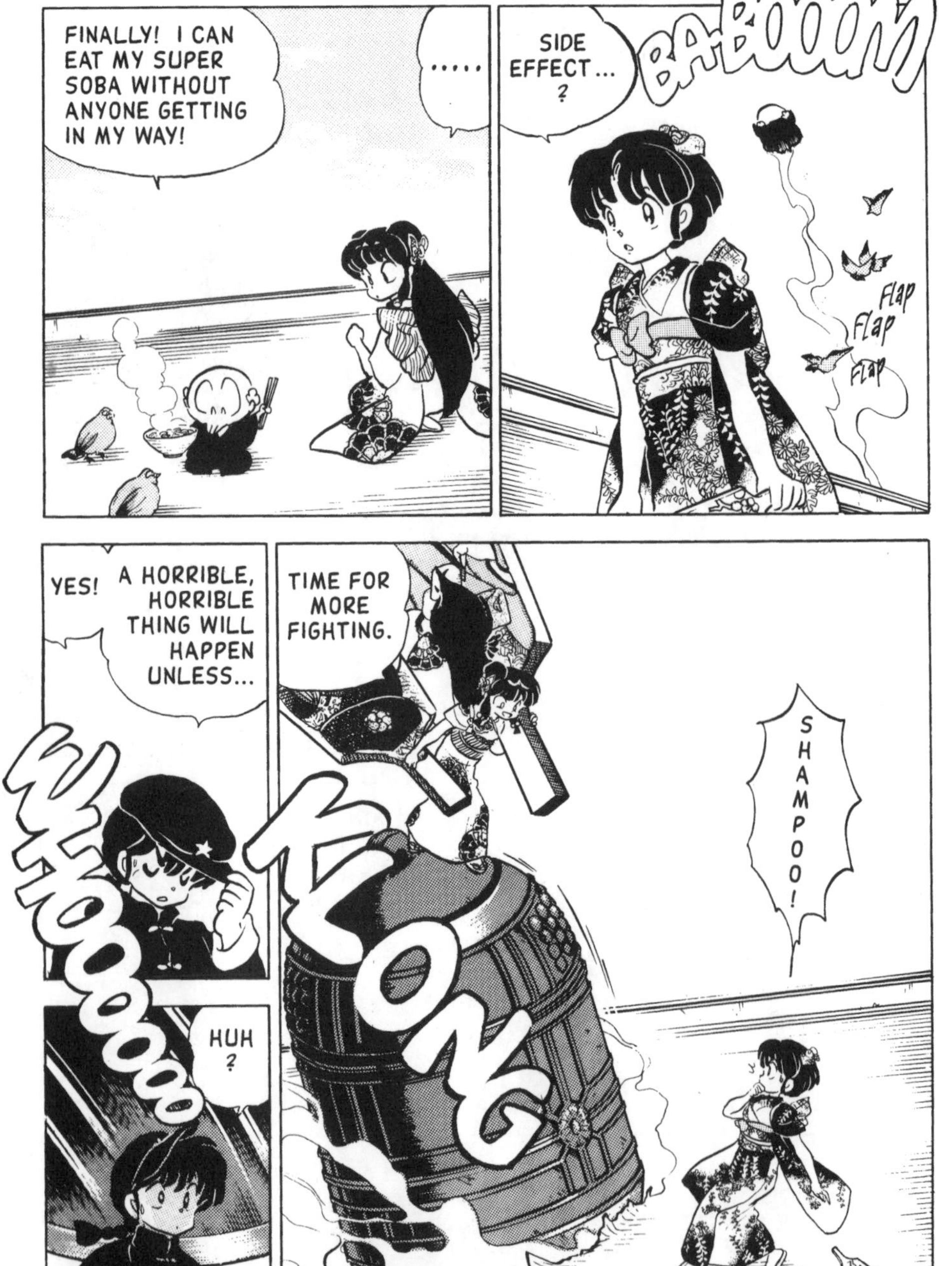
FINALLY! I CAN EAT MY SUPER SOBA WITHOUT ANYONE GETTING IN MY WAY!
.....
SIDE EFFECT... ?
BA-BOOOM
FLAP
FLAP
FLAP
YES!
A HORRIBLE, HORRIBLE THING WILL HAPPEN UNLESS...
WHOOOOOO
HUH ?
TIME FOR MORE FIGHTING.
KLONG
SHAMPOO!

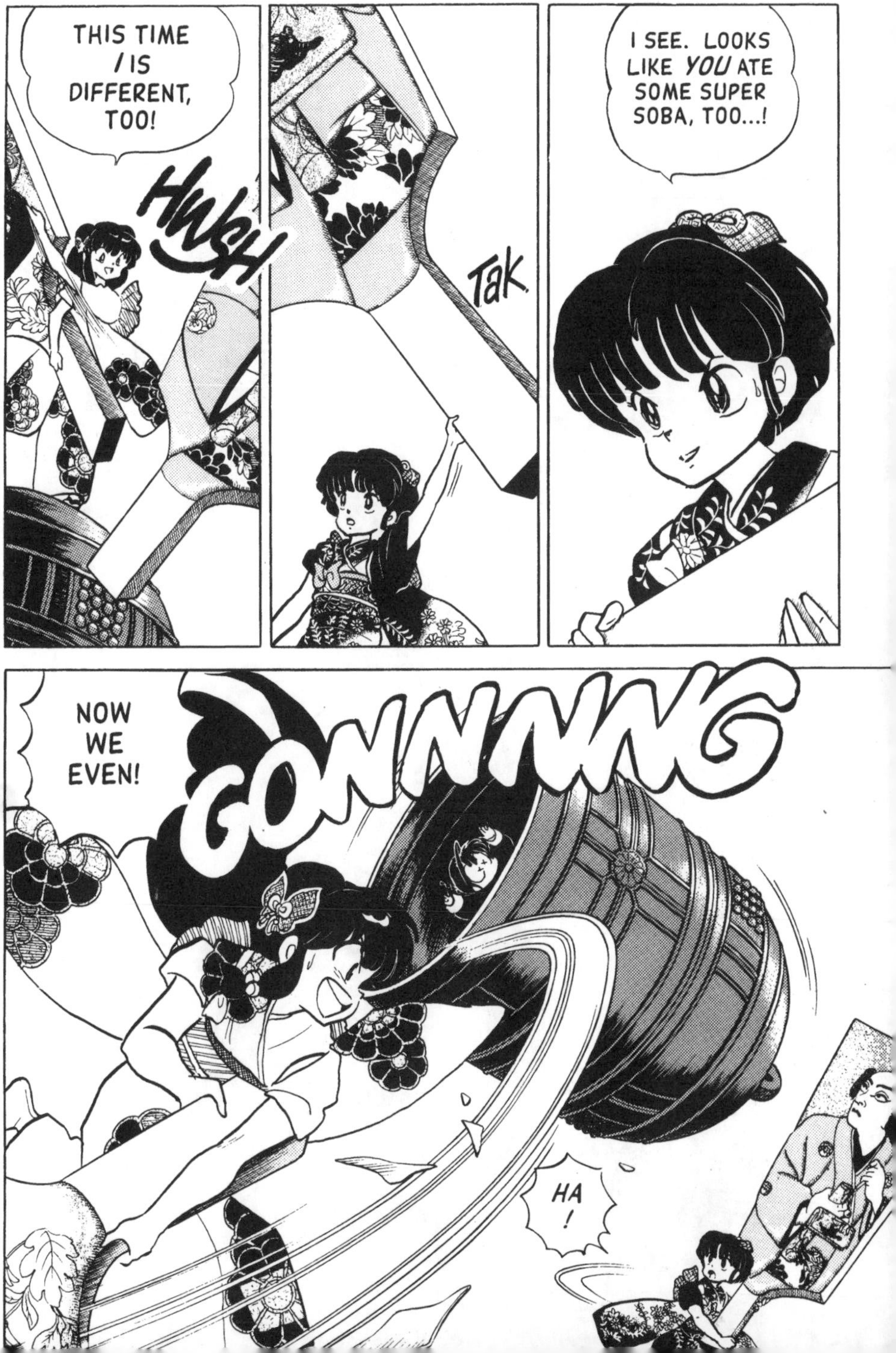
THIS TIME I IS DIFFERENT, TOO!
HWGH
TAK
I SEE. LOOKS LIKE YOU ATE SOME SUPER SOBA, TOO...!
NOW WE EVEN!
GONNNNG
HA!

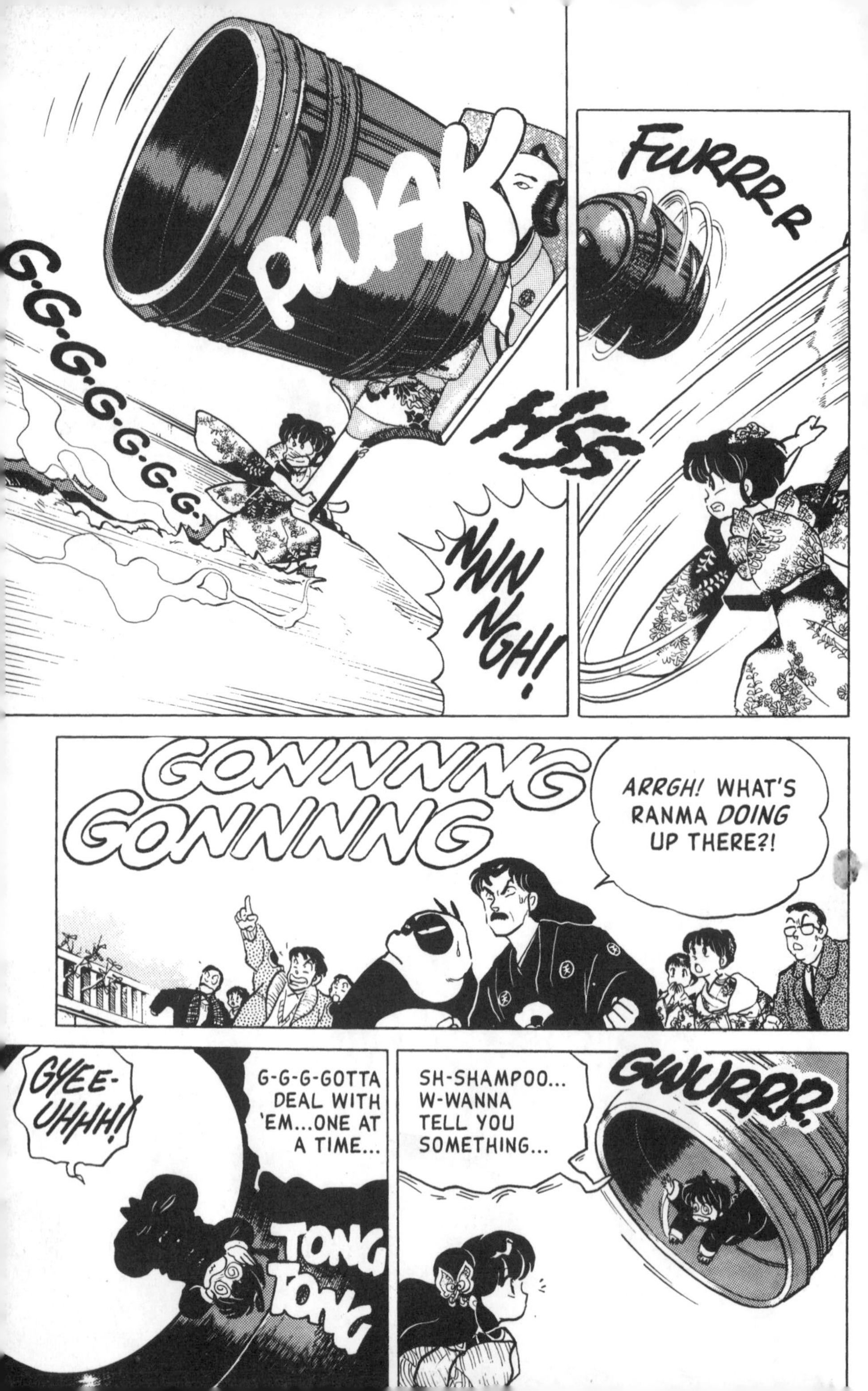
G-G-G-G-G-G-G-G-G
PWAK
FURRRR
HSS
NNNNGH!
GONNNNG
GONNNNG
ARRGH! WHAT'S RANMA DOING UP THERE?!
GYEE-UHHH!
G-G-G-GOTTA DEAL WITH 'EM...ONE AT A TIME...
TONG
TONG
SH-SHAMPOO... W-WANNA TELL YOU SOMETHING...
GWURRR

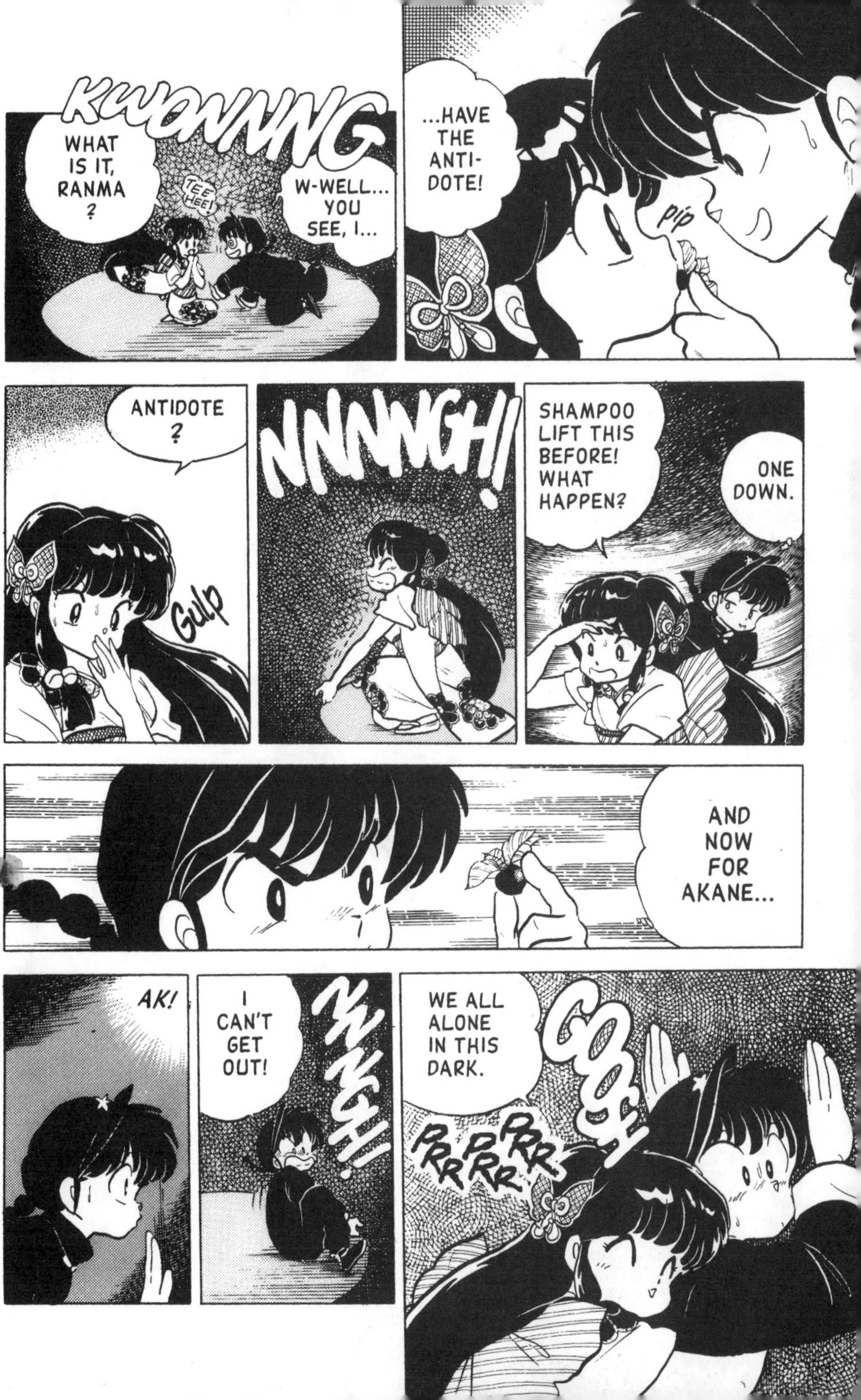
KWONNNG
WHAT IS IT, RANMA?
TEE HEE!
W-WELL... YOU SEE, I...
...HAVE THE ANTI-DOTE!
pip
ANTIDOTE?
Gulp
NNNNGH!
SHAMPOO LIFT THIS BEFORE! WHAT HAPPEN?
ONE DOWN.
AND NOW FOR AKANE...
AK!
I CAN'T GET OUT!
NNNGH!
WE ALL ALONE IN THIS DARK.
GOOH
PRRRRRRRR

H-HEY! TH-THIS IS NO TIME FOR--

?

KLANG KLONG

OF COURSE! I KNOW HOW TO GET US OUT OF HERE...!

WAAAAAH! SHAMPOO! PUT YOUR CLOTHES BACK ON!

POONG

FSSHH

WHAT ARE YOU TWO *DOING* IN THERE?!

SHAMPOO NO TAKE CLOTHES OFF. *HMPH.*

YOU DUMMY! YOU MAY HAVE MUSCLES, BUT YOU'VE STILL GOT NO BRAINS.

GRRR...

WHAT DID YOU SAY?!

KA-TONNG

THERE HE GOES MAKING HER MAD AGAIN.

AKANE... PLEASE TAKE THE ANTI-DOTE!

SOB SOB SOB SOB

PART 5
SERIOUS SIDE EFFECTS

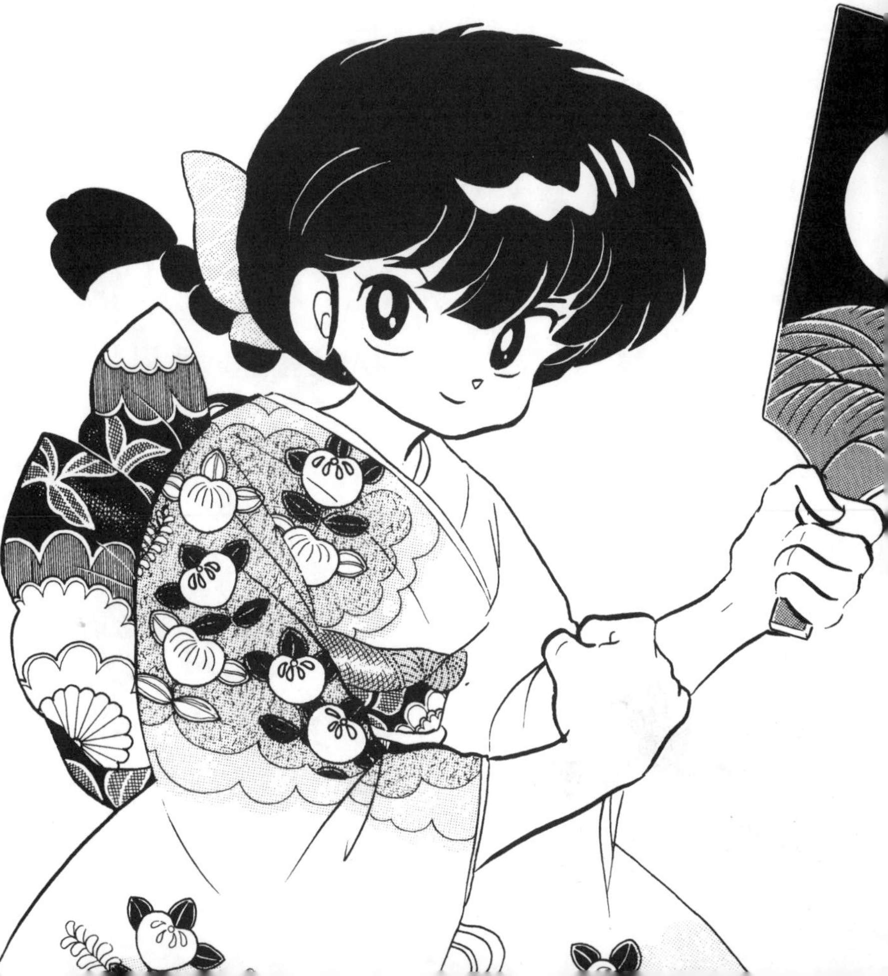

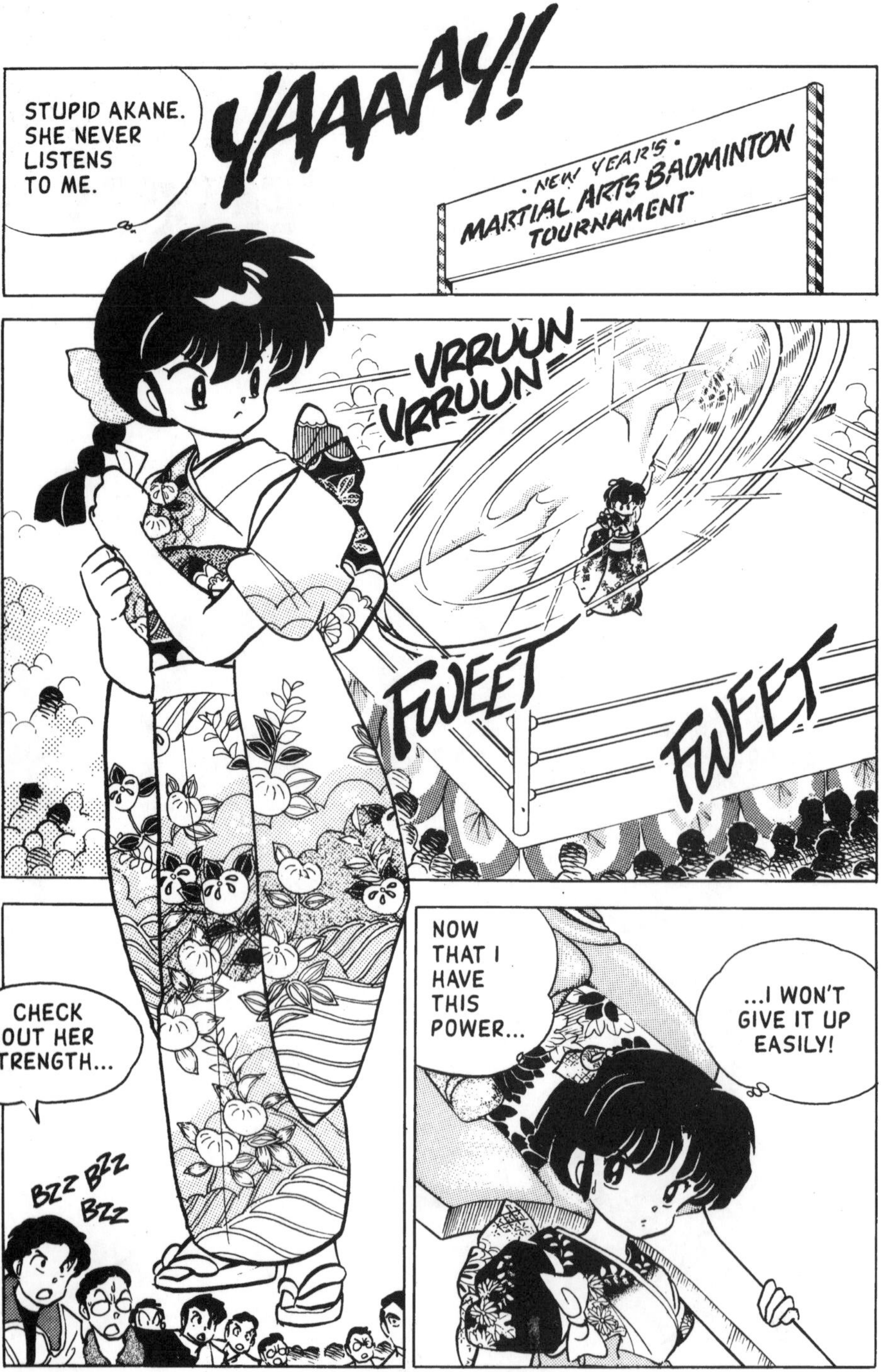
STUPID AKANE. SHE NEVER LISTENS TO ME.
YAAAAY!
·NEW YEAR'S· MARTIAL ARTS BADMINTON TOURNAMENT
VRRUUN VRRUUN
FWEET
FWEET
CHECK OUT HER STRENGTH...
BZZ BZZ BZZ
NOW THAT I HAVE THIS POWER...
...I WON'T GIVE IT UP EASILY!

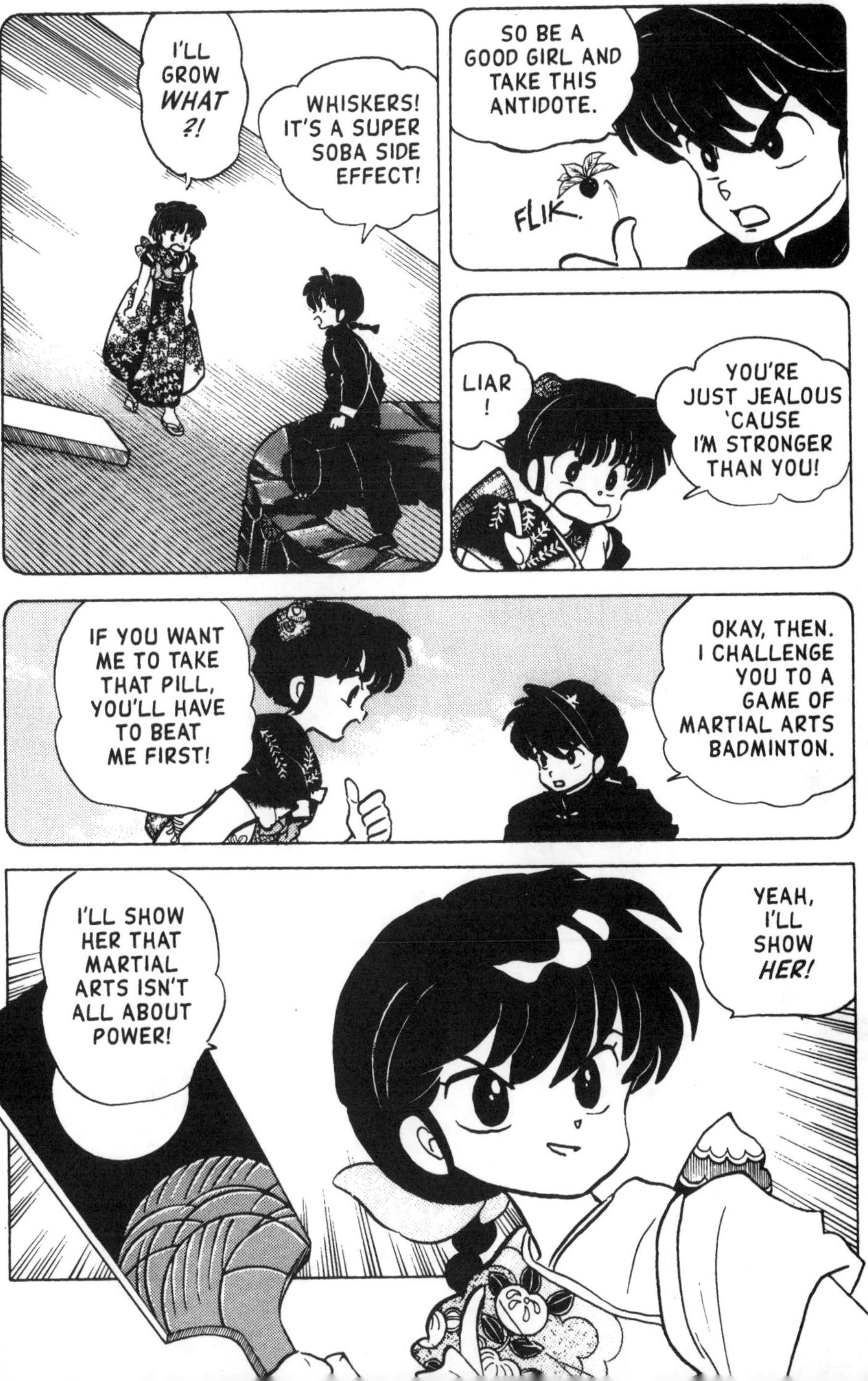
I'LL GROW *WHAT* ?!
WHISKERS! IT'S A SUPER SOBA SIDE EFFECT!
SO BE A GOOD GIRL AND TAKE THIS ANTIDOTE.
FLIK
LIAR!
YOU'RE JUST JEALOUS 'CAUSE I'M STRONGER THAN YOU!
IF YOU WANT ME TO TAKE THAT PILL, YOU'LL HAVE TO BEAT ME FIRST!
OKAY, THEN. I CHALLENGE YOU TO A GAME OF MARTIAL ARTS BADMINTON.
I'LL SHOW HER THAT MARTIAL ARTS ISN'T ALL ABOUT POWER!
YEAH, I'LL SHOW *HER!*

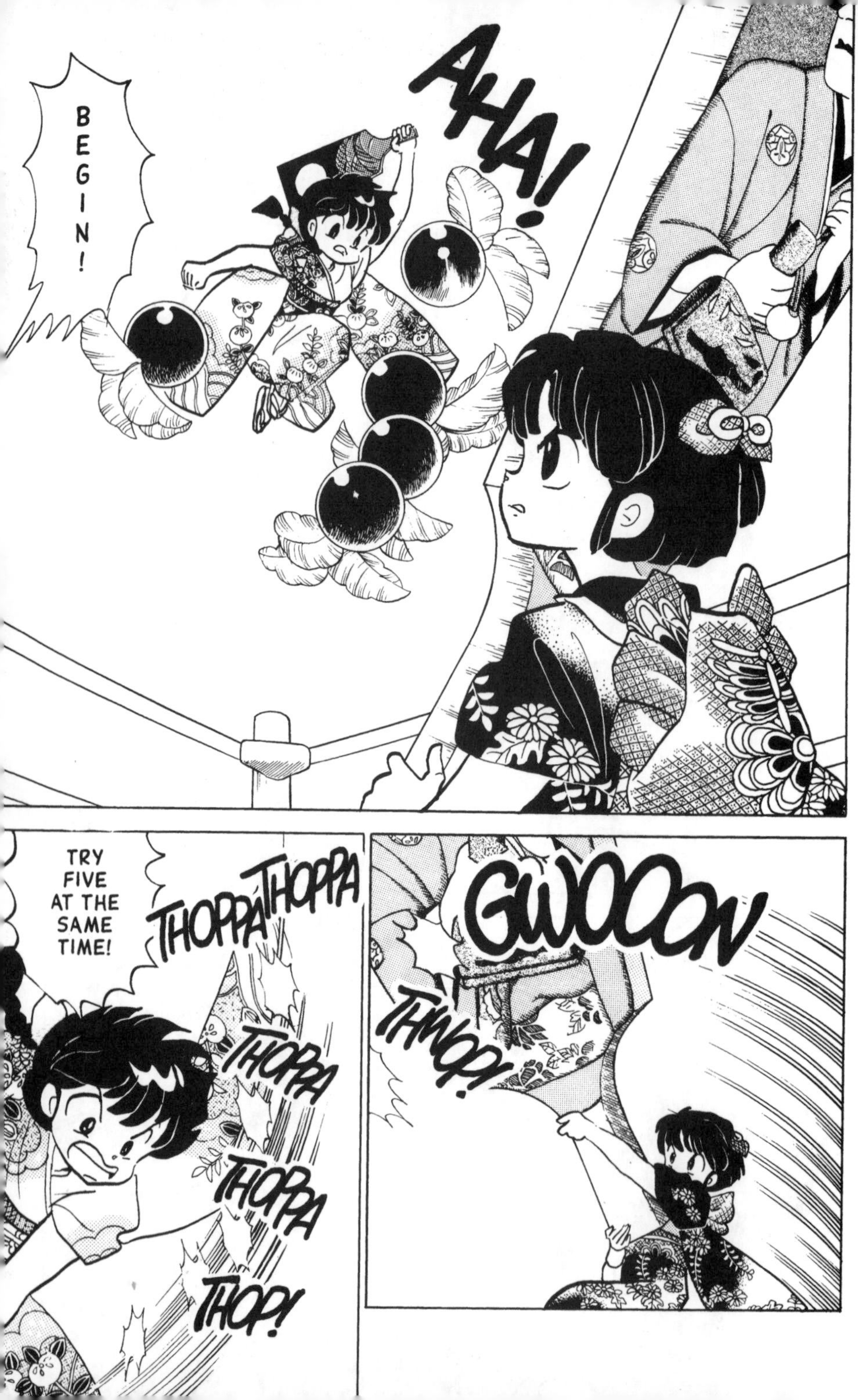
BEGIN!
AHA!
TRY FIVE AT THE SAME TIME!
THOPPA THOPPA
THOPPA
THOPPA
THOP!
GWOOON
THWOP!

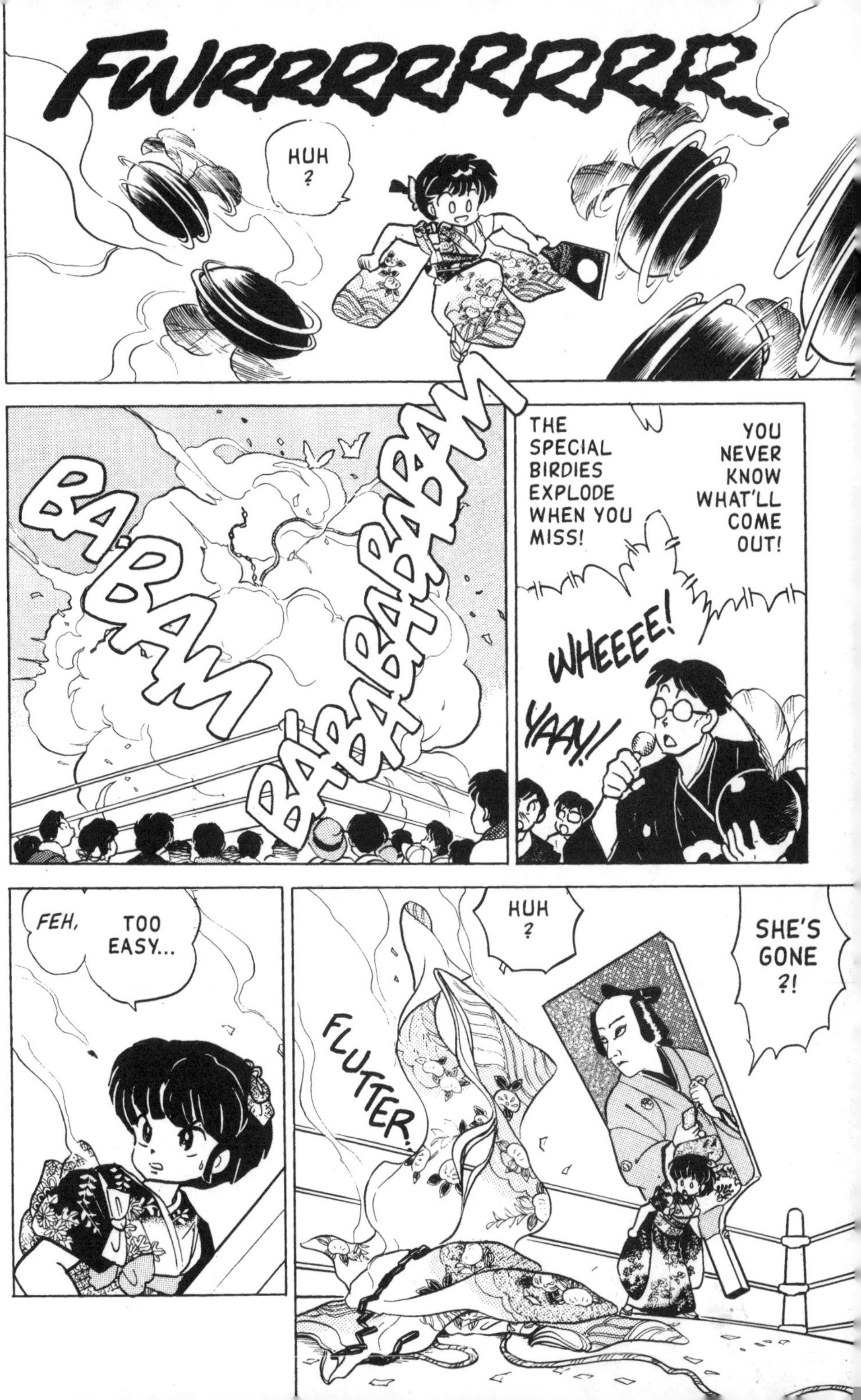
FWRRRRRRRRR
HUH?
BABABAM
BABABABABAM
THE SPECIAL BIRDIES EXPLODE WHEN YOU MISS!
YOU NEVER KNOW WHAT'LL COME OUT!
WHEEEE!
YAAAY!
FEH, TOO EASY...
HUH?
SHE'S GONE?!
FLUTTER

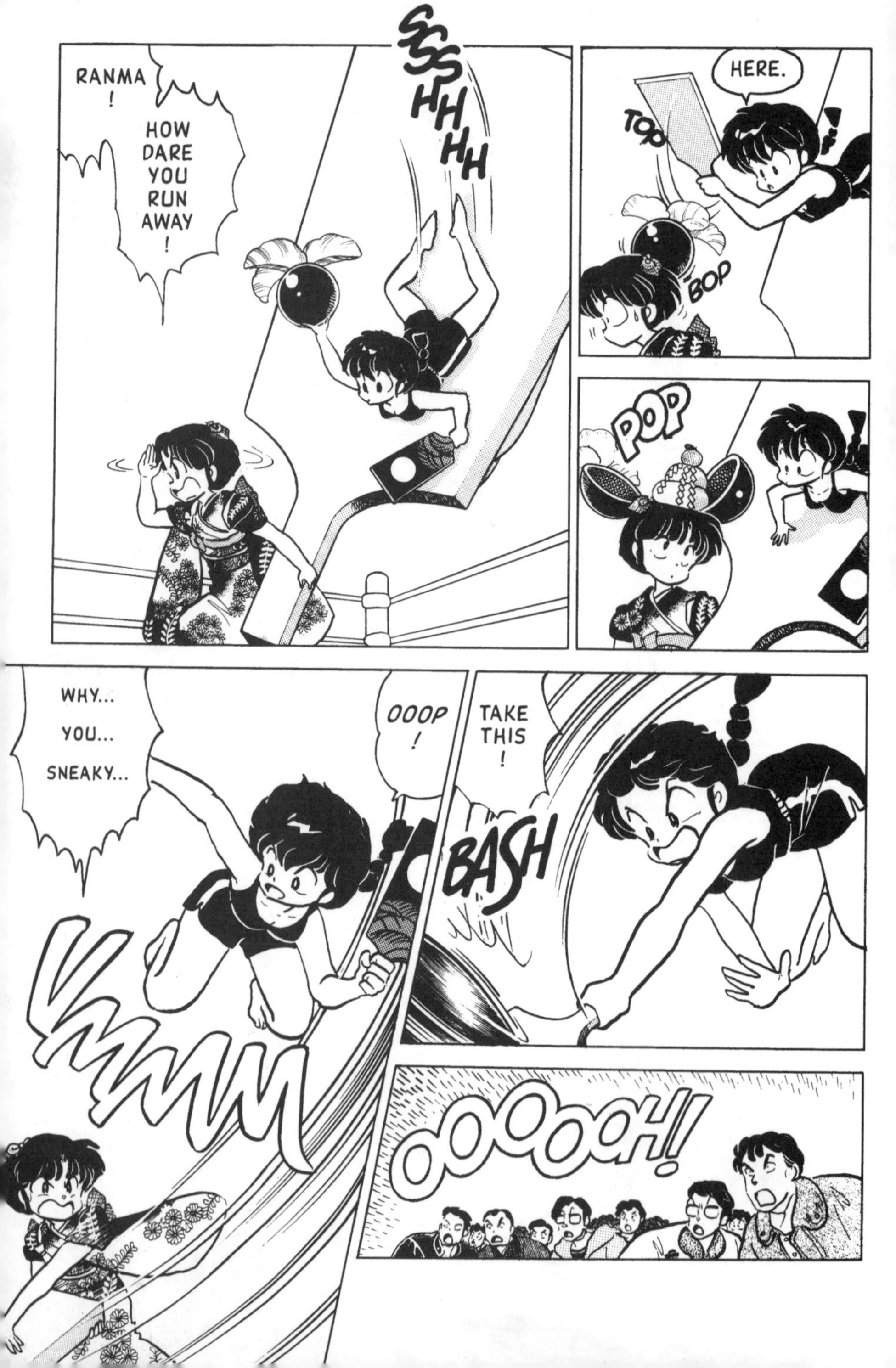
RANMA!
HOW DARE YOU RUN AWAY!
SSSHHHHH
HERE.
TOP
BOP
POP
WHY... YOU... SNEAKY...
VMMM
OOOP!
TAKE THIS!
BASH
OOOOOH!

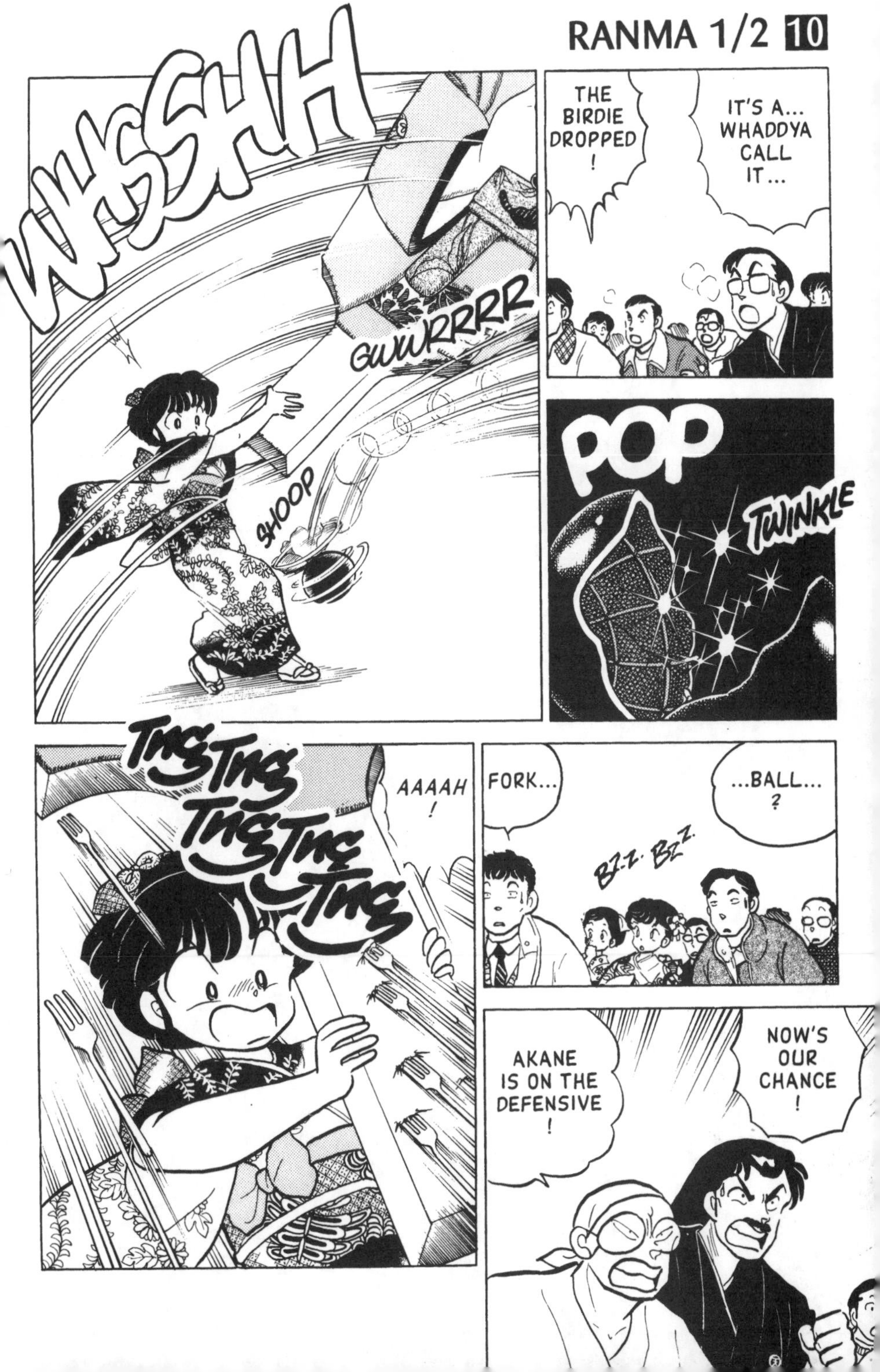
WHSHH
GWURRRR
SHOOP
THE BIRDIE DROPPED !
IT'S A... WHADDYA CALL IT...
POP
TWINKLE
TING TING TING TING TING TING
AAAAH !
FORK...
...BALL... ?
BZ-Z- BZ-Z-
AKANE IS ON THE DEFENSIVE !
NOW'S OUR CHANCE !

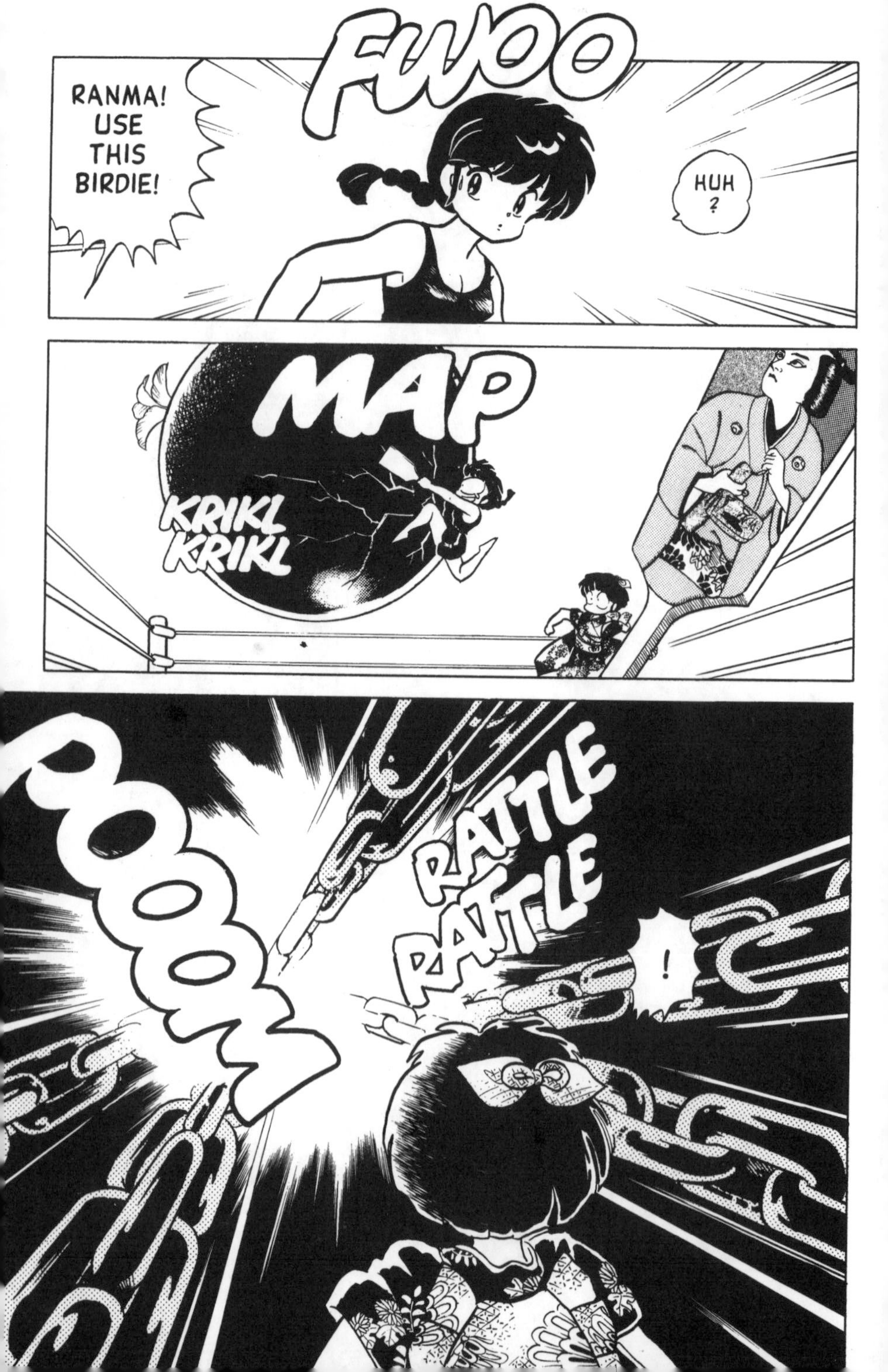
FWOO
RANMA! USE THIS BIRDIE!
HUH?
MAP
KRIKL KRIKL
ROOOOM
RATTLE RATTLE
!

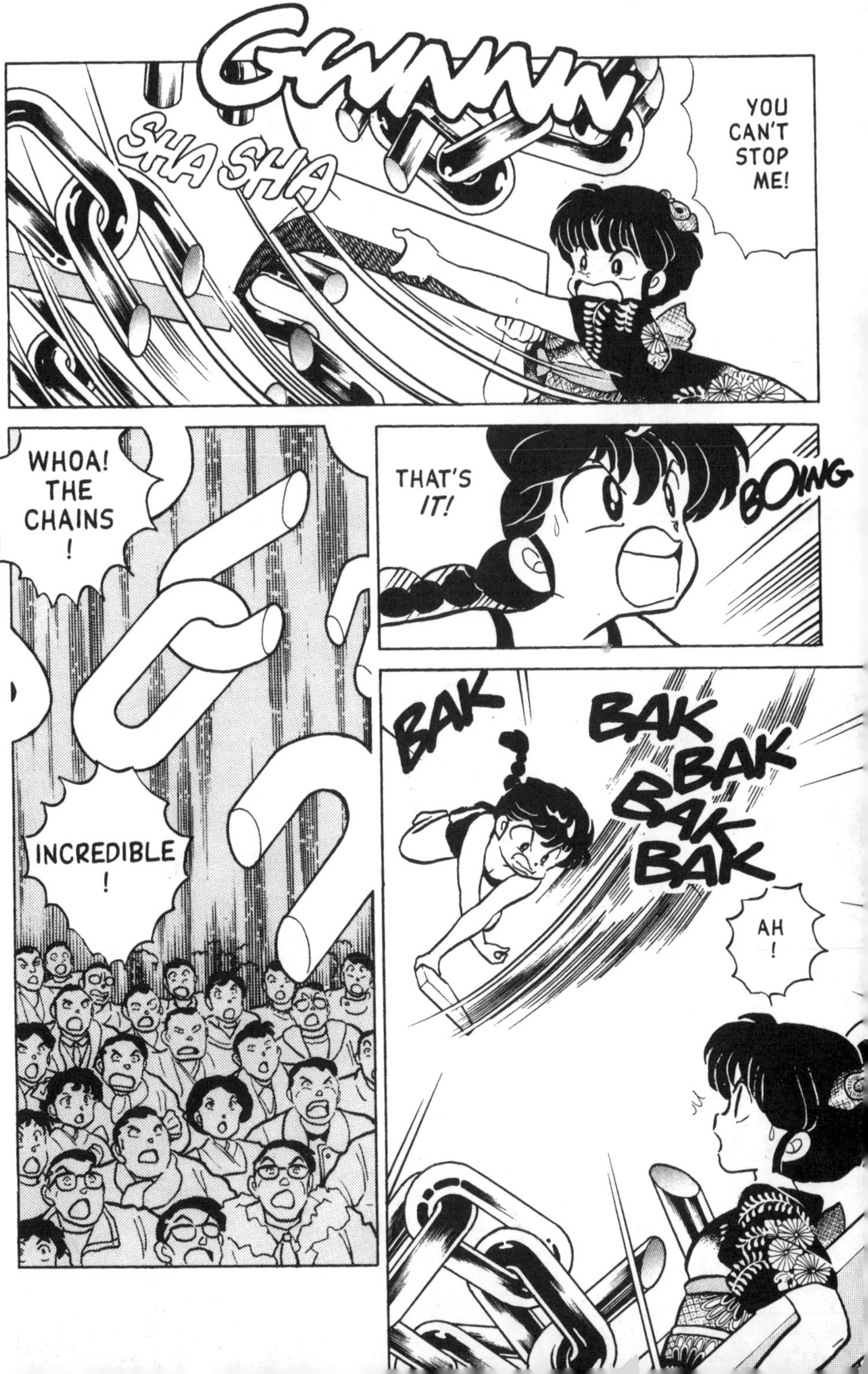
SHA SHA
YOU CAN'T STOP ME!
WHOA! THE CHAINS!
INCREDIBLE!
THAT'S IT!
BOING
BAK
BAK BAK BAK BAK
AH!

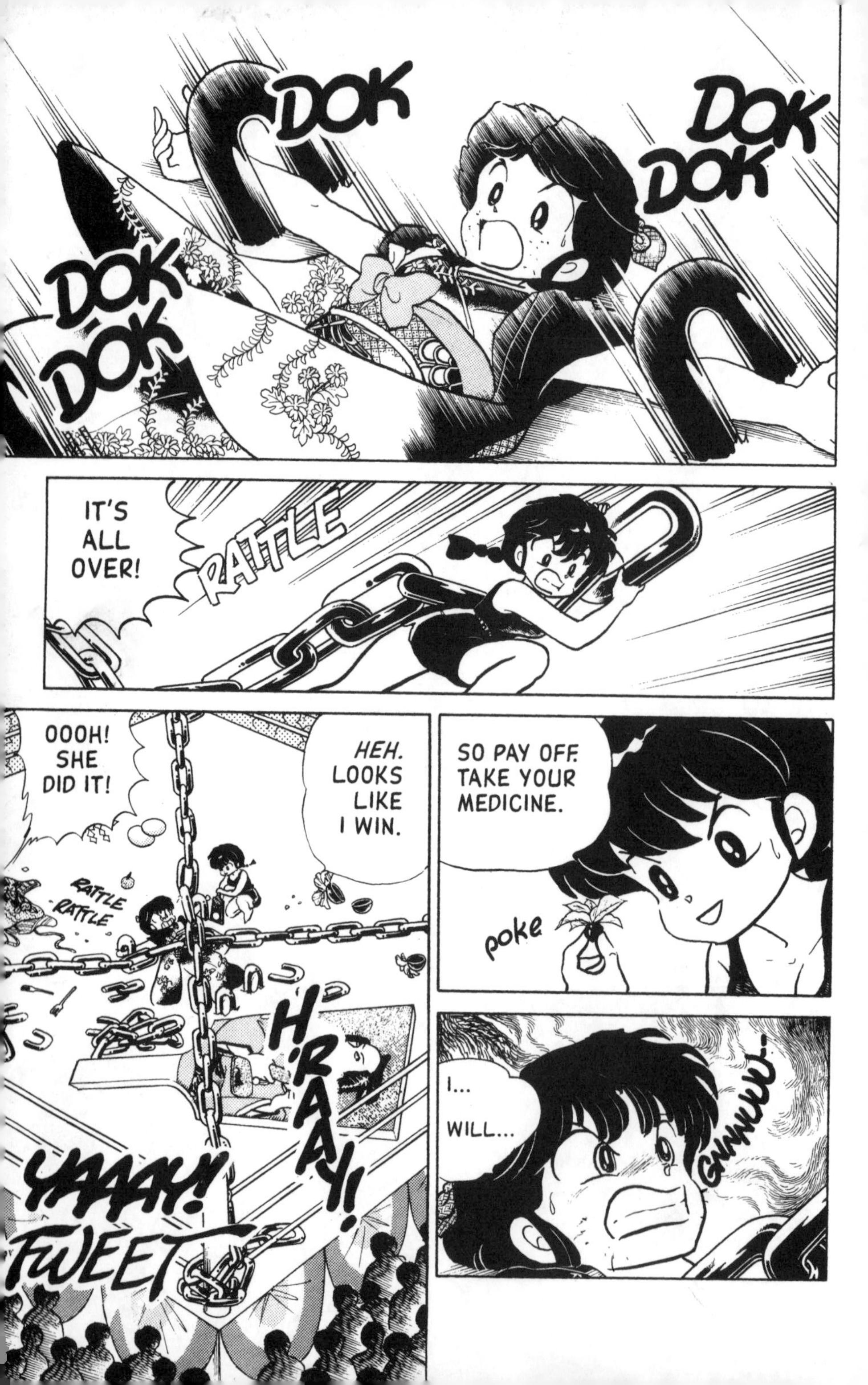
DOK
DOK DOK
DOK DOK
IT'S ALL OVER!
RATTLE
OOOH! SHE DID IT!
RATTLE RATTLE
HEH. LOOKS LIKE I WIN.
HRAAY!!
YAAAY!
TWEET
SO PAY OFF. TAKE YOUR MEDICINE.
poke
I... WILL...
GNNNUUU...

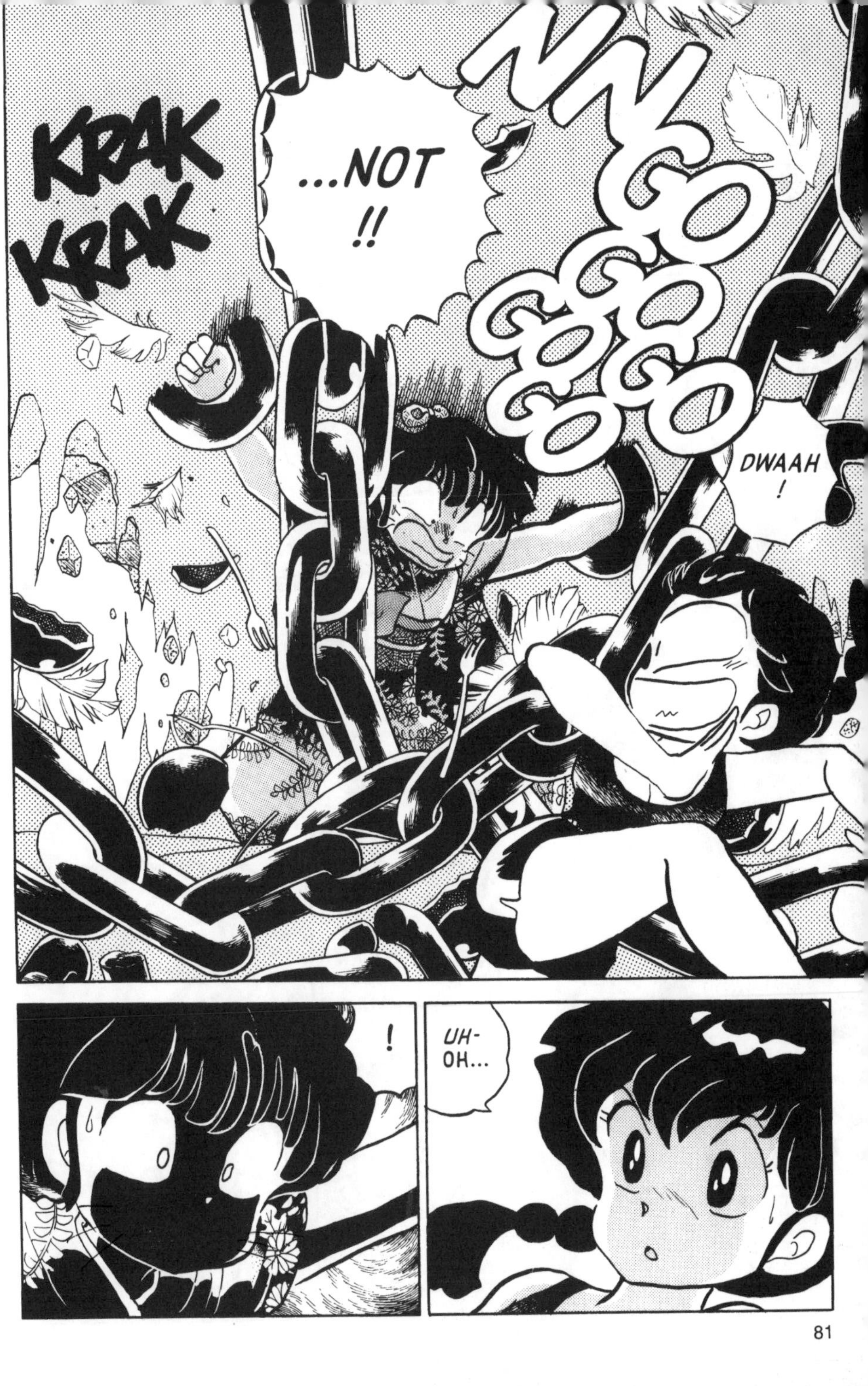
KRAK KRAK
...NOT !!
NNGOGOGOGO
DWAAH !
!
UH- OH...

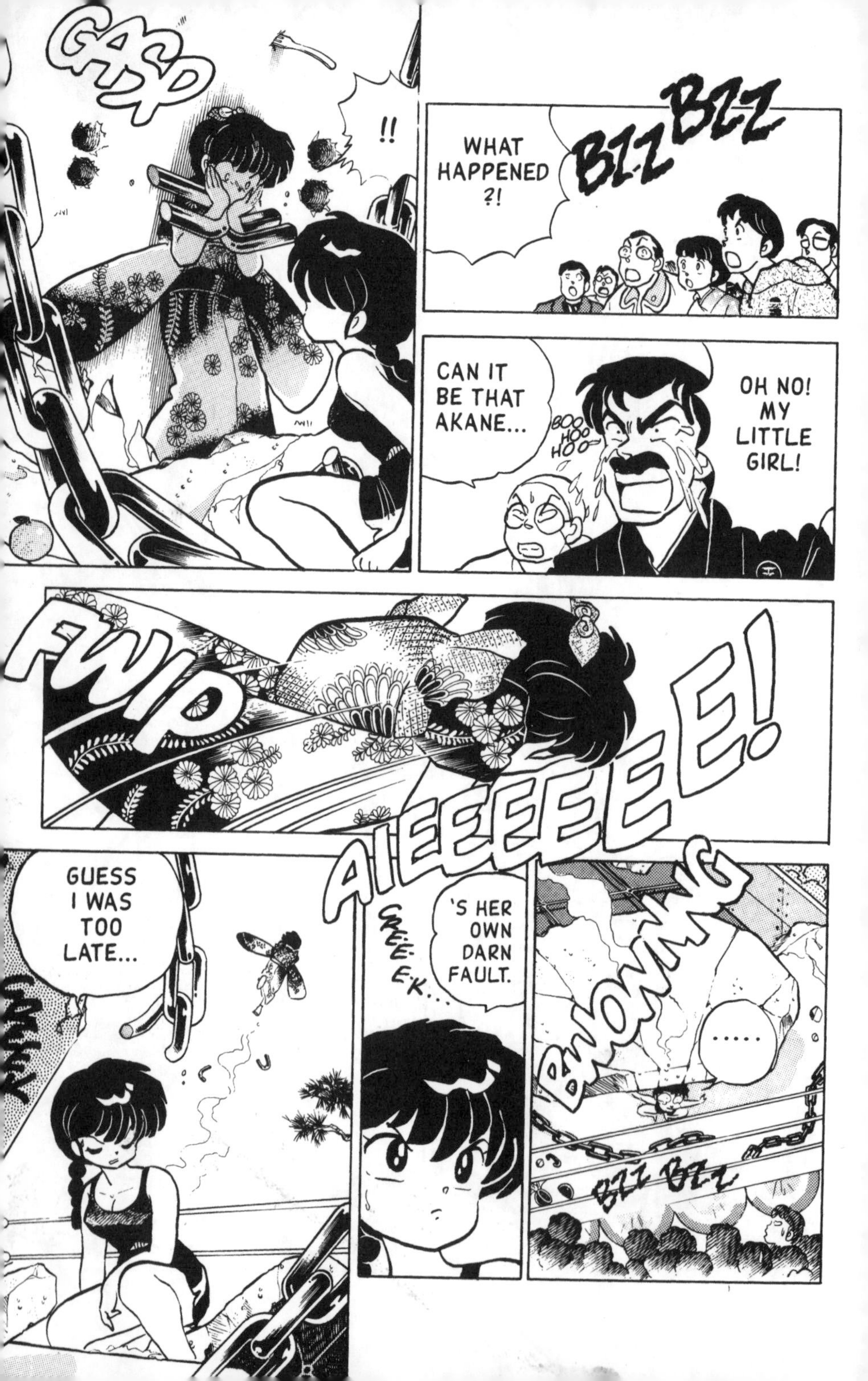
GACP
!!
WHAT HAPPENED ?!
BZZ BZZ
CAN IT BE THAT AKANE...
BOO HOO HOO
OH NO! MY LITTLE GIRL!
FWIP
AIEEEEEEE!
GUESS I WAS TOO LATE...
'S HER OWN DARN FAULT.
.....
BZZ BZZ

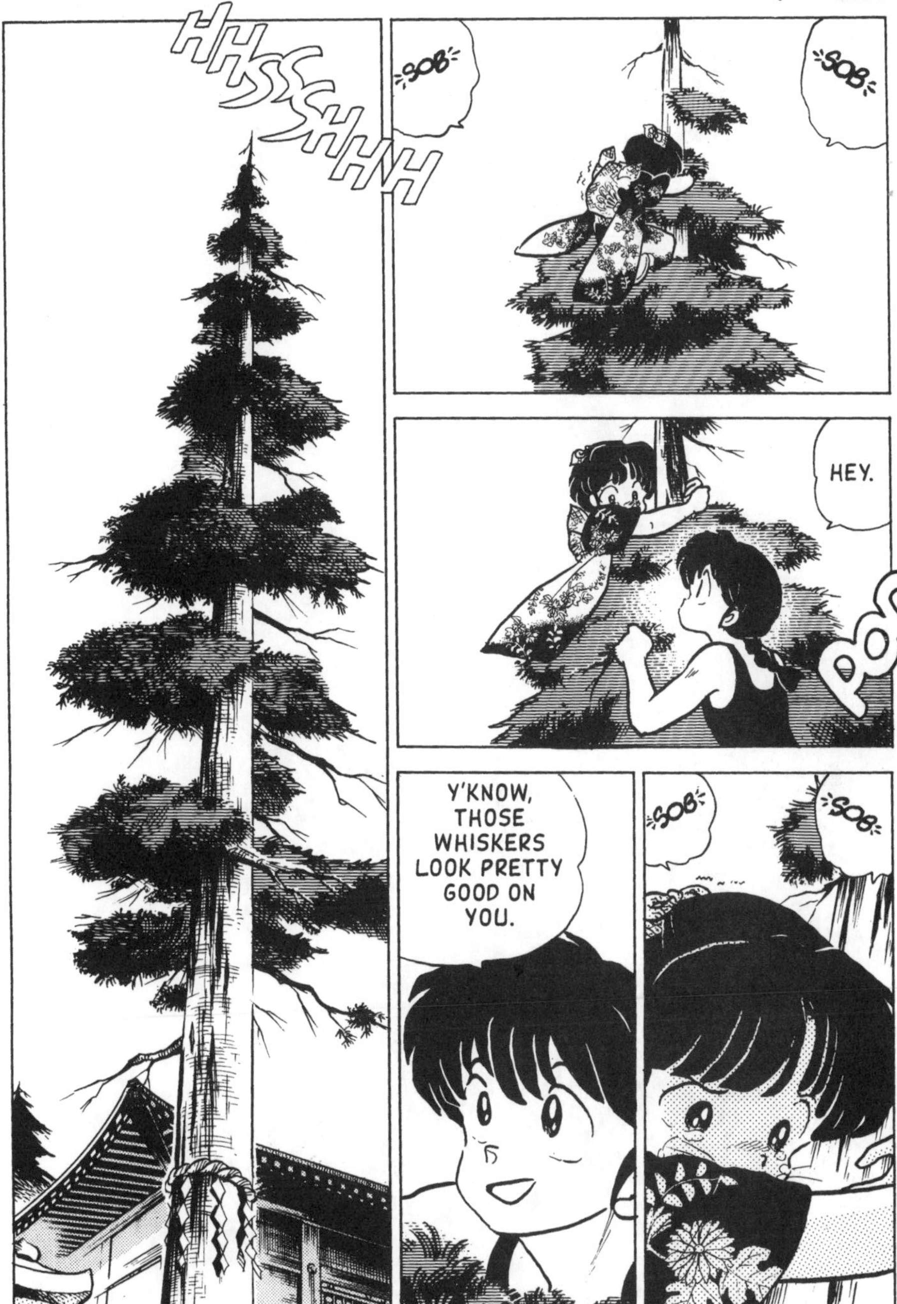
HHSSSHHHH
SOB
SOB
HEY.
POP
Y'KNOW, THOSE WHISKERS LOOK PRETTY GOOD ON YOU.
SOB
SOB

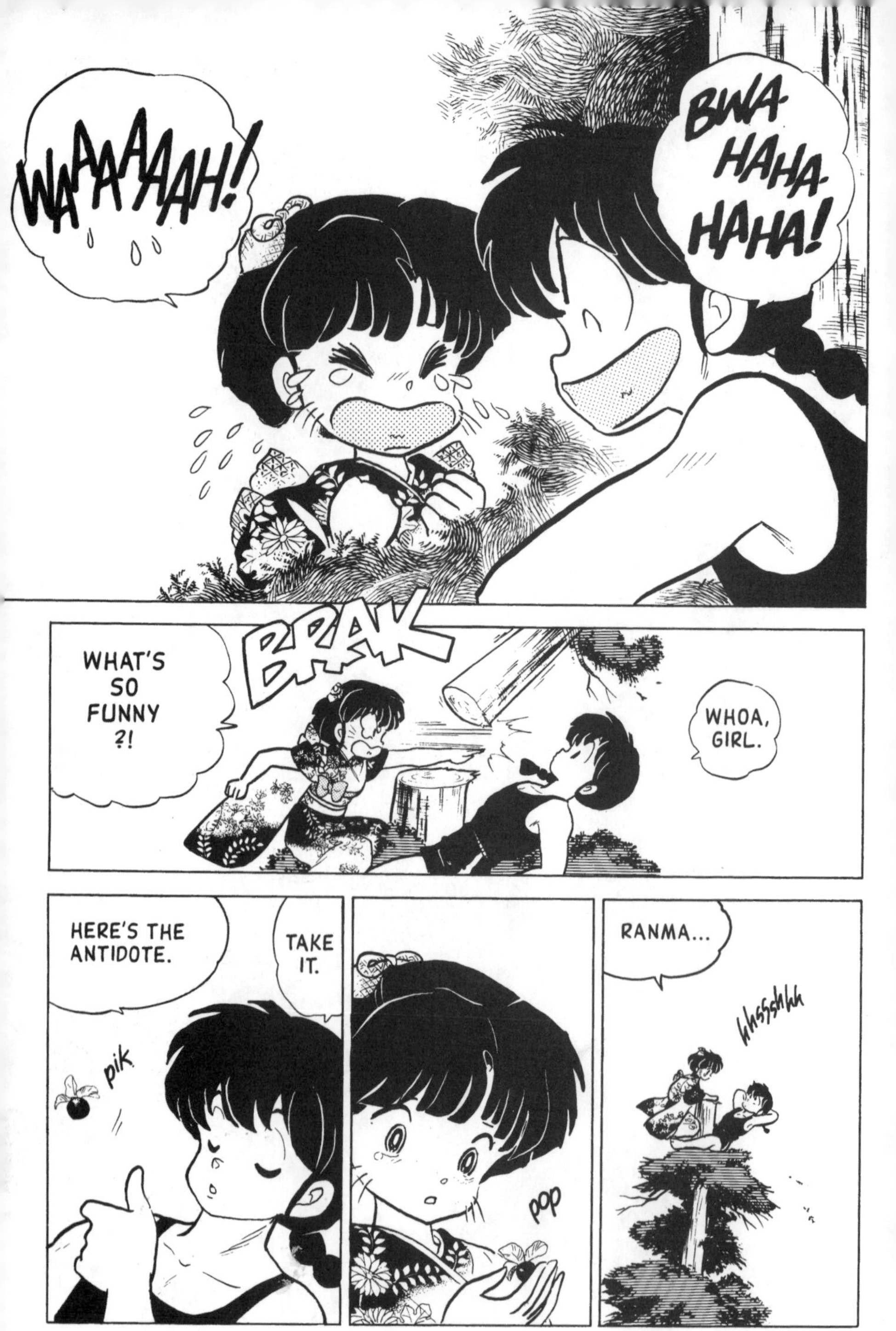
WAAAAAAH!
BWA HAHA HAHA HAHA!
WHAT'S SO FUNNY ?!
BRAK
WHOA, GIRL.
HERE'S THE ANTIDOTE.
pik
TAKE IT.
pop
RANMA...
hhsssshhh

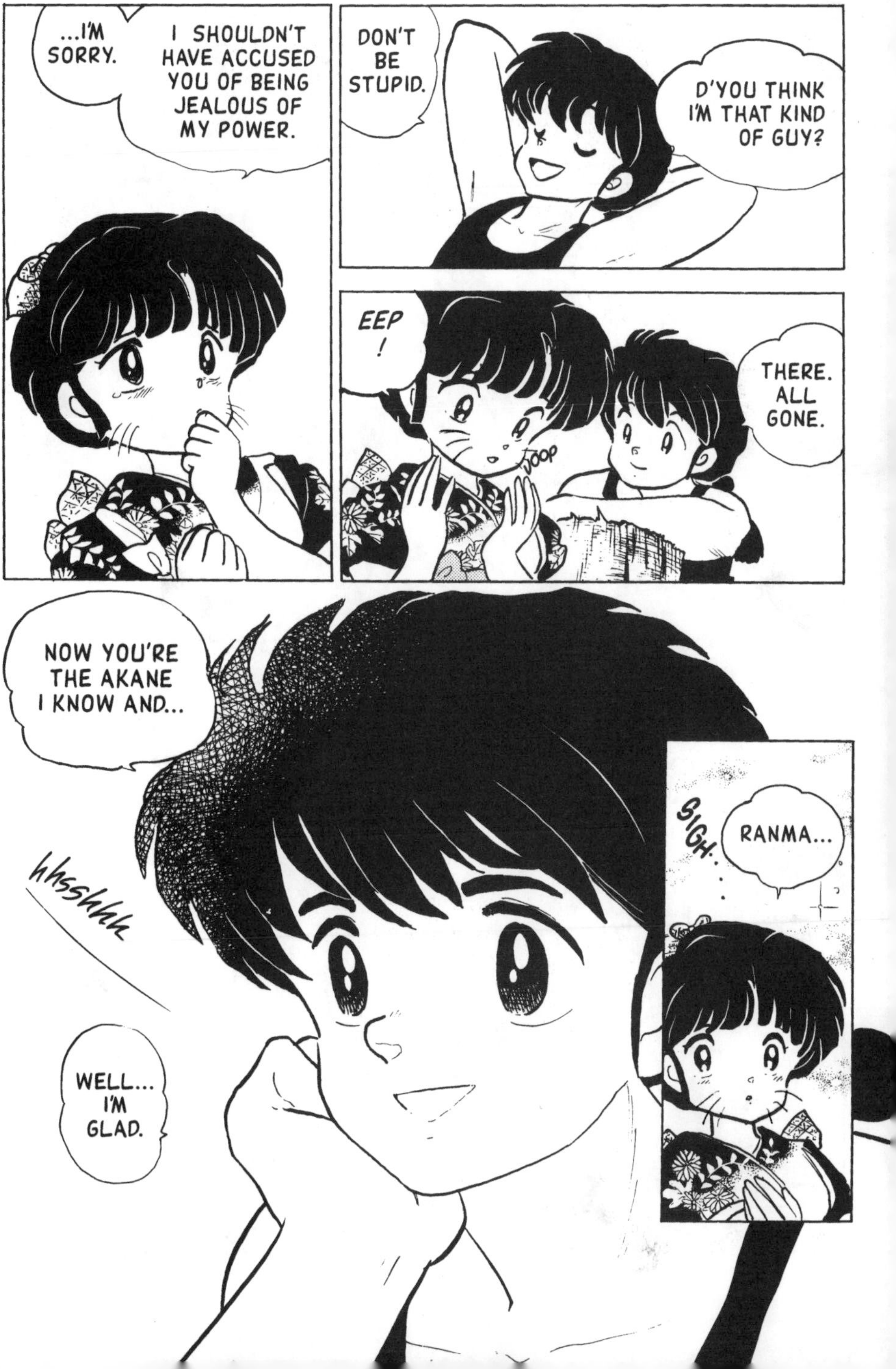
...I'M SORRY.
I SHOULDN'T HAVE ACCUSED YOU OF BEING JEALOUS OF MY POWER.
DON'T BE STUPID.
D'YOU THINK I'M THAT KIND OF GUY?
EEP!
JOOP
THERE. ALL GONE.
NOW YOU'RE THE AKANE I KNOW AND...
hhsshhh
WELL... I'M GLAD.
SIGH...
RANMA...

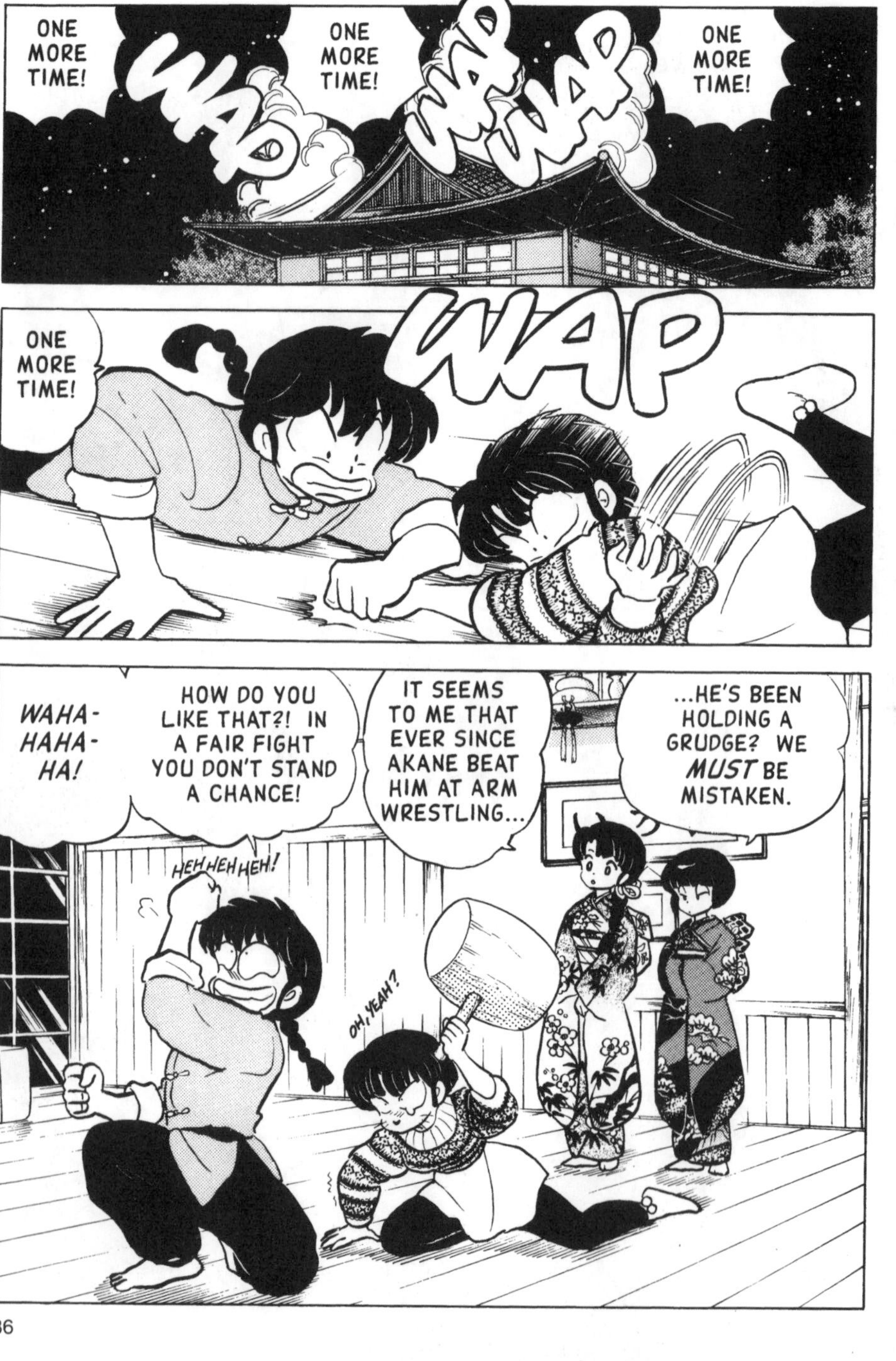
ONE MORE TIME!
WAP
ONE MORE TIME!
WAP WAP
ONE MORE TIME!
ONE MORE TIME!
WAP
WAHA-HAHA-HA!
HOW DO YOU LIKE THAT?! IN A FAIR FIGHT YOU DON'T STAND A CHANCE!
HEH HEH HEH!
IT SEEMS TO ME THAT EVER SINCE AKANE BEAT HIM AT ARM WRESTLING...
...HE'S BEEN HOLDING A GRUDGE? WE *MUST* BE MISTAKEN.
OH, YEAH?

PART 6
THE RETURN OF THE PRINCIPAL

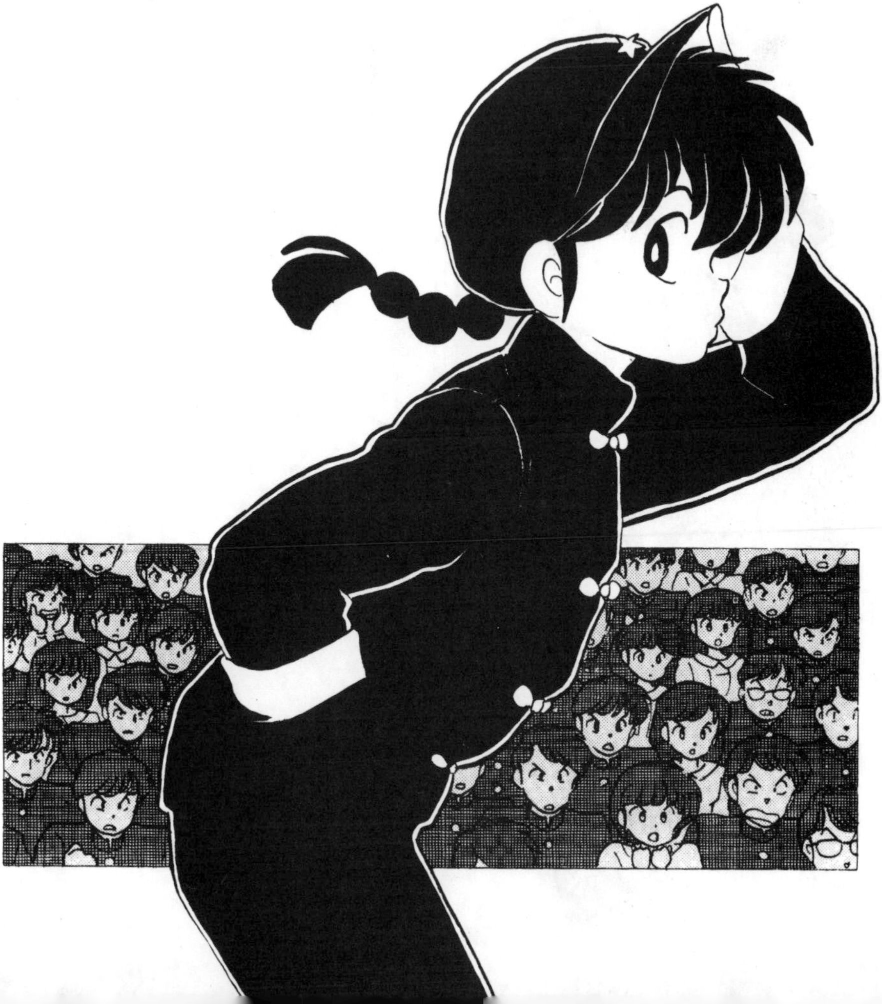

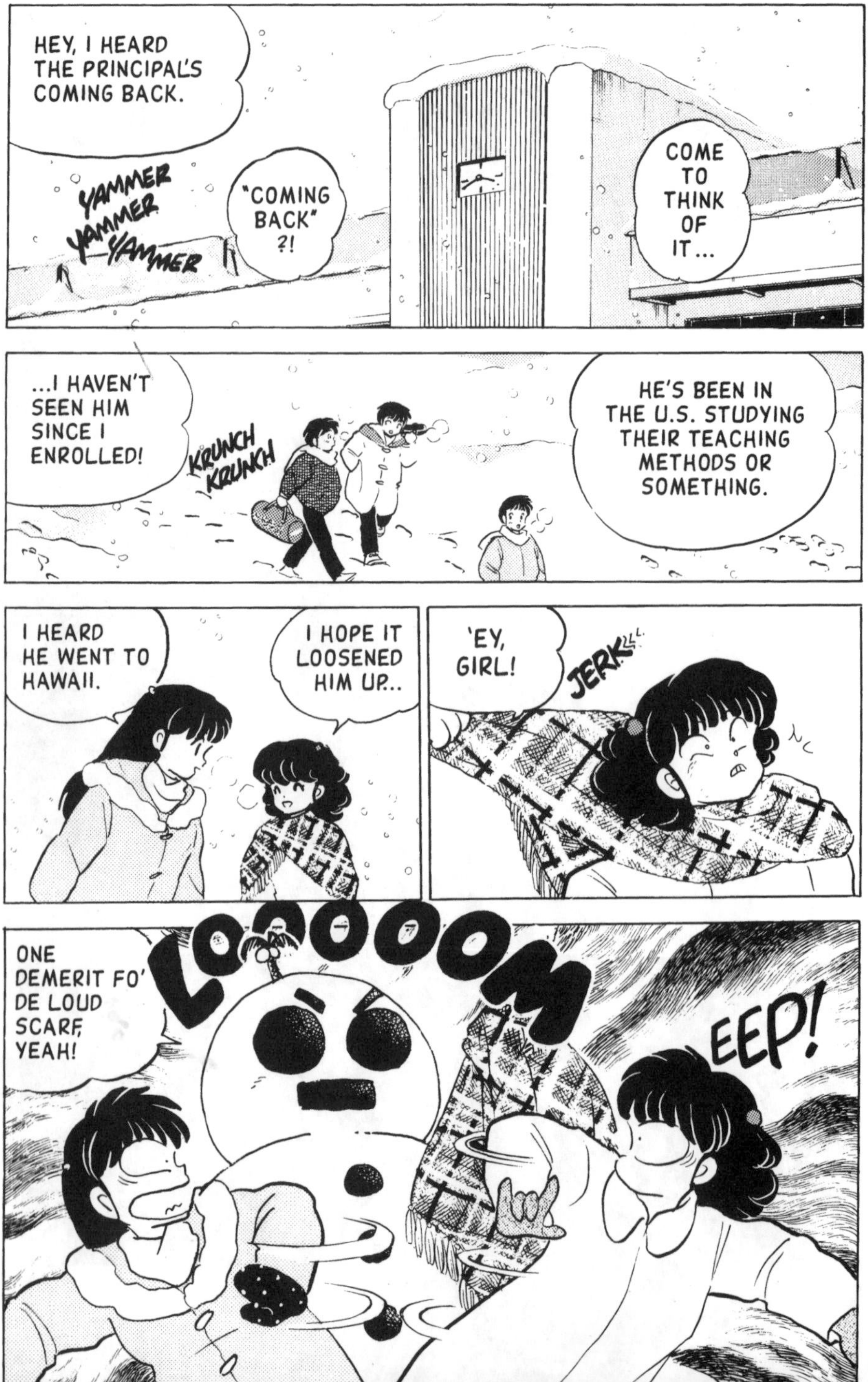
HEY, I HEARD THE PRINCIPAL'S COMING BACK.
YAMMER YAMMER YAMMER
"COMING BACK" ?!
COME TO THINK OF IT...
...I HAVEN'T SEEN HIM SINCE I ENROLLED!
KRUNCH KRUNCH
HE'S BEEN IN THE U.S. STUDYING THEIR TEACHING METHODS OR SOMETHING.
I HEARD HE WENT TO HAWAII.
I HOPE IT LOOSENED HIM UP...
'EY, GIRL!
JERK
LOOOOOM
ONE DEMERIT FO' DE LOUD SCARF, YEAH!
EEP!

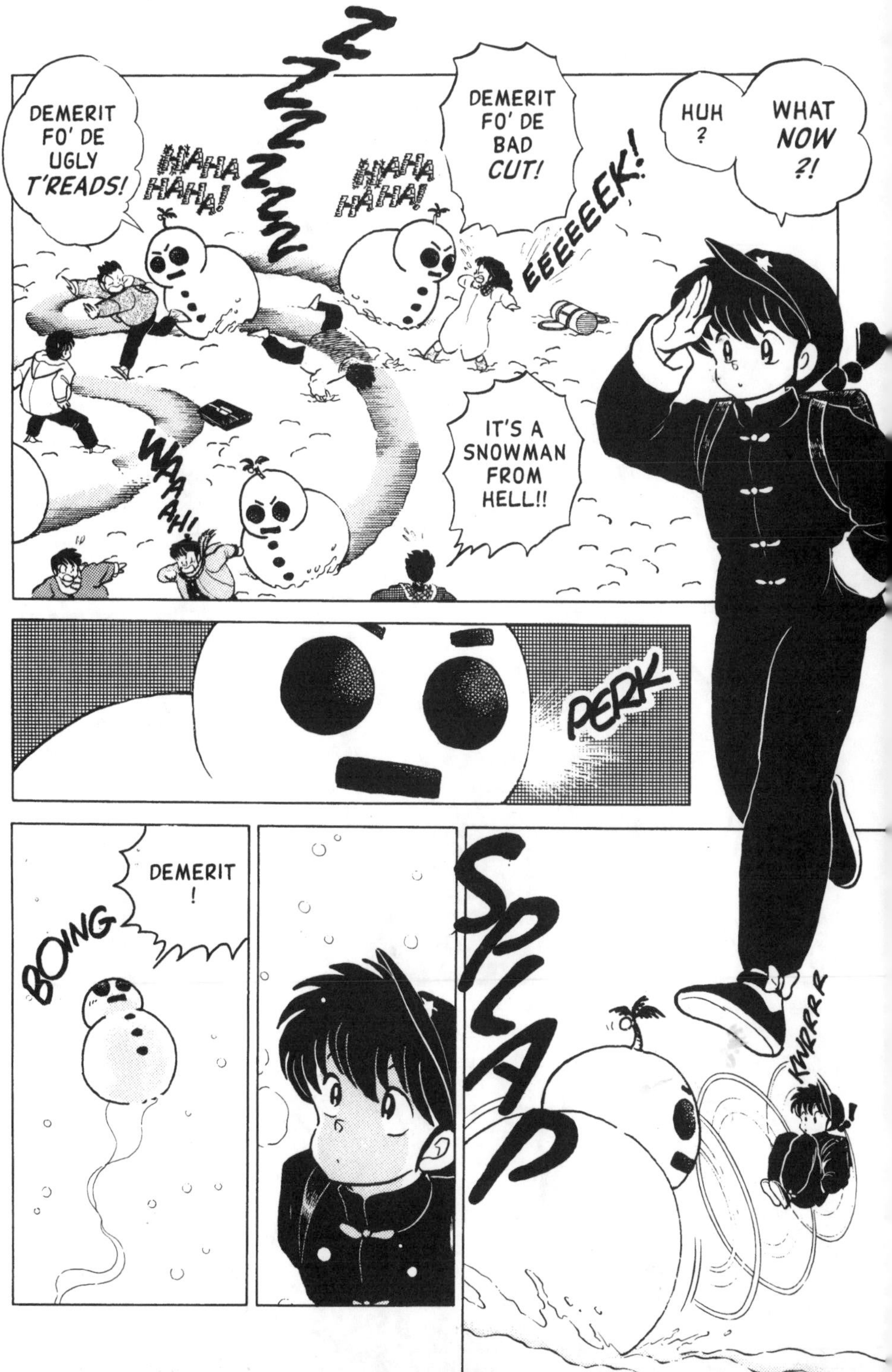

DEMERIT FO' DE UGLY T'READS!
HAHA HAHA!
ZZZZZZZZ
HAHA HAHA!
DEMERIT FO' DE BAD CUT!
EEEEEEK!
HUH ?
WHAT NOW ?!
WAAAAH!
IT'S A SNOWMAN FROM HELL!!
PERK
DEMERIT !
BOING
SPLAT
KWRRRR

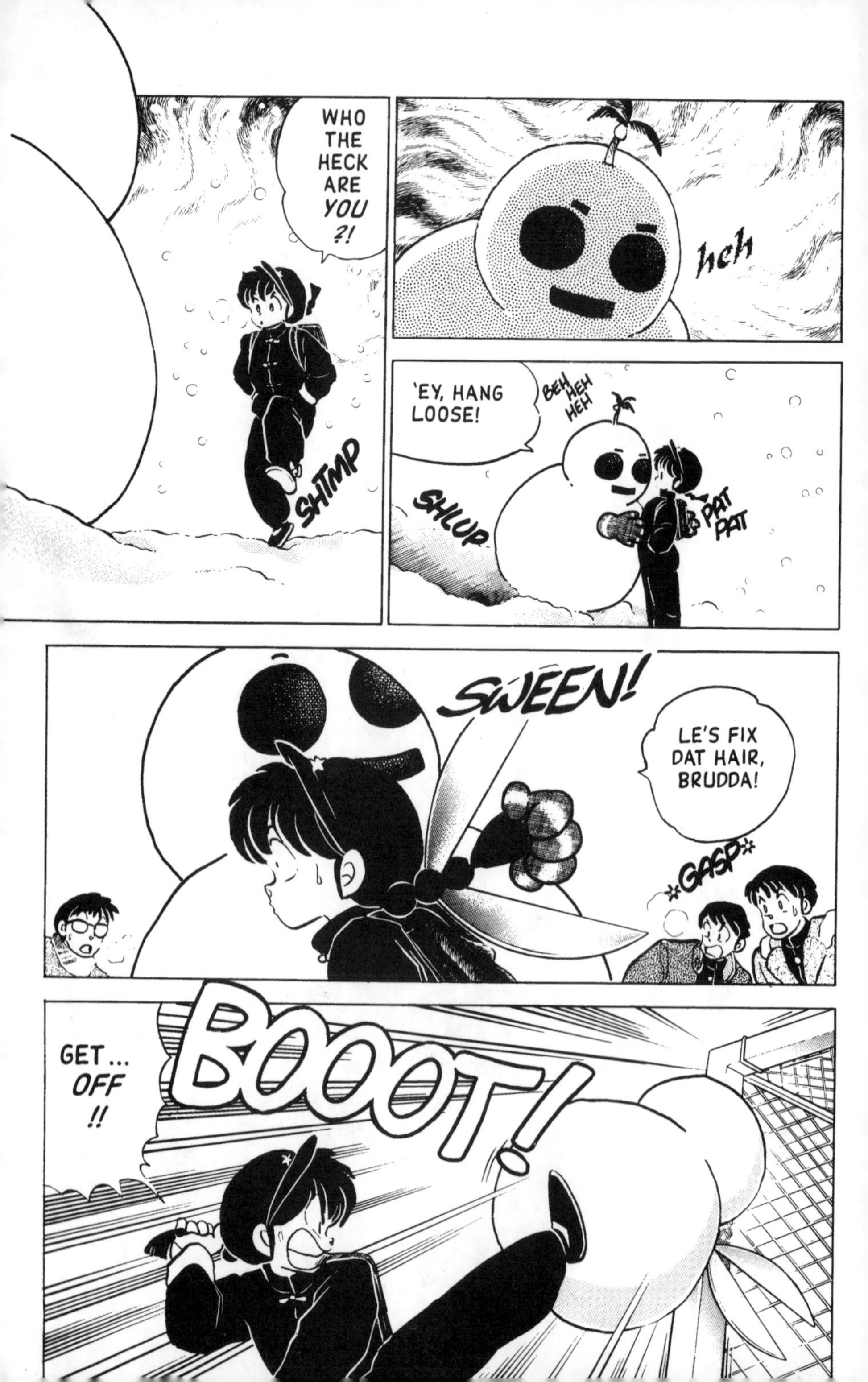
WHO THE HECK ARE YOU ?!
SHTMP
hch
'EY, HANG LOOSE!
BEH HEH HEH
SHLUP
PAT PAT
SWEEN!
LE'S FIX DAT HAIR, BRUDDA!
GASP
GET... OFF !!
BOOOT!

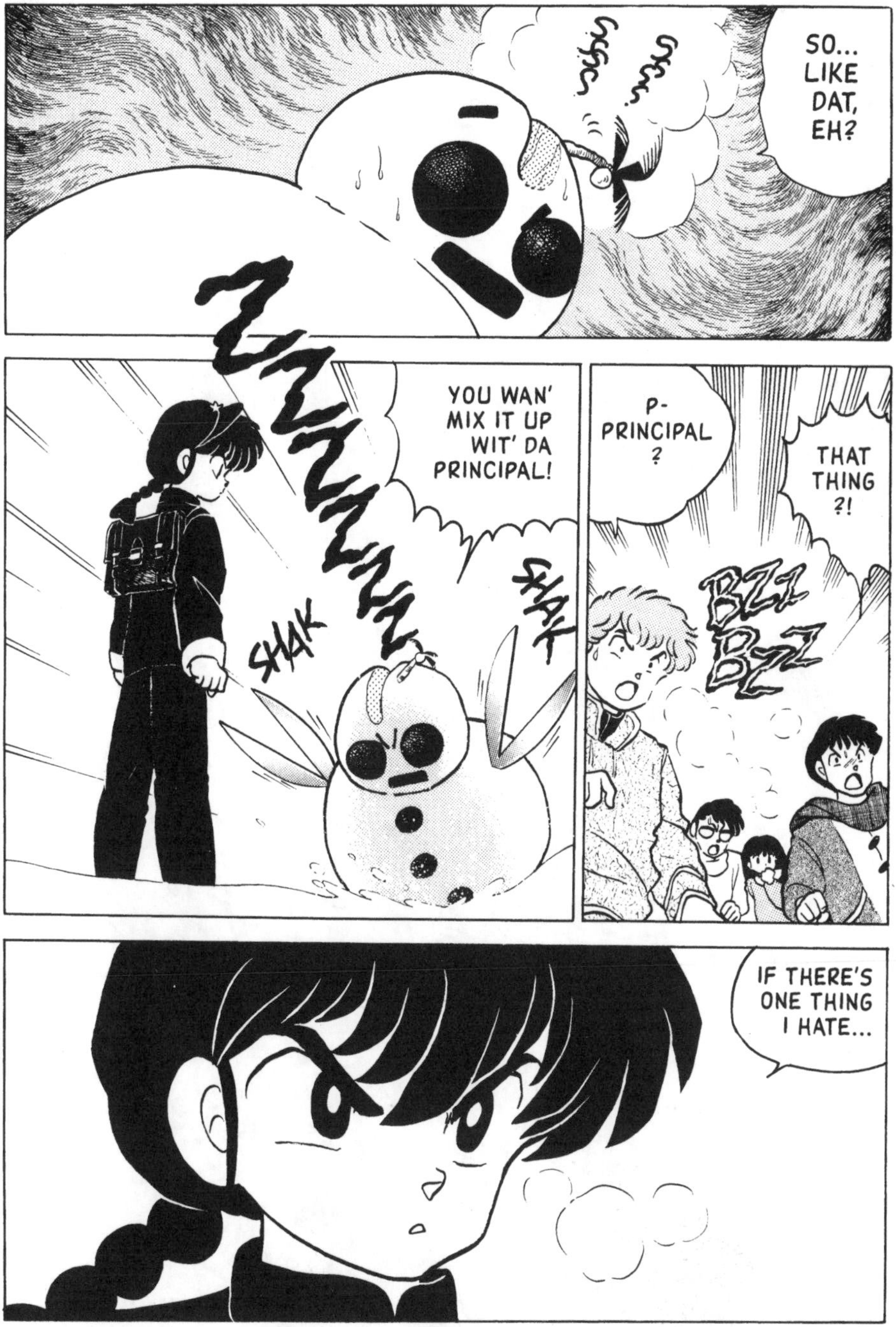
SO... LIKE DAT, EH?
GRRR... GRRR...
ZUNNNNNNN
YOU WAN' MIX IT UP WIT' DA PRINCIPAL!
SHAK
SHAK
P-PRINCIPAL?
THAT THING?!
BZZ BZZ
IF THERE'S ONE THING I HATE...

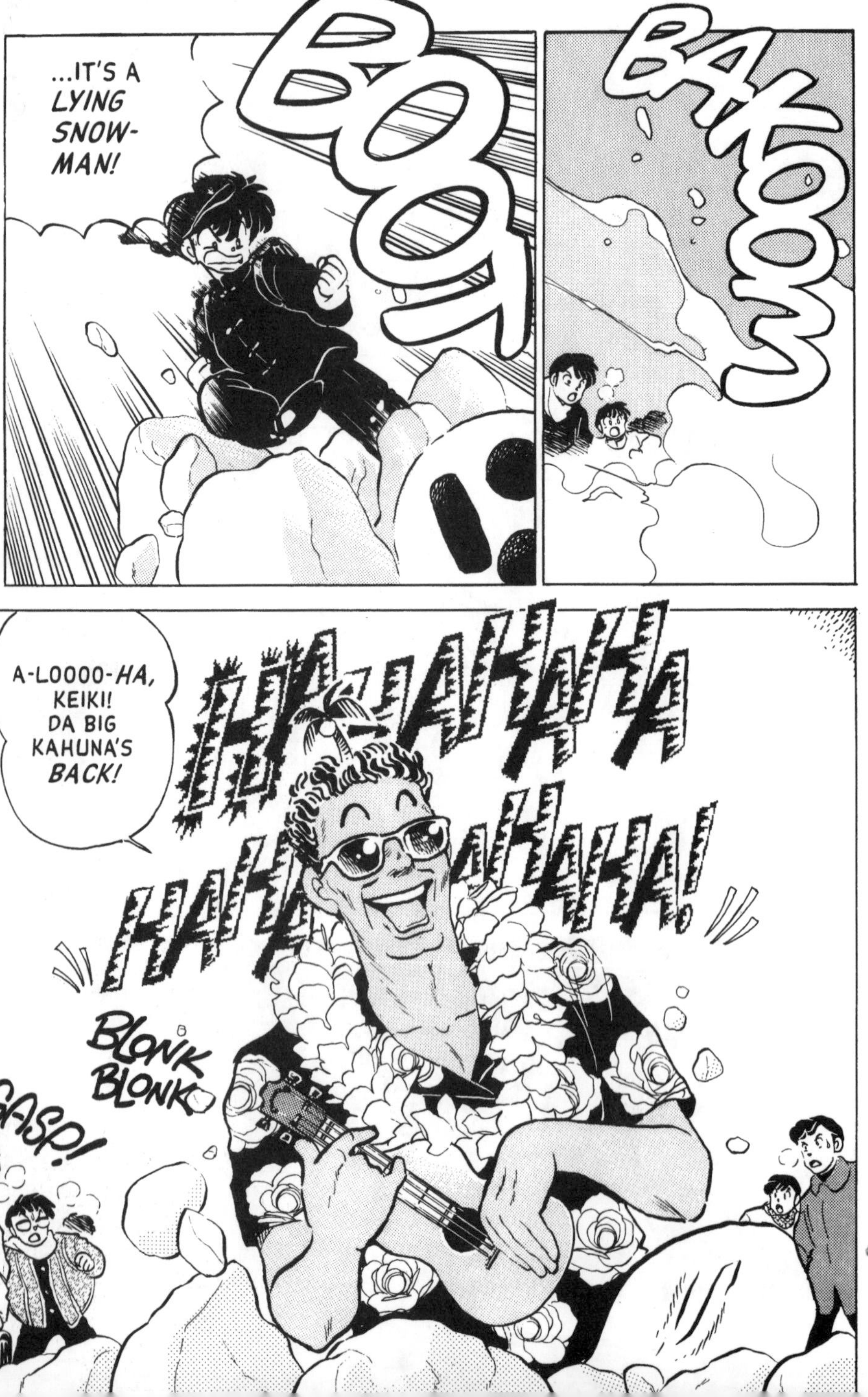
...IT'S A LYING SNOW-MAN!
BOOOT
BAKOOM
A-LOOOO-HA, KEIKI! DA BIG KAHUNA'S BACK!
HAHAHAHAHA
HAHAHAHAHA!
BLONK BLONK
GASP!

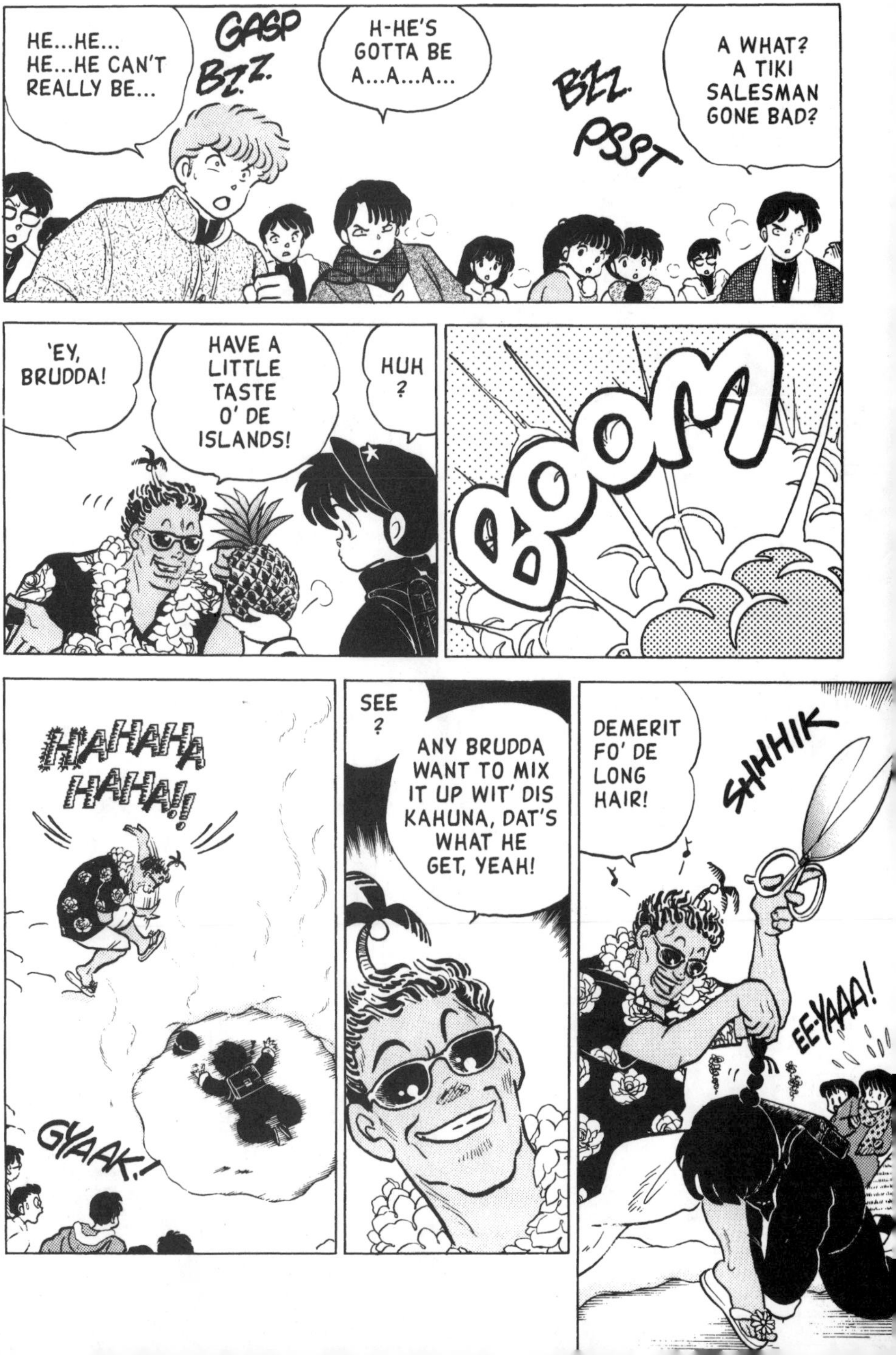
HE...HE...
HE...HE CAN'T
REALLY BE...
GASP
BZZ.
H-HE'S
GOTTA BE
A...A...A...
BZZ.
PSST
A WHAT?
A TIKI
SALESMAN
GONE BAD?
'EY,
BRUDDA!
HAVE A
LITTLE
TASTE
O' DE
ISLANDS!
HUH
?
BOOM
HAHAHA
HAHA!!
GYAAK!
SEE
?
ANY BRUDDA
WANT TO MIX
IT UP WIT' DIS
KAHUNA, DAT'S
WHAT HE
GET, YEAH!
DEMERIT
FO' DE
LONG
HAIR!
SHHHIK
EE-YAAA!

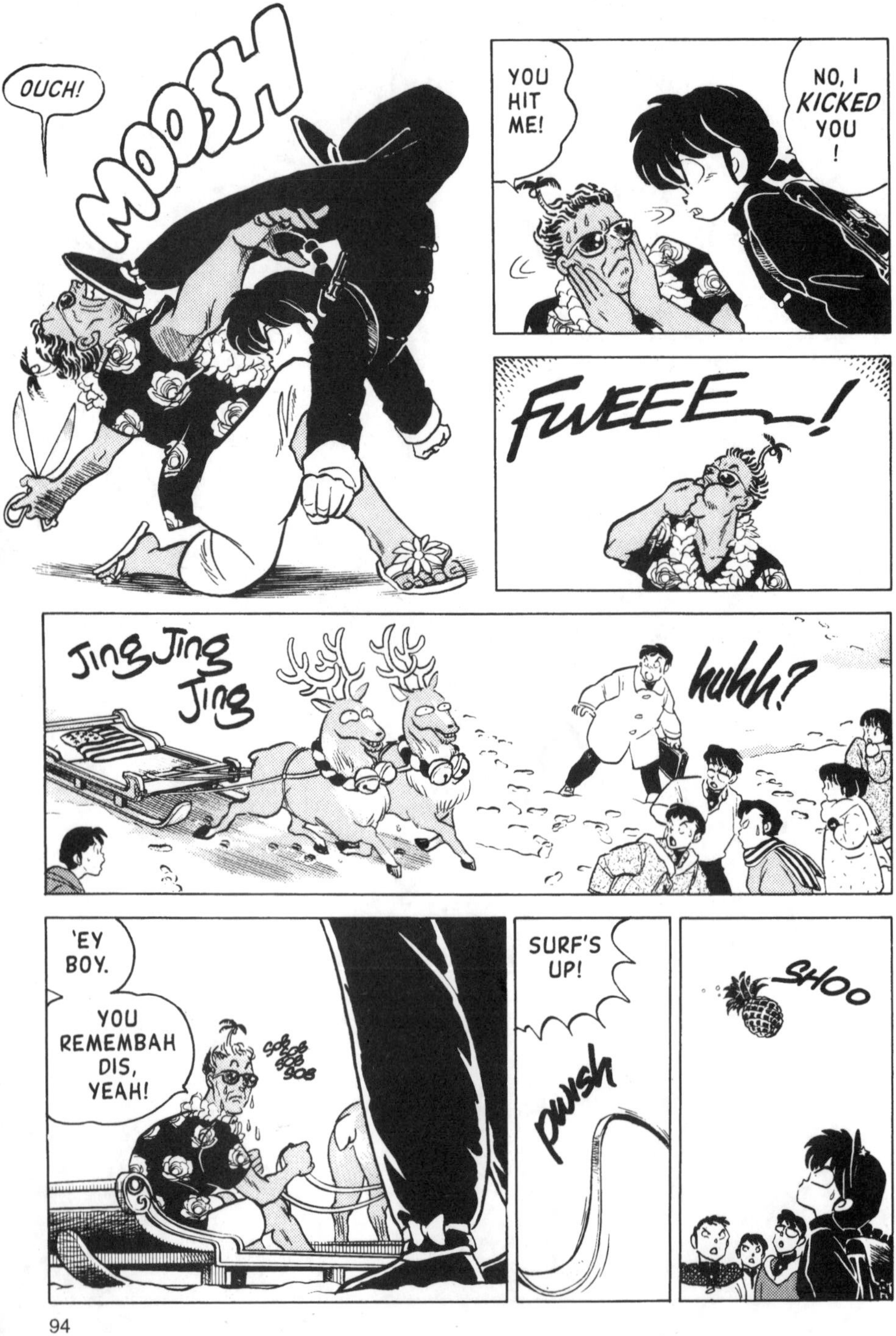
OUCH!
MOOSH
YOU HIT ME!
NO, I KICKED YOU!
FWEEE—!
Jing Jing Jing
huhh?
'EY BOY.
YOU REMEMBAH DIS, YEAH!
sob sob sob sob
SURF'S UP!
pwsh
SHOO

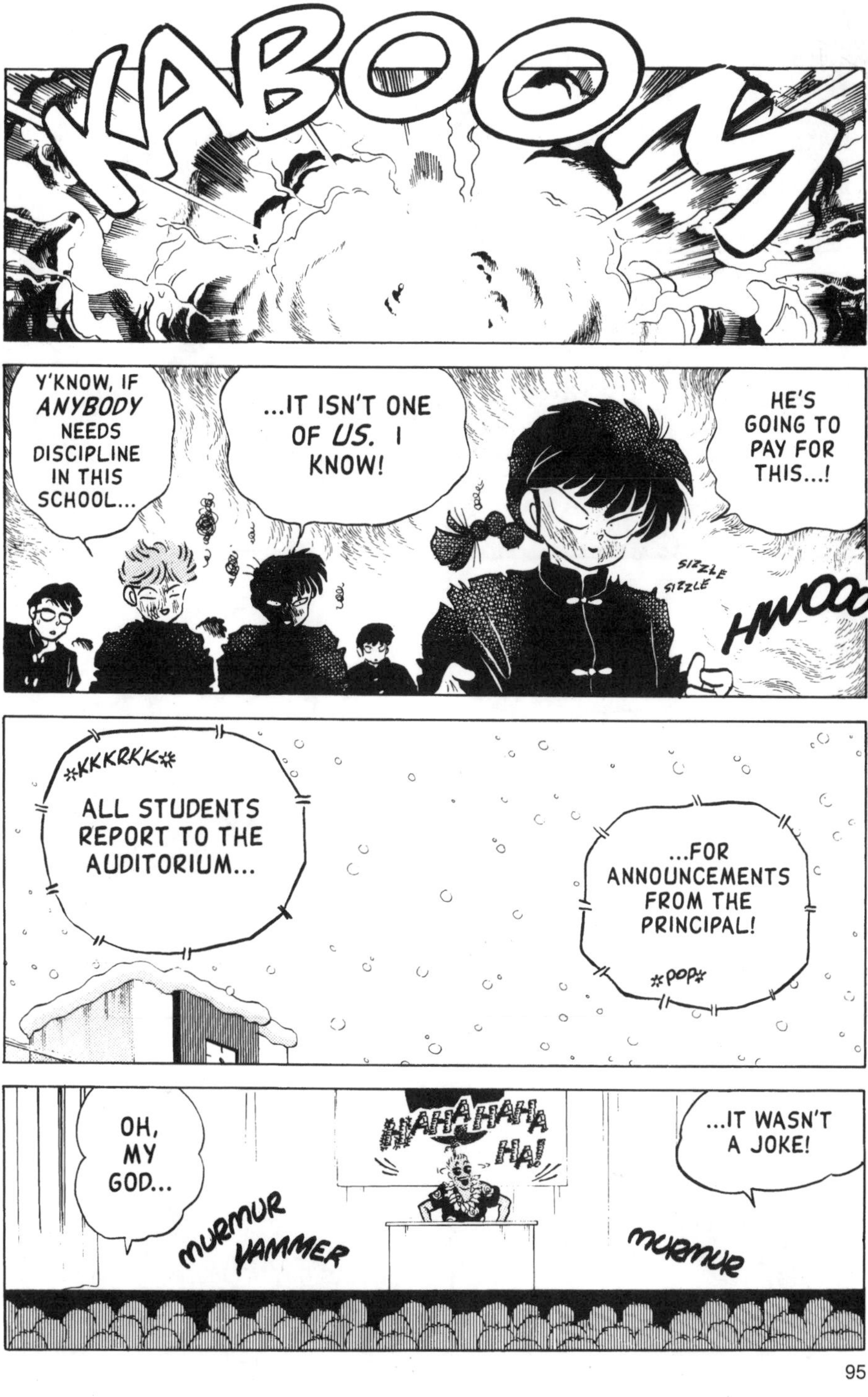
KABOOM
Y'KNOW, IF ANYBODY NEEDS DISCIPLINE IN THIS SCHOOL...
...IT ISN'T ONE OF US. I KNOW!
HE'S GOING TO PAY FOR THIS...!
SIZZLE SIZZLE
HWOOOOO
KKKRKK
ALL STUDENTS REPORT TO THE AUDITORIUM...
...FOR ANNOUNCEMENTS FROM THE PRINCIPAL!
POP
OH, MY GOD...
HAHAHAHA HA!
...IT WASN'T A JOKE!
MURMUR YAMMER
MURMUR

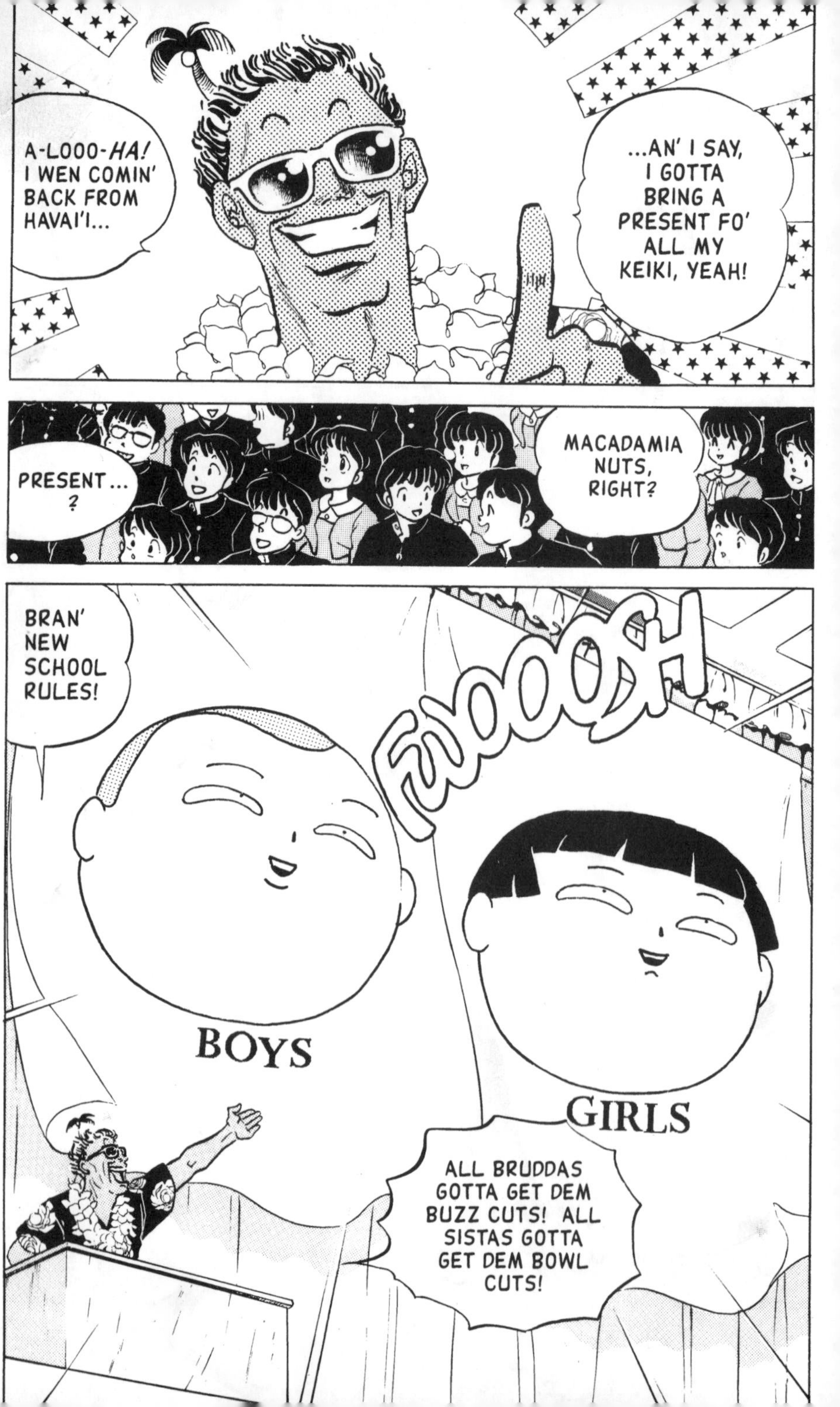
A-LOOO-*HA!* I WEN COMIN' BACK FROM HAVAI'I...
...AN' I SAY, I GOTTA BRING A PRESENT FO' ALL MY KEIKI, YEAH!
PRESENT... ?
MACADAMIA NUTS, RIGHT?
BRAN' NEW SCHOOL RULES!
FWOOOSH
BOYS
GIRLS
ALL BRUDDAS GOTTA GET DEM BUZZ CUTS! ALL SISTAS GOTTA GET DEM BOWL CUTS!

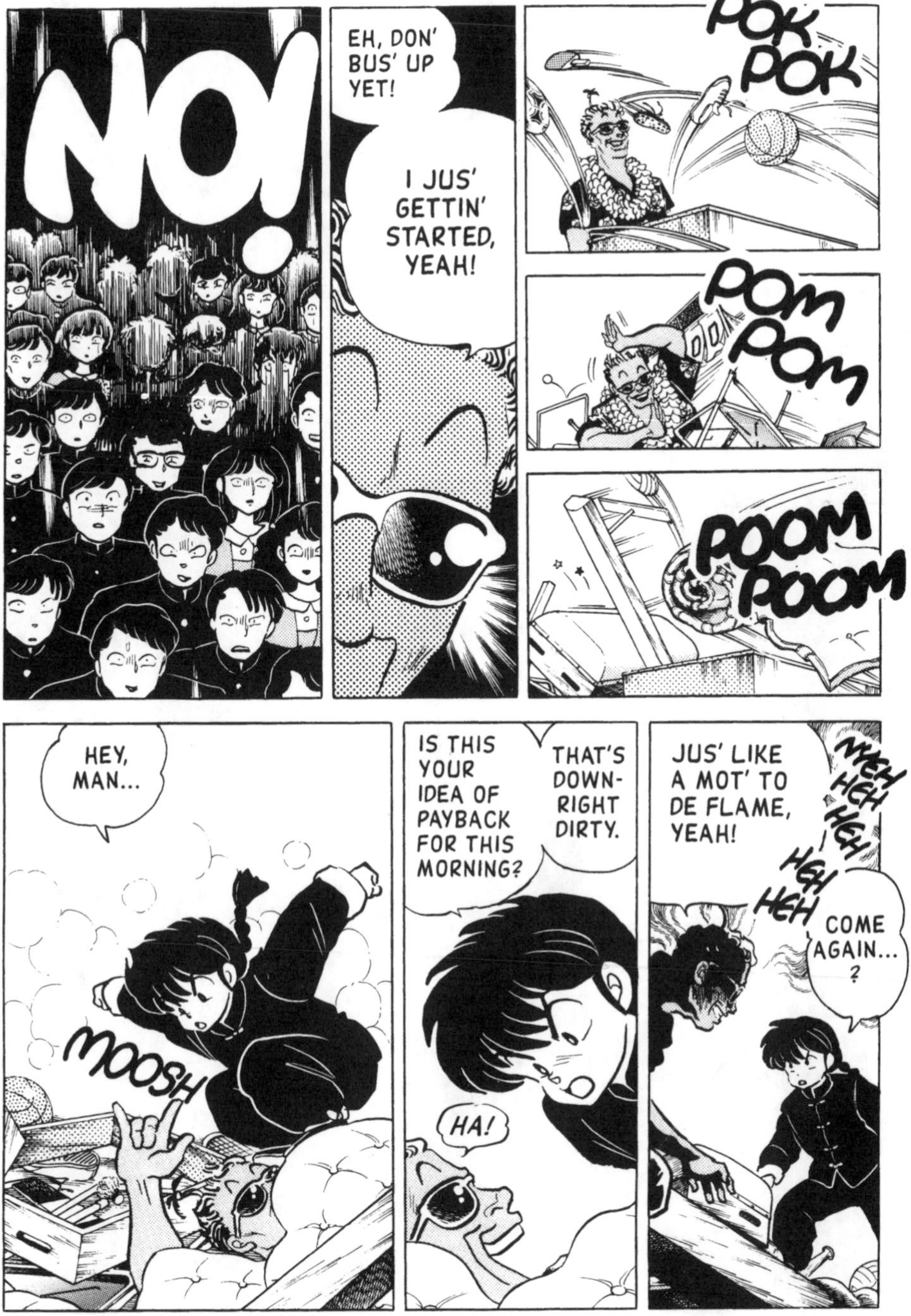
NO!
EH, DON' BUS' UP YET!
I JUS' GETTIN' STARTED, YEAH!
POK POK
POM POM
POOM POOM
HEY, MAN...
MOOSH
IS THIS YOUR IDEA OF PAYBACK FOR THIS MORNING?
THAT'S DOWN-RIGHT DIRTY.
HA!
JUS' LIKE A MOT' TO DE FLAME, YEAH!
NYEH HEH HEH! HEH HEH
COME AGAIN...?

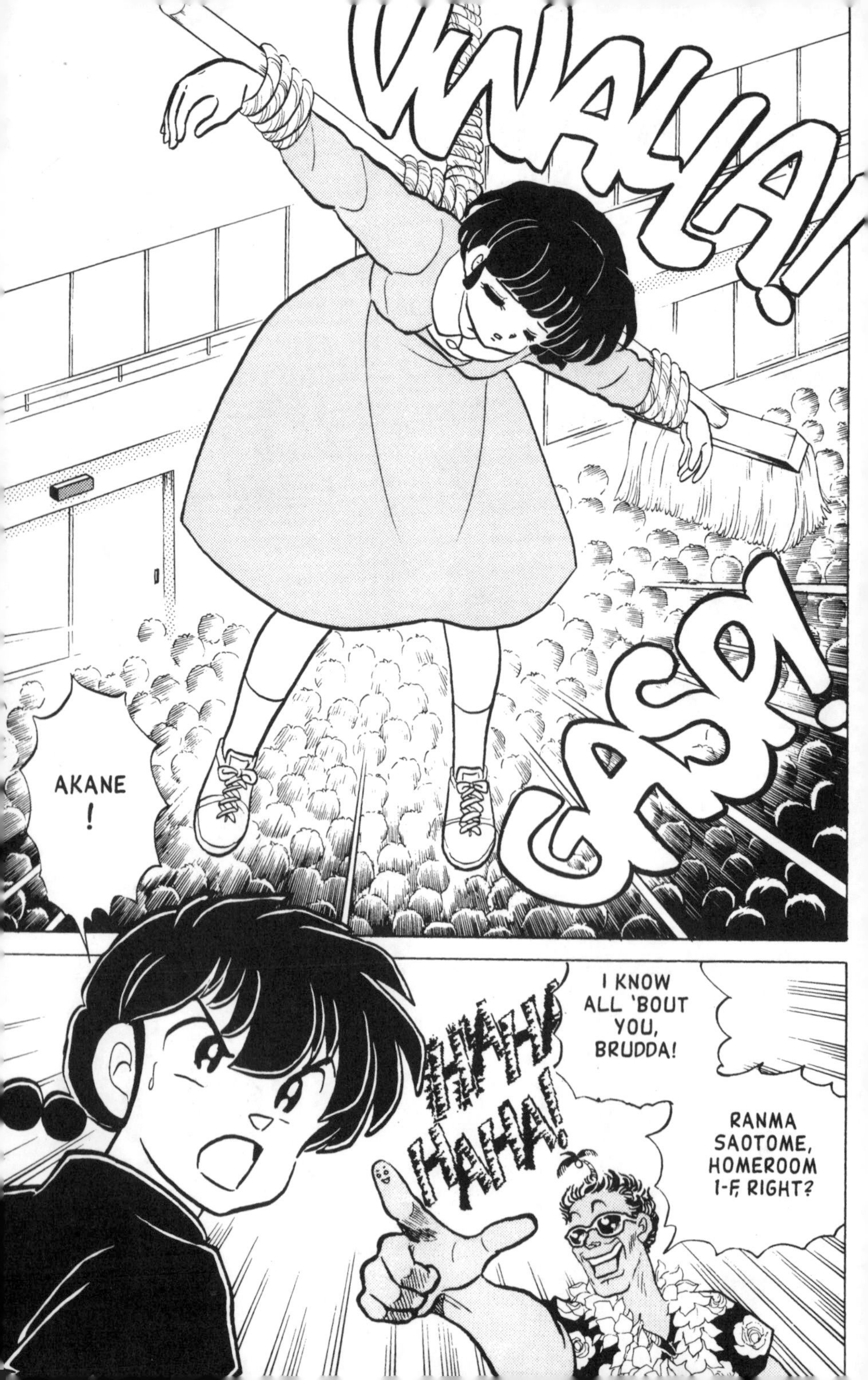
WHALA!
CASP!
AKANE!
I KNOW ALL 'BOUT YOU, BRUDDA!
HAHA! HAHA!
RANMA SAOTOME, HOMEROOM 1-F, RIGHT?

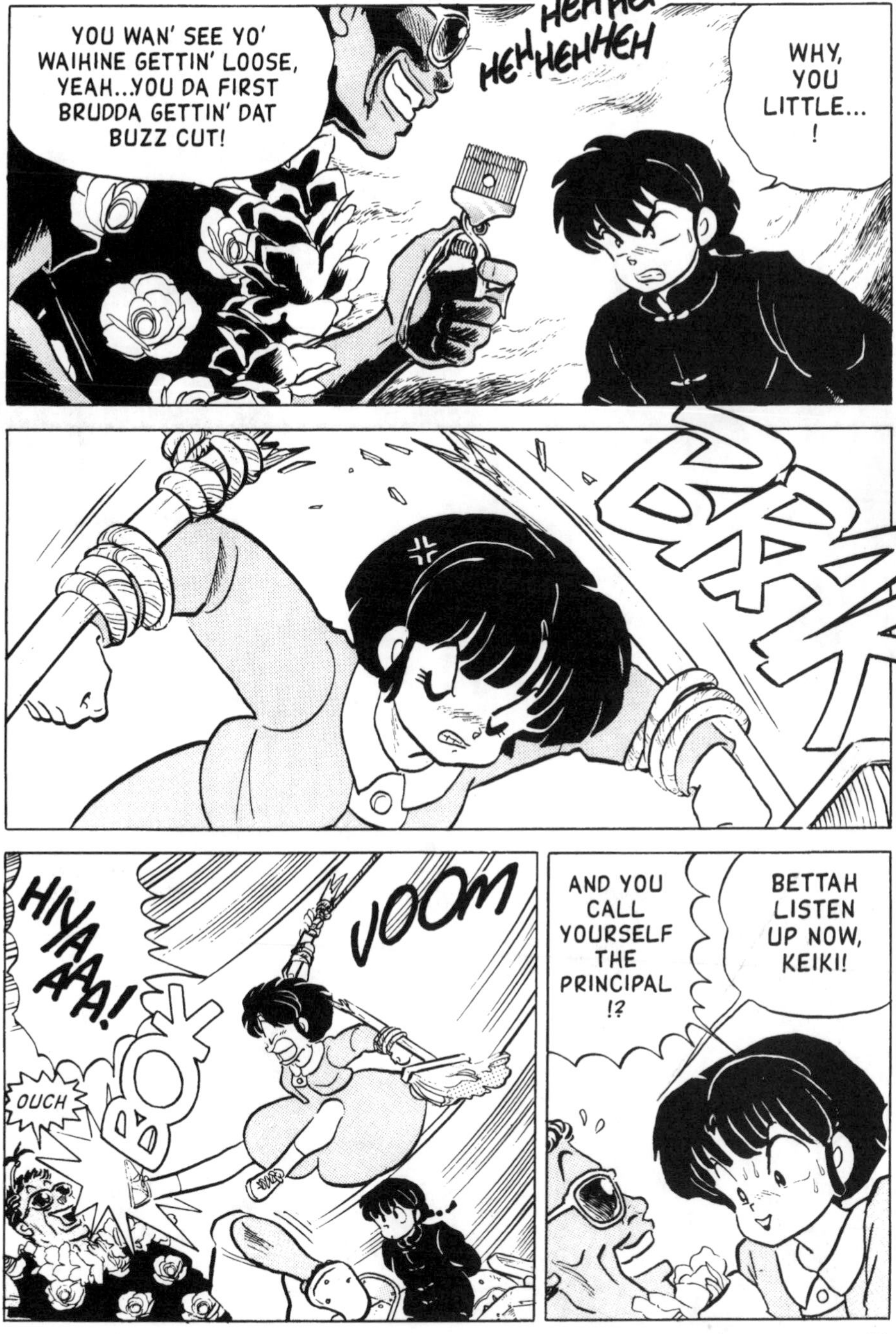
YOU WAN' SEE YO' WAIHINE GETTIN' LOOSE, YEAH...YOU DA FIRST BRUDDA GETTIN' DAT BUZZ CUT!
HEH HEH HEH HEH HEH HEH
WHY, YOU LITTLE... !
DRAK
HIYAAAAA!
VOOM
BOK
OUCH
AND YOU CALL YOURSELF THE PRINCIPAL !?
BETTAH LISTEN UP NOW, KEIKI!

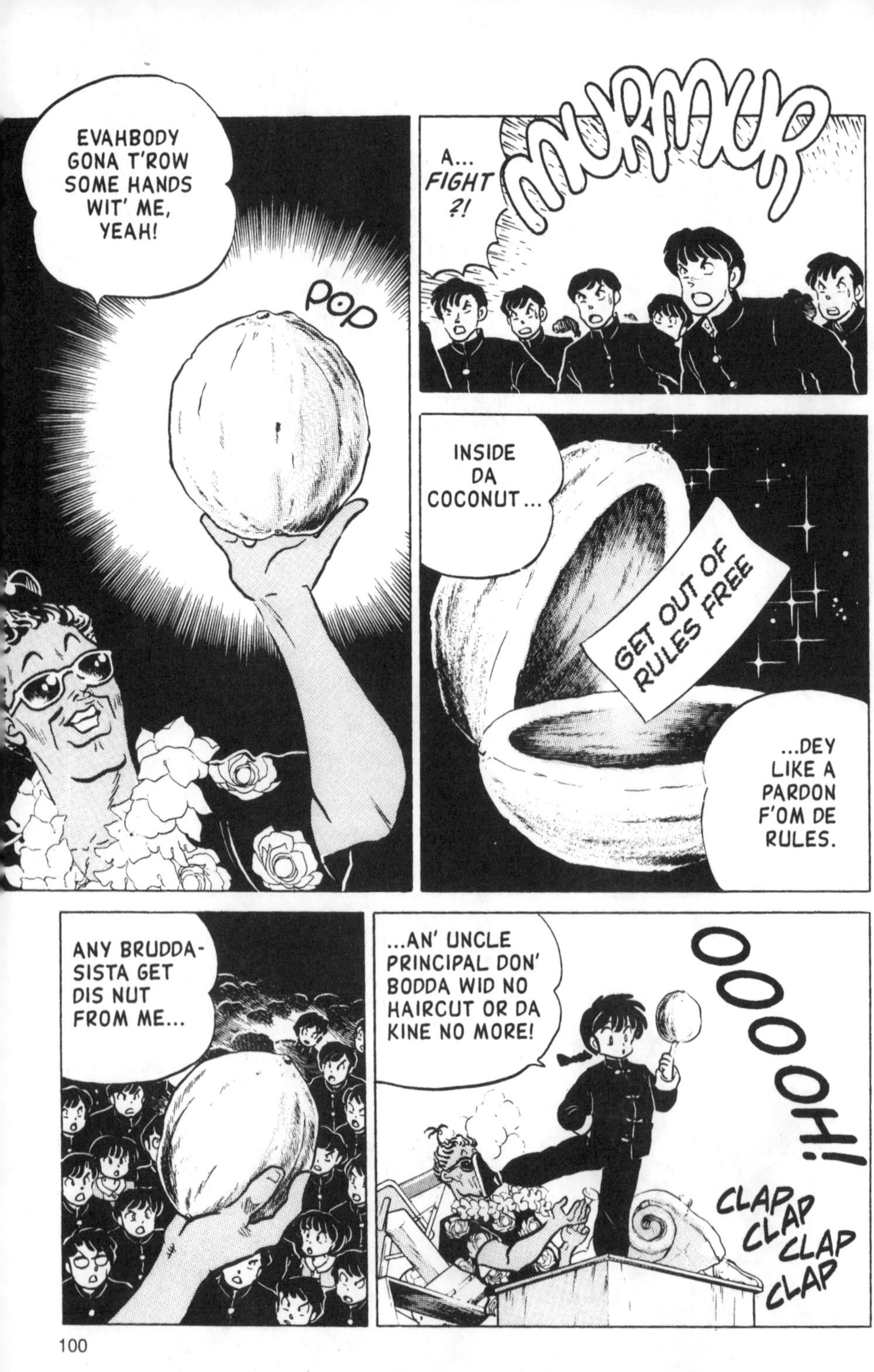
EVAHBODY GONA T'ROW SOME HANDS WIT' ME, YEAH!
POP
A... FIGHT ?!
MURMUR
INSIDE DA COCONUT...
GET OUT OF RULES FREE
...DEY LIKE A PARDON F'OM DE RULES.
ANY BRUDDA-SISTA GET DIS NUT FROM ME...
...AN' UNCLE PRINCIPAL DON' BODDA WID NO HAIRCUT OR DA KINE NO MORE!
OOOOOH!
CLAP CLAP CLAP CLAP

YOU GOT T'REE DAYS FO' DO IT!

I LIKE WAITIN' IN MY OFFICE!

THREE DAYS, HUH?!

YEAH! YEAH! YEAH!

WE'LL GET IT IF IT KILLS US!

HE HASN'T CHANGED ONE BIT...

HE'S ALWAYS BEEN LIKE THIS?!

HE'LL DO ANYTHING TO ANNOY THE STUDENTS.

YEAH! YEAH! YEAH!

'EY, BOY!

POIK.

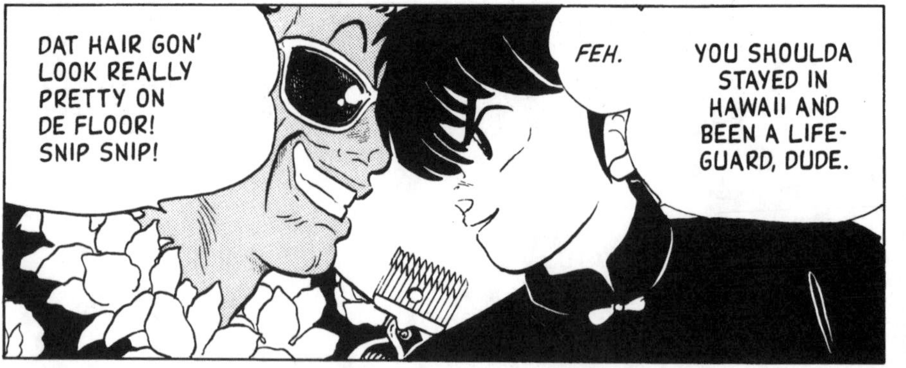
DAT HAIR GON' LOOK REALLY PRETTY ON DE FLOOR! SNIP SNIP!
FEH.
YOU SHOULDA STAYED IN HAWAII AND BEEN A LIFE-GUARD, DUDE.
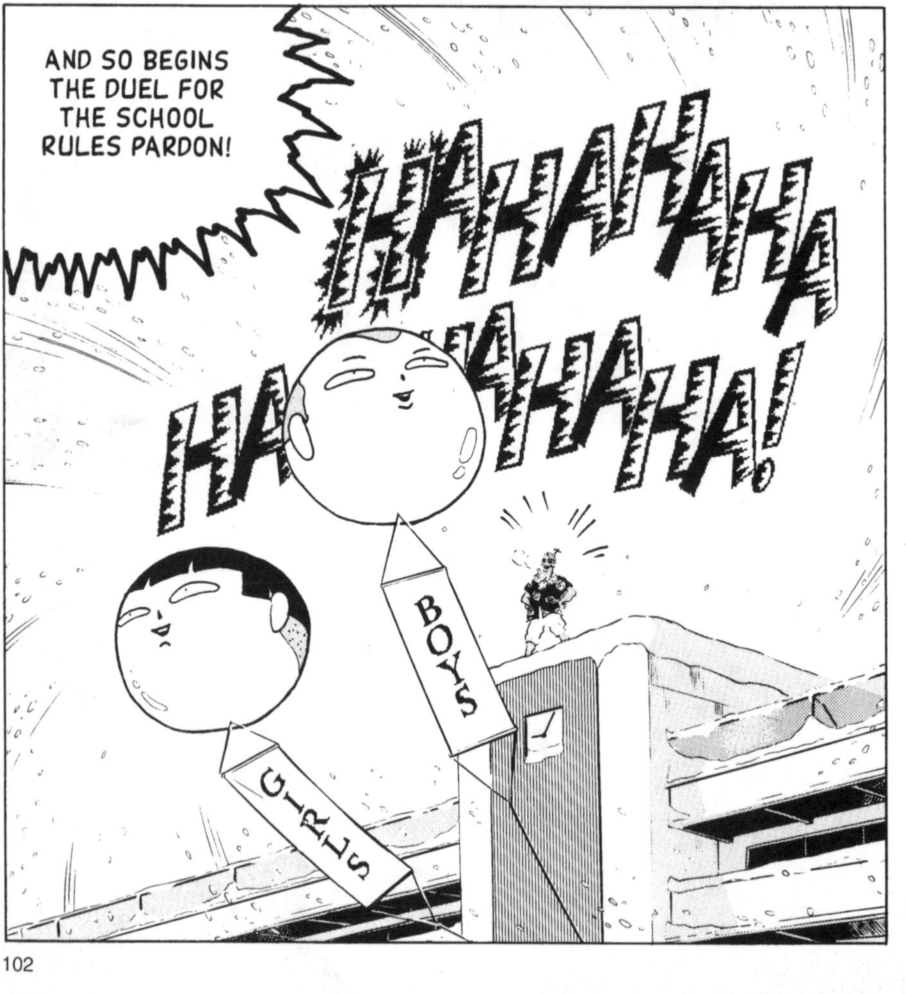
AND SO BEGINS THE DUEL FOR THE SCHOOL RULES PARDON!
HAHAHAHAHA HAHAHAHAHA!
BOYS
GIRLS

PART 7

JOURNEY INTO THE PRINCIPAL'S OFFICE

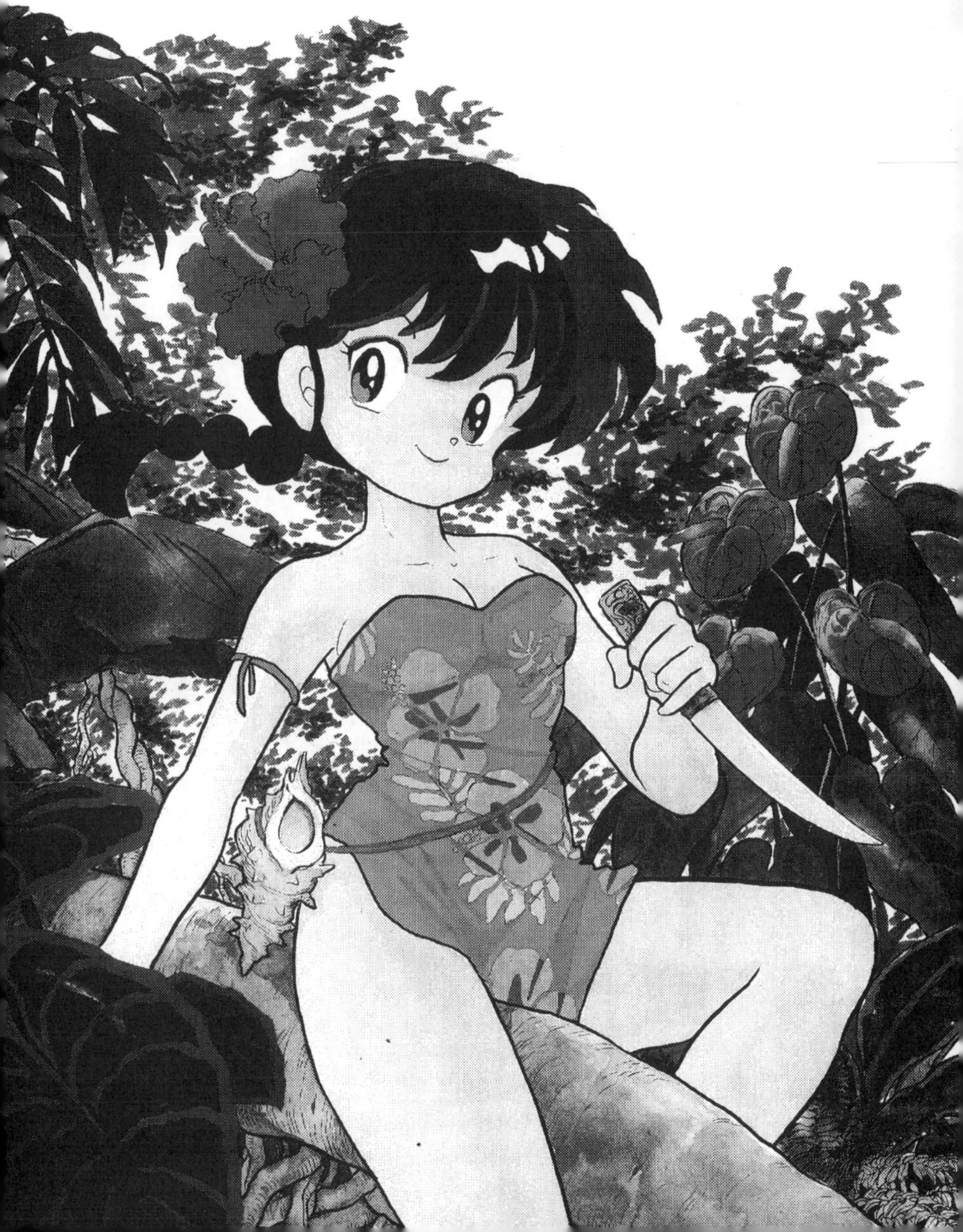

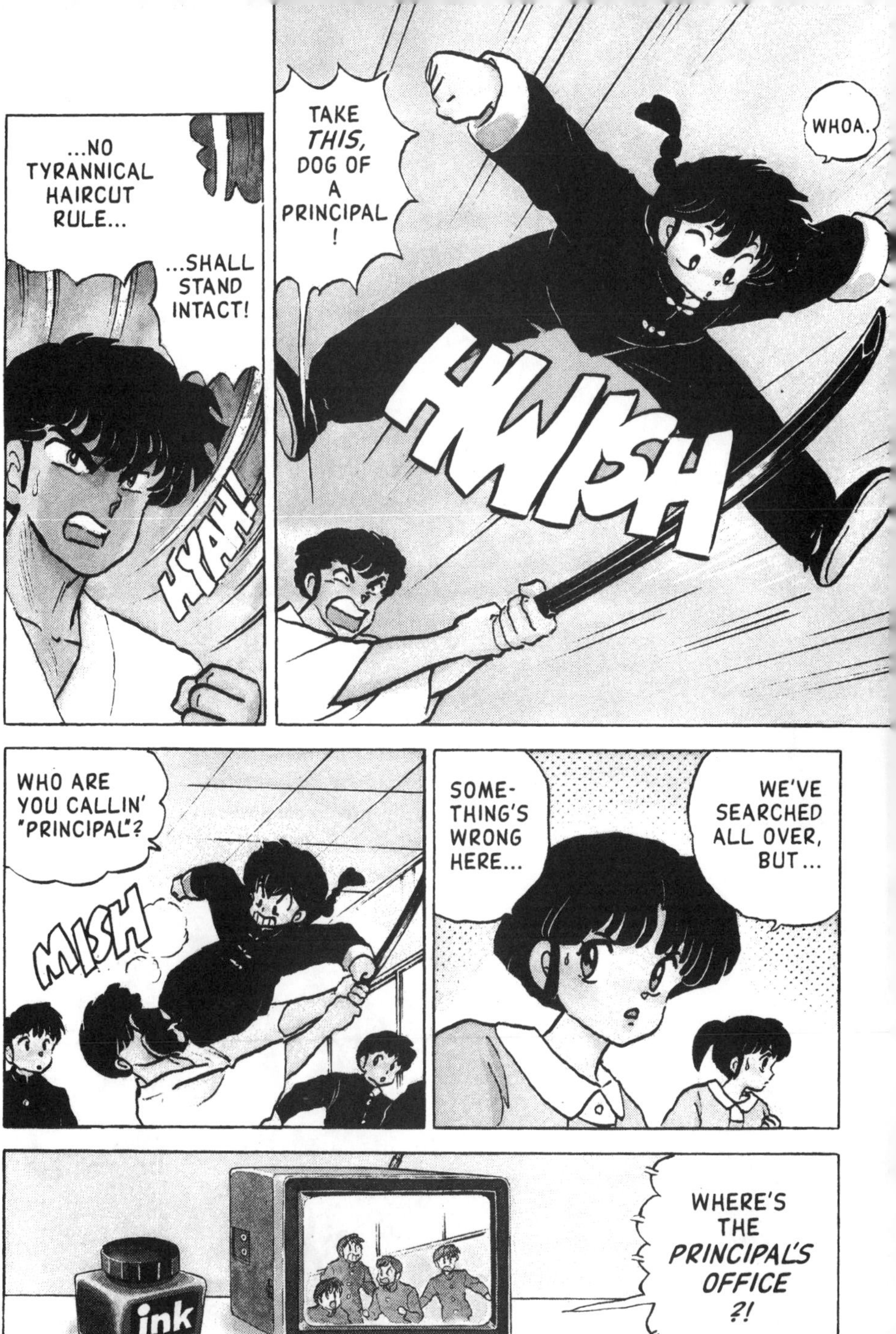
...NO TYRANNICAL HAIRCUT RULE...
...SHALL STAND INTACT!
HYAH!
TAKE *THIS,* DOG OF A PRINCIPAL!
WHOA.
HWISH
WHO ARE YOU CALLIN' "PRINCIPAL"?
MISH
SOME-THING'S WRONG HERE...
WE'VE SEARCHED ALL OVER, BUT...
ink
WHERE'S THE *PRINCIPAL'S OFFICE* ?!

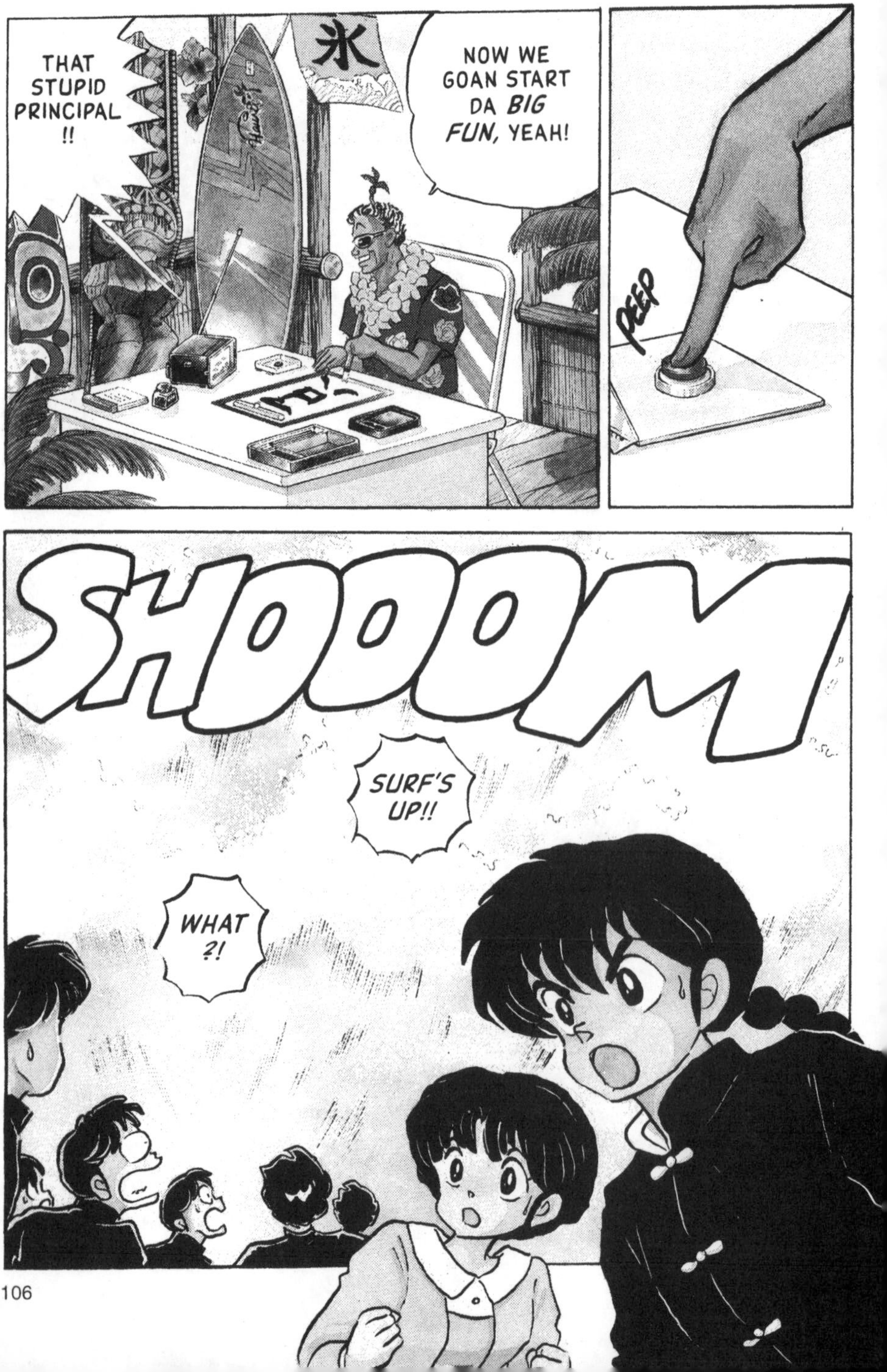
THAT STUPID PRINCIPAL !!
NOW WE GOAN START DA BIG FUN, YEAH!
PEEP
SHOOOM
SURF'S UP!!
WHAT ?!

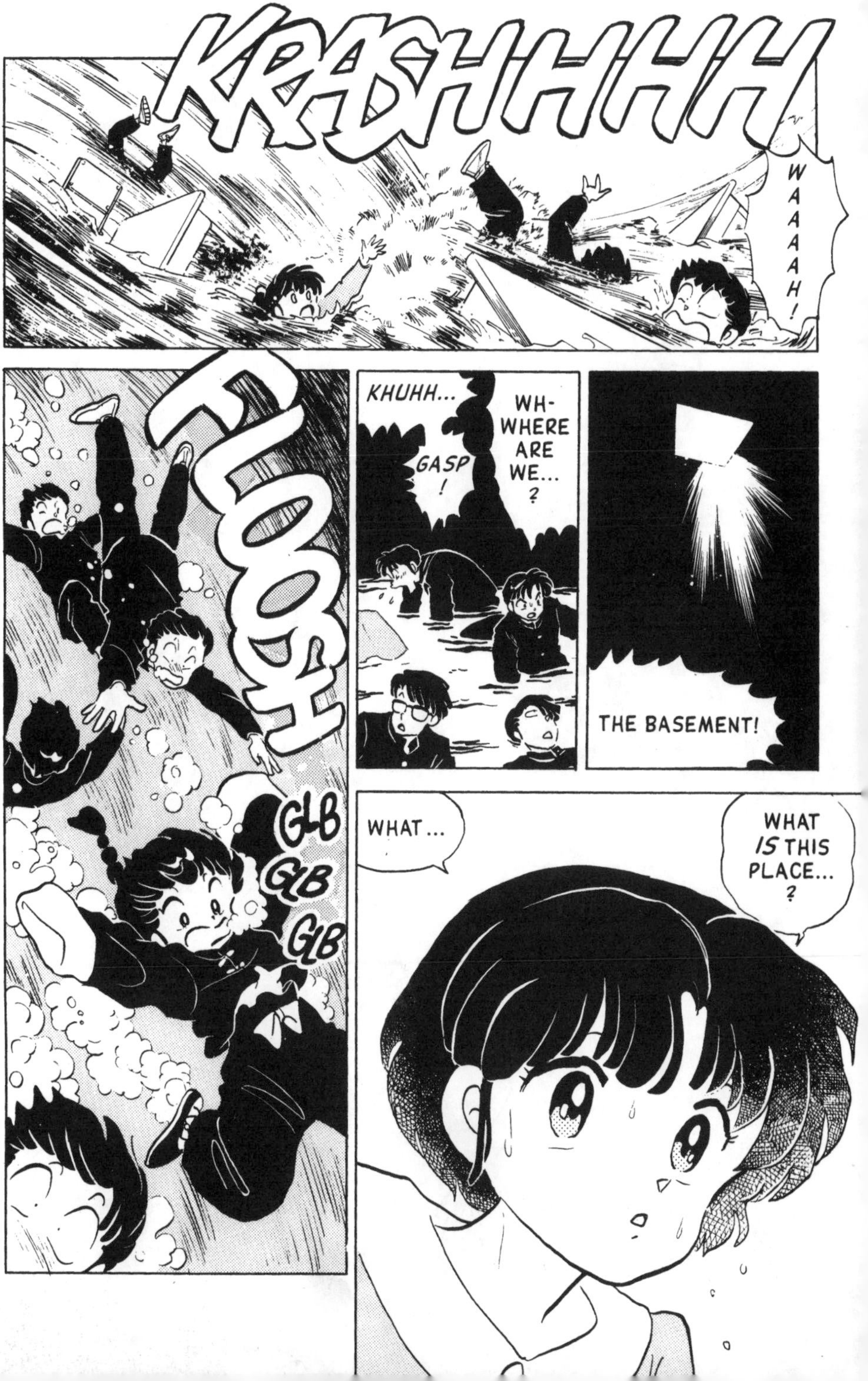
KRASHHHHH
WAAAAAH!
FLOOSH
GLB
GLB
GLB
KHUHH...
GASP!
WH-WHERE ARE WE...?
THE BASEMENT!
WHAT...
WHAT IS THIS PLACE...?

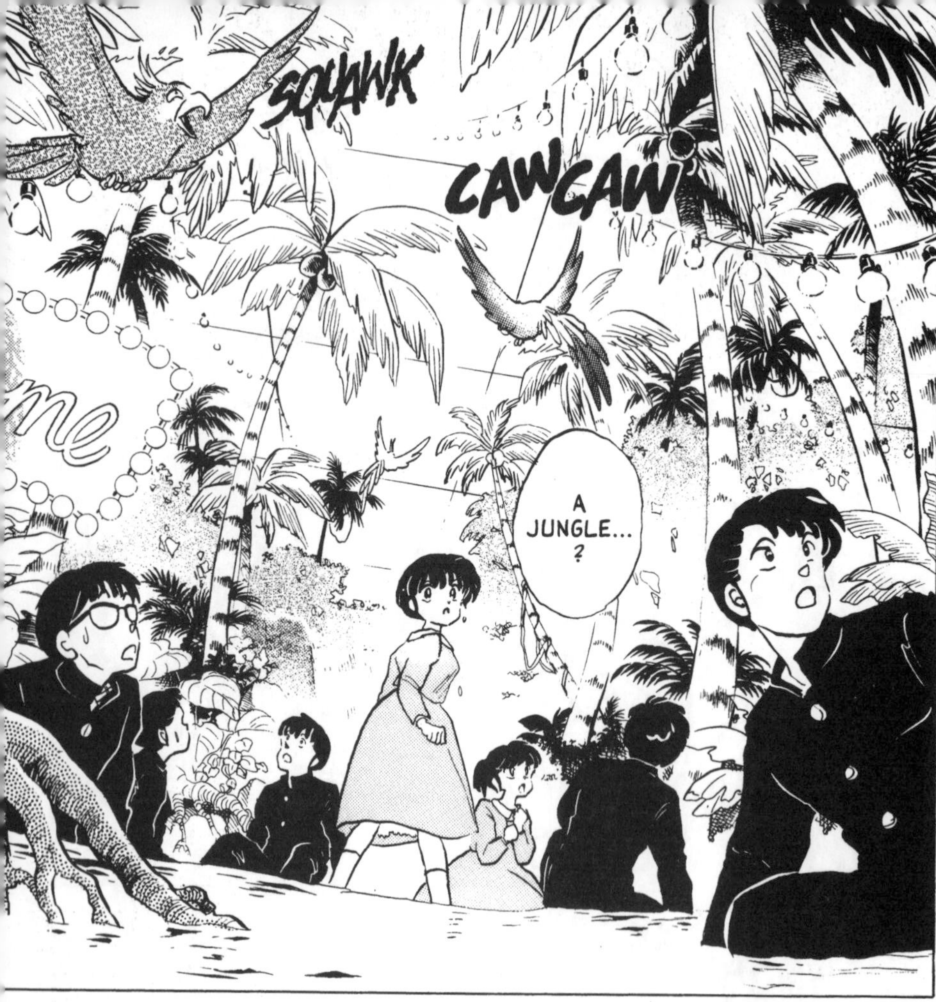
SQUAWK
CAW CAW
A JUNGLE... ?
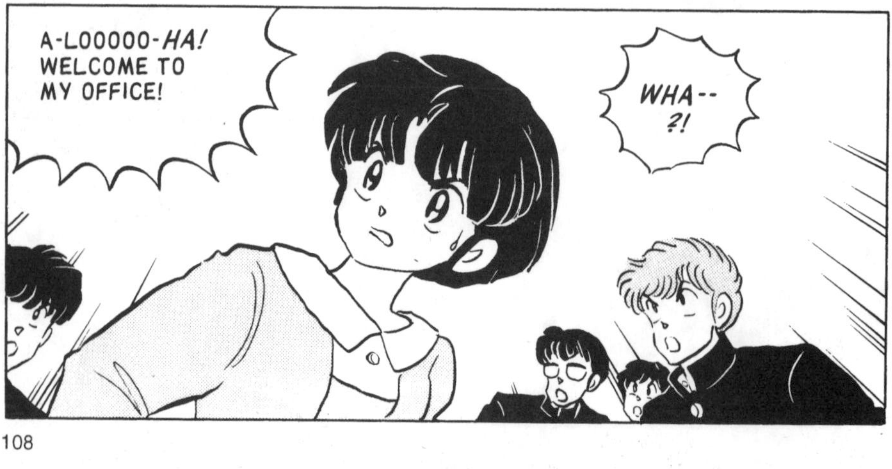
A-LOOOOO-*HA!* WELCOME TO MY OFFICE!
WHA-- ?!

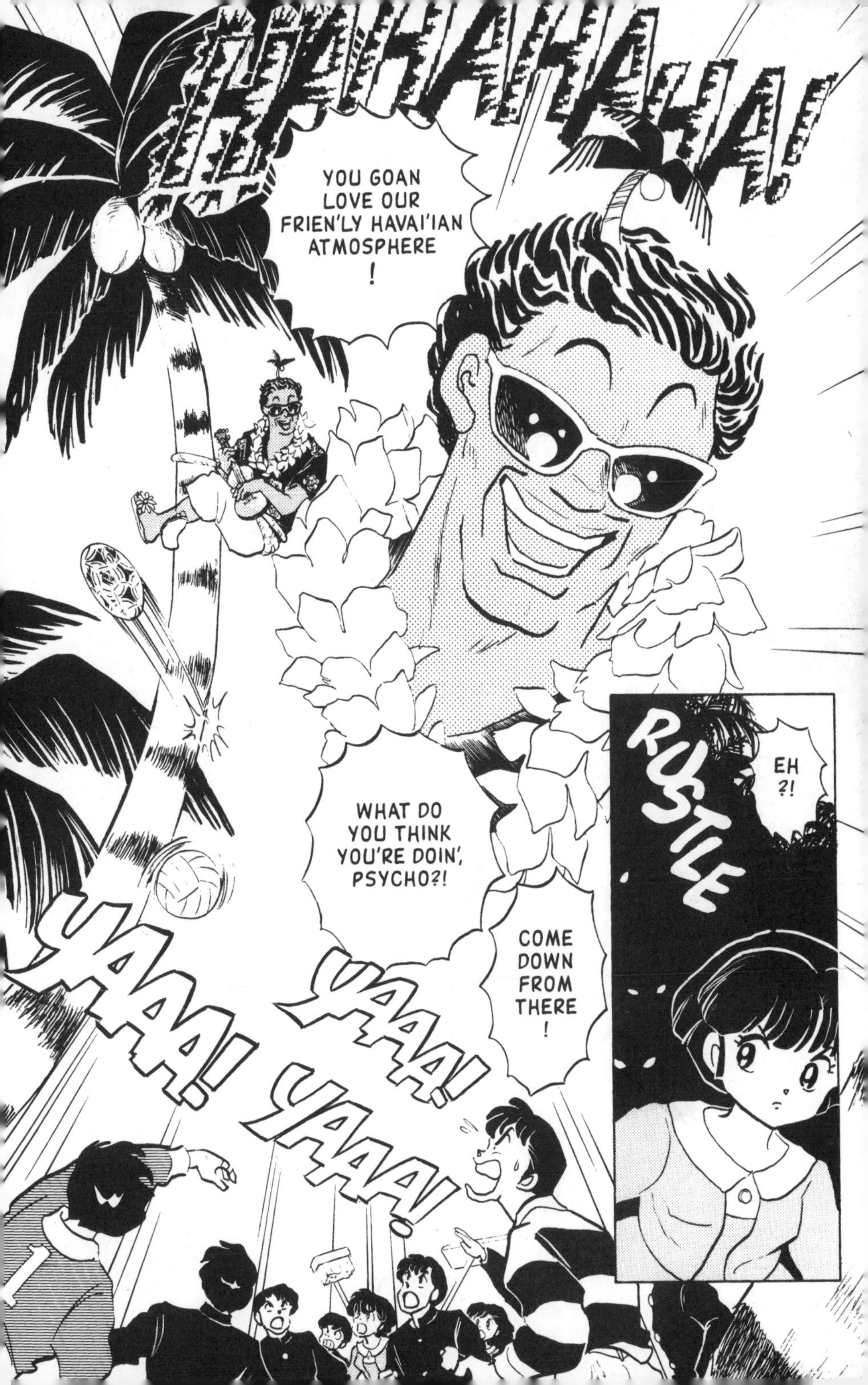
HAHAHAHA!
YOU GOAN LOVE OUR FRIEN'LY HAVAI'IAN ATMOSPHERE !
RUSTLE
EH ?!
WHAT DO YOU THINK YOU'RE DOIN', PSYCHO?!
COME DOWN FROM THERE !
YAAA! YAAA! YAAA!

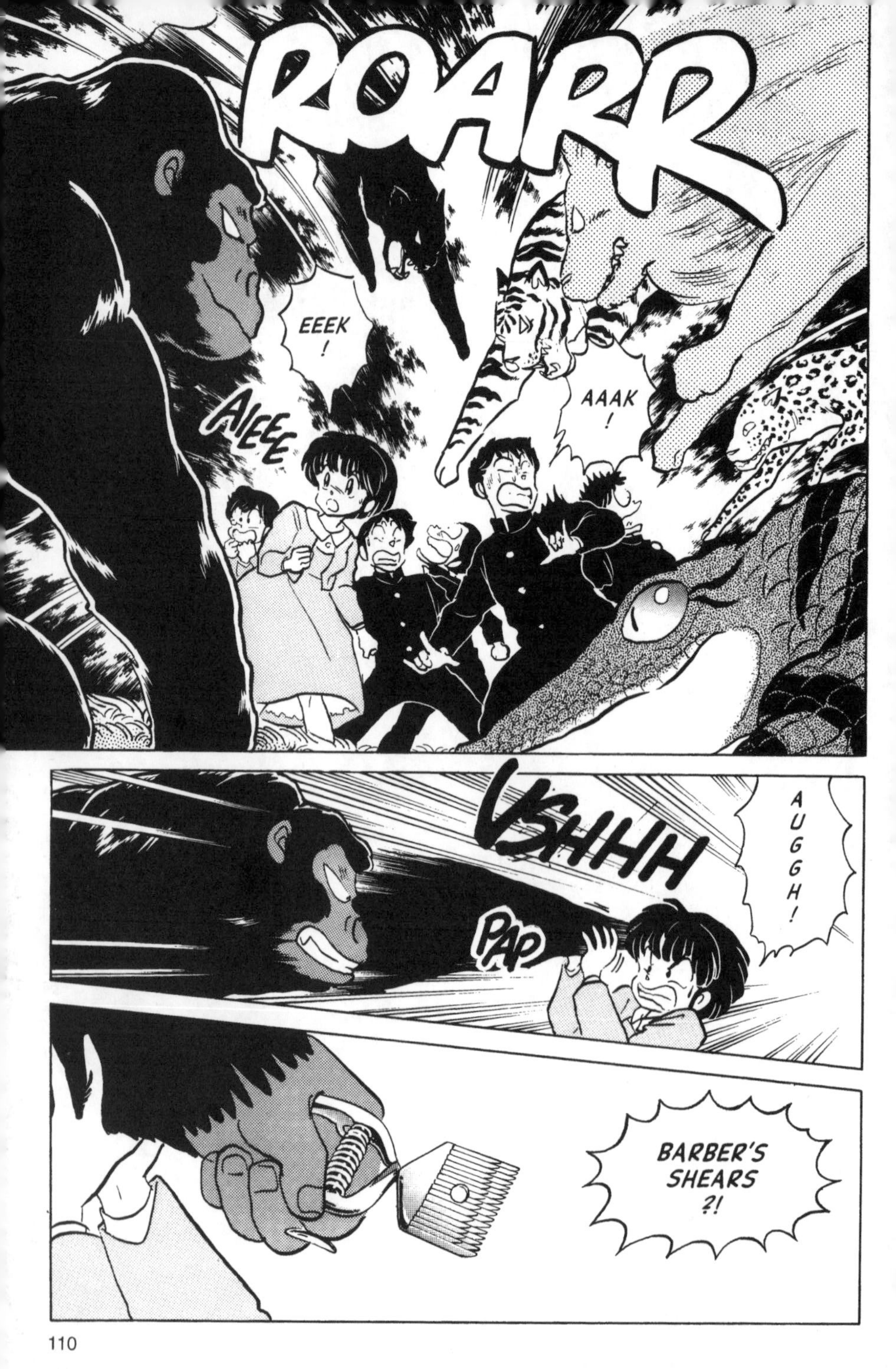
ROARR
EEEK!
AIEEE
AAAK!
VSHHH
PAP
AUGGH!
BARBER'S SHEARS ?!

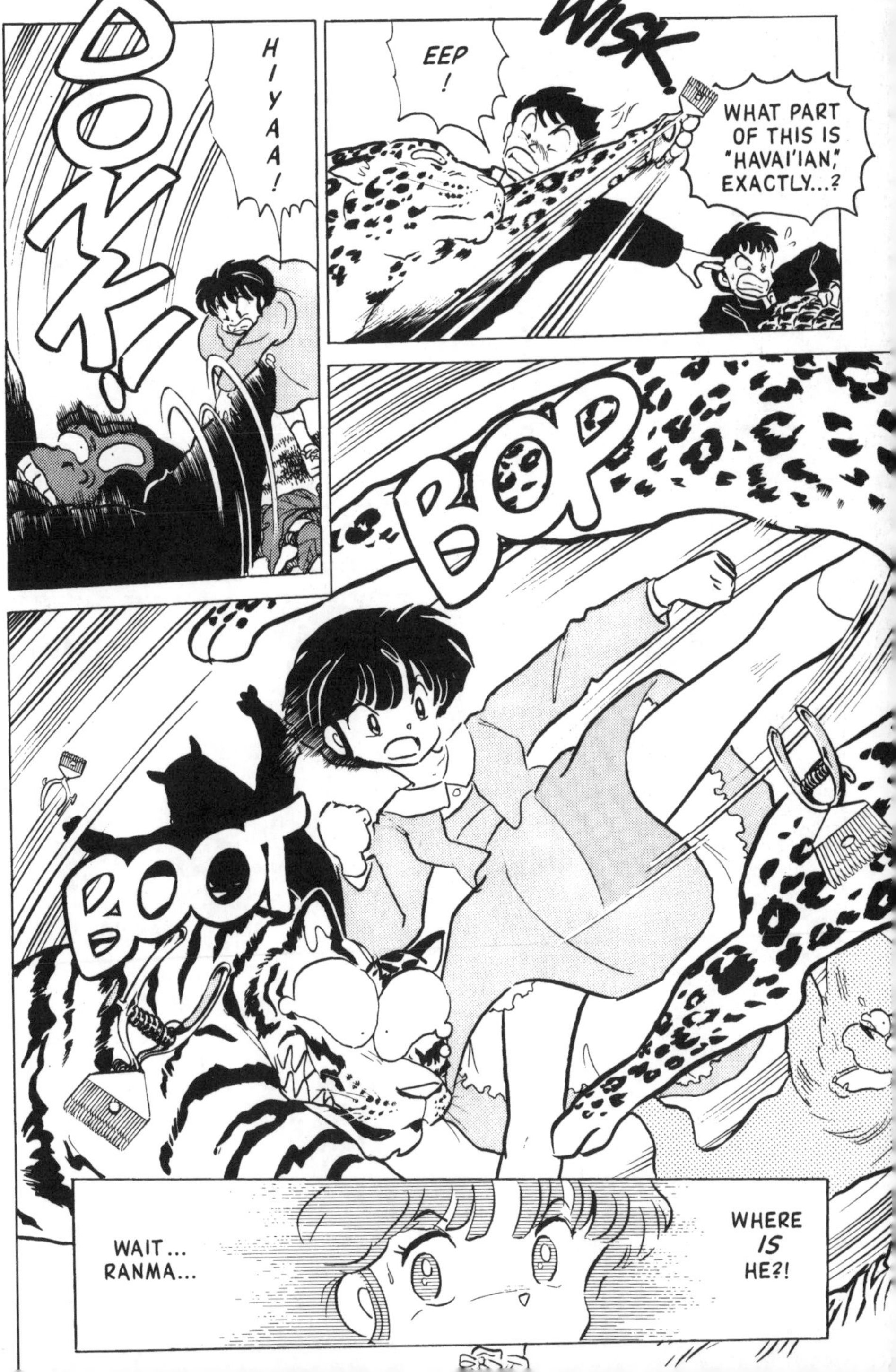
DONK!
HIYAAA!
WISK!
EEP!
WHAT PART OF THIS IS "HAVAI'IAN," EXACTLY...?
BOP
BOOT
WAIT... RANMA...
WHERE IS HE?!

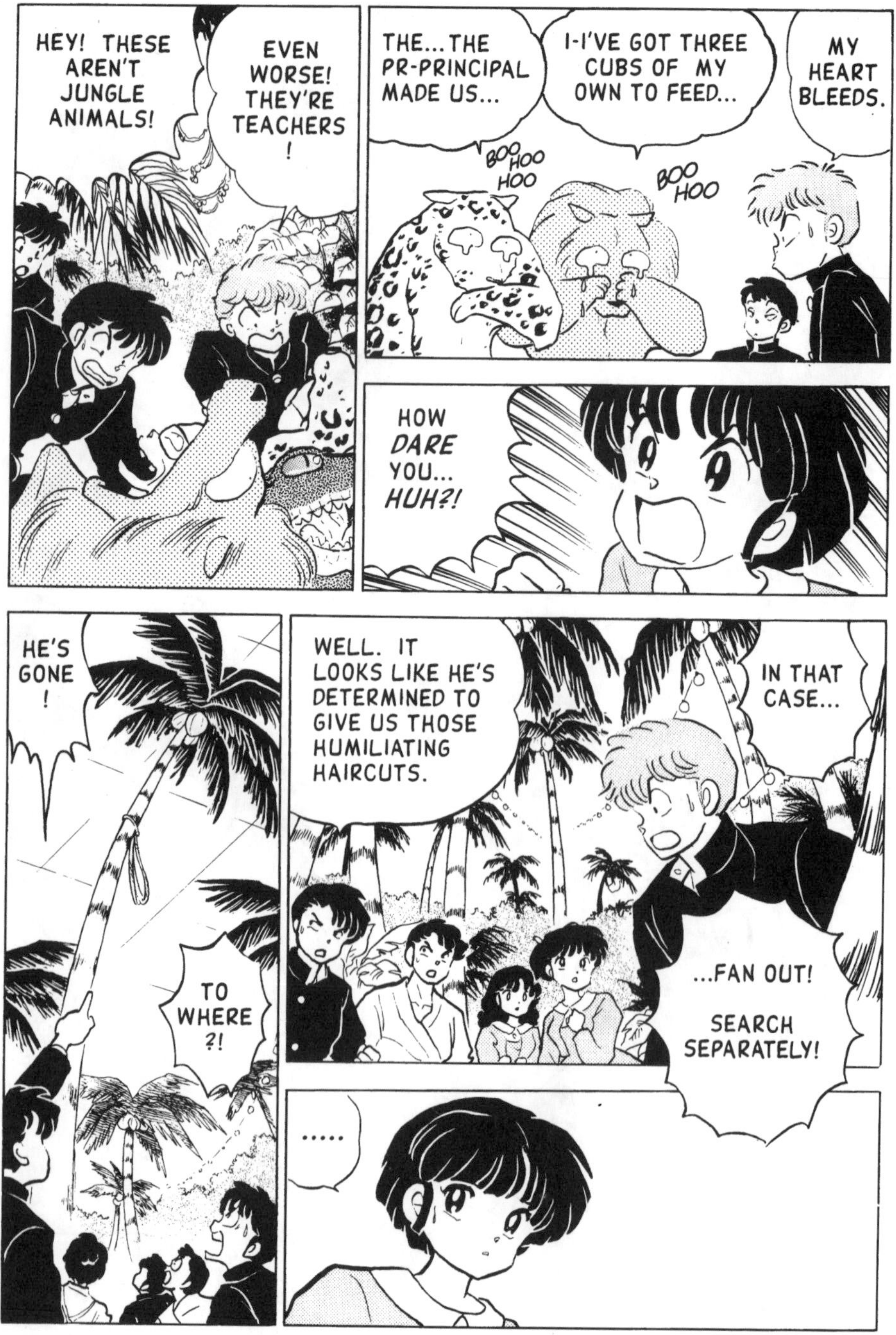
HEY! THESE AREN'T JUNGLE ANIMALS!
EVEN WORSE! THEY'RE TEACHERS!
THE...THE PR-PRINCIPAL MADE US...
BOO HOO HOO
I-I'VE GOT THREE CUBS OF MY OWN TO FEED...
BOO HOO
MY HEART BLEEDS.
HOW *DARE* YOU... *HUH?!*
HE'S GONE!
TO WHERE?!
WELL. IT LOOKS LIKE HE'S DETERMINED TO GIVE US THOSE HUMILIATING HAIRCUTS.
IN THAT CASE...
...FAN OUT! SEARCH SEPARATELY!
.....

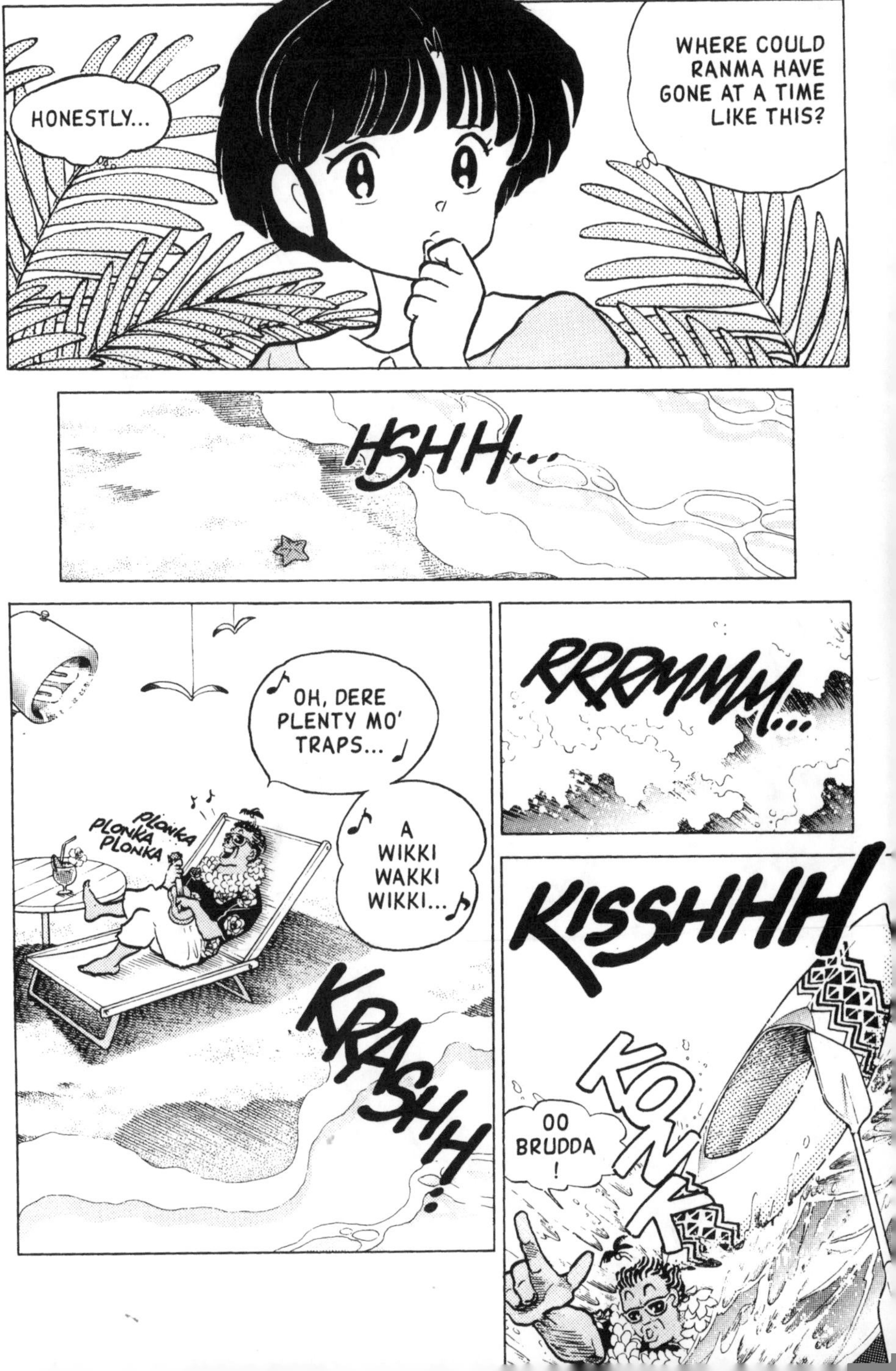
HONESTLY...
WHERE COULD RANMA HAVE GONE AT A TIME LIKE THIS?
HSHH...
OH, DERE PLENTY MO' TRAPS...
PLONKA PLONKA PLONKA
A WIKKI WAKKI WIKKI...
KRASHH!
RRRMMM...
KISSHHH
KON
OO BRUDDA!

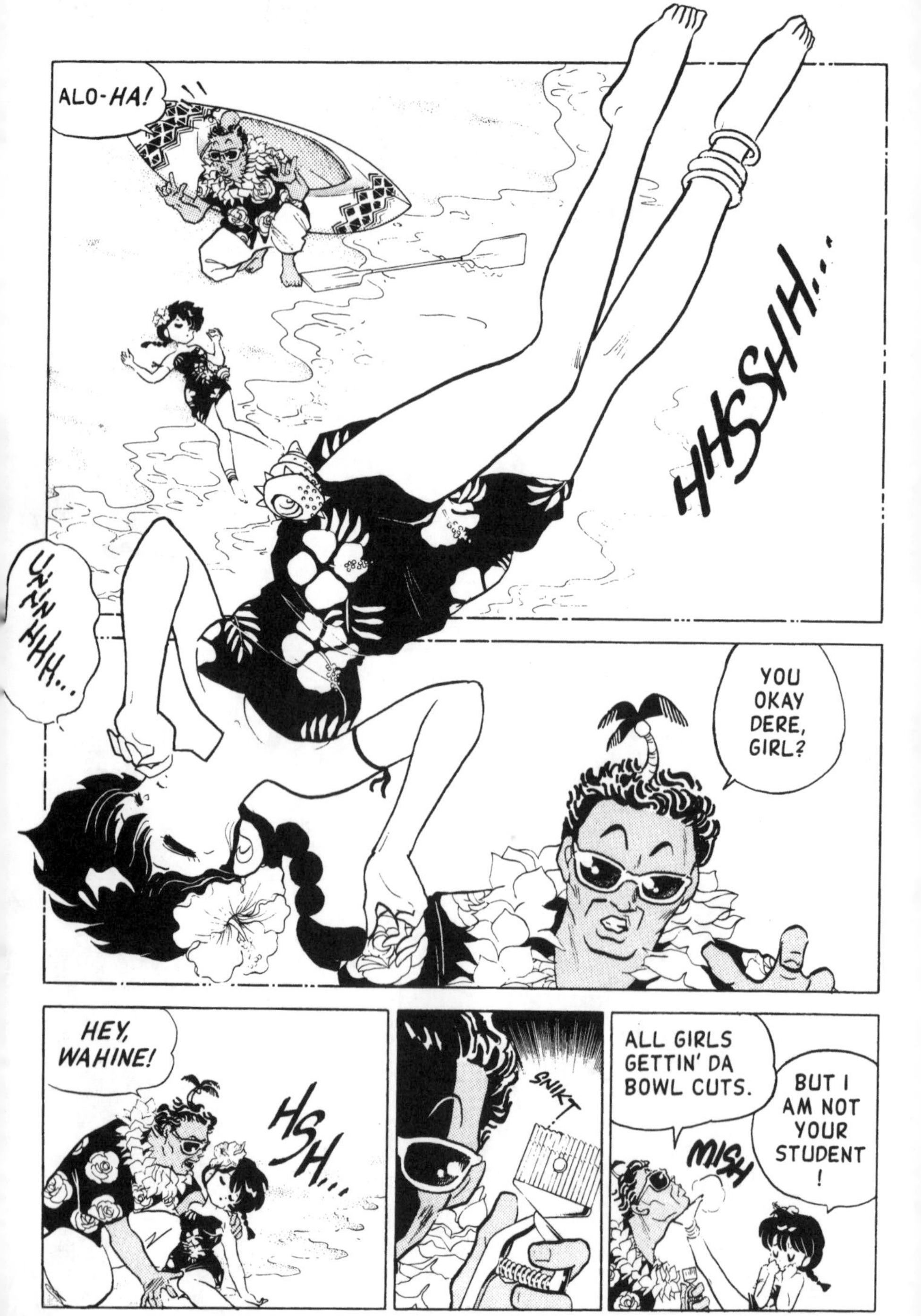
ALO-HA!
HHSHH...
UNNN HHH...
YOU OKAY DERE, GIRL?
HEY, WAHINE!
HSH...
SNIKT
ALL GIRLS GETTIN' DA BOWL CUTS.
MISH
BUT I AM NOT YOUR STUDENT!

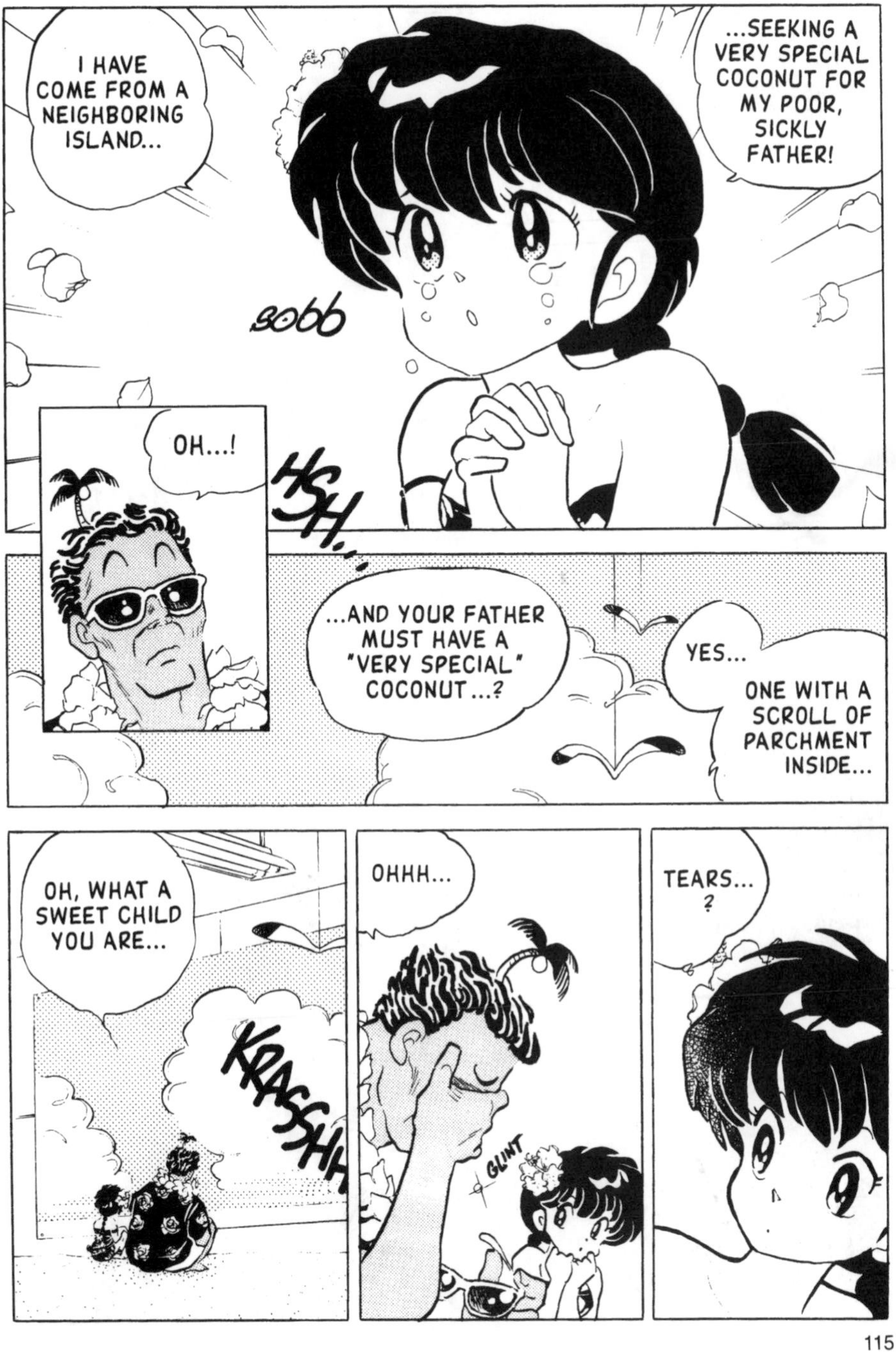
I HAVE COME FROM A NEIGHBORING ISLAND...
...SEEKING A VERY SPECIAL COCONUT FOR MY POOR, SICKLY FATHER!
sobb
OH...!
HSH...
...AND YOUR FATHER MUST HAVE A "VERY SPECIAL" COCONUT...?
YES...
ONE WITH A SCROLL OF PARCHMENT INSIDE...
OH, WHAT A SWEET CHILD YOU ARE...
KRASSHH
OHHH...
GLINT
TEARS...?

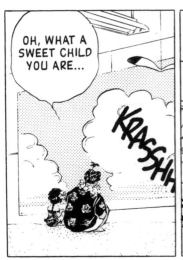

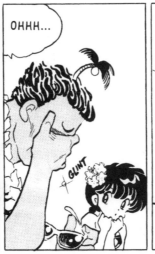

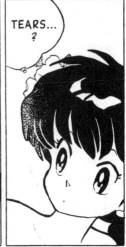

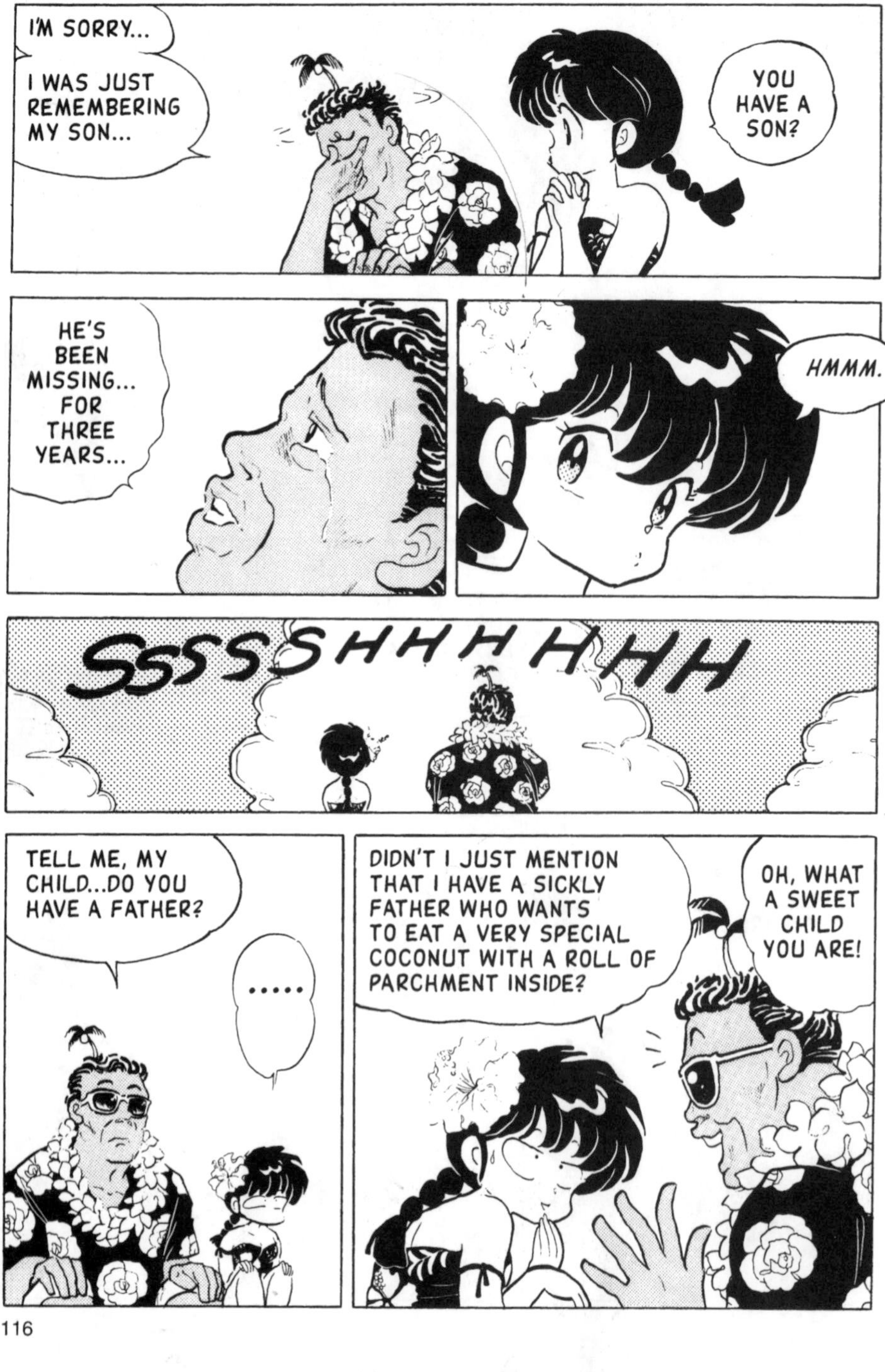
I'M SORRY...
I WAS JUST REMEMBERING MY SON...
YOU HAVE A SON?
HE'S BEEN MISSING... FOR THREE YEARS...
HMMM.
SSSSHHHHHHH
TELL ME, MY CHILD...DO YOU HAVE A FATHER?
.....
DIDN'T I JUST MENTION THAT I HAVE A SICKLY FATHER WHO WANTS TO EAT A VERY SPECIAL COCONUT WITH A ROLL OF PARCHMENT INSIDE?
OH, WHAT A SWEET CHILD YOU ARE!

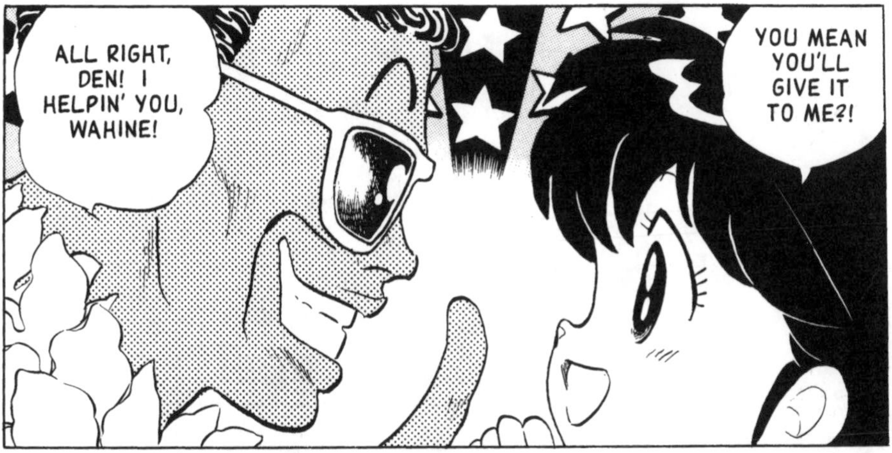
ALL RIGHT, DEN! I HELPIN' YOU, WAHINE!
YOU MEAN YOU'LL GIVE IT TO ME?!

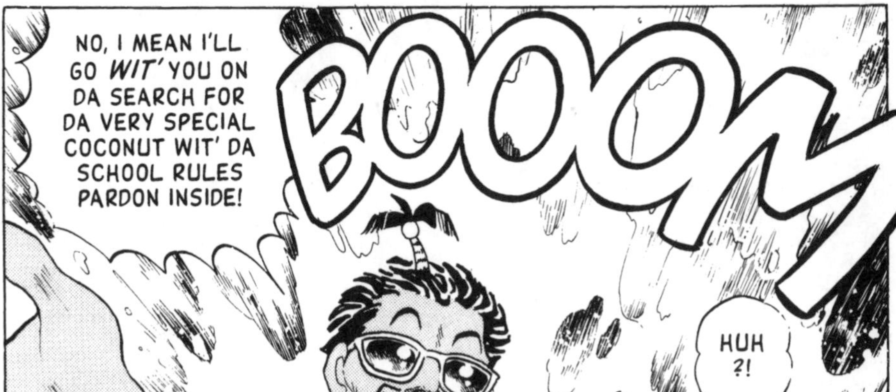
NO, I MEAN I'LL GO *WIT'* YOU ON DA SEARCH FOR DA VERY SPECIAL COCONUT WIT' DA SCHOOL RULES PARDON INSIDE!
BOOOM
HUH ?!

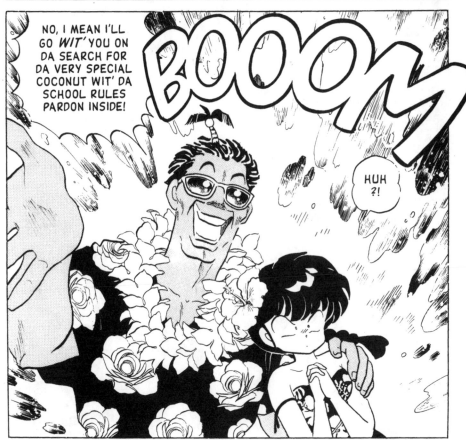

PART 8
THE PRINCIPAL OF THE THING

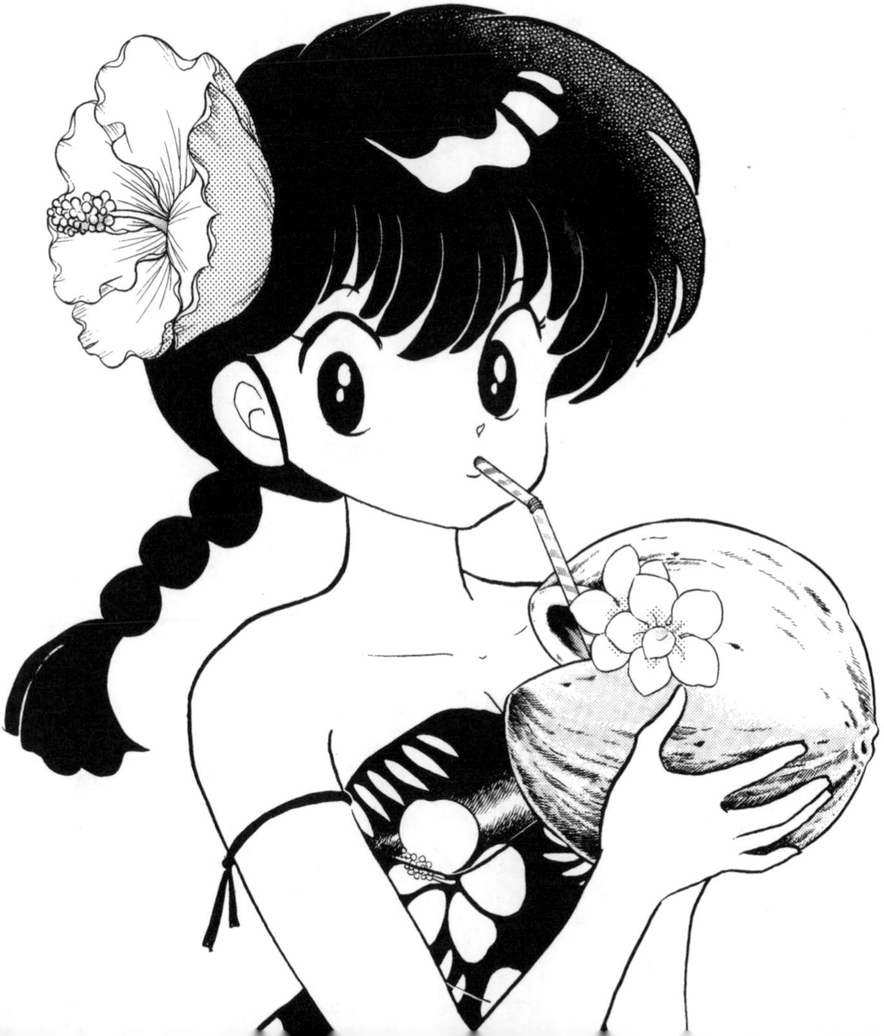

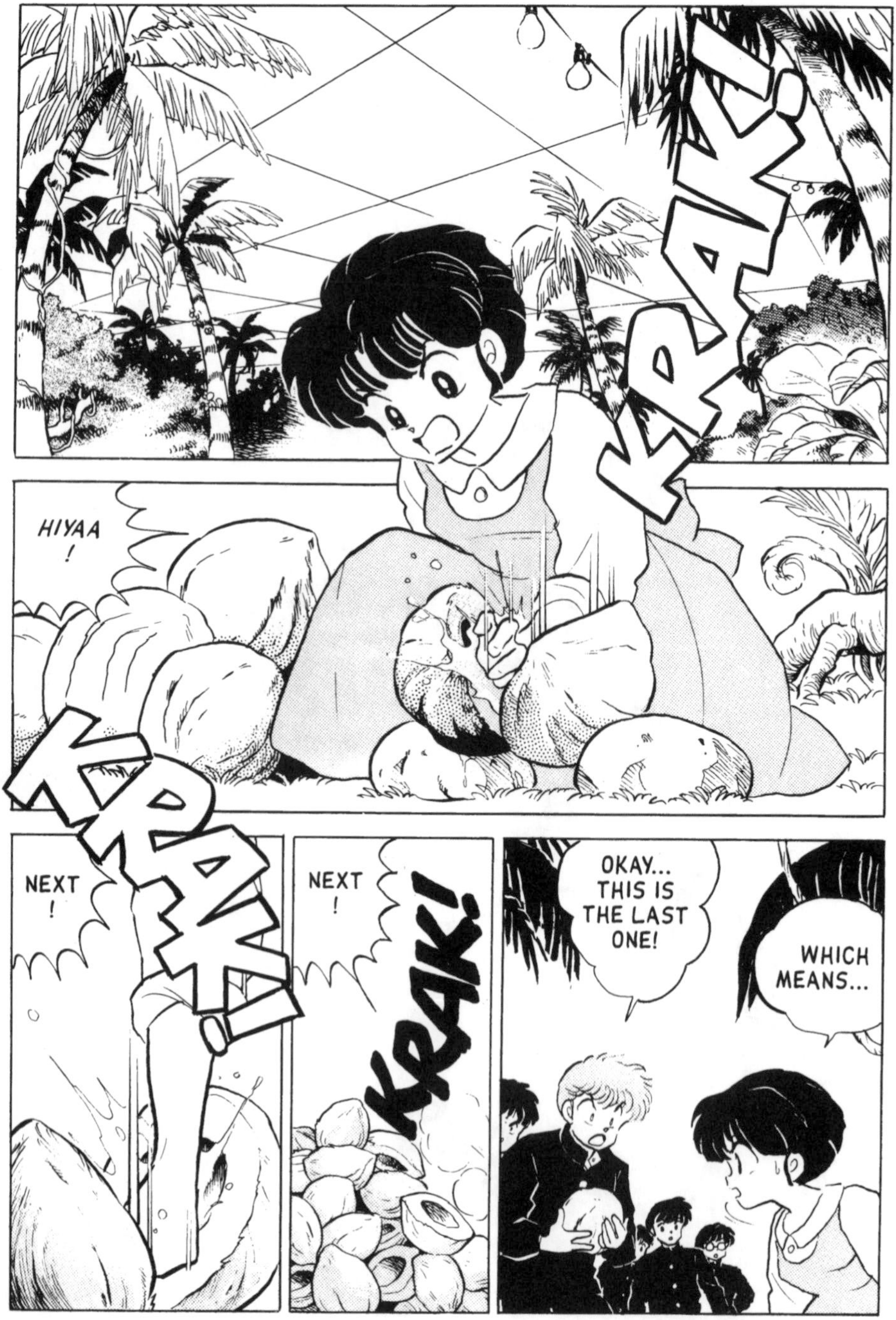
KRAK!
HIYAA!
KRAK!
NEXT!
KRAK!
NEXT!
KRAK!
OKAY... THIS IS THE LAST ONE!
WHICH MEANS...

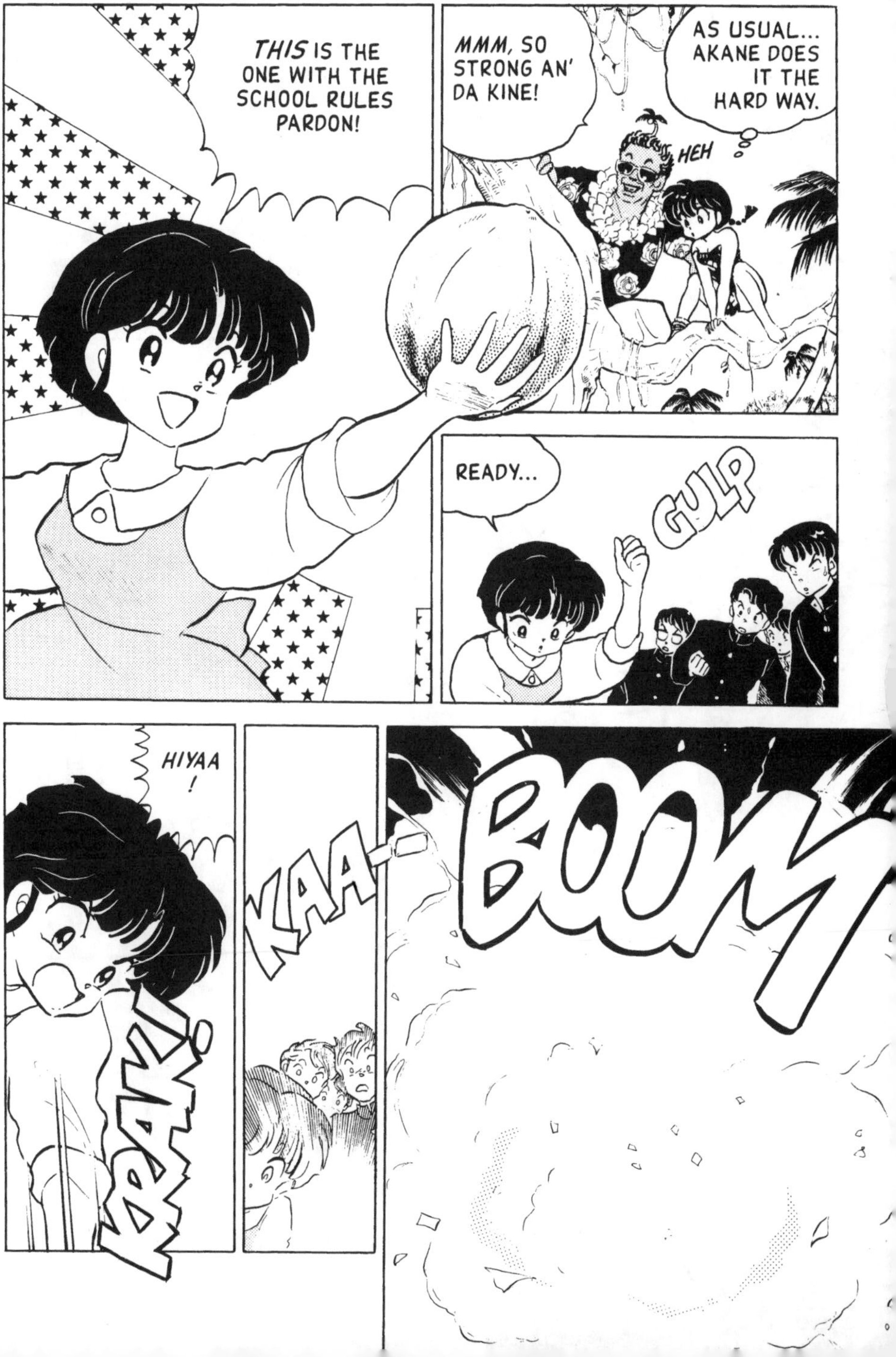
THIS IS THE ONE WITH THE SCHOOL RULES PARDON!
MMM, SO STRONG AN' DA KINE!
AS USUAL... AKANE DOES IT THE HARD WAY.
HEH
READY...
GULP
HIYAA !
KRAK!
KAA-
BOOM

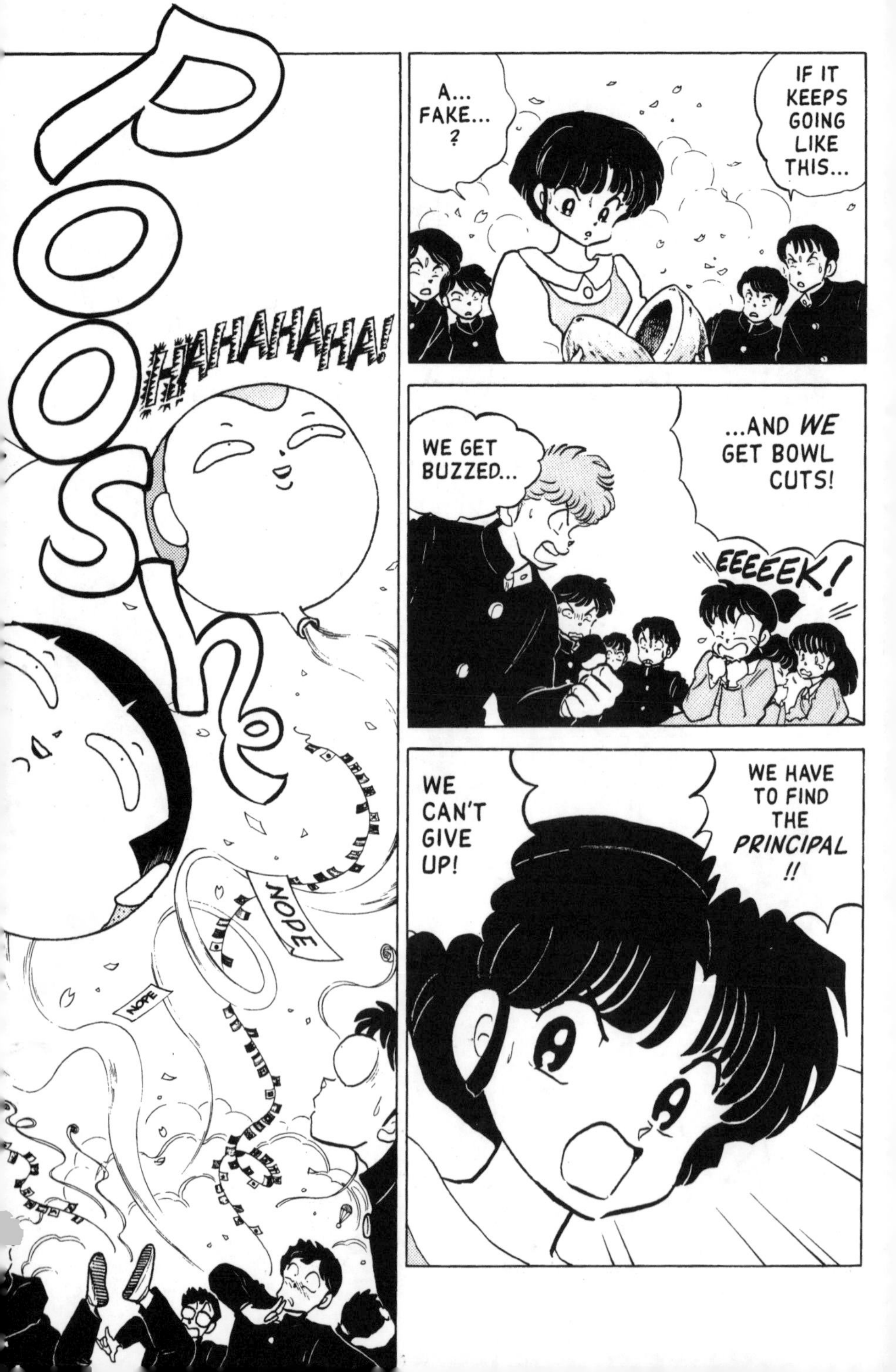
POOSH
HAHAHAHA!
NOPE
NOPE
A... FAKE...?
IF IT KEEPS GOING LIKE THIS...
WE GET BUZZED...
...AND *WE* GET BOWL CUTS!
EEEEEK!
WE CAN'T GIVE UP!
WE HAVE TO FIND THE *PRINCIPAL*!!

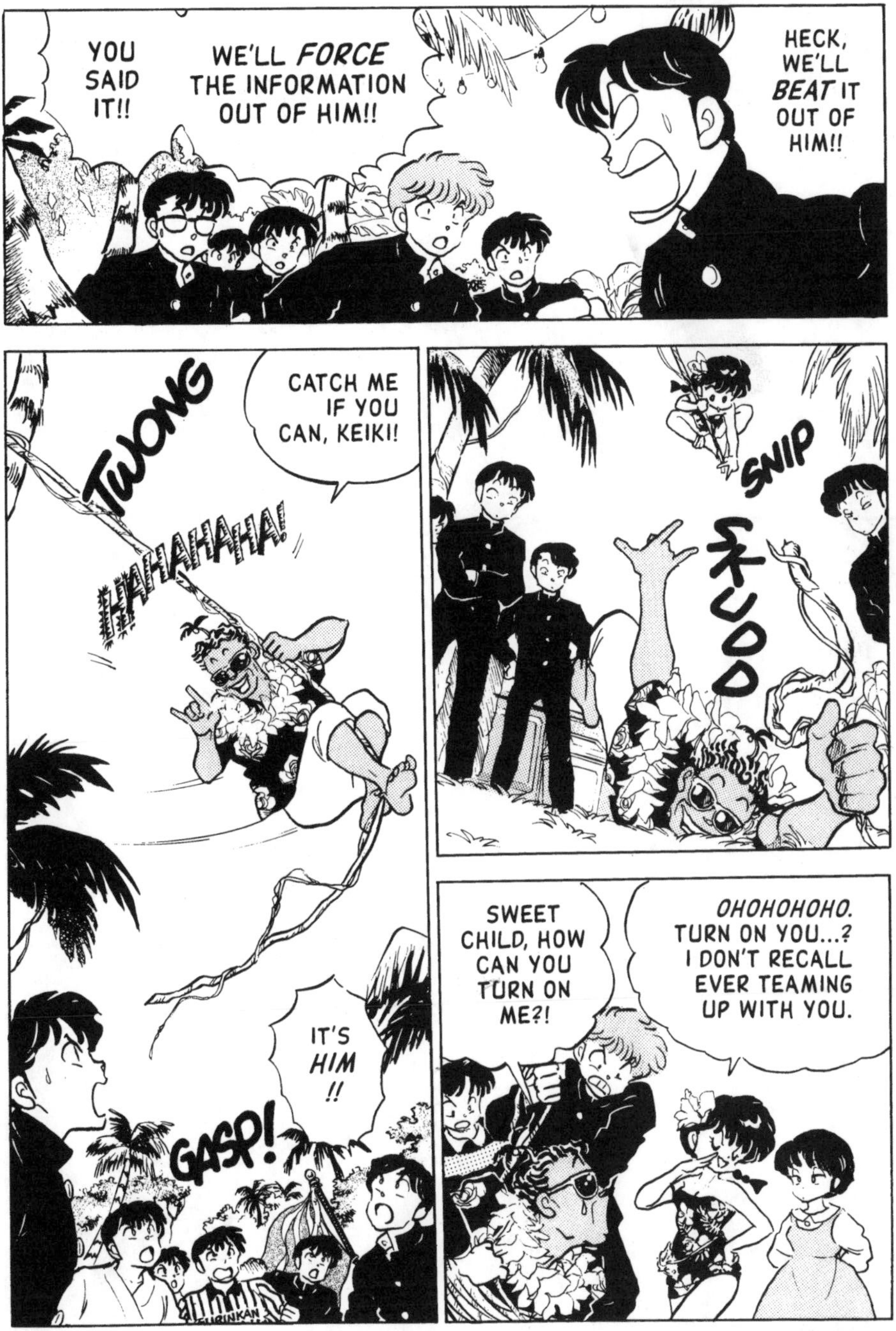
YOU SAID IT!!
WE'LL *FORCE* THE INFORMATION OUT OF HIM!!
HECK, WE'LL *BEAT* IT OUT OF HIM!!
TWONG
CATCH ME IF YOU CAN, KEIKI!
HAHAHAHA!
SNIP
THUD
IT'S *HIM* !!
GASP!
SWEET CHILD, HOW CAN YOU TURN ON ME?!
OHOHOHOHO. TURN ON YOU...? I DON'T RECALL EVER TEAMING UP WITH YOU.

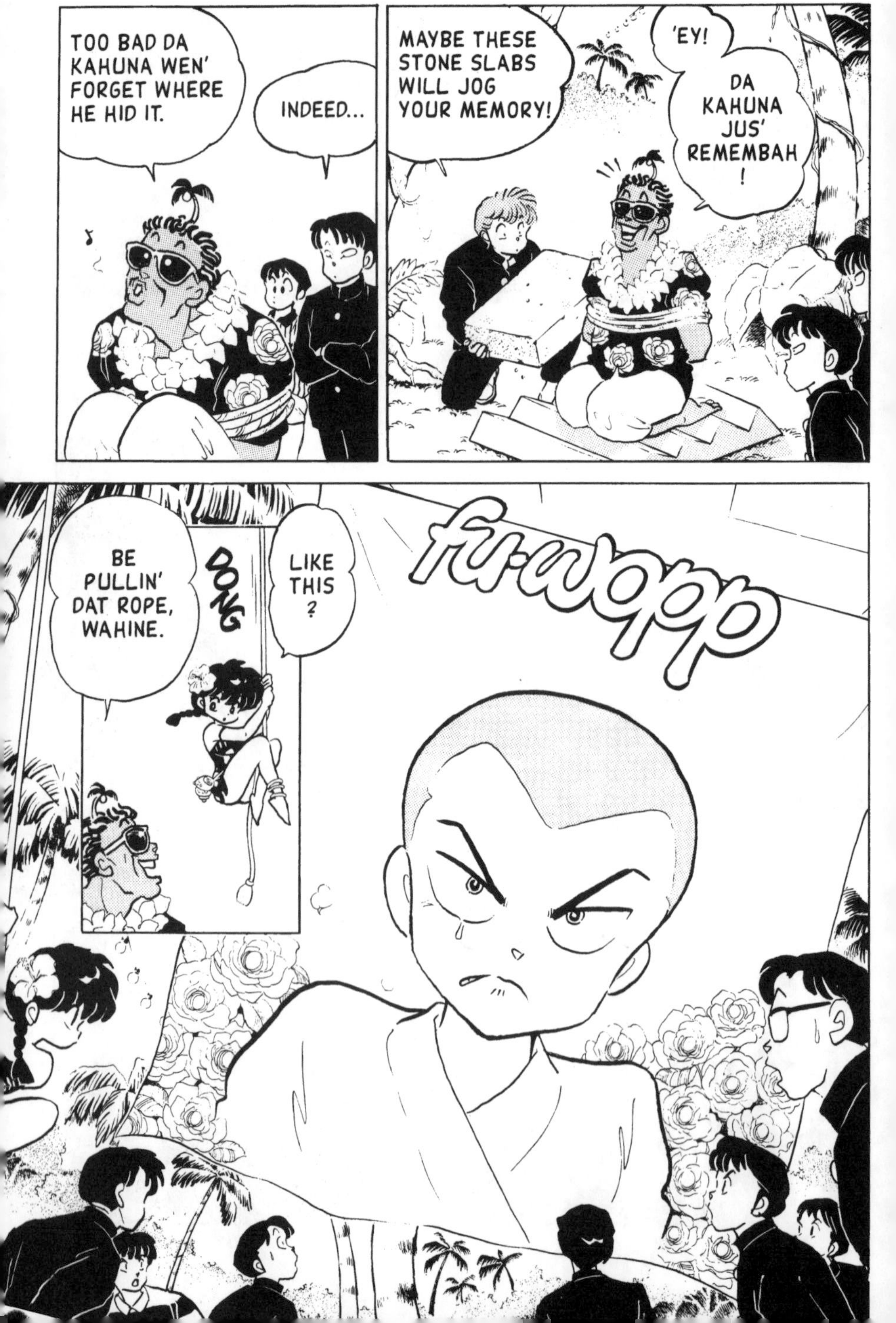
TOO BAD DA KAHUNA WEN' FORGET WHERE HE HID IT.
INDEED...
MAYBE THESE STONE SLABS WILL JOG YOUR MEMORY!
'EY!
DA KAHUNA JUS' REMEMBAH!
BE PULLIN' DAT ROPE, WAHINE.
DONG
LIKE THIS?
fu-wopp

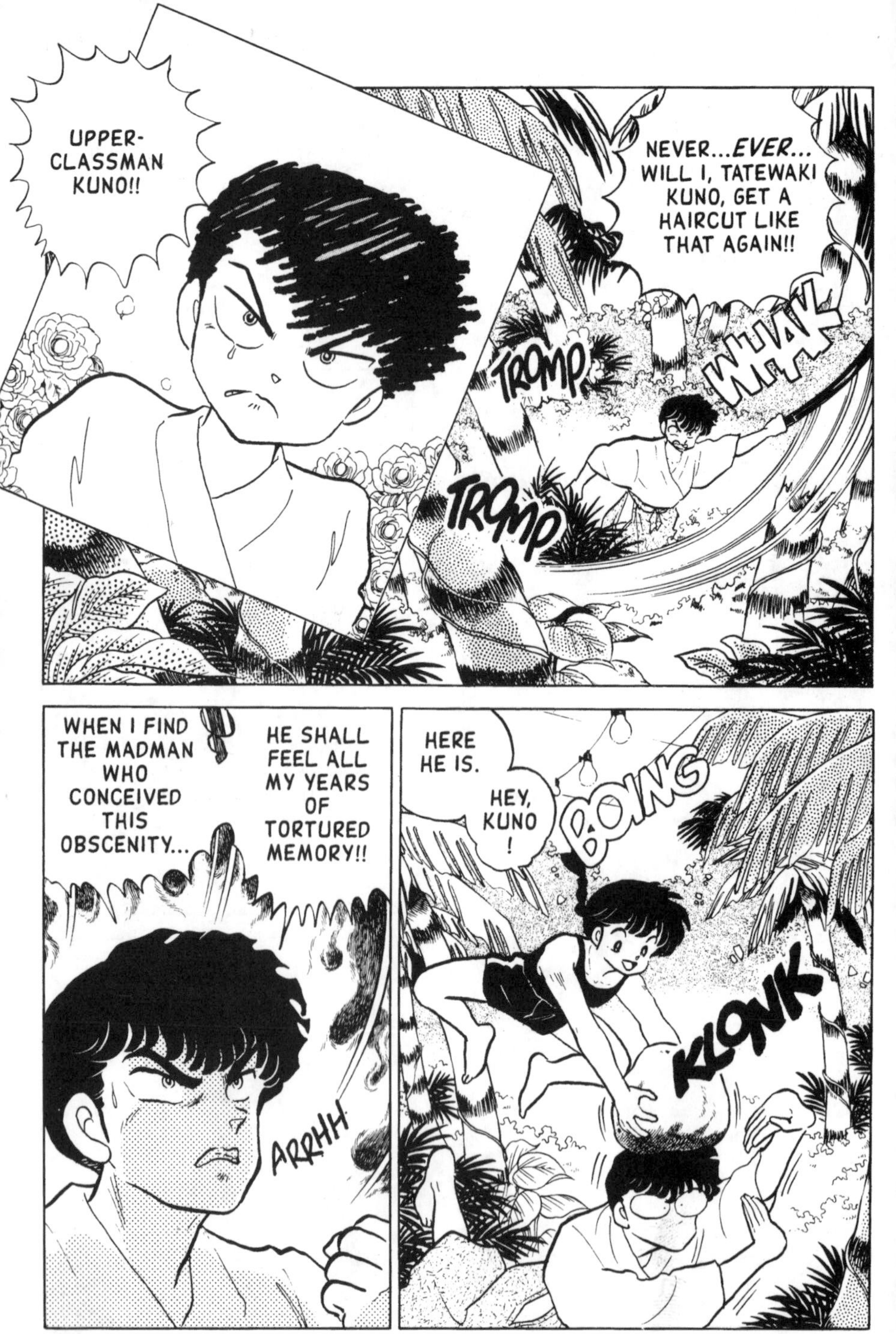
UPPER-CLASSMAN KUNO!!
NEVER...*EVER*... WILL I, TATEWAKI KUNO, GET A HAIRCUT LIKE THAT AGAIN!!
TROMP
WHAK
TROMP
WHEN I FIND THE MADMAN WHO CONCEIVED THIS OBSCENITY...
HE SHALL FEEL ALL MY YEARS OF TORTURED MEMORY!!
ARRHH
HERE HE IS.
HEY, KUNO!
BOING
KLONK

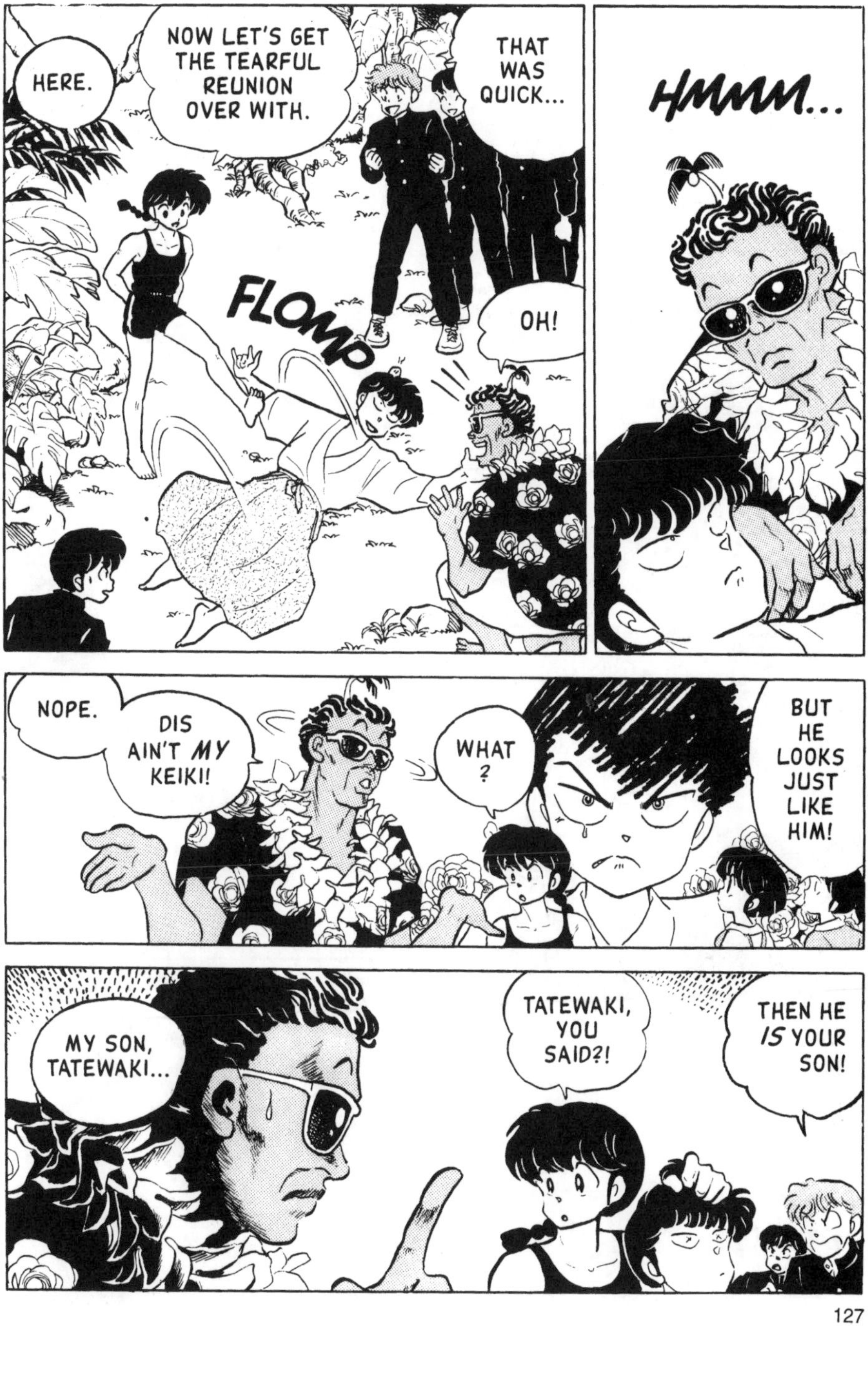
HERE.
NOW LET'S GET THE TEARFUL REUNION OVER WITH.
THAT WAS QUICK...
FLOMP
OH!
HMMM...
NOPE.
DIS AIN'T *MY* KEIKI!
WHAT?
BUT HE LOOKS JUST LIKE HIM!
MY SON, TATEWAKI...
TATEWAKI, YOU SAID?!
THEN HE *IS* YOUR SON!

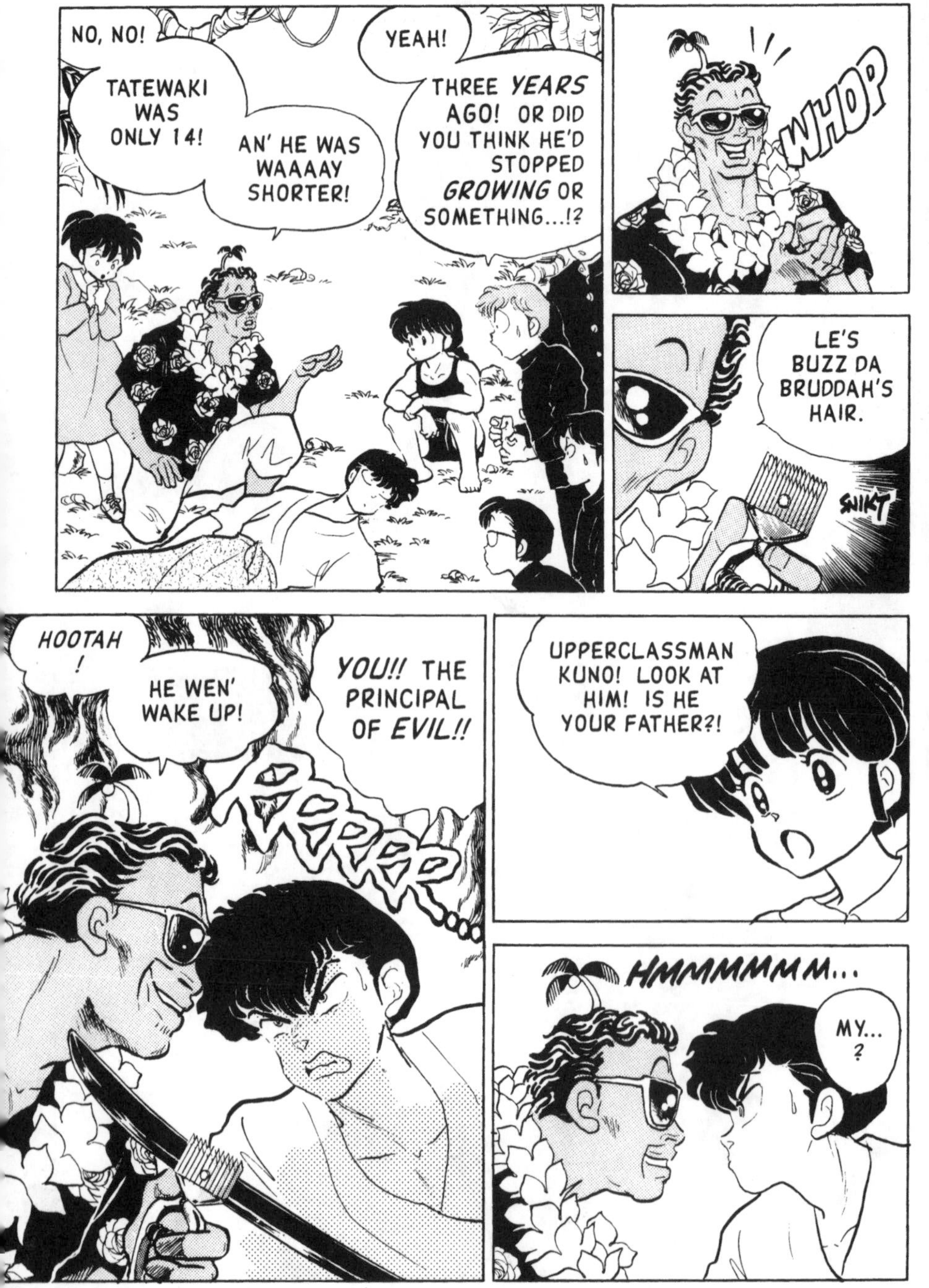
NO, NO!
TATEWAKI WAS ONLY 14!
AN' HE WAS WAAAAY SHORTER!
YEAH!
THREE *YEARS* AGO! OR DID YOU THINK HE'D STOPPED *GROWING* OR SOMETHING...!?
WHOP
LE'S BUZZ DA BRUDDAH'S HAIR.
SNIKT
HOOTAH!
HE WEN' WAKE UP!
YOU!! THE PRINCIPAL OF *EVIL!!*
UPPERCLASSMAN KUNO! LOOK AT HIM! IS HE YOUR FATHER?!
HMMMMMM...
MY...?

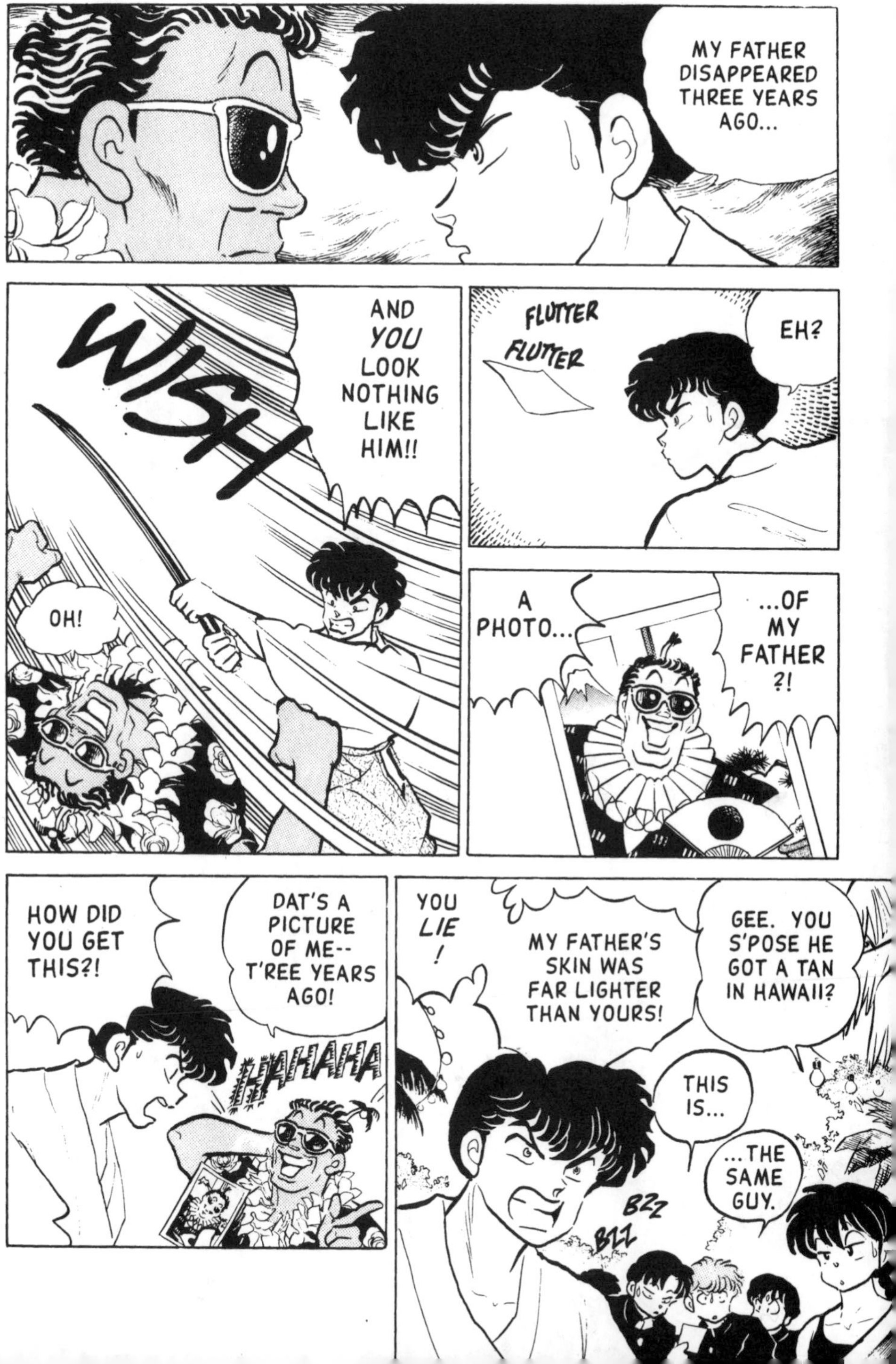
MY FATHER DISAPPEARED THREE YEARS AGO...
WISH
AND YOU LOOK NOTHING LIKE HIM!!
OH!
FLUTTER
FLUTTER
EH?
A PHOTO...
...OF MY FATHER ?!
HOW DID YOU GET THIS?!
DAT'S A PICTURE OF ME-- T'REE YEARS AGO!
HAHAHA
YOU LIE !
MY FATHER'S SKIN WAS FAR LIGHTER THAN YOURS!
GEE. YOU S'POSE HE GOT A TAN IN HAWAII?
THIS IS...
...THE SAME GUY.
BZZ
BZZ

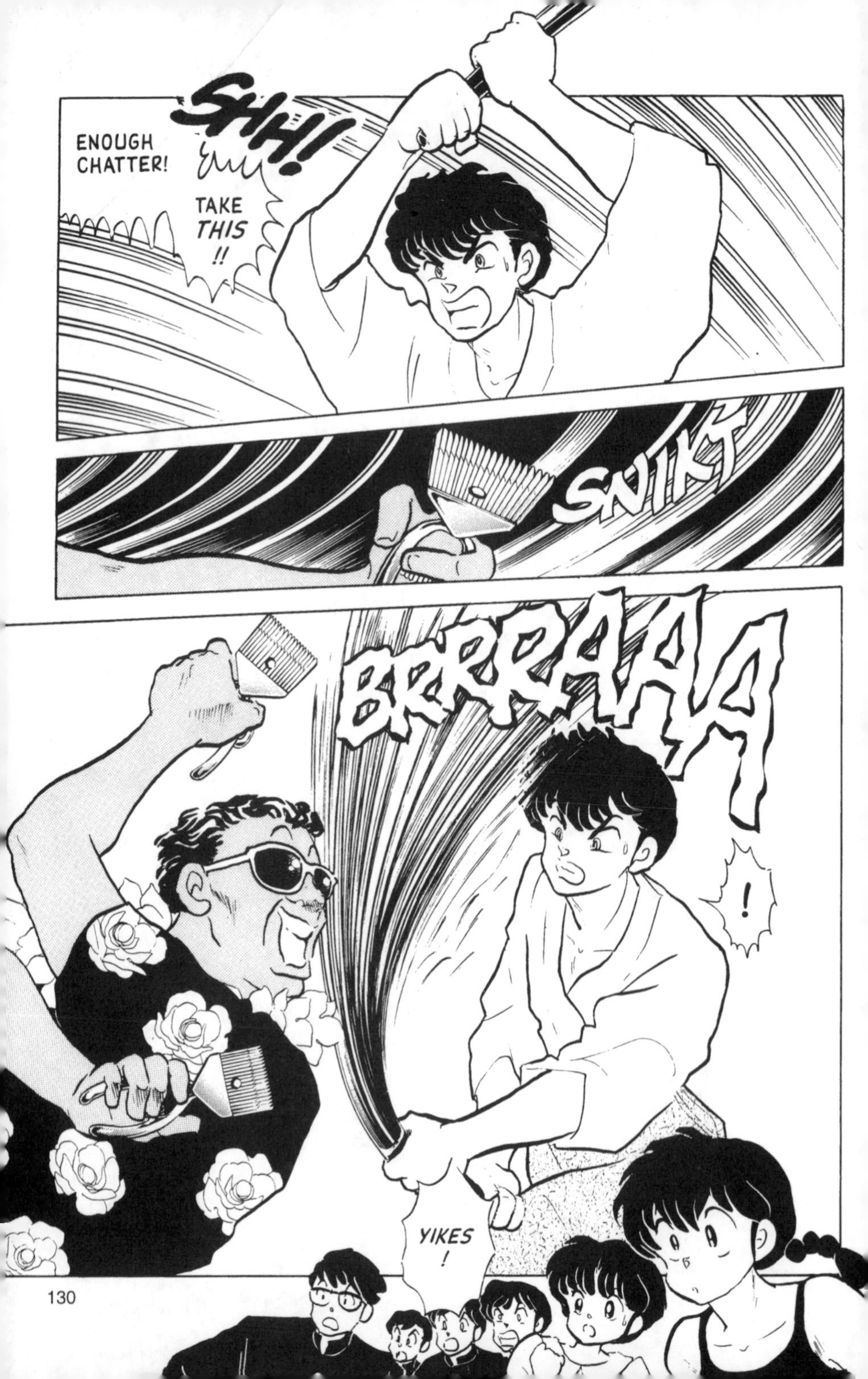
SHH!
ENOUGH CHATTER!
TAKE THIS !!
SNIKT
BRRRAAAA
!
YIKES !

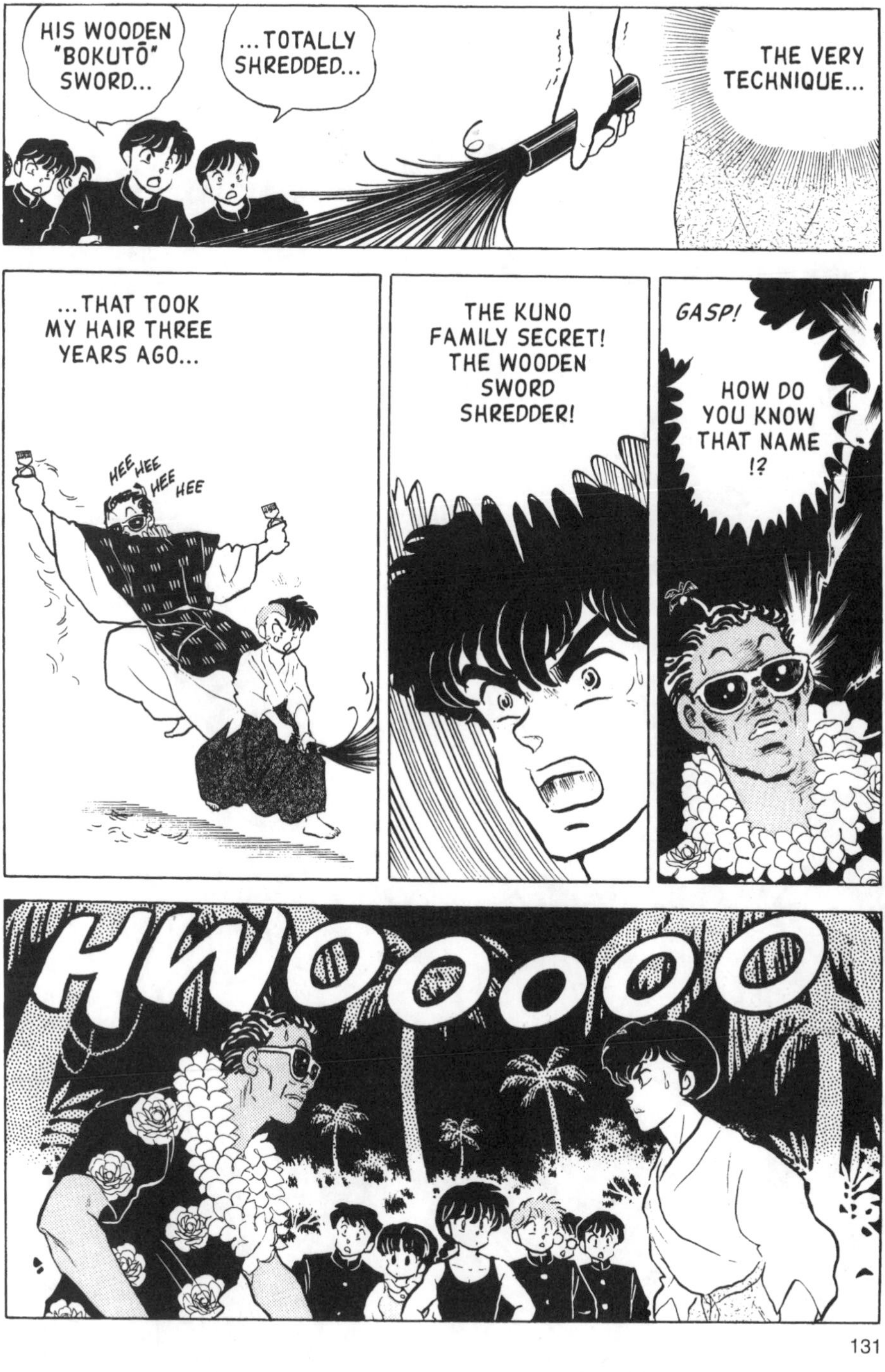
HIS WOODEN "BOKUTŌ" SWORD...
...TOTALLY SHREDDED...
THE VERY TECHNIQUE...
...THAT TOOK MY HAIR THREE YEARS AGO...
HEE HEE HEE HEE
THE KUNO FAMILY SECRET! THE WOODEN SWORD SHREDDER!
GASP!
HOW DO YOU KNOW THAT NAME !?
HWOOOOO

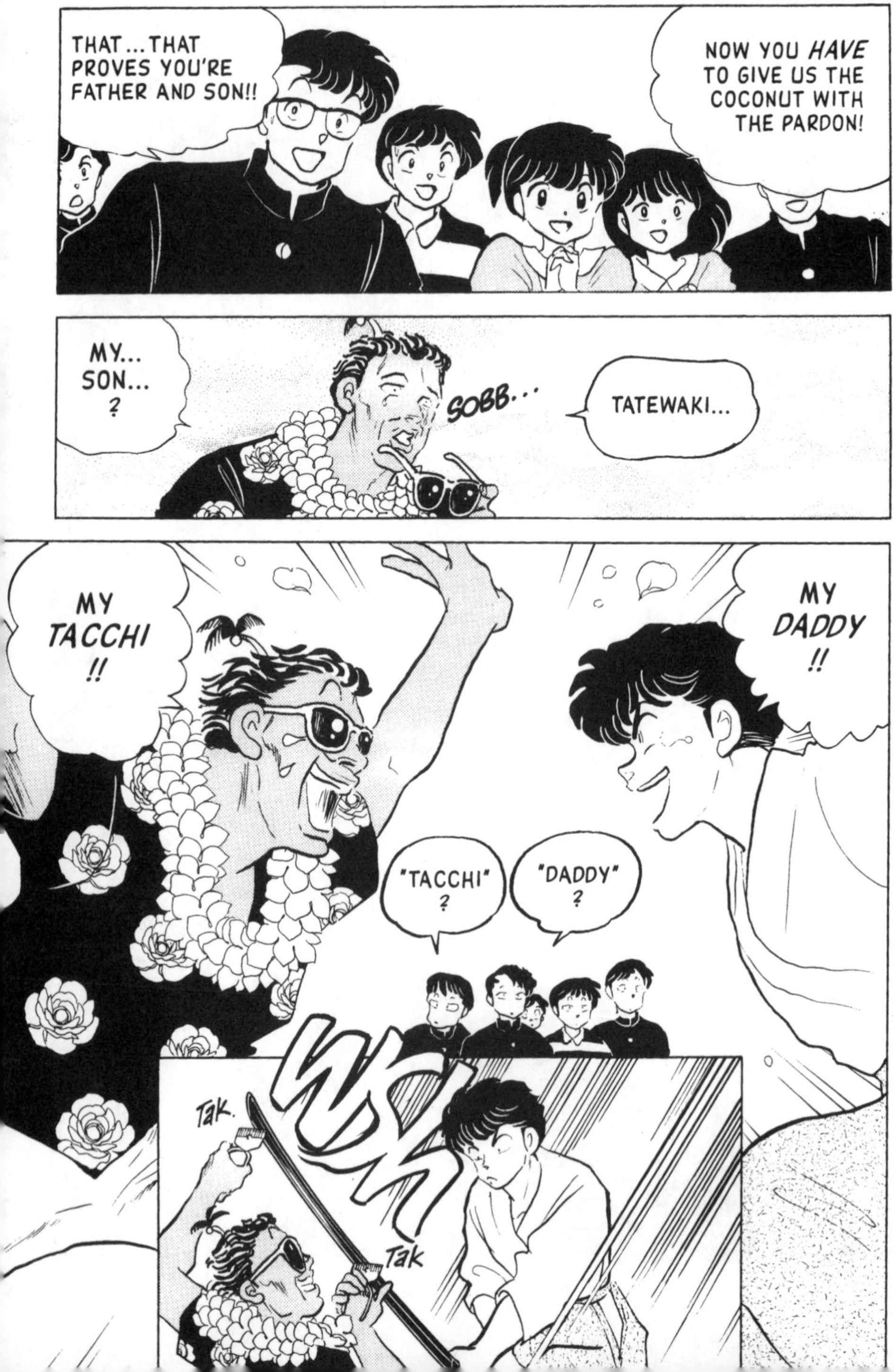
THAT... THAT PROVES YOU'RE FATHER AND SON!!
NOW YOU *HAVE* TO GIVE US THE COCONUT WITH THE PARDON!
MY... SON... ?
SOBB...
TATEWAKI...
MY *TACCHI* !!
MY *DADDY* !!
"TACCHI" ?
"DADDY" ?
Tak.
Tak

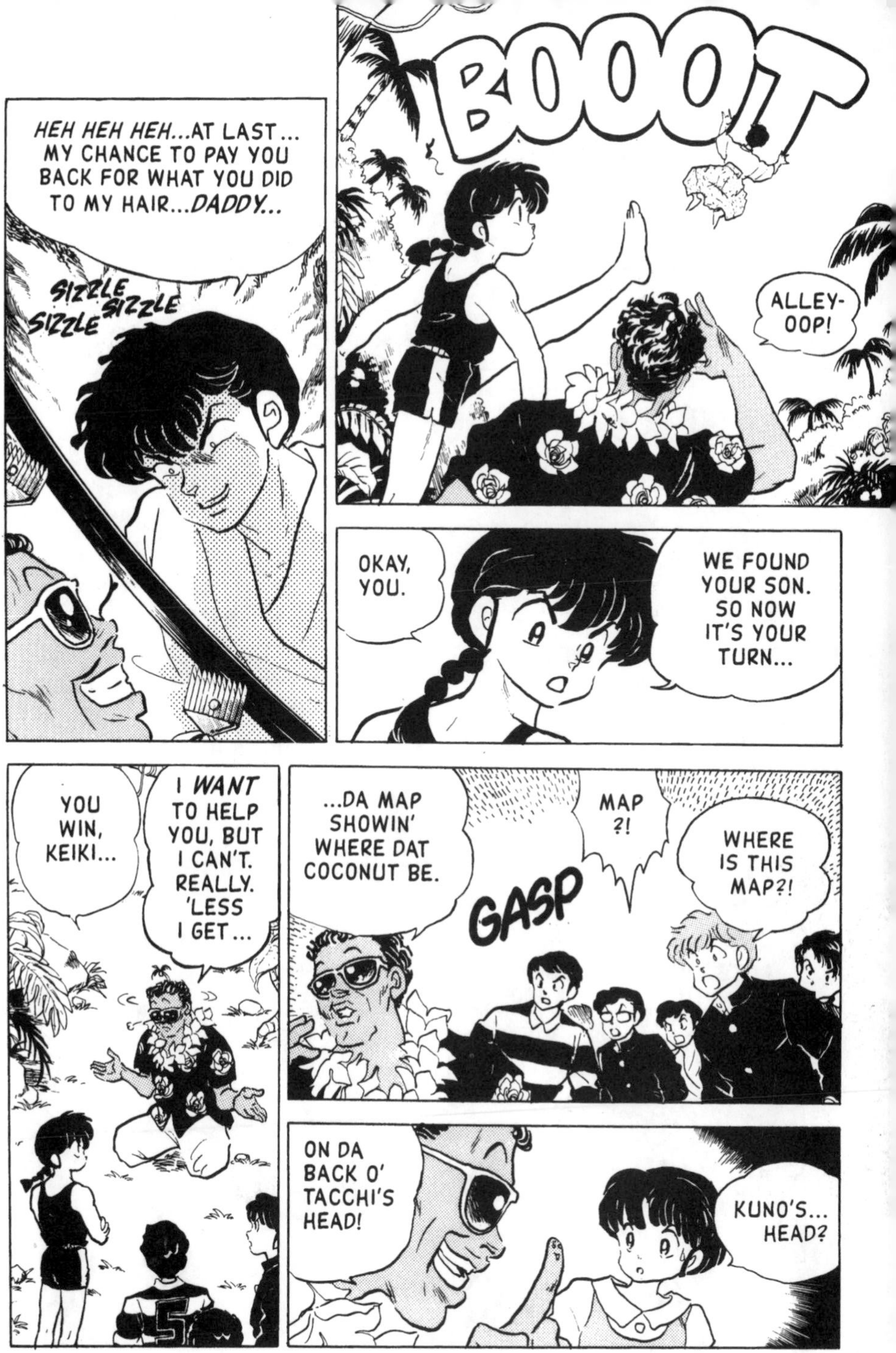
HEH HEH HEH...AT LAST... MY CHANCE TO PAY YOU BACK FOR WHAT YOU DID TO MY HAIR...*DADDY*...
SIZZLE SIZZLE SIZZLE
BOOOOT
ALLEY-OOP!
OKAY, YOU.
WE FOUND YOUR SON. SO NOW IT'S YOUR TURN...
YOU WIN, KEIKI...
I *WANT* TO HELP YOU, BUT I CAN'T. REALLY. 'LESS I GET...
...DA MAP SHOWIN' WHERE DAT COCONUT BE.
MAP ?!
GASP
WHERE IS THIS MAP?!
ON DA BACK O' TACCHI'S HEAD!
KUNO'S... HEAD?

PART 9
ONE HAIRY DAY

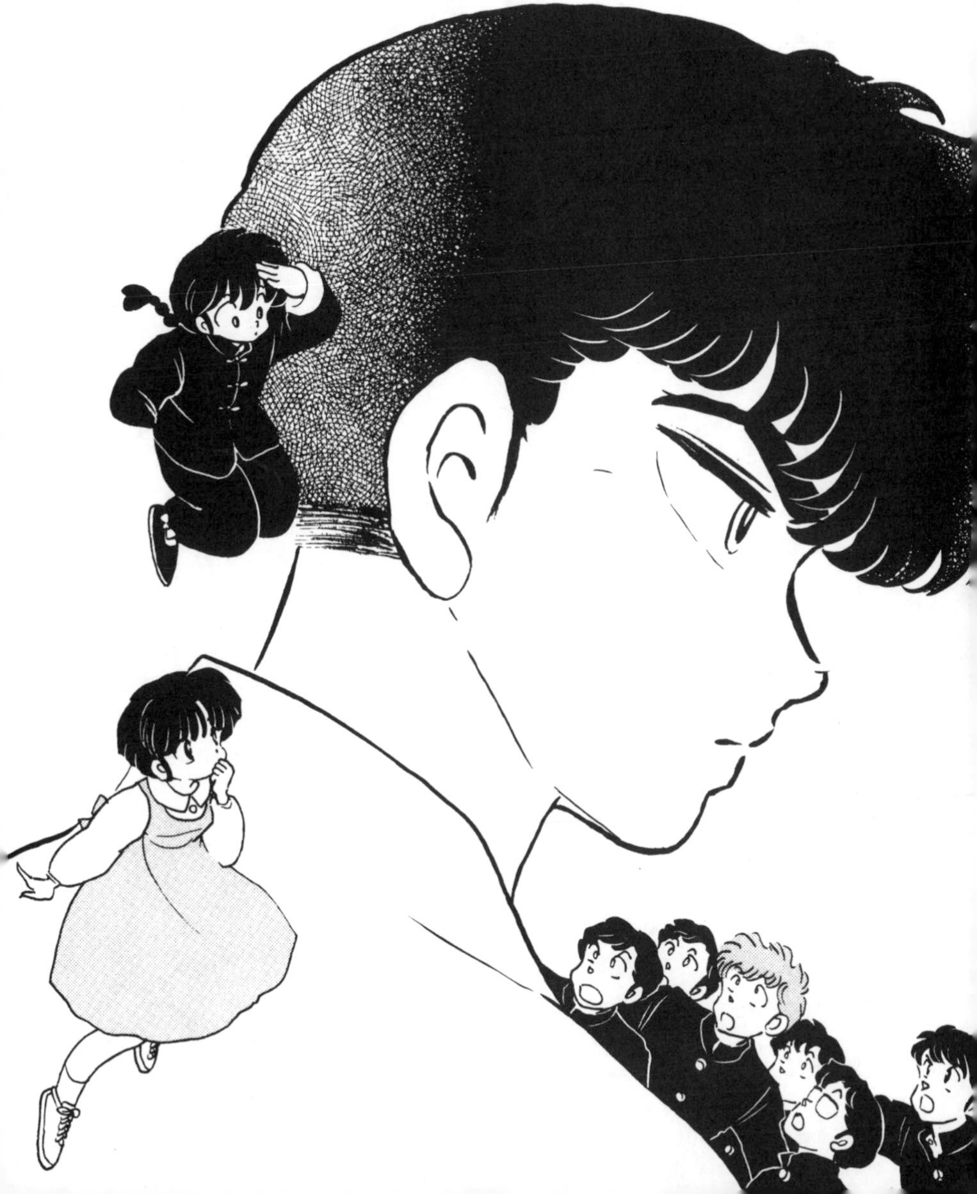

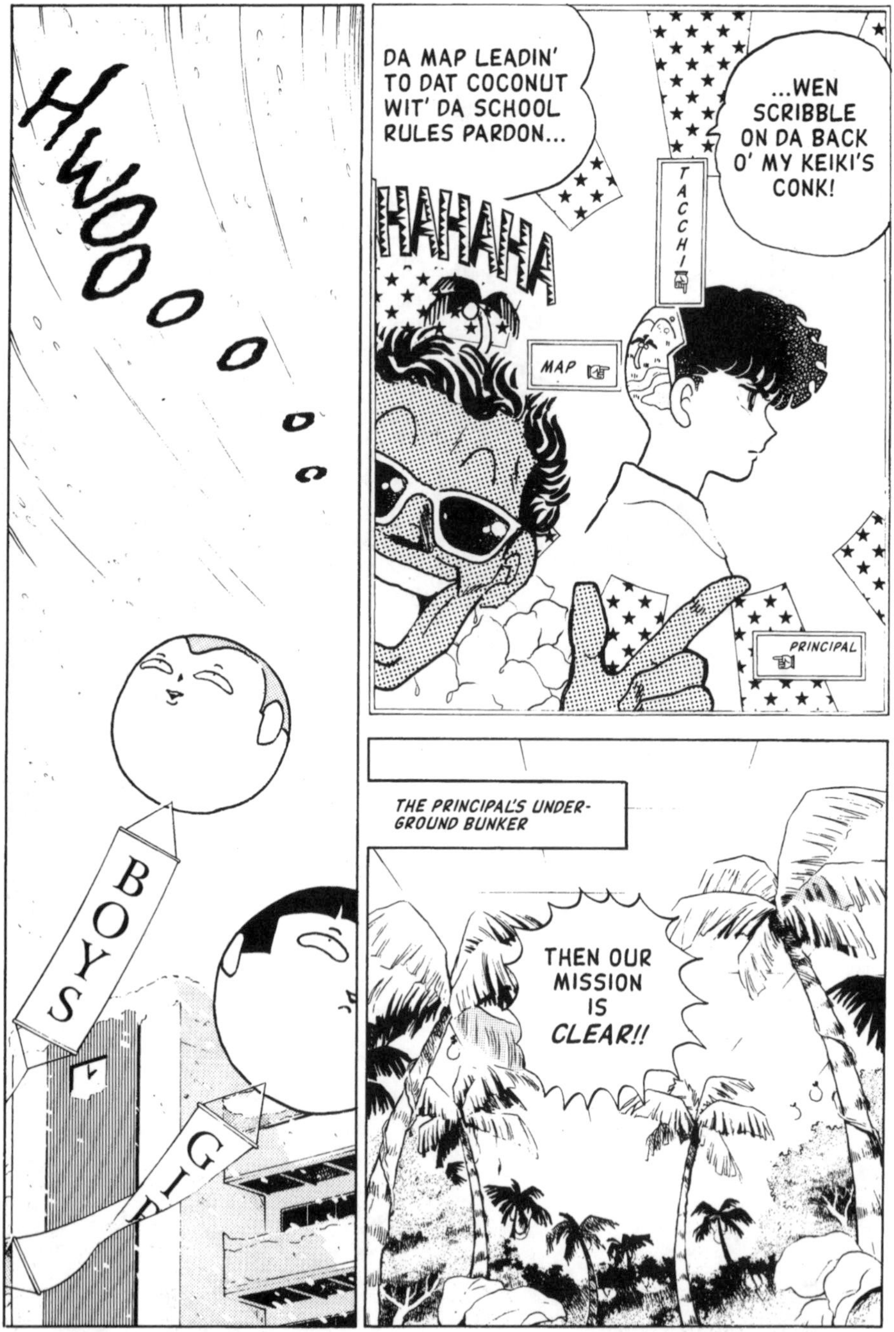
HWOOOOOOOO
BOYS
DA MAP LEADIN' TO DAT COCONUT WIT' DA SCHOOL RULES PARDON...
...WEN SCRIBBLE ON DA BACK O' MY KEIKI'S CONK!
HAHAHA
TACCHI
MAP
PRINCIPAL
THE PRINCIPAL'S UNDER-GROUND BUNKER
THEN OUR MISSION IS CLEAR!!

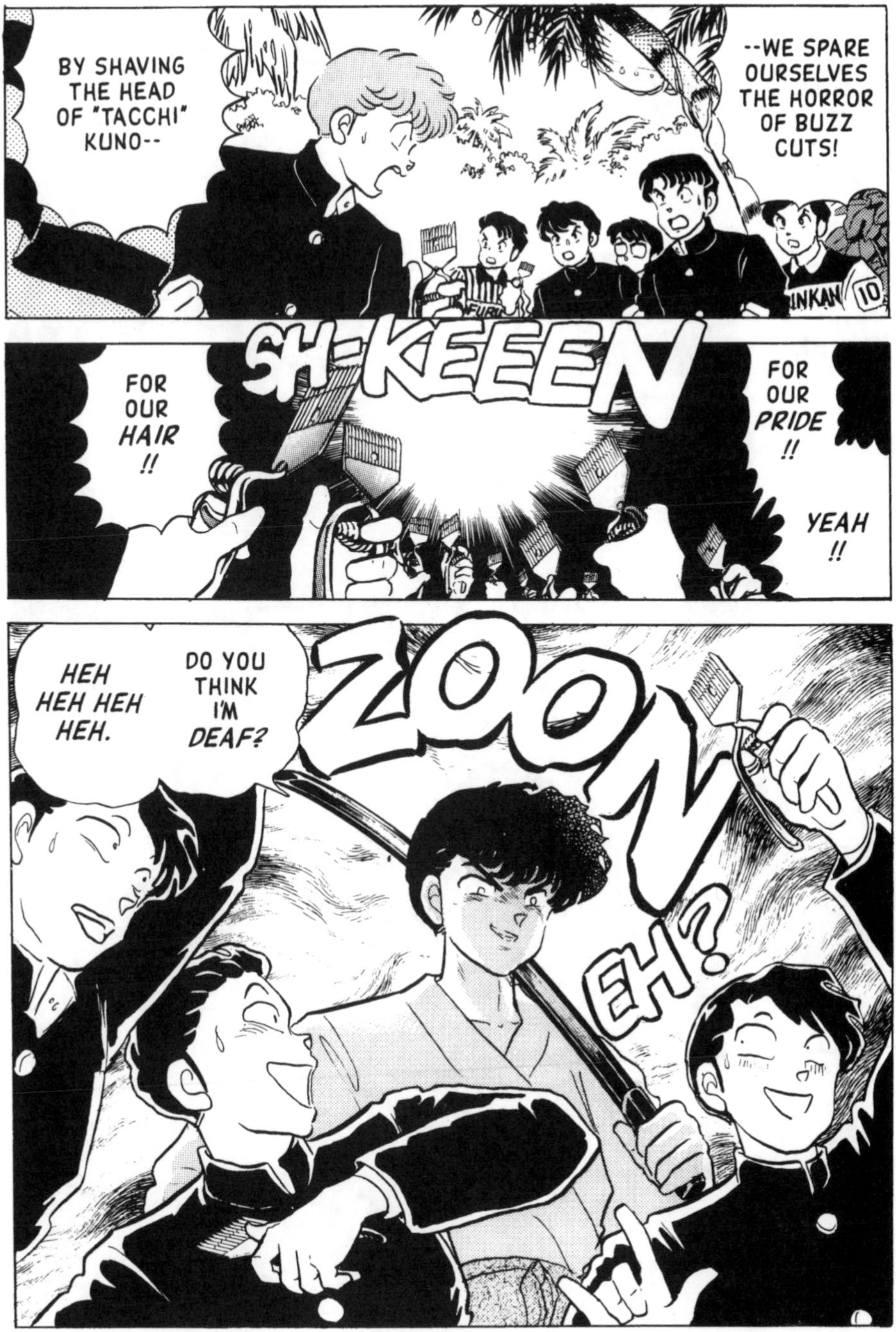
BY SHAVING THE HEAD OF "TACCHI" KUNO--
--WE SPARE OURSELVES THE HORROR OF BUZZ CUTS!
SH-KEEEN
FOR OUR HAIR !!
FOR OUR PRIDE !!
YEAH !!
HEH HEH HEH HEH.
DO YOU THINK I'M DEAF?
ZOOON
EH?

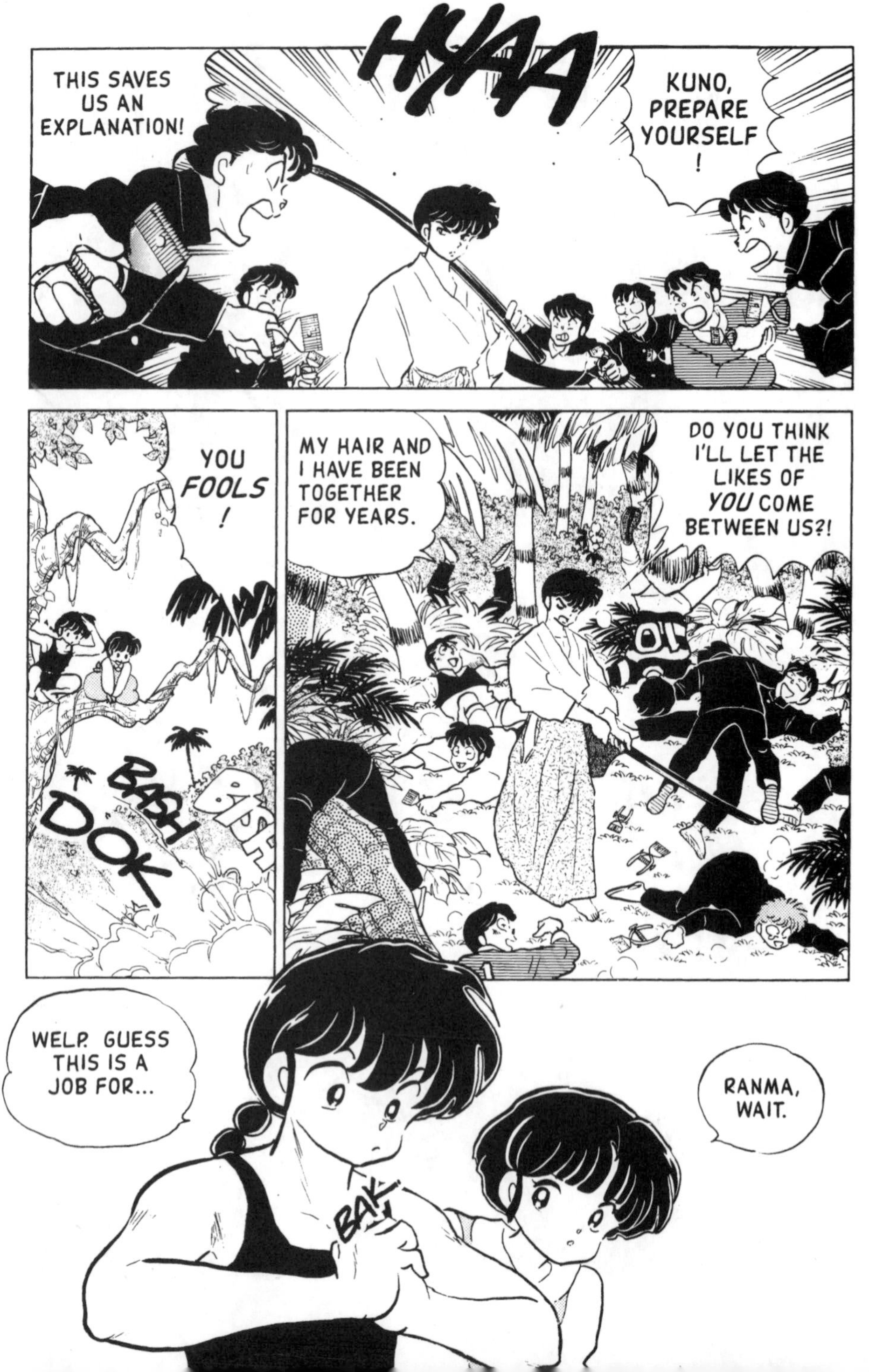
HYAA
THIS SAVES US AN EXPLANATION!
KUNO, PREPARE YOURSELF!
YOU FOOLS!
BASH
DOK
BISH
MY HAIR AND I HAVE BEEN TOGETHER FOR YEARS.
DO YOU THINK I'LL LET THE LIKES OF YOU COME BETWEEN US?!
WELP. GUESS THIS IS A JOB FOR...
BAK
RANMA, WAIT.

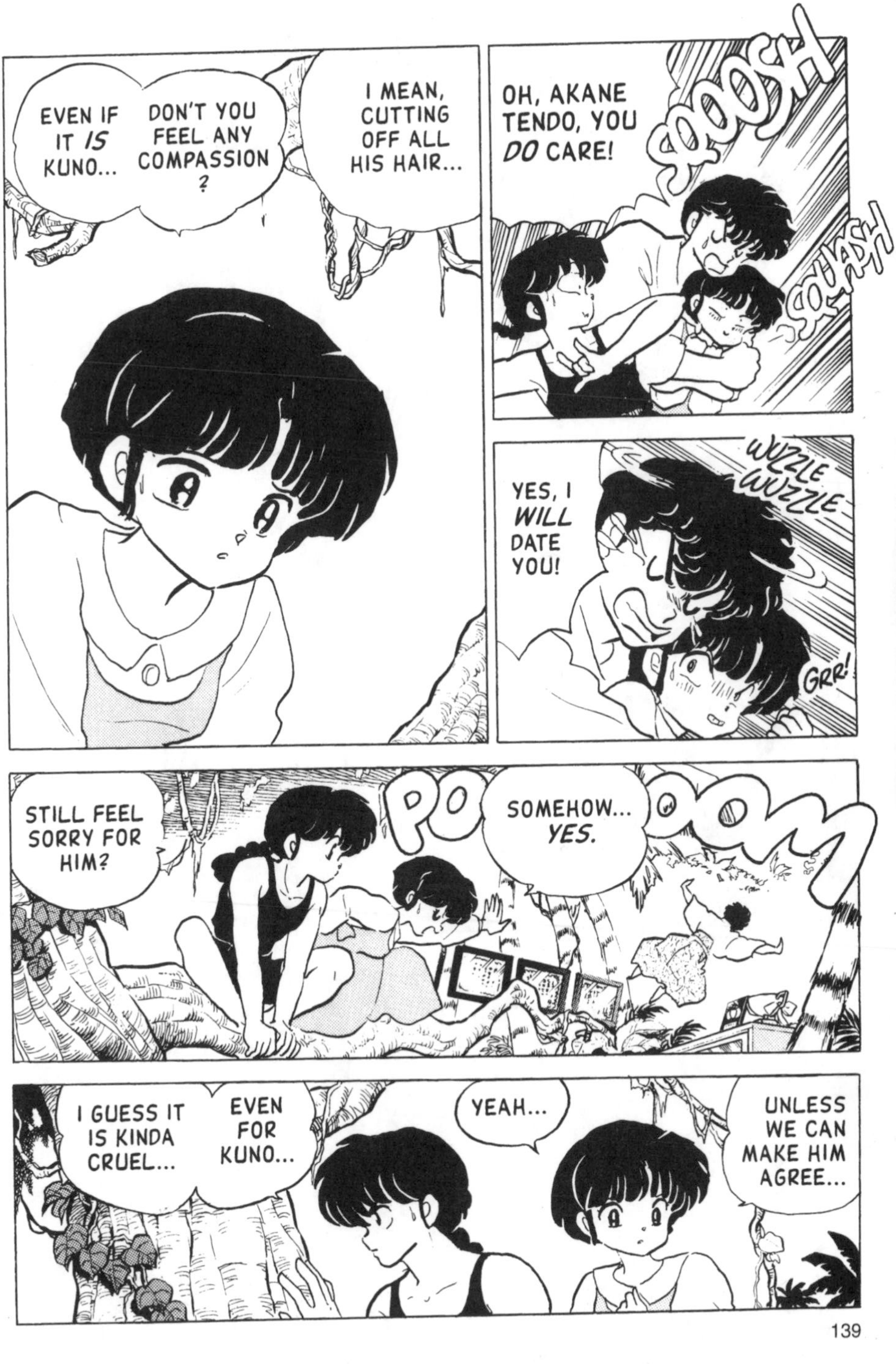
EVEN IF IT IS KUNO...
DON'T YOU FEEL ANY COMPASSION?
I MEAN, CUTTING OFF ALL HIS HAIR...
SQOOSH
OH, AKANE TENDO, YOU DO CARE!
SQUASH
WUZZLE WUZZLE
YES, I WILL DATE YOU!
GRR!
STILL FEEL SORRY FOR HIM?
PO
OOM
SOMEHOW... YES.
I GUESS IT IS KINDA CRUEL...
EVEN FOR KUNO...
YEAH...
UNLESS WE CAN MAKE HIM AGREE...

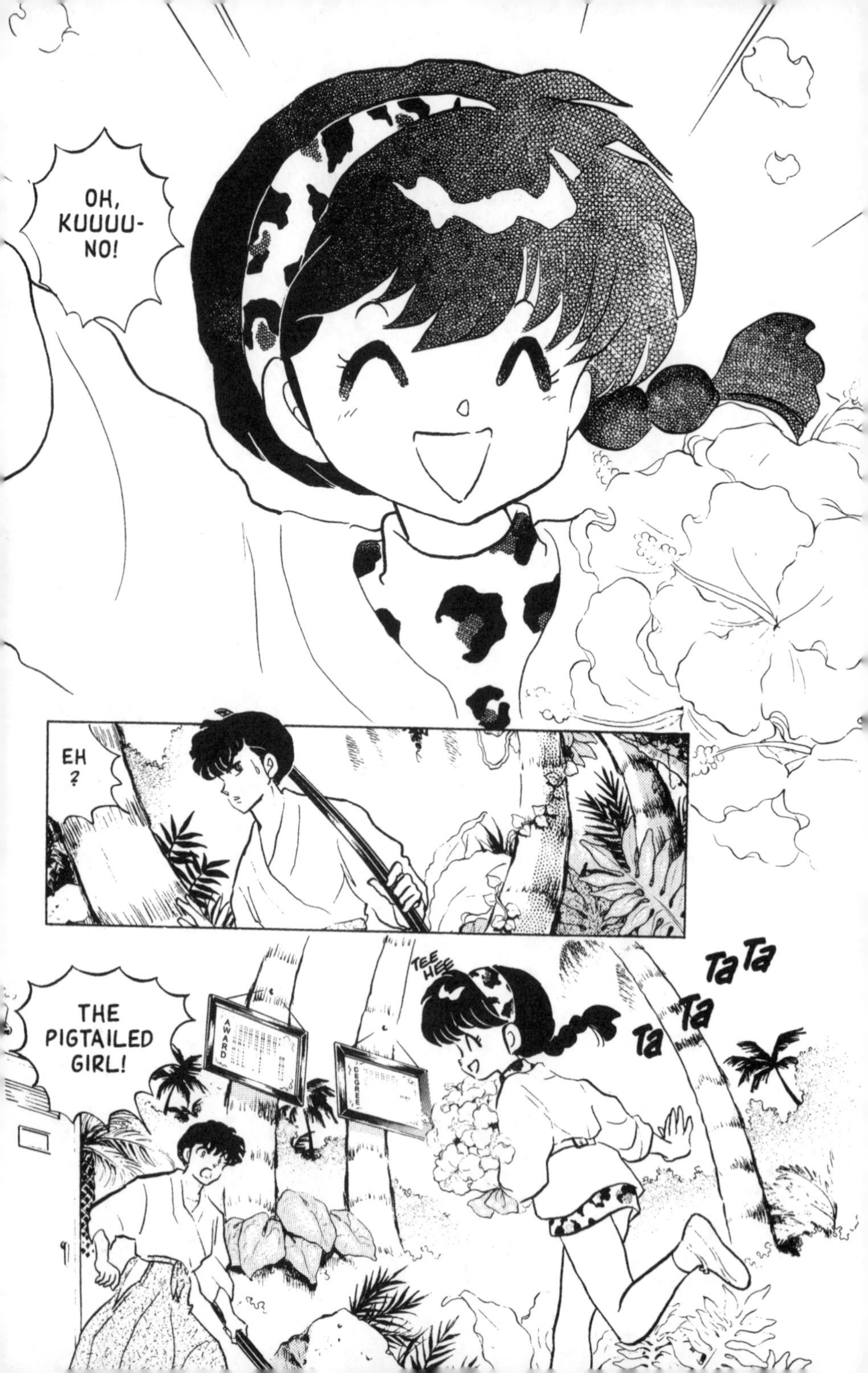
OH, KUUUU-NO!
EH?
THE PIGTAILED GIRL!
TEE HEE
AWARD
DEGREE
TA TA TA TA

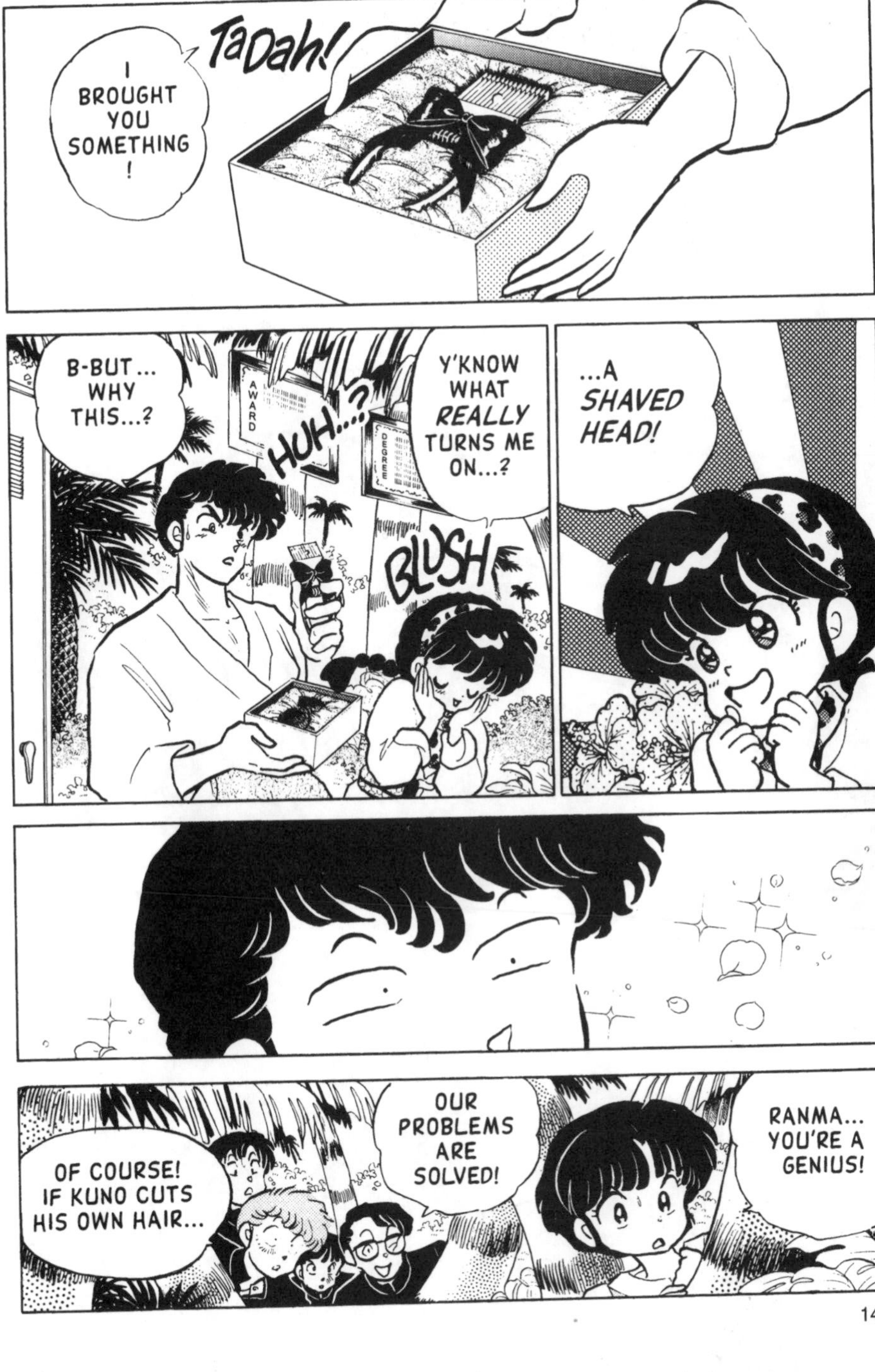
TaDah!
I BROUGHT YOU SOMETHING!
B-BUT... WHY THIS...?
AWARD
HUH...?
DEGREE
Y'KNOW WHAT REALLY TURNS ME ON...?
BLUSH
...A SHAVED HEAD!
OF COURSE! IF KUNO CUTS HIS OWN HAIR...
OUR PROBLEMS ARE SOLVED!
RANMA... YOU'RE A GENIUS!

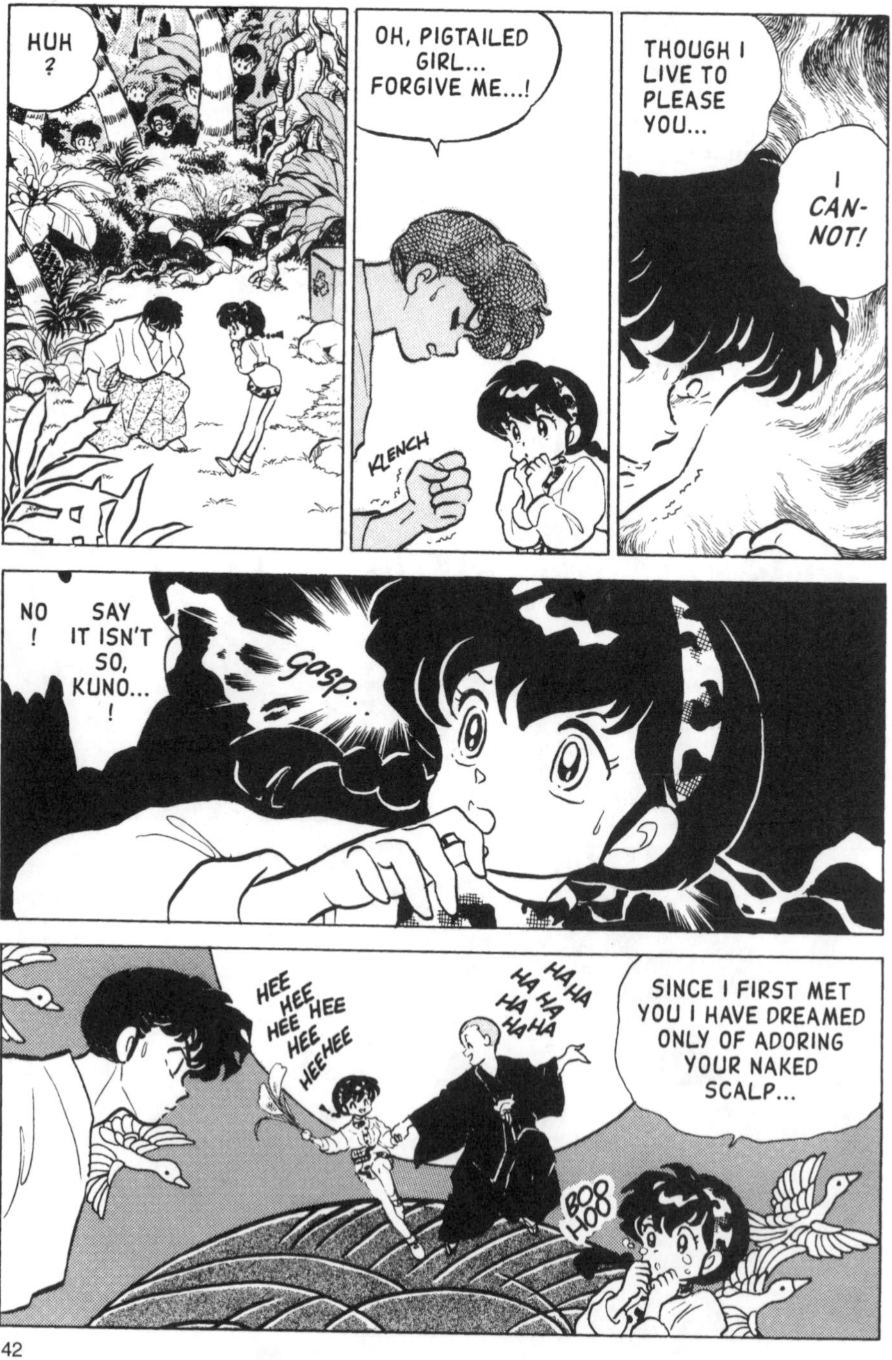
HUH ?
OH, PIGTAILED GIRL... FORGIVE ME...!
KLENCH
THOUGH I LIVE TO PLEASE YOU...
I CAN-NOT!
NO !
SAY IT ISN'T SO, KUNO... !
Gasp...
HEE HEE HEE HEE HEE HEEHEE
HA HA HA HA HA HA HA HA
SINCE I FIRST MET YOU I HAVE DREAMED ONLY OF ADORING YOUR NAKED SCALP...
BOO HOO

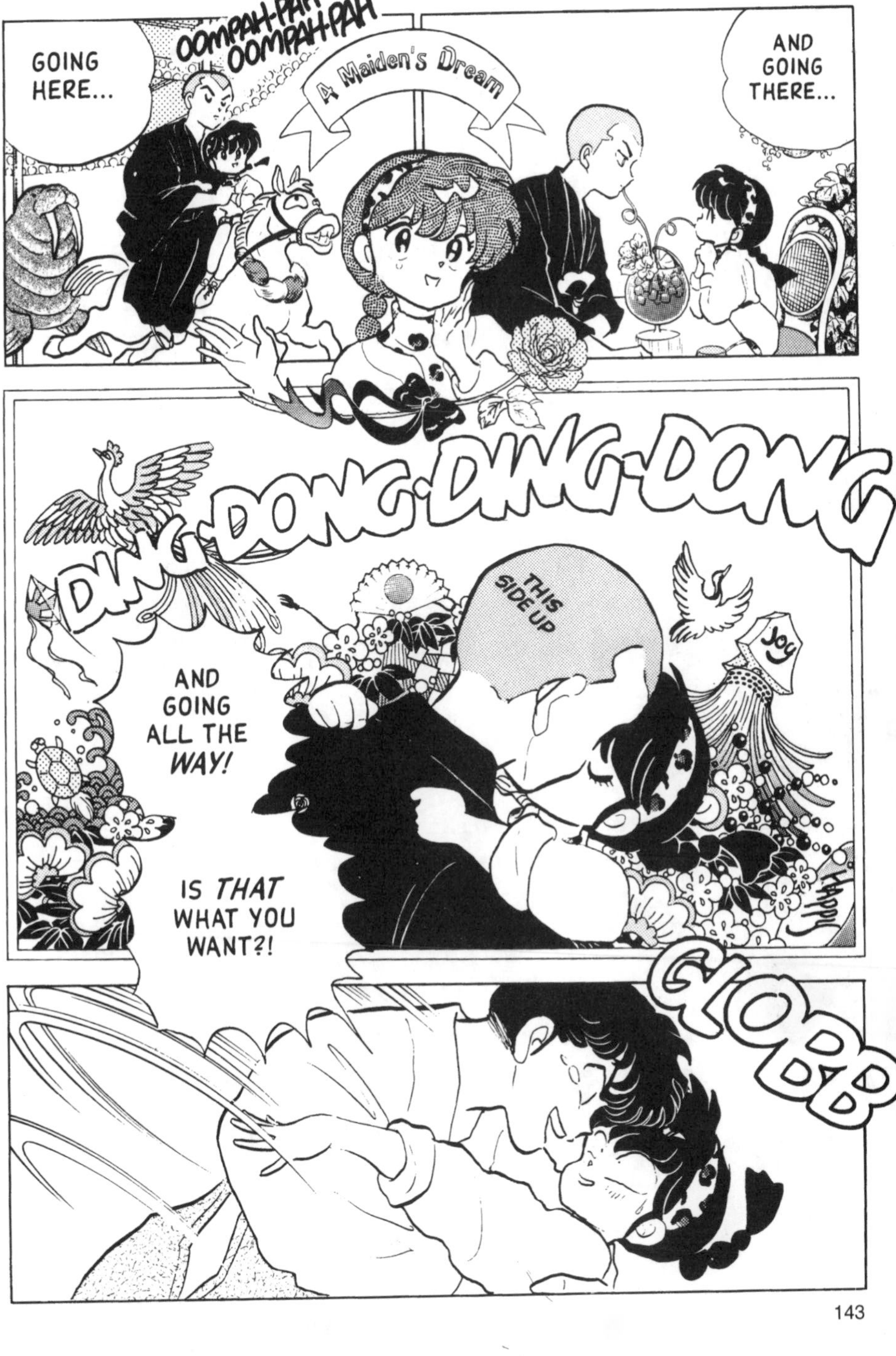
GOING HERE...
OOMPAH-PAH OOMPAH-PAH
A Maiden's Dream
AND GOING THERE...
DING-DONG-DING-DONG
THIS SIDE UP
Joy
AND GOING ALL THE WAY!
IS THAT WHAT YOU WANT?!
HAPPY
GLOBB

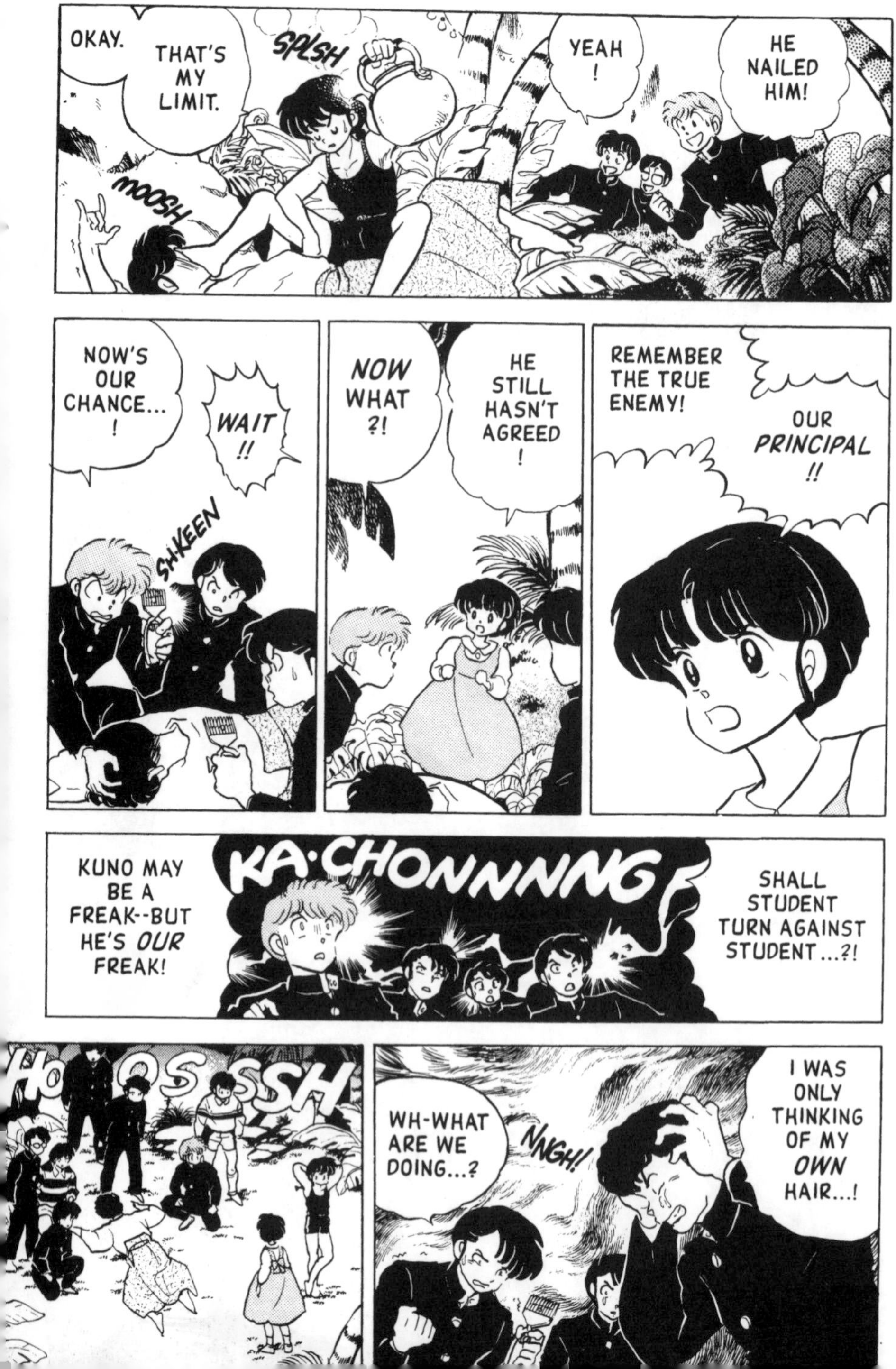
OKAY.
THAT'S MY LIMIT.
SPLSH
MOOSH
YEAH !
HE NAILED HIM!
NOW'S OUR CHANCE... !
WAIT !!
SH-KEEN
NOW WHAT ?!
HE STILL HASN'T AGREED !
REMEMBER THE TRUE ENEMY!
OUR PRINCIPAL !!
KUNO MAY BE A FREAK--BUT HE'S OUR FREAK!
KA-CHONNNNG
SHALL STUDENT TURN AGAINST STUDENT...?!
HOOSSSH
WH-WHAT ARE WE DOING...?
NNGH!
I WAS ONLY THINKING OF MY OWN HAIR...!

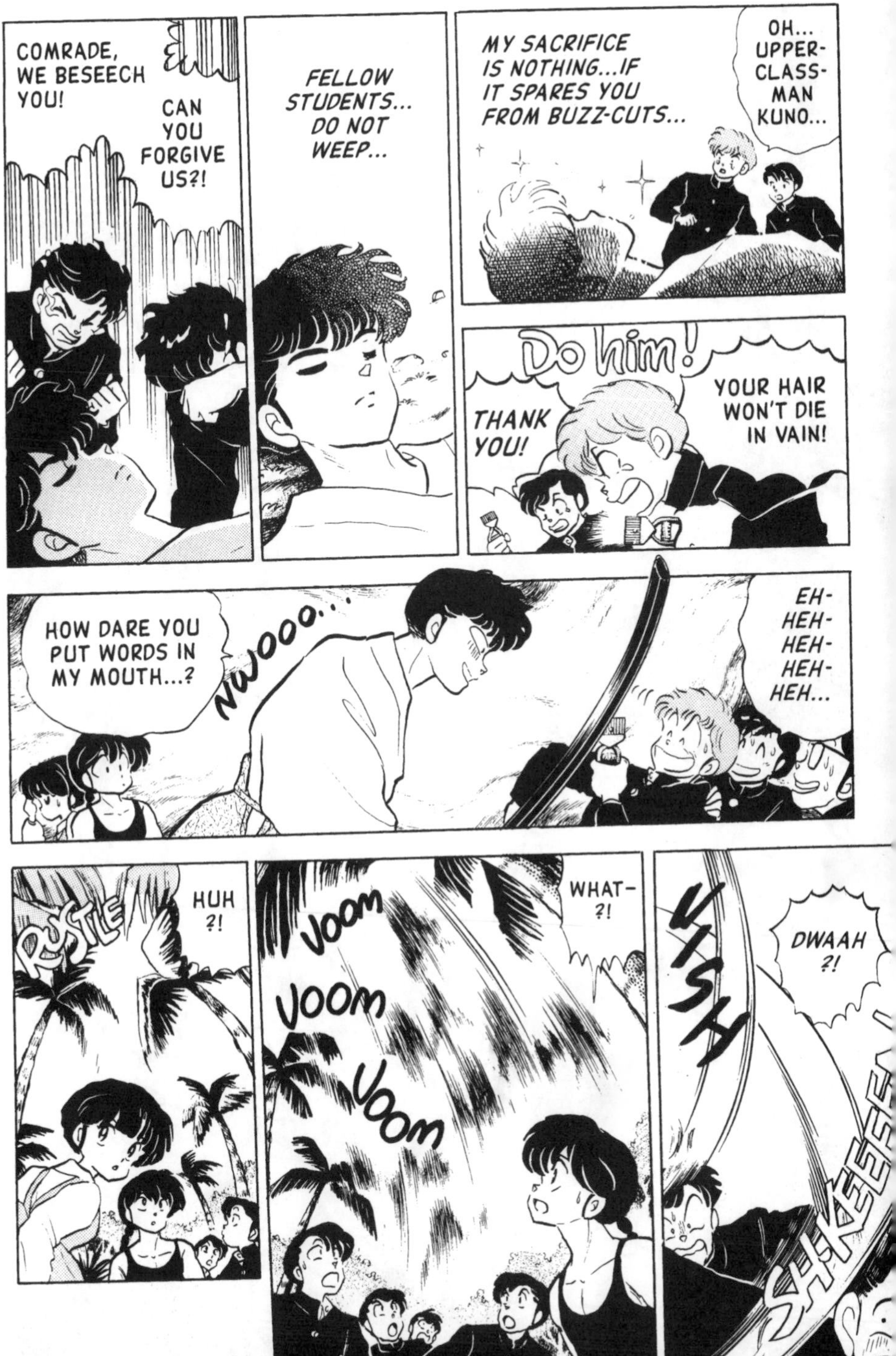
COMRADE, WE BESEECH YOU!
CAN YOU FORGIVE US?!
FELLOW STUDENTS... DO NOT WEEP...
MY SACRIFICE IS NOTHING...IF IT SPARES YOU FROM BUZZ-CUTS...
OH... UPPER-CLASS-MAN KUNO...
Do him!
THANK YOU!
YOUR HAIR WON'T DIE IN VAIN!
HOW DARE YOU PUT WORDS IN MY MOUTH...?
NWOOO...
EH-HEH-HEH-HEH-HEH...
RUSTLE
HUH ?!
VOOM
VOOM
VOOM
VOOM
WHAT- ?!
VISH
DWAAH ?!
SHKEEEE

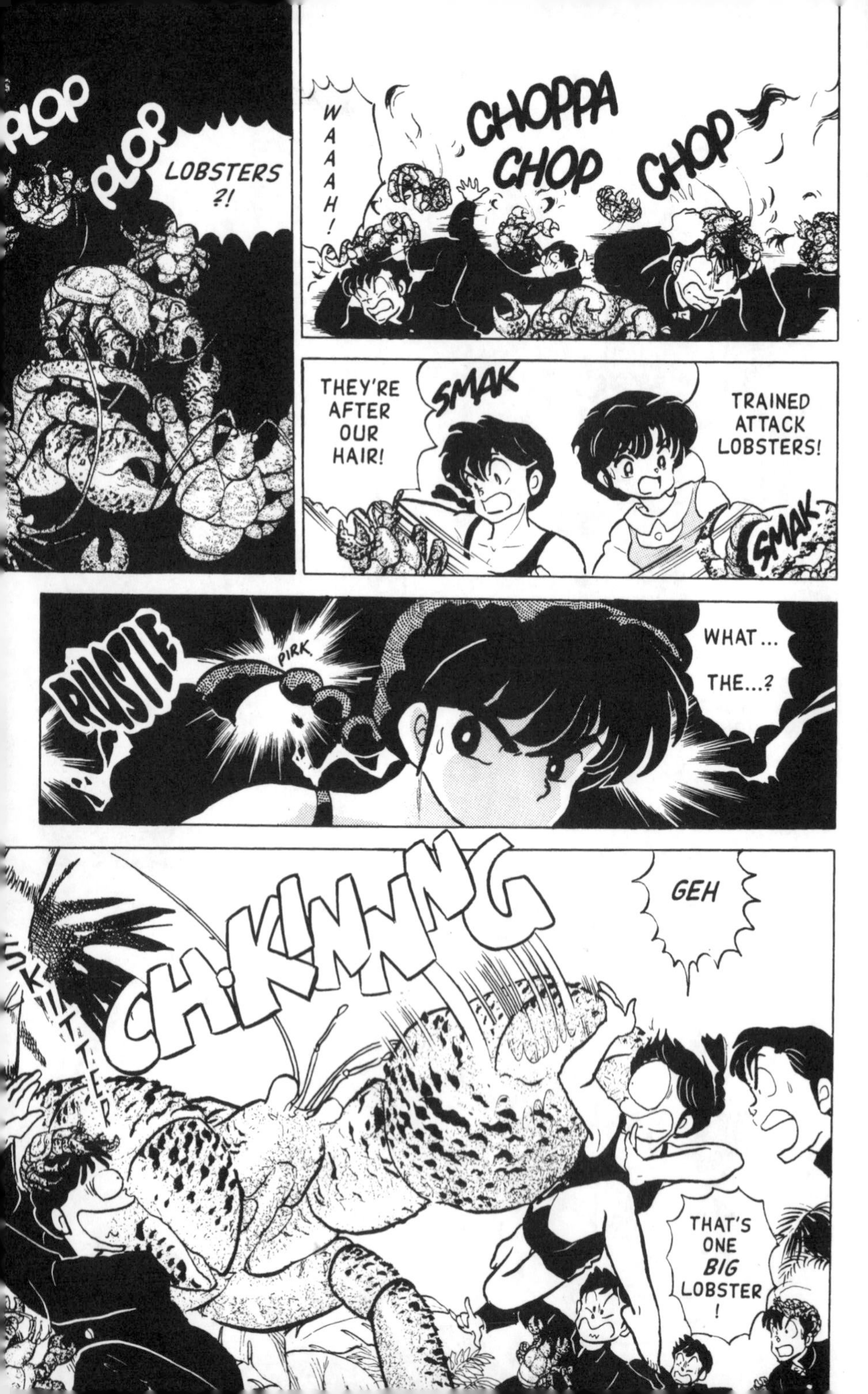
PLOP
PLOP
LOBSTERS ?!
WAAAAH!
CHOPPA CHOP CHOP
THEY'RE AFTER OUR HAIR!
SMAK
TRAINED ATTACK LOBSTERS!
SMAK
RUSTLE
PIRK
WHAT...
THE...?
SKITTER
CHKINNNG
GEH
THAT'S ONE *BIG* LOBSTER!

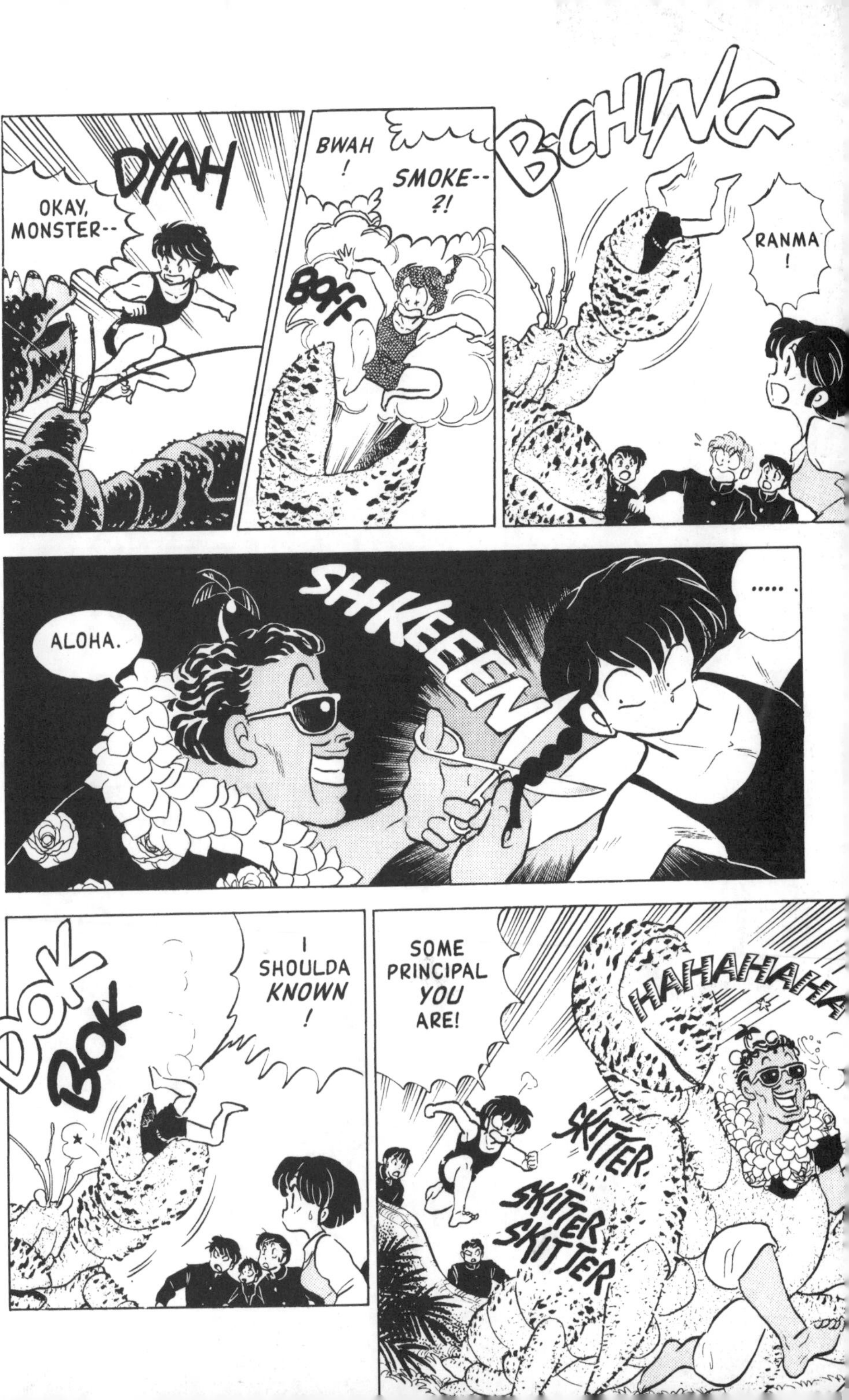
OKAY, MONSTER--
DYAH
BWAH!
SMOKE--?!
BOFF
B-CHING
RANMA!
ALOHA.
SHKEEEN
......
DOK
BOK
I SHOULDA KNOWN!
SOME PRINCIPAL YOU ARE!
HAHAHAHAHA
SKITTER
SKITTER SKITTER

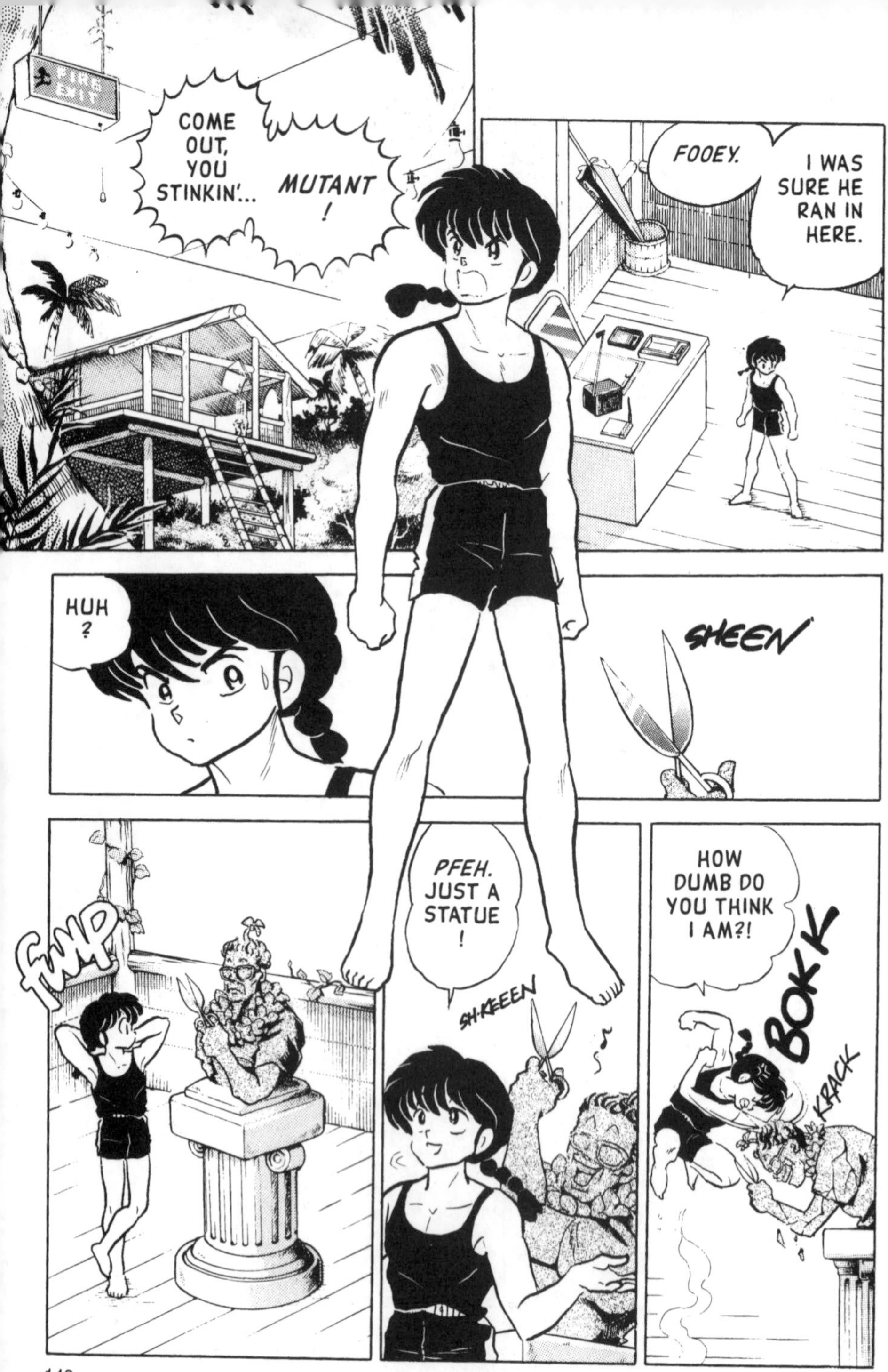
FIRE EXIT
COME OUT, YOU STINKIN'...
MUTANT!
FOOEY.
I WAS SURE HE RAN IN HERE.
HUH?
SHEEN
FWIP
PFEH. JUST A STATUE!
SH-KEEEN
HOW DUMB DO YOU THINK I AM?!
BOKK
KRACK

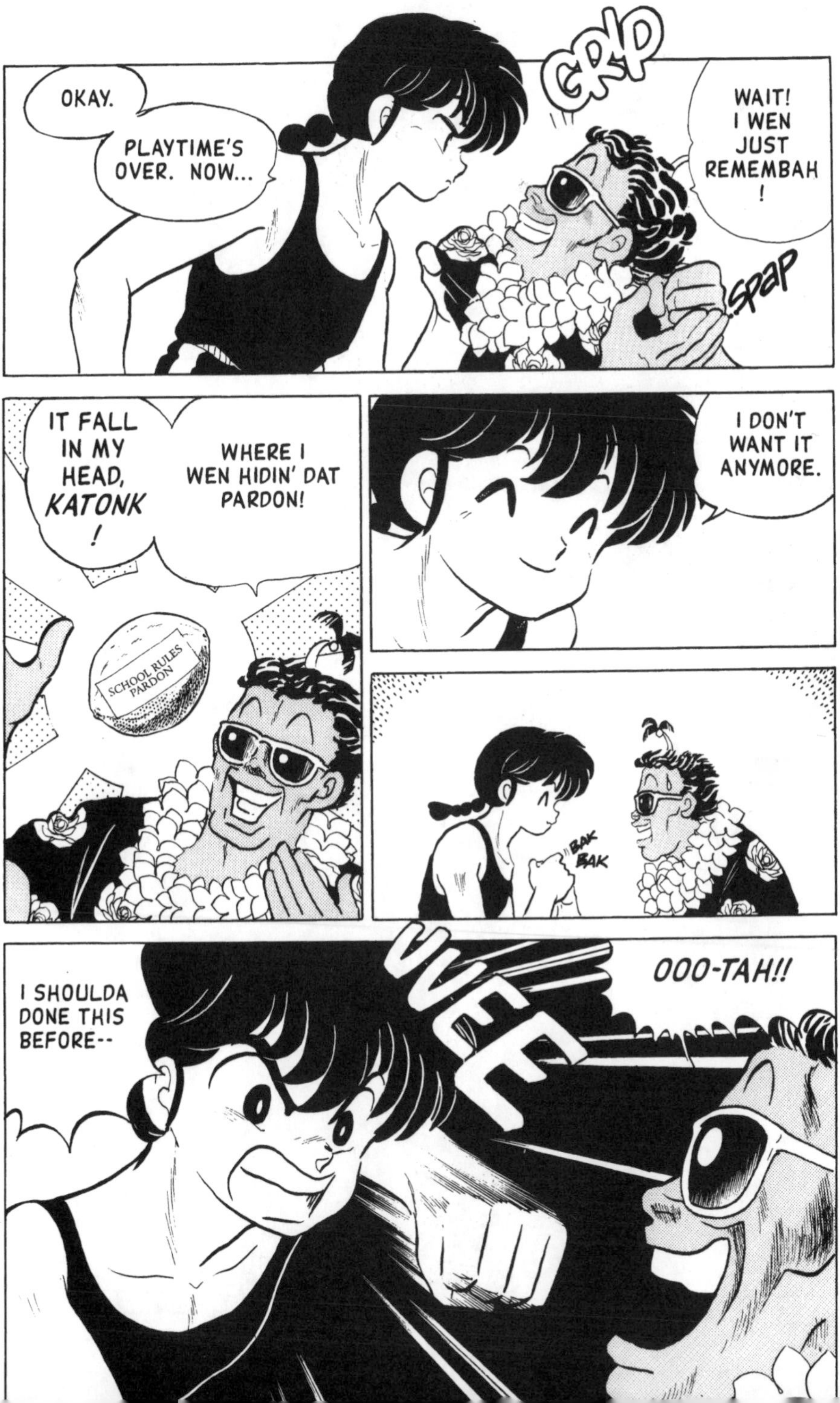
GRIP
OKAY.
PLAYTIME'S OVER. NOW...
WAIT! I WEN JUST REMEMBAH!
SPAP
IT FALL IN MY HEAD, *KATONK*!
WHERE I WEN HIDIN' DAT PARDON!
SCHOOL RULES PARDON
I DON'T WANT IT ANYMORE.
BAK BAK
I SHOULDA DONE THIS BEFORE--
SWEE
OOO-TAH!!

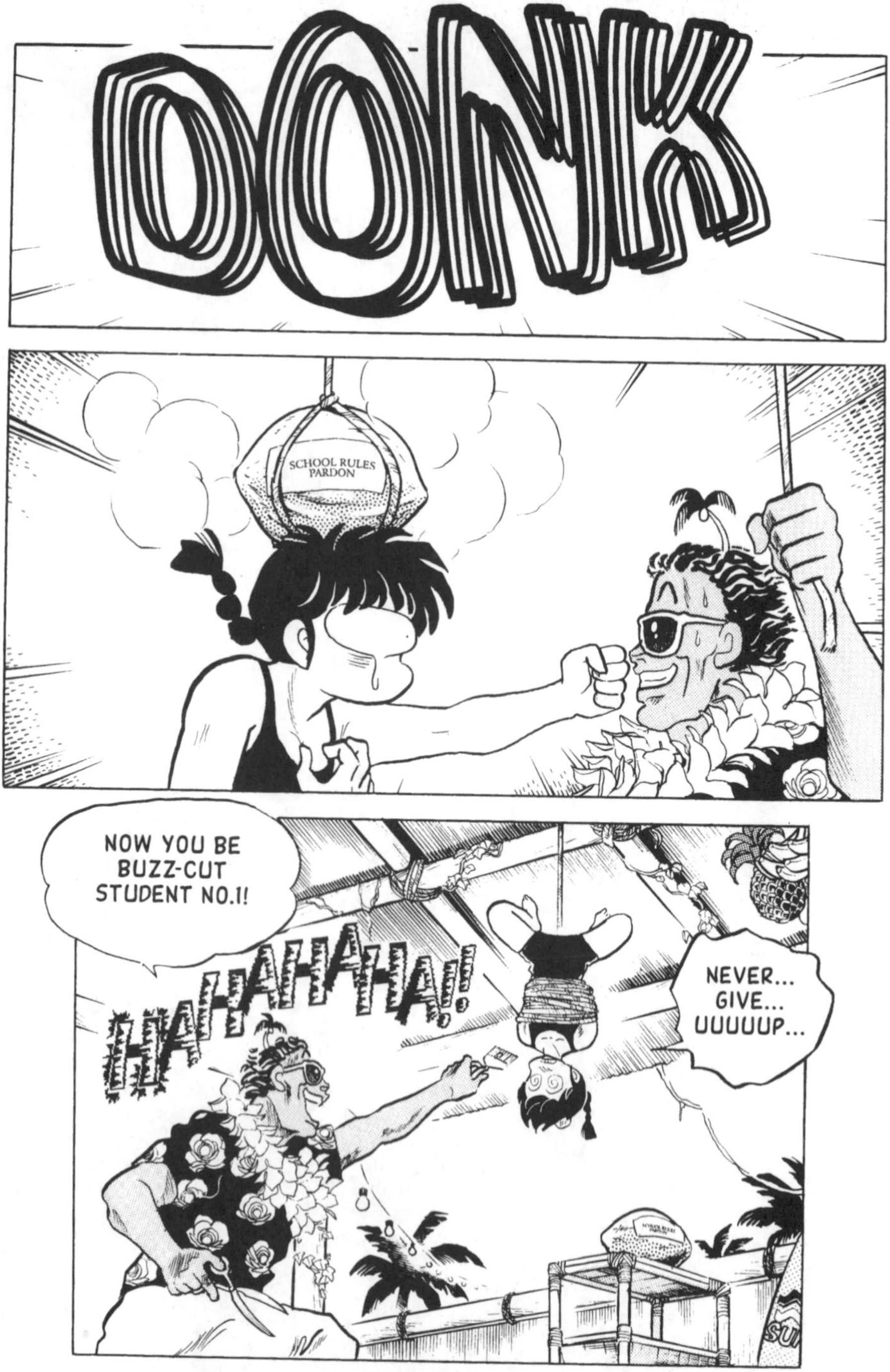
DONK
SCHOOL RULES PARDON
NOW YOU BE BUZZ-CUT STUDENT NO.1!
HAHAHAHA!
NEVER... GIVE... UUUUUP...

PART 10
SHEAR FOLLY

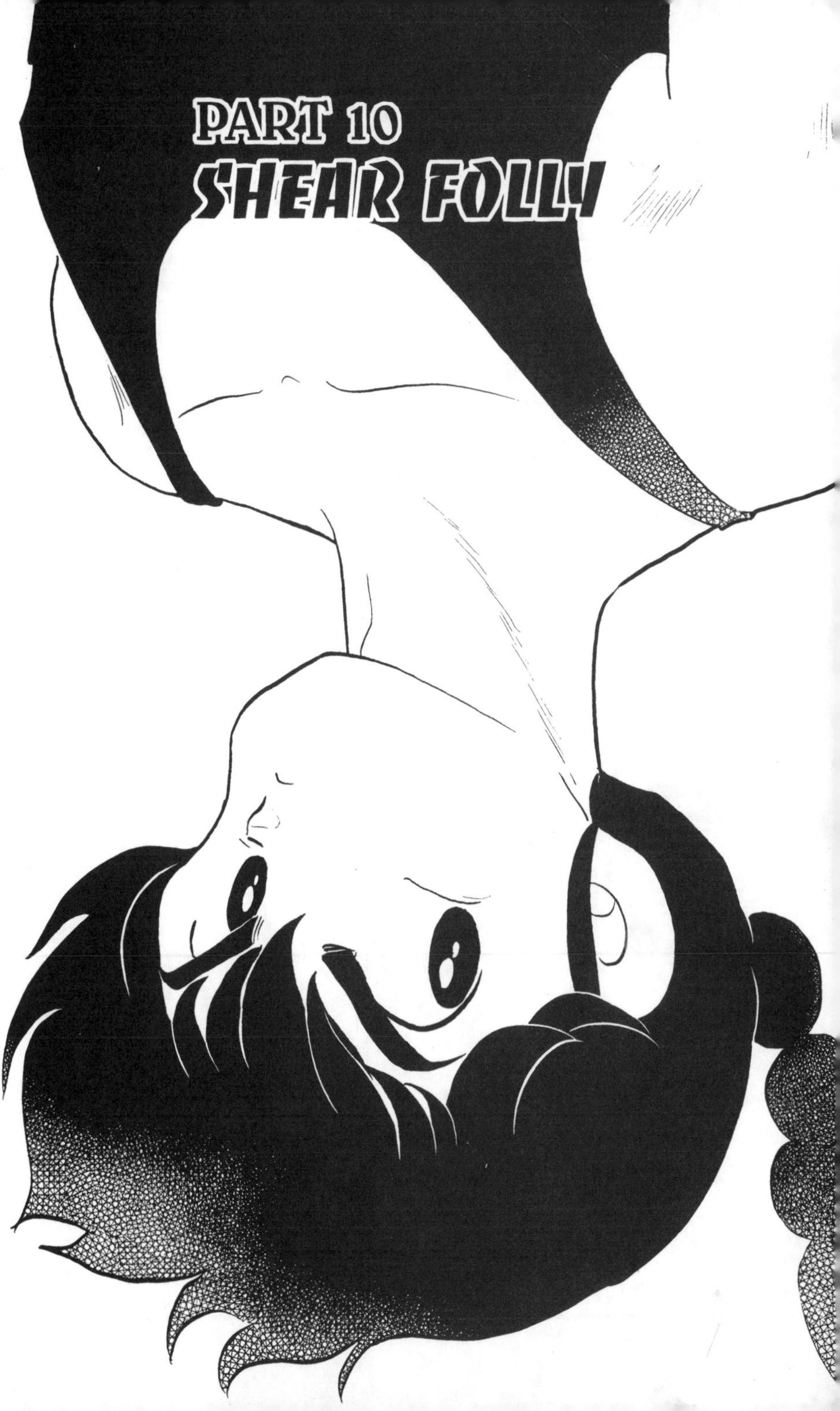

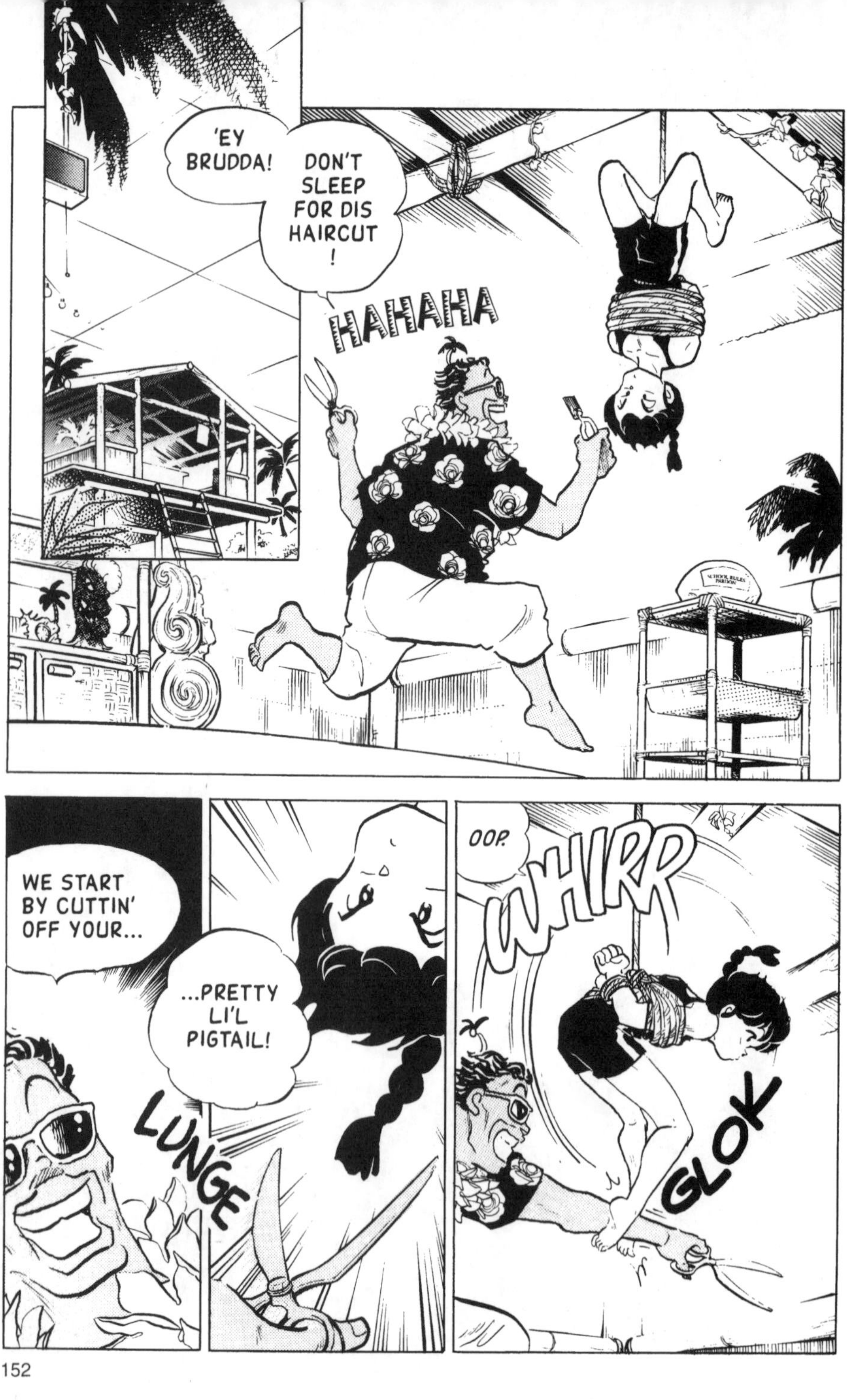
'EY BRUDDA!
DON'T SLEEP FOR DIS HAIRCUT !
HAHAHA
WE START BY CUTTIN' OFF YOUR...
...PRETTY LI'L PIGTAIL!
LUNGE
OOP.
WHIRR
GLOK

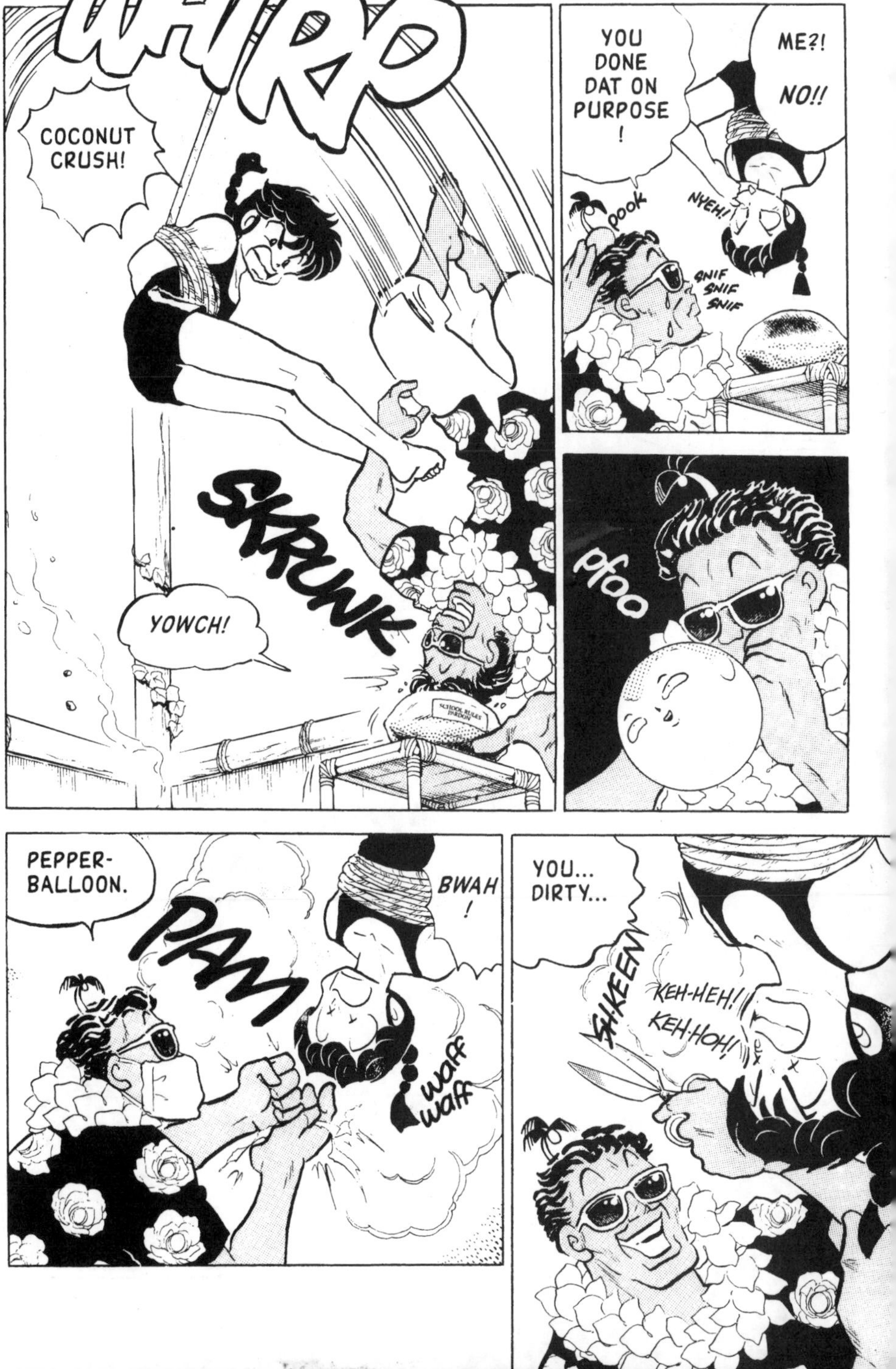
WHIRP
COCONUT CRUSH!
SKRUNK
YOWCH!
YOU DONE DAT ON PURPOSE!
ME?! NO!!
pook
NYEH!
SNIF SNIF SNIF
pfoo
PEPPER-BALLOON.
BWAH!
PAM
waff waff
YOU... DIRTY...
SHKEEN
KEH-HEH! KEH-HOH!

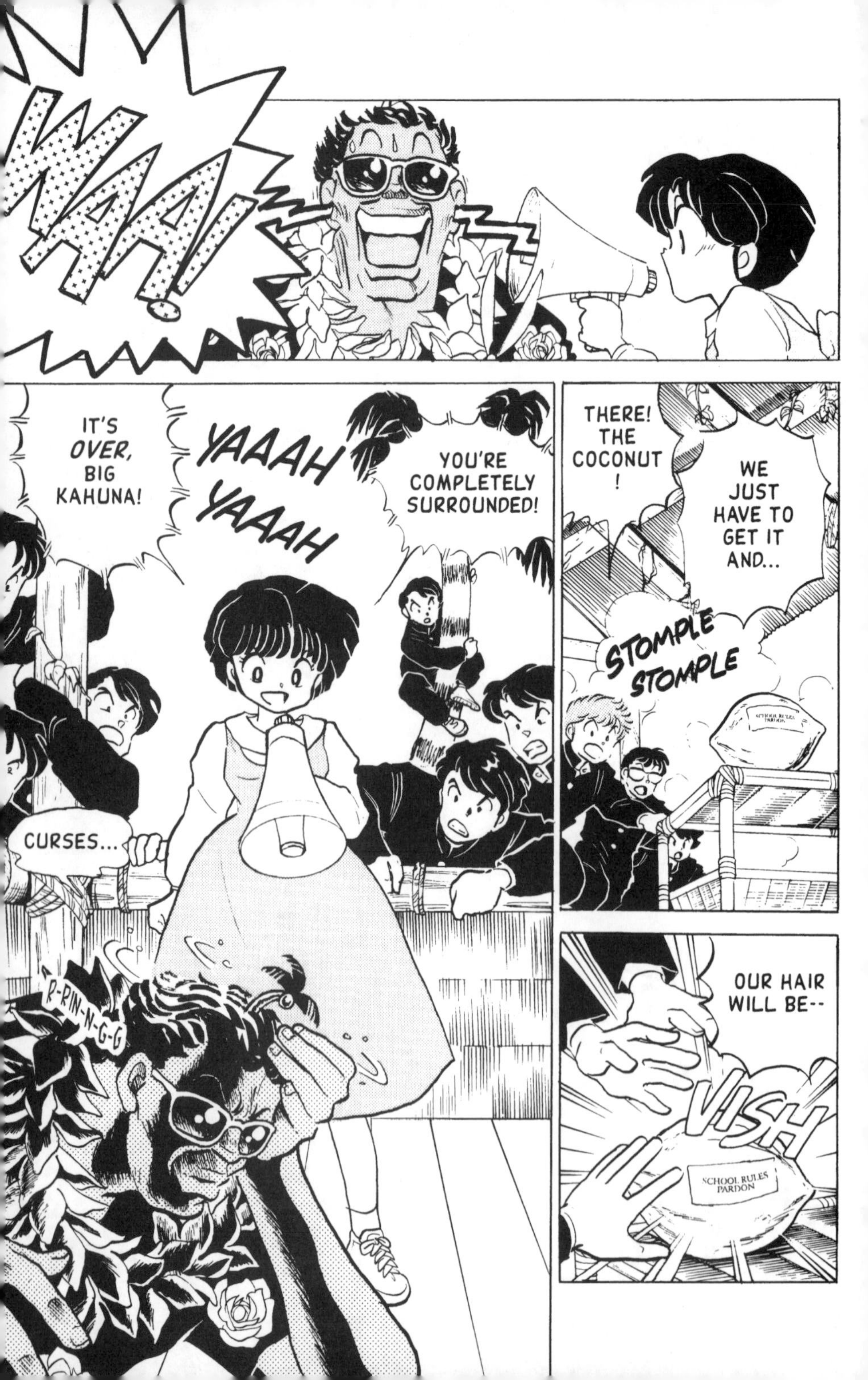
WAA!
IT'S OVER, BIG KAHUNA!
YAAAH YAAAH
YOU'RE COMPLETELY SURROUNDED!
CURSES...
R-RIN-N-G-G
THERE! THE COCONUT!
WE JUST HAVE TO GET IT AND...
STOMPLE STOMPLE
SCHOOL RULES PARDON
OUR HAIR WILL BE--
VISH
SCHOOL RULES PARDON

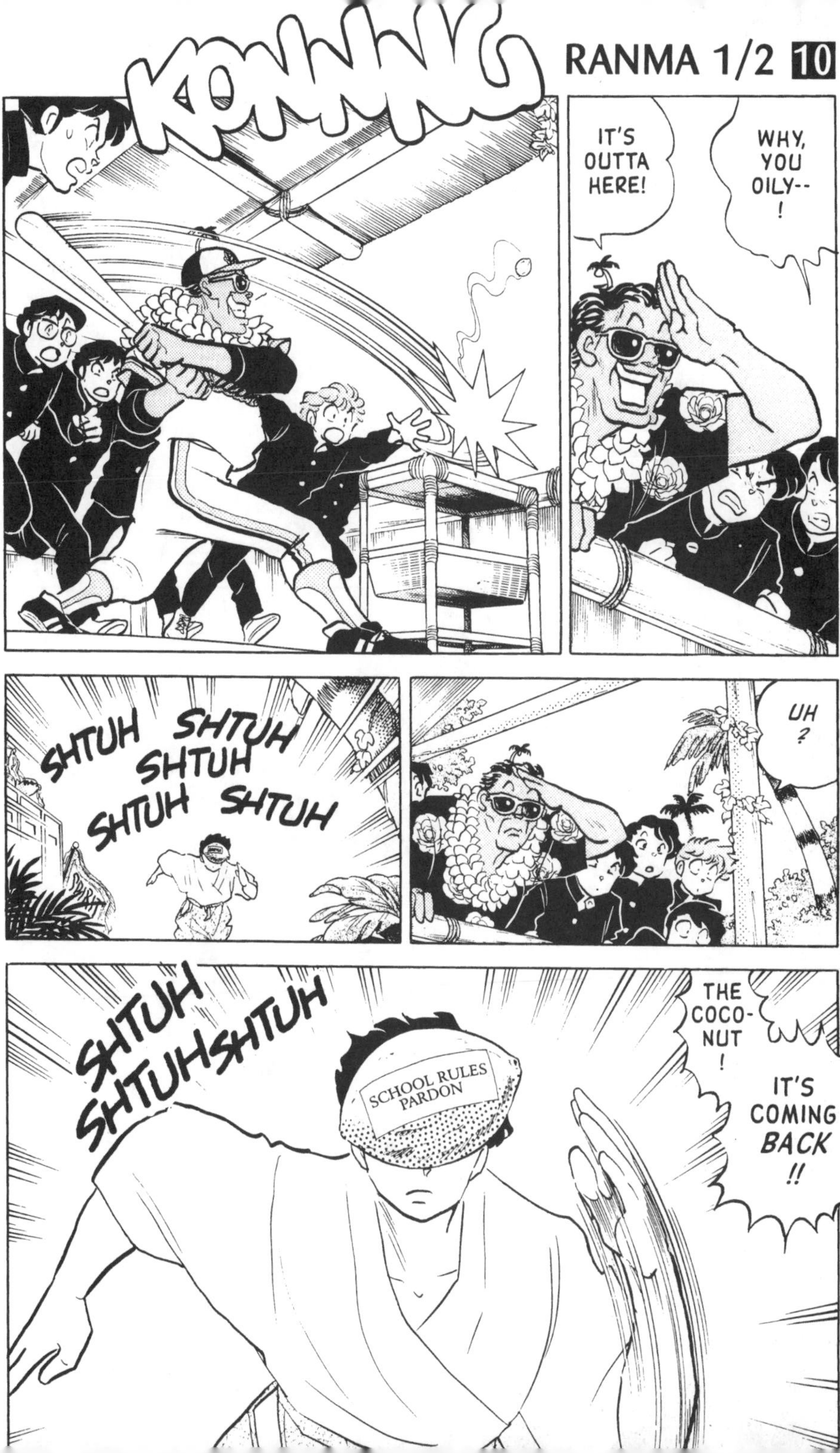
KONNNG
IT'S OUTTA HERE!
WHY, YOU OILY-- !
SHTUH SHTUH SHTUH SHTUH SHTUH
UH ?
SHTUH SHTUHSHTUH
SCHOOL RULES PARDON
THE COCONUT !
IT'S COMING BACK !!

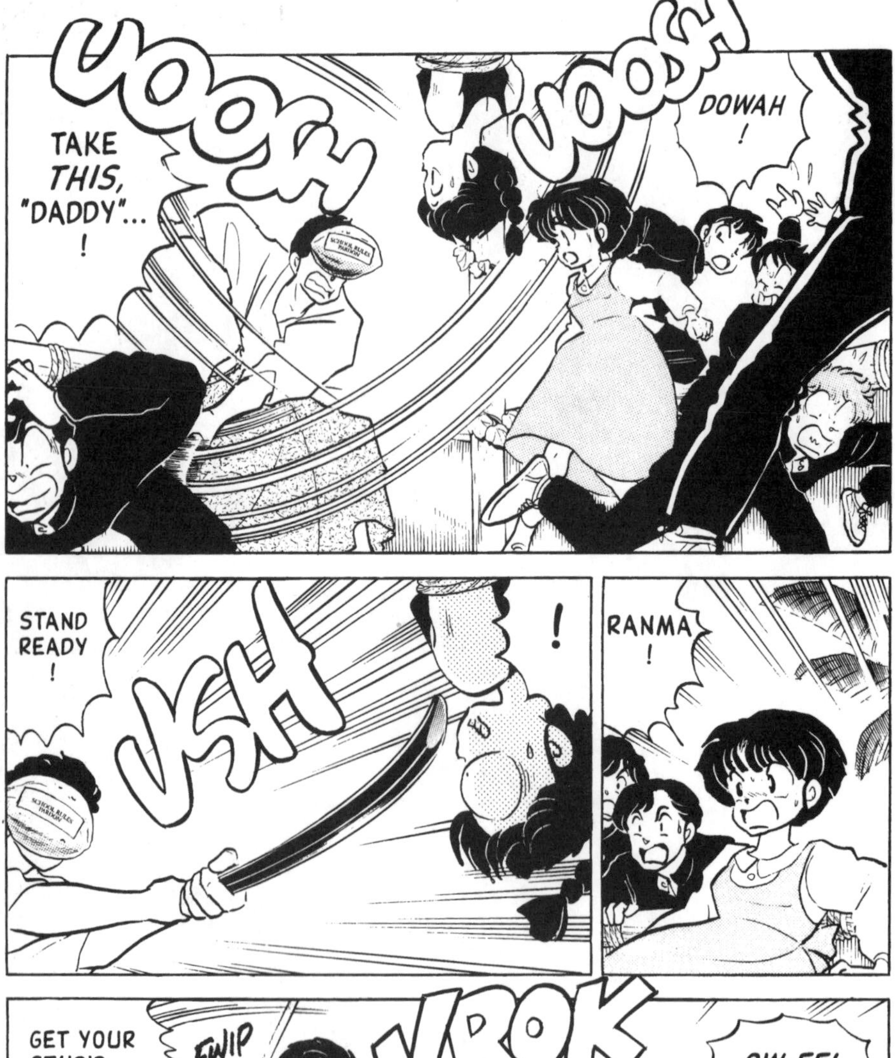
VOOSH
TAKE THIS, "DADDY"... !
VOOSH
DOWAH !
STAND READY !
VSH
!
RANMA !
GET YOUR STUPID FATHER, MORON!
FWIP
KROK
OW-EE!

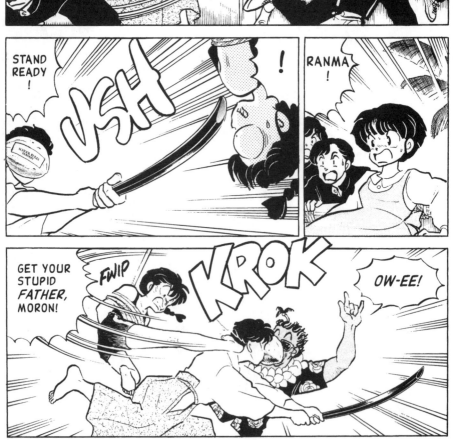

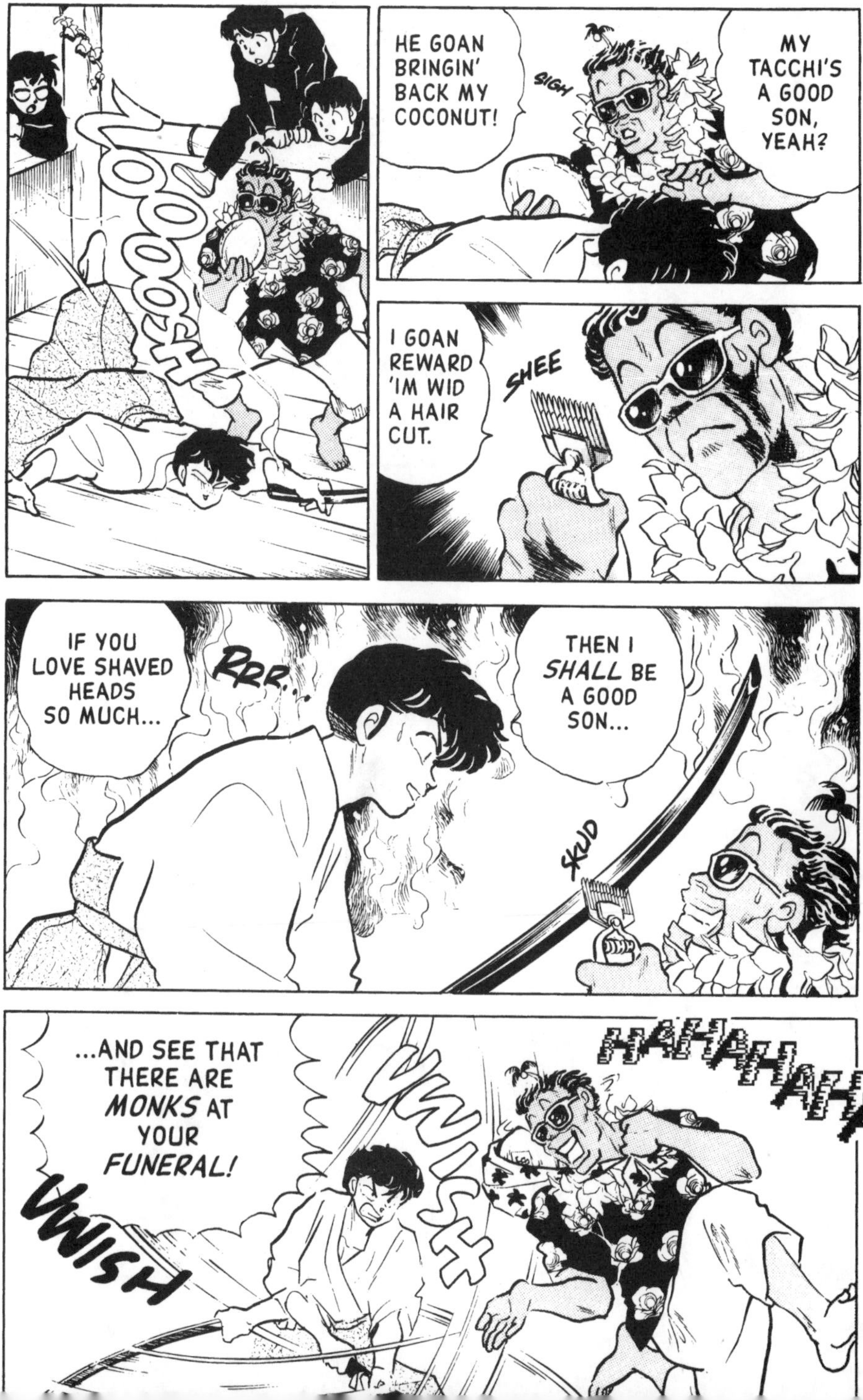
WOOOOSH
HE GOAN BRINGIN' BACK MY COCONUT!
SIGH
MY TACCHI'S A GOOD SON, YEAH?
I GOAN REWARD 'IM WID A HAIR CUT.
SHEE
IF YOU LOVE SHAVED HEADS SO MUCH...
RRR...
THEN I *SHALL* BE A GOOD SON...
SKUD
...AND SEE THAT THERE ARE *MONKS* AT YOUR *FUNERAL!*
HAHAHAHA
WWISH
WWISH

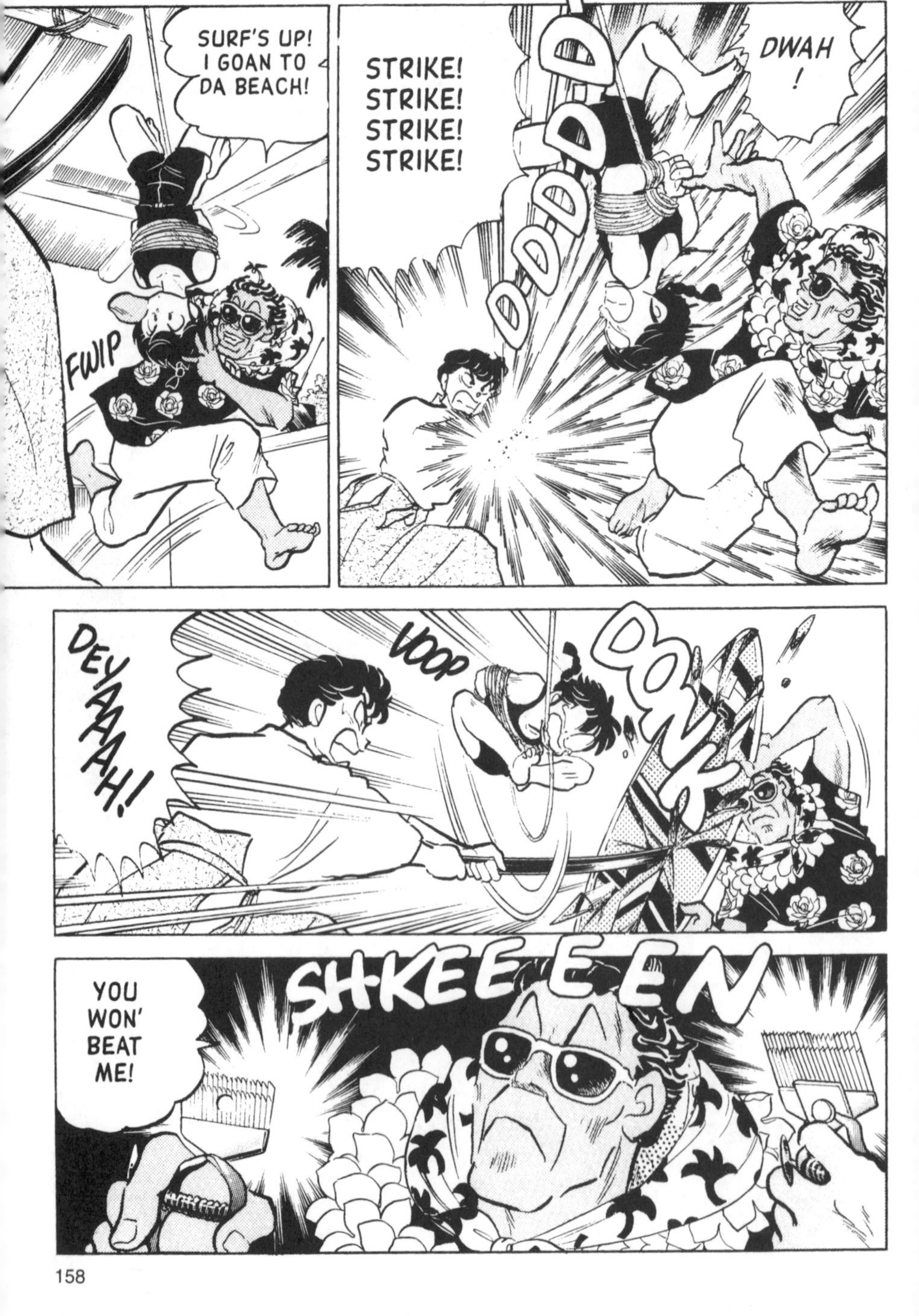
SURF'S UP! I GOAN TO DA BEACH!
FWIP
STRIKE! STRIKE! STRIKE! STRIKE!
DDDDDD
DWAH!
DEYAAAAH!
VOOP
DONK
SHKEEEEEN
YOU WON' BEAT ME!

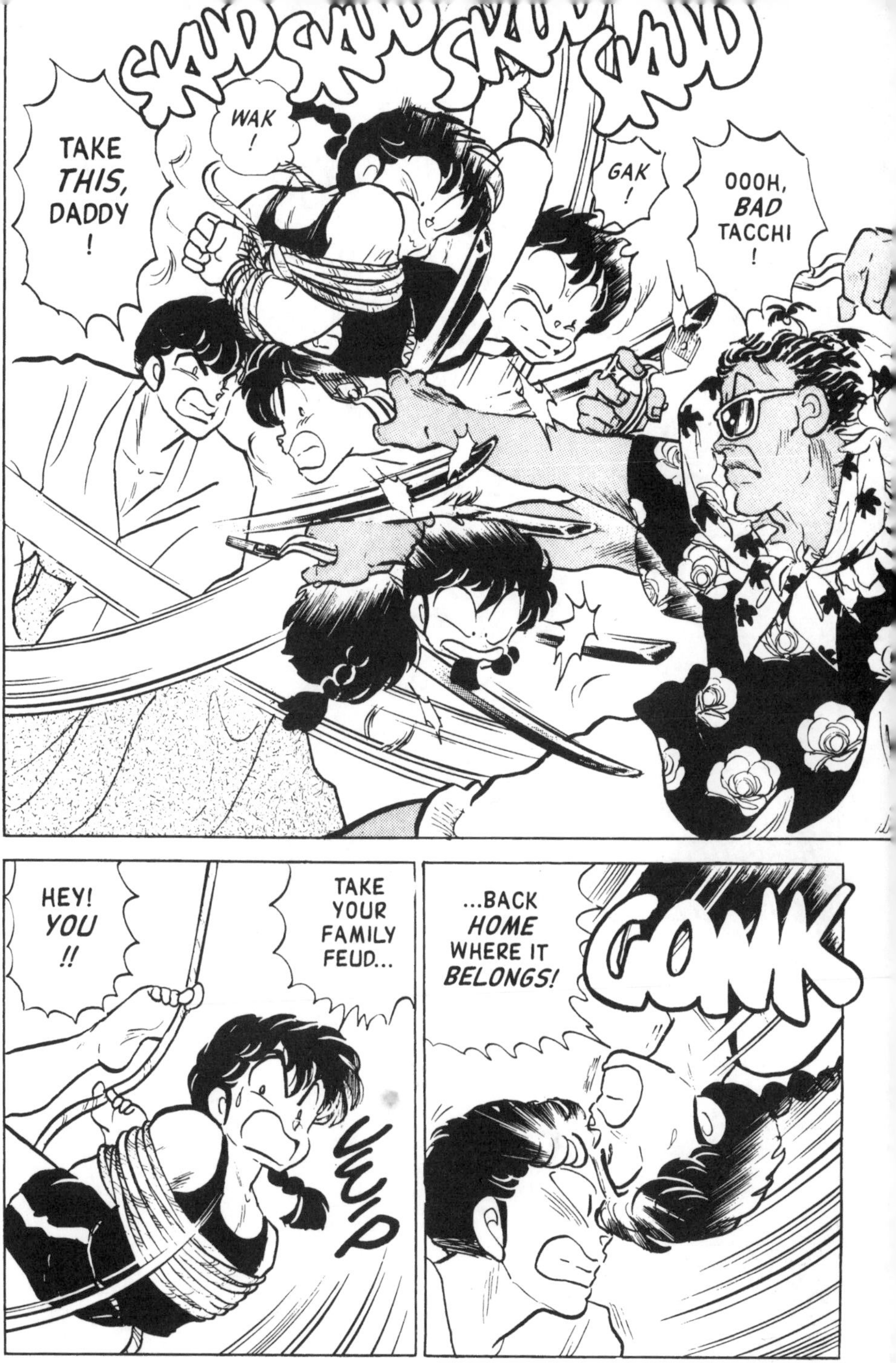
SKUD SKUD SKUD SKUD
TAKE THIS, DADDY!
WAK!
GAK!
OOOH, BAD TACCHI!
HEY! YOU!!
TAKE YOUR FAMILY FEUD...
WHIP
...BACK HOME WHERE IT BELONGS!
GONK

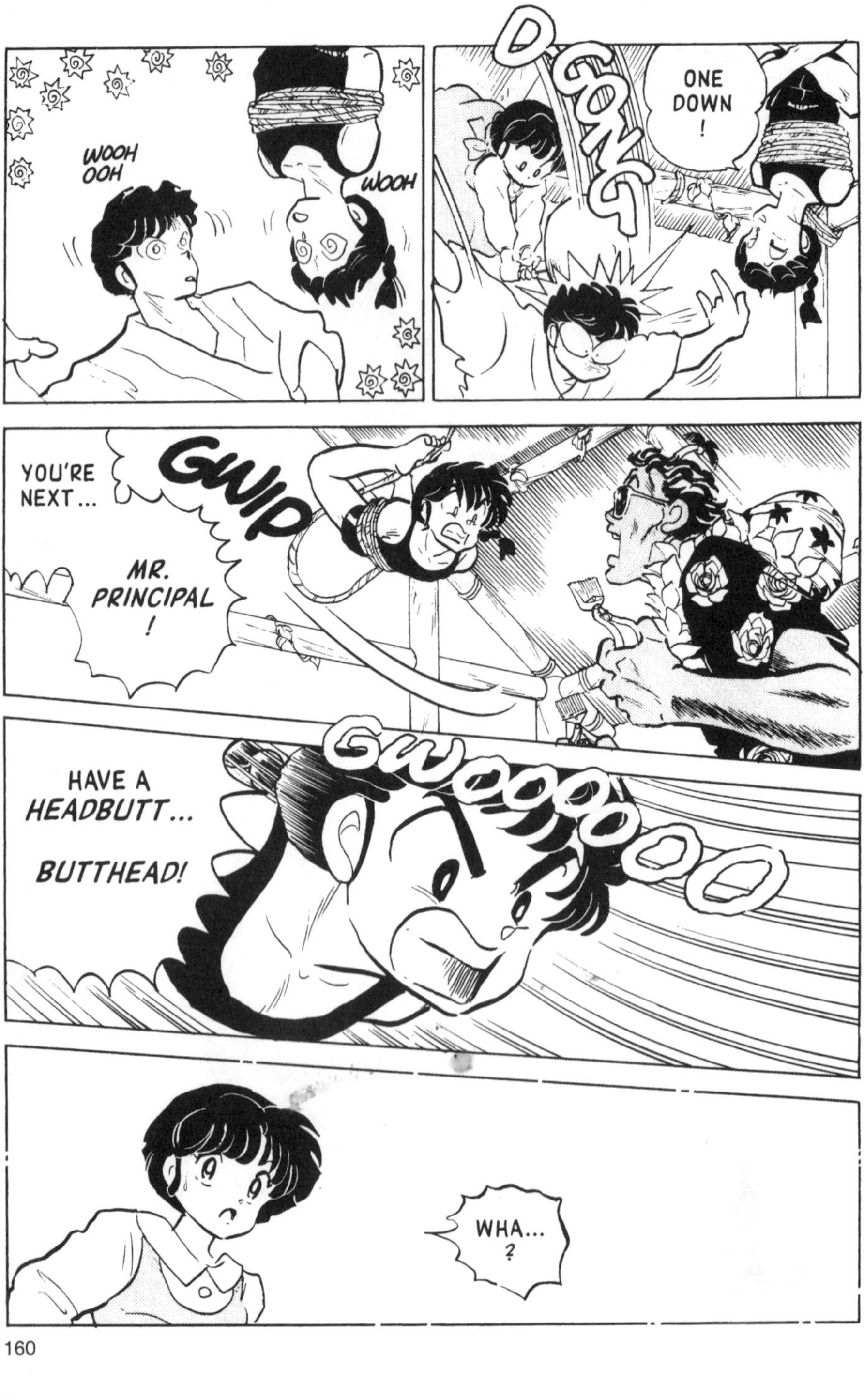
WOOH OOH
WOOH
D GONG
ONE DOWN !
YOU'RE NEXT...
GWIP
MR. PRINCIPAL !
HAVE A HEADBUTT...
BUTTHEAD!
GWOOOOOOO
WHA... ?

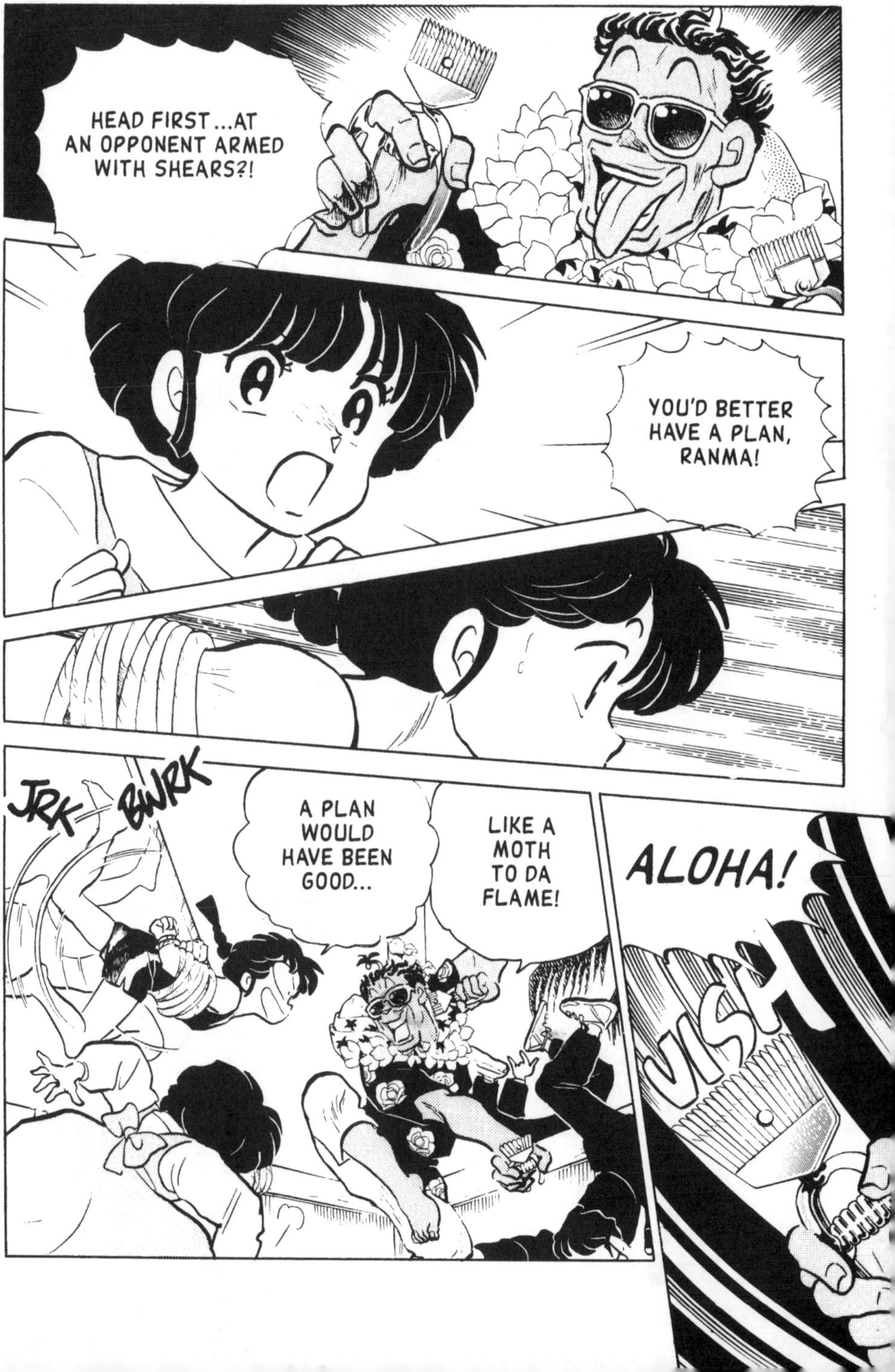
HEAD FIRST ...AT AN OPPONENT ARMED WITH SHEARS?!
YOU'D BETTER HAVE A PLAN, RANMA!
JRK
BWRK
A PLAN WOULD HAVE BEEN GOOD...
LIKE A MOTH TO DA FLAME!
ALOHA!
VISH

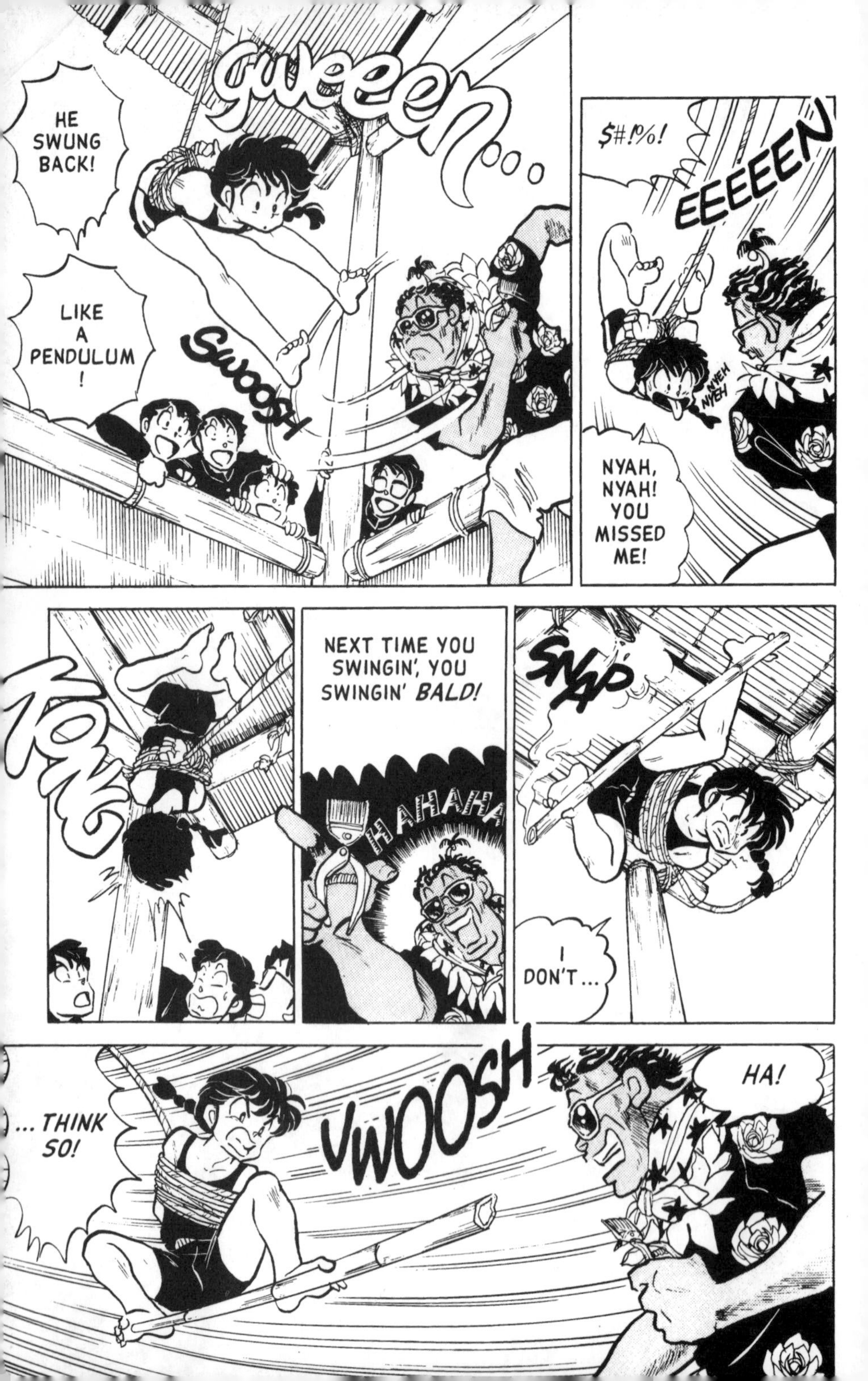

HE SWUNG BACK!
GWEEEN
OOO
LIKE A PENDULUM!
SWOOSH
$#!%!
EEEEEEN
NYEH NYEH
NYAH, NYAH! YOU MISSED ME!
TONG
NEXT TIME YOU SWINGIN', YOU SWINGIN' *BALD!*
HAHAHA
SNAP
I DON'T...
...THINK SO!
VWOOSH
HA!

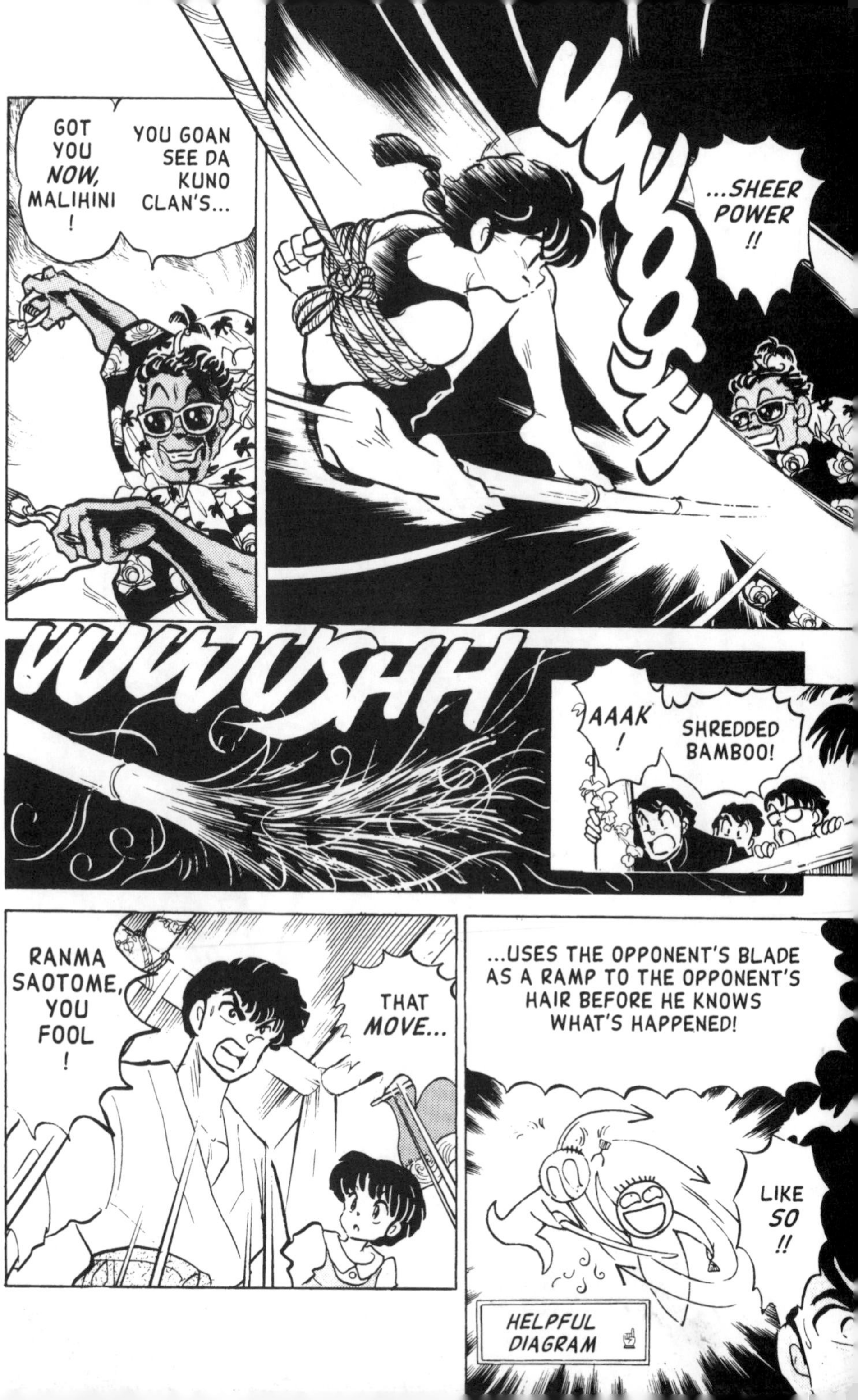
GOT YOU NOW, MALIHINI!
YOU GOAN SEE DA KUNO CLAN'S...
...SHEER POWER!!
VWOOOSH
VVVVUSHH
AAAK!
SHREDDED BAMBOO!
RANMA SAOTOME, YOU FOOL!
THAT MOVE...
...USES THE OPPONENT'S BLADE AS A RAMP TO THE OPPONENT'S HAIR BEFORE HE KNOWS WHAT'S HAPPENED!
LIKE SO!!
HELPFUL DIAGRAM

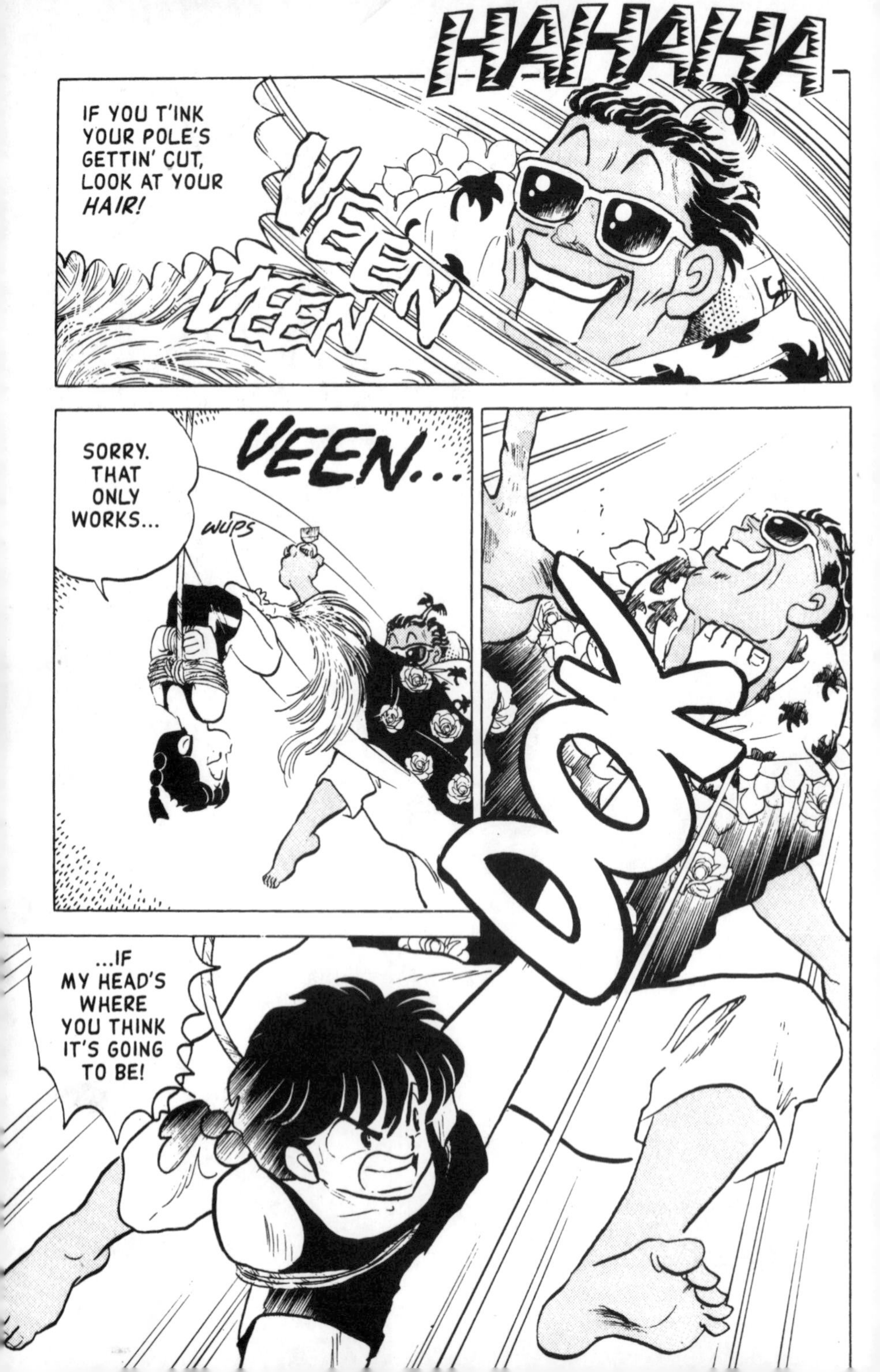
HAHAHA
IF YOU T'INK YOUR POLE'S GETTIN' CUT, LOOK AT YOUR *HAIR!*
VEEN VEEN
SORRY. THAT ONLY WORKS...
VEEN...
WUPS
DOK
...IF MY HEAD'S WHERE YOU THINK IT'S GOING TO BE!

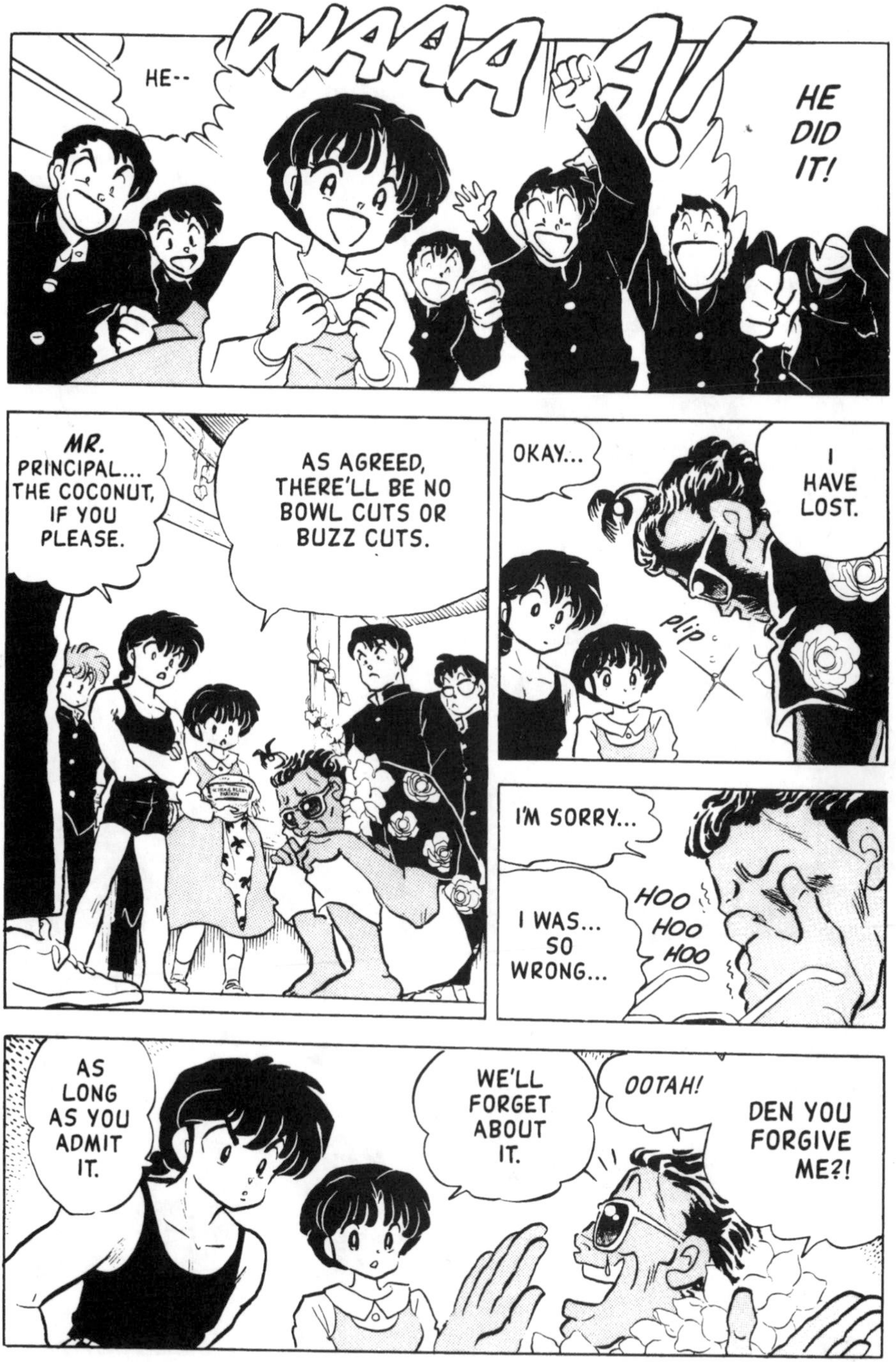
HE--
WAAAA A!
HE DID IT!
MR. PRINCIPAL... THE COCONUT, IF YOU PLEASE.
AS AGREED, THERE'LL BE NO BOWL CUTS OR BUZZ CUTS.
OKAY...
I HAVE LOST.
plip
I'M SORRY...
I WAS... SO WRONG...
HOO HOO HOO
AS LONG AS YOU ADMIT IT.
WE'LL FORGET ABOUT IT.
OOTAH!
DEN YOU FORGIVE ME?!

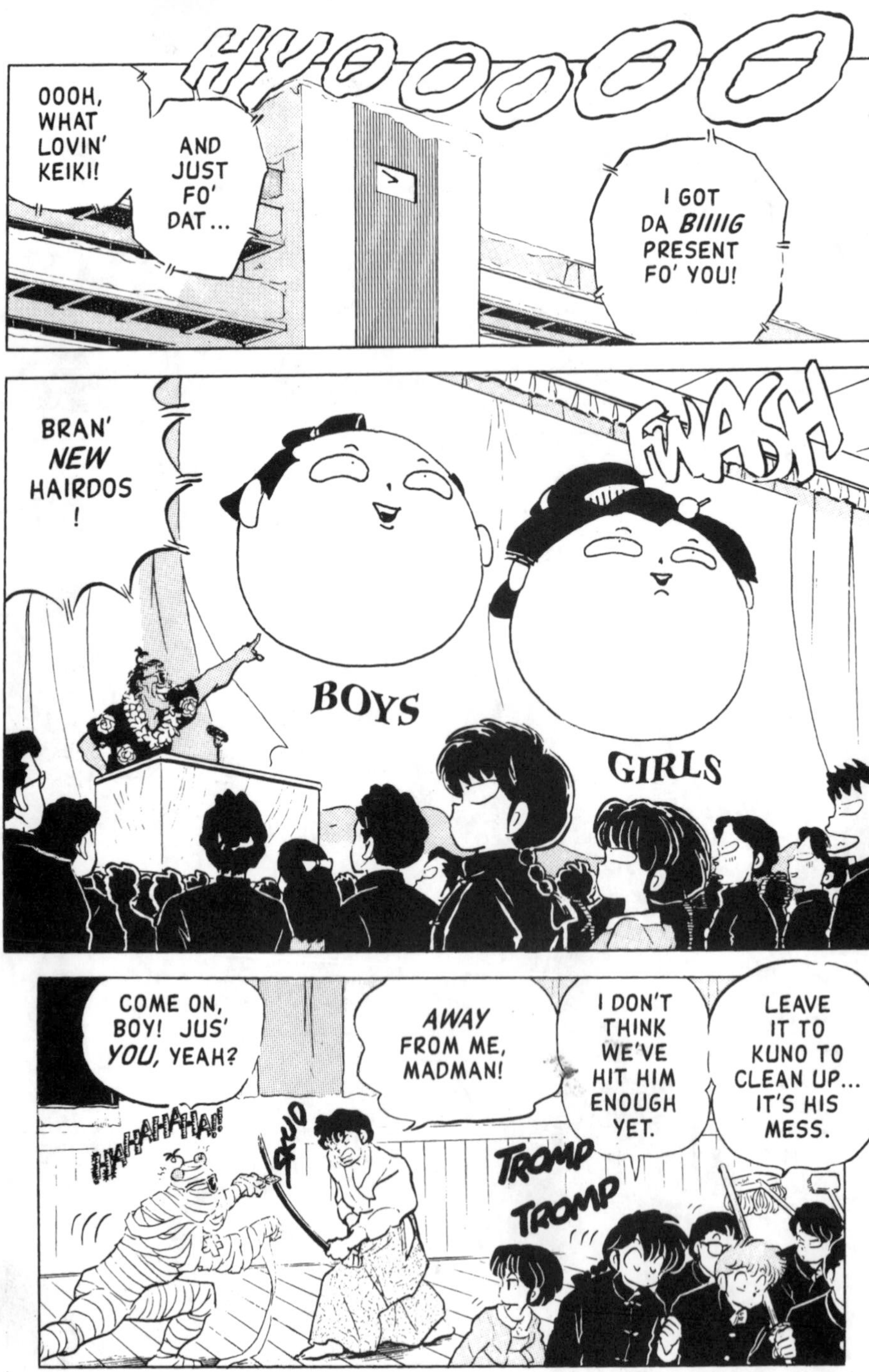
HYOOOOOO
OOOH, WHAT LOVIN' KEIKI!
AND JUST FO' DAT...
I GOT DA BIIIIG PRESENT FO' YOU!
BRAN' NEW HAIRDOS!
FWASH
BOYS
GIRLS
COME ON, BOY! JUS' YOU, YEAH?
AWAY FROM ME, MADMAN!
I DON'T THINK WE'VE HIT HIM ENOUGH YET.
LEAVE IT TO KUNO TO CLEAN UP... IT'S HIS MESS.
HAHAHAHA!
TROMP
TROMP

PART 11
GONNA MAKE YOU TARDY!

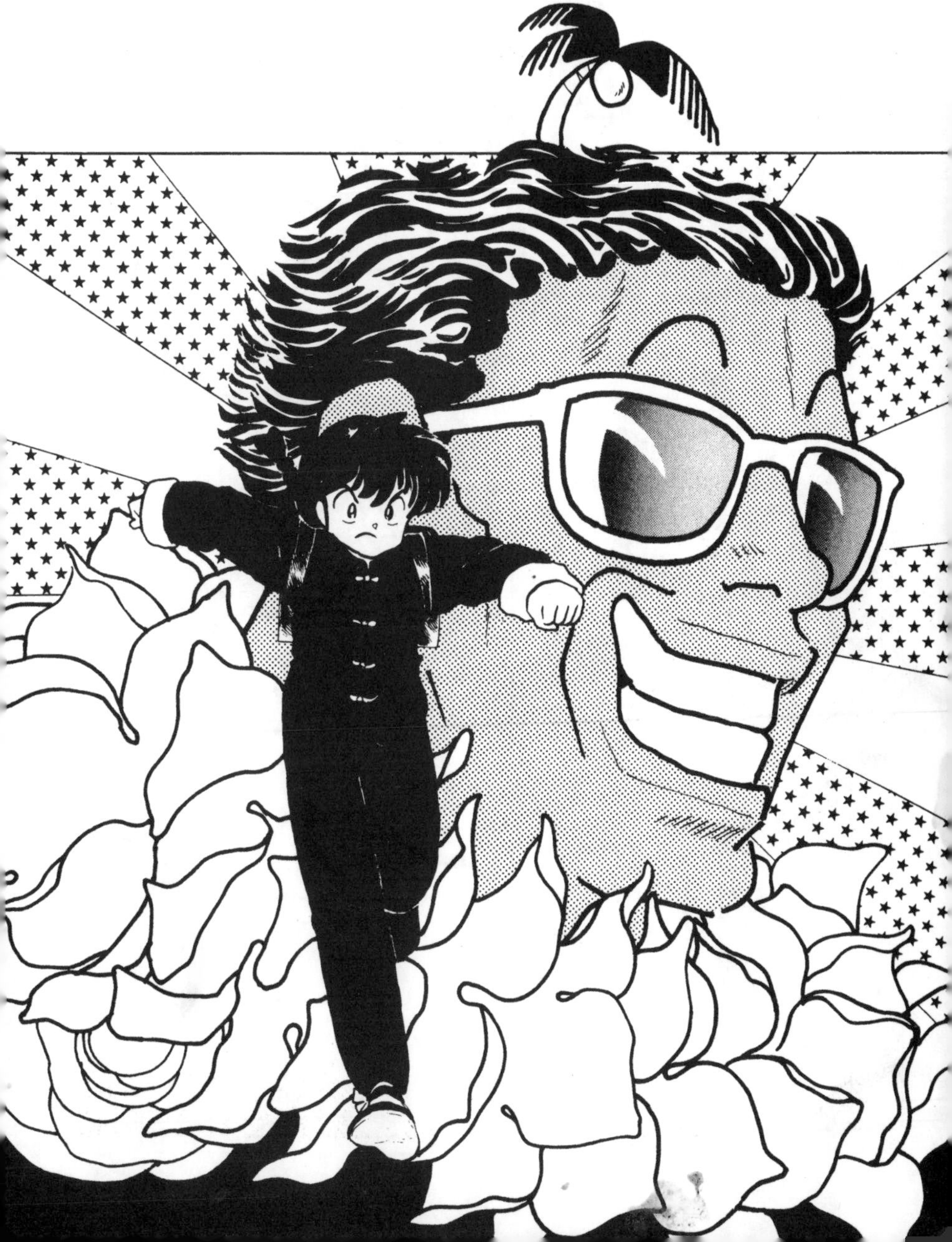

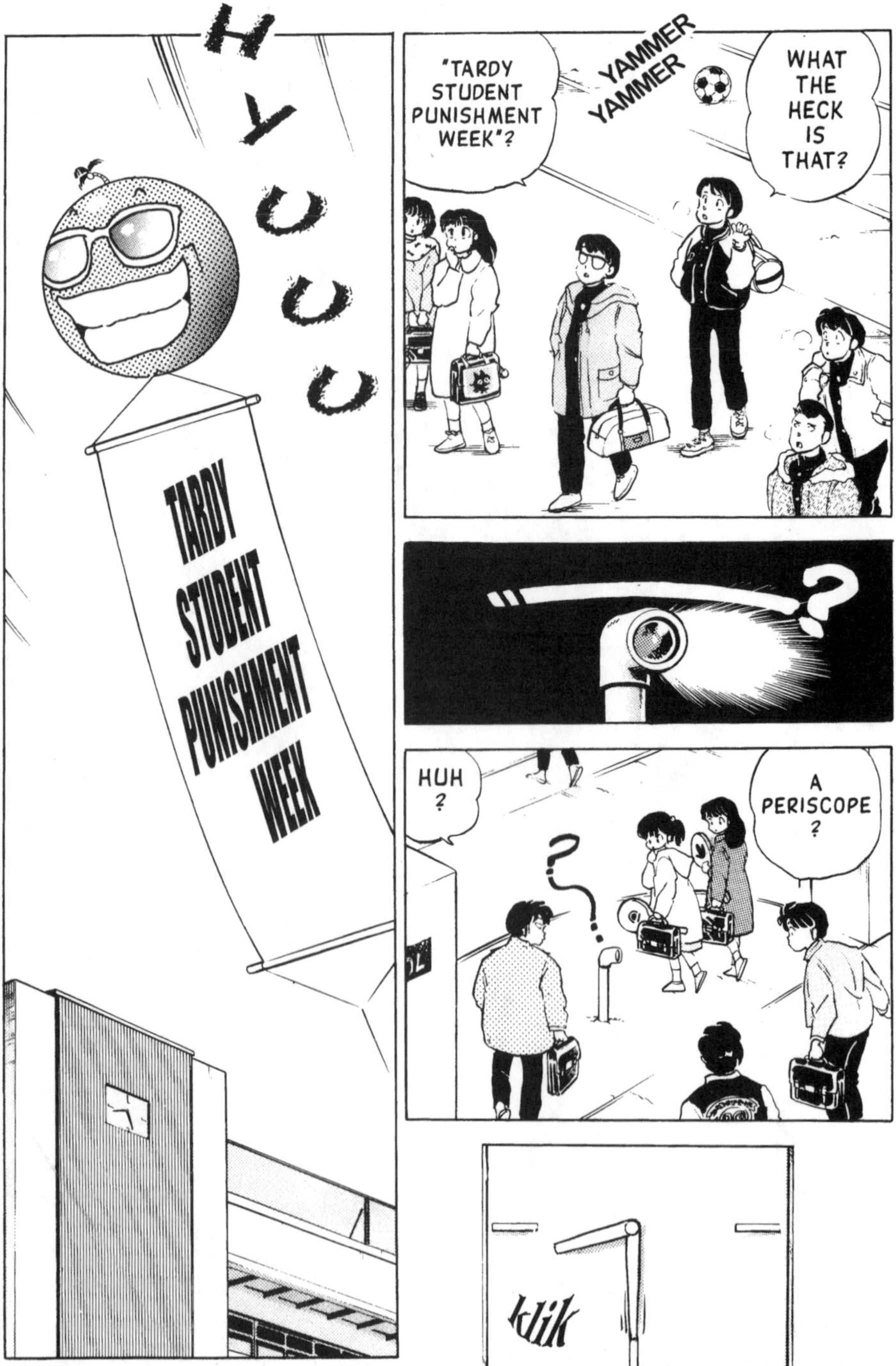
HYUUU
TARDY STUDENT PUNISHMENT WEEK
"TARDY STUDENT PUNISHMENT WEEK"?
YAMMER YAMMER
WHAT THE HECK IS THAT?
HUH?
A PERISCOPE?
klik

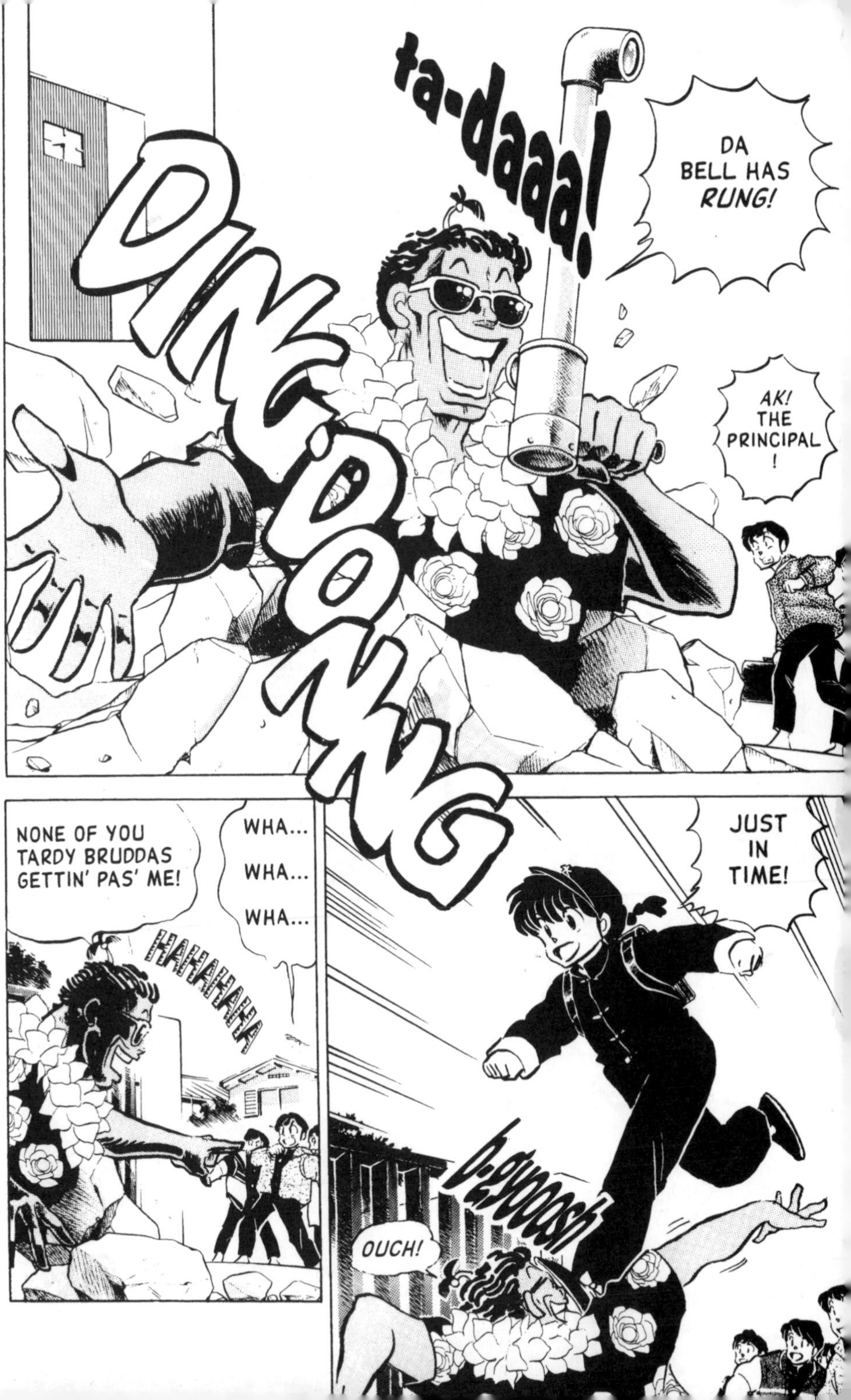
ta-daaa!
DING-DONG
DA BELL HAS RUNG!
AK! THE PRINCIPAL!
NONE OF YOU TARDY BRUDDAS GETTIN' PAS' ME!
WHA... WHA... WHA...
JUST IN TIME!
b-gyoosh!
OUCH!

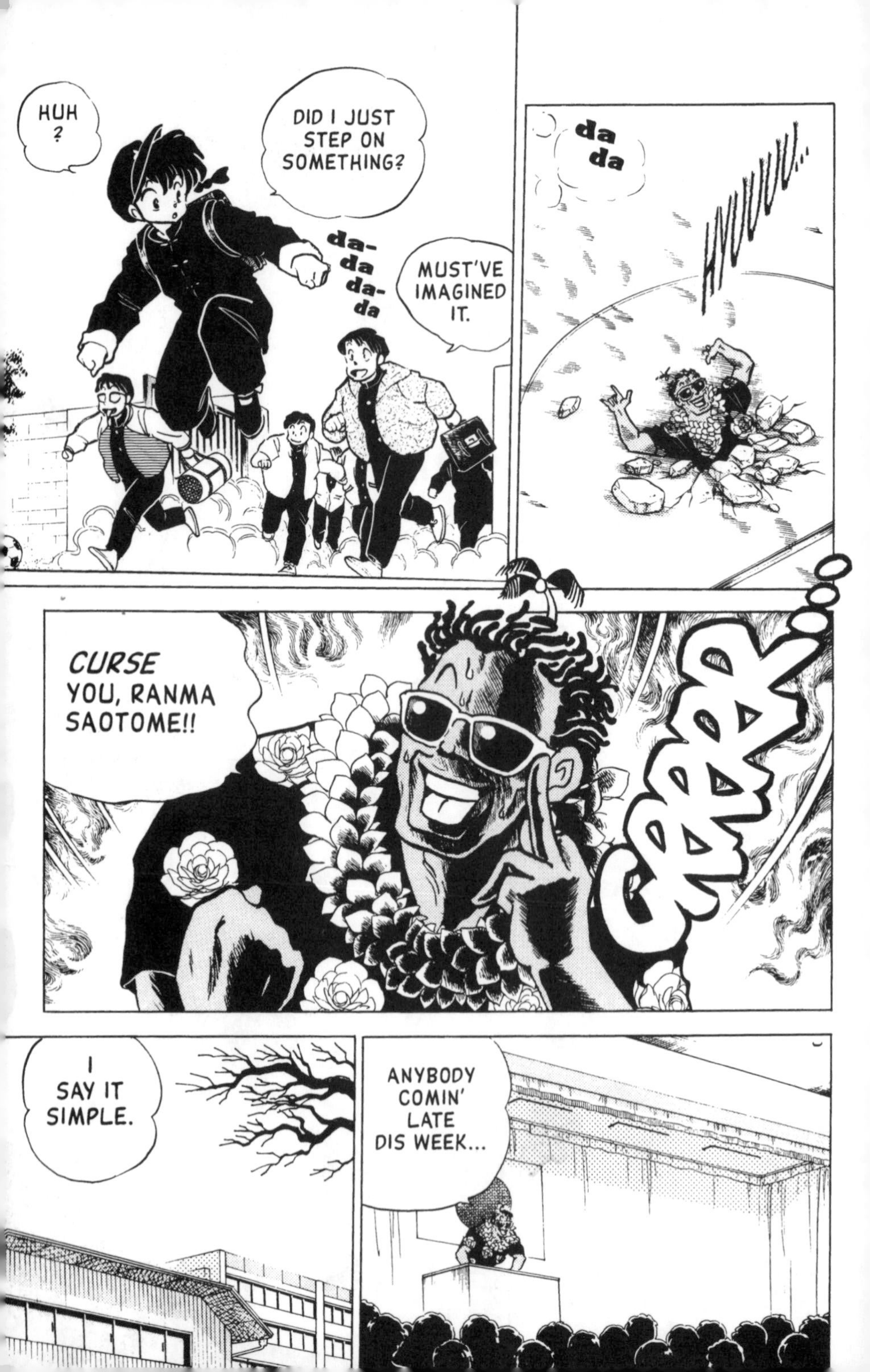
HUH ?
DID I JUST STEP ON SOMETHING?
da-da da-da
MUST'VE IMAGINED IT.
da da
HYUUUU...
CURSE YOU, RANMA SAOTOME!!
GRRRR...
I SAY IT SIMPLE.
ANYBODY COMIN' LATE DIS WEEK...

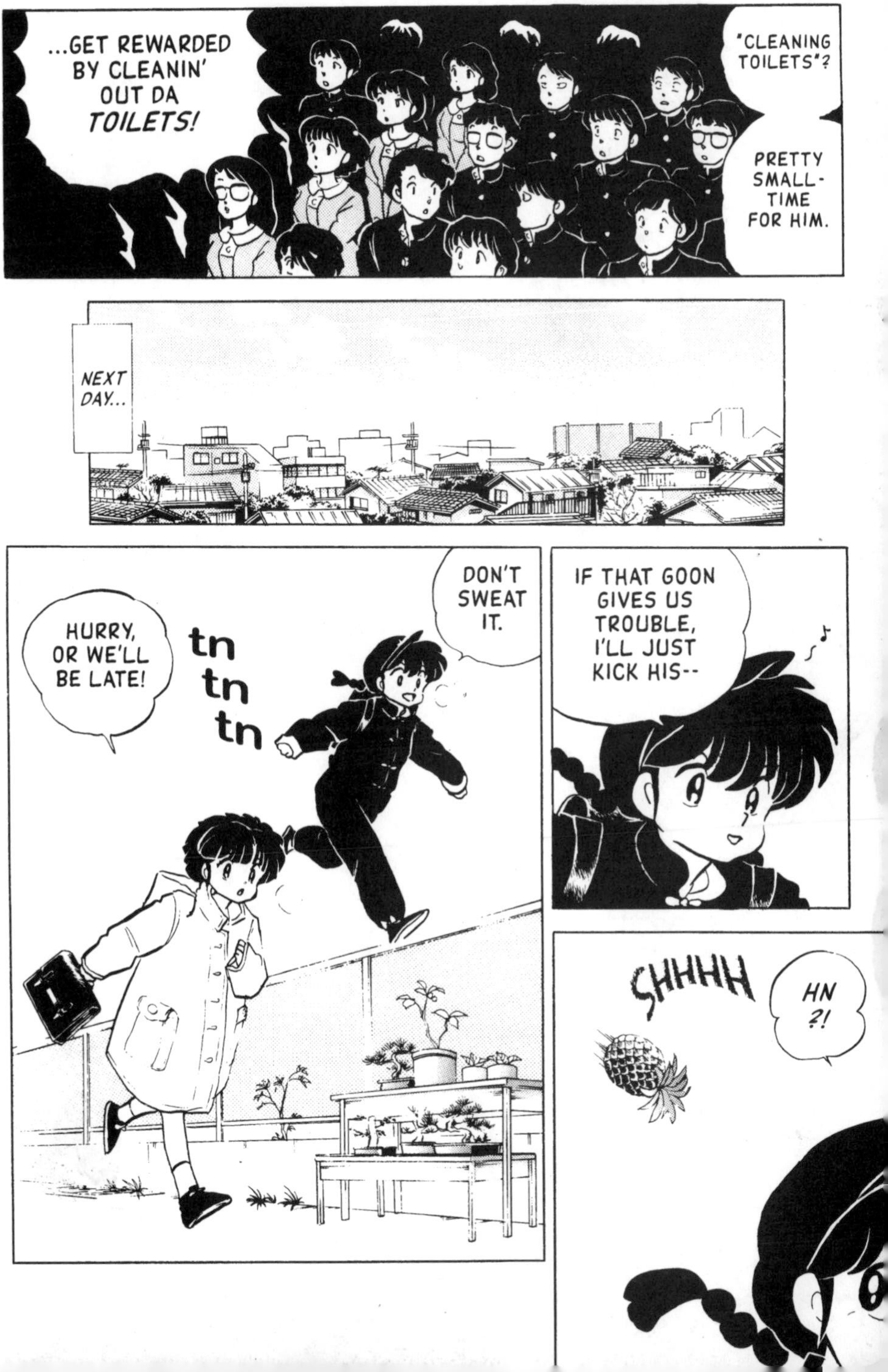
...GET REWARDED BY CLEANIN' OUT DA TOILETS!
"CLEANING TOILETS"?
PRETTY SMALL-TIME FOR HIM.
NEXT DAY...
HURRY, OR WE'LL BE LATE!
tn tn tn
DON'T SWEAT IT.
IF THAT GOON GIVES US TROUBLE, I'LL JUST KICK HIS--
SHHHH
HN ?!

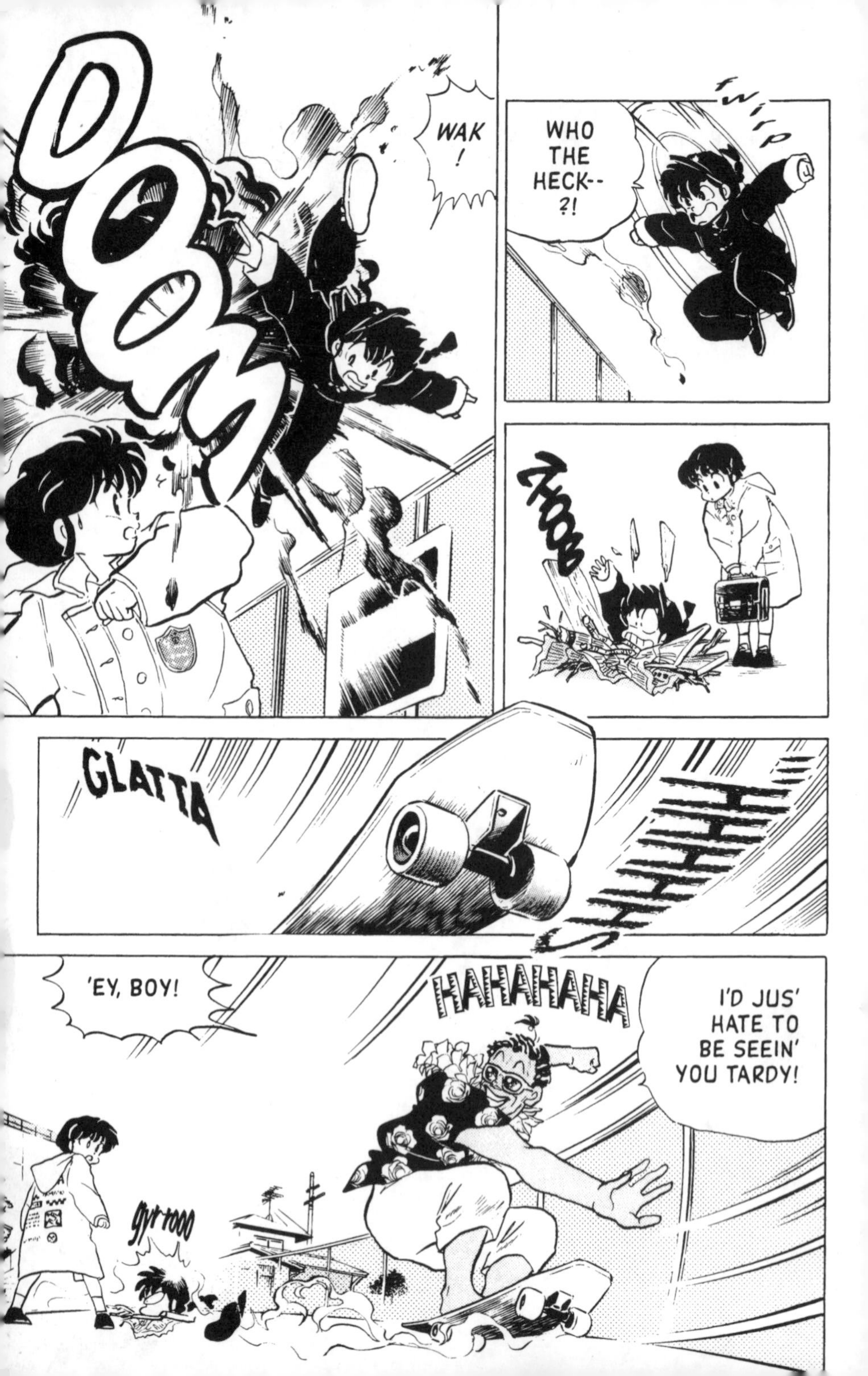

DOOM
WAK!
WHO THE HECK--?!
fwirp
ZOOB
GLATTA
'EY, BOY!
HAHAHAHA
I'D JUS' HATE TO BE SEEIN' YOU TARDY!
gyrtooo

WHY...
YOU...
YOU...

Boing

YOU!!

ta ta ta ta ta

WHAT'RE YOU UP TO NOW?!

SSHHAAAAH

RANMA SAOTOME...

...I KNOW HOW YOU GET TO SCHOOL!

YEAH?!

SO WHAT GOOD'LL THAT --

BING

'RACTIC

A MAN GOTTA BE CREATIVE, YEAH?

GET READY TO SPEN' DIS WEEK POLISHIN' PORCELAIN!

BONK

SHHA

HAHAHAHA

D.BOOOSH

RANMA!

EEARGH!

GWAAH

SHK SHK

TAKE YOUR TIME, LI'L SISTA!

GRRR...

HAHAHAHA

CHIR-RING

AT LAST! THE PIG-TAILED GIRL!

MY LOVE!

ACK! KUNO?!

GO OUT WITH ME!

ZH-DA-DA-DA-DA

POK

YOU MORON!

DO *YOU* WANNA SPEND A WEEK SCRUBBING TOILETS *TOO?!*

EH ?!

WHAT ?!

LHWA

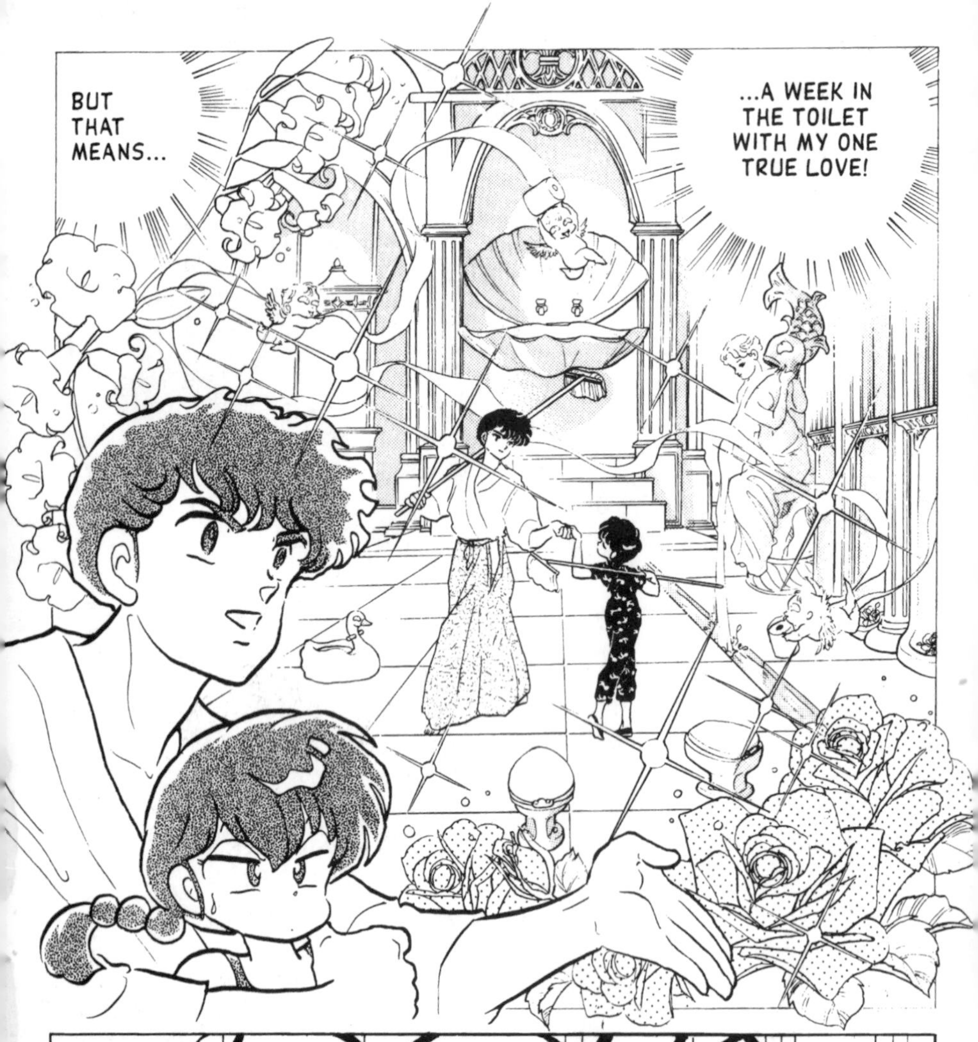
BUT THAT MEANS...
...A WEEK IN THE TOILET WITH MY ONE TRUE LOVE!
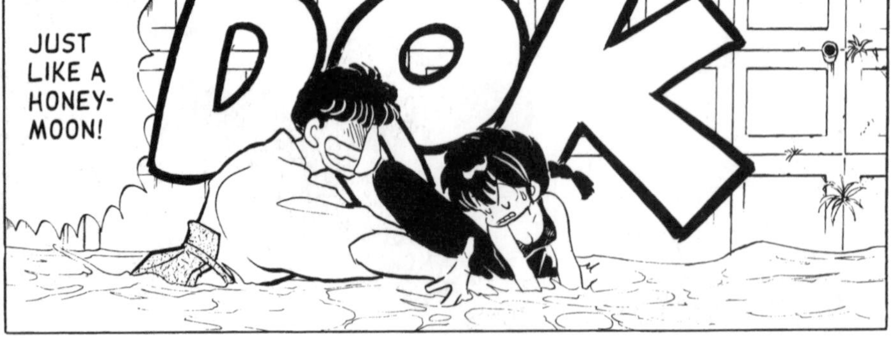
JUST LIKE A HONEY-MOON!
DOK

shtop
shtop

AUGH! TALK ABOUT A WASTE OF TIME...

ON ON ON ON ON ON ON ON

HEY RANMA! YOU FORGOT YOUR LUNCH!

HEY RANMA!

I'M TALKING TO YOU!

DADADADA

AT LEAST ANSWER ME...

PANG

¡FOOL!

HOW DO I KNOW YOU'RE THERE...

CHUMP!

BONG

CAN YOU DO THIS *AFTER* SCHOOL ?!

KAK KAK KAK KAK

TAAA!

TAKE THIS!

HYUN

TAKE THAT!

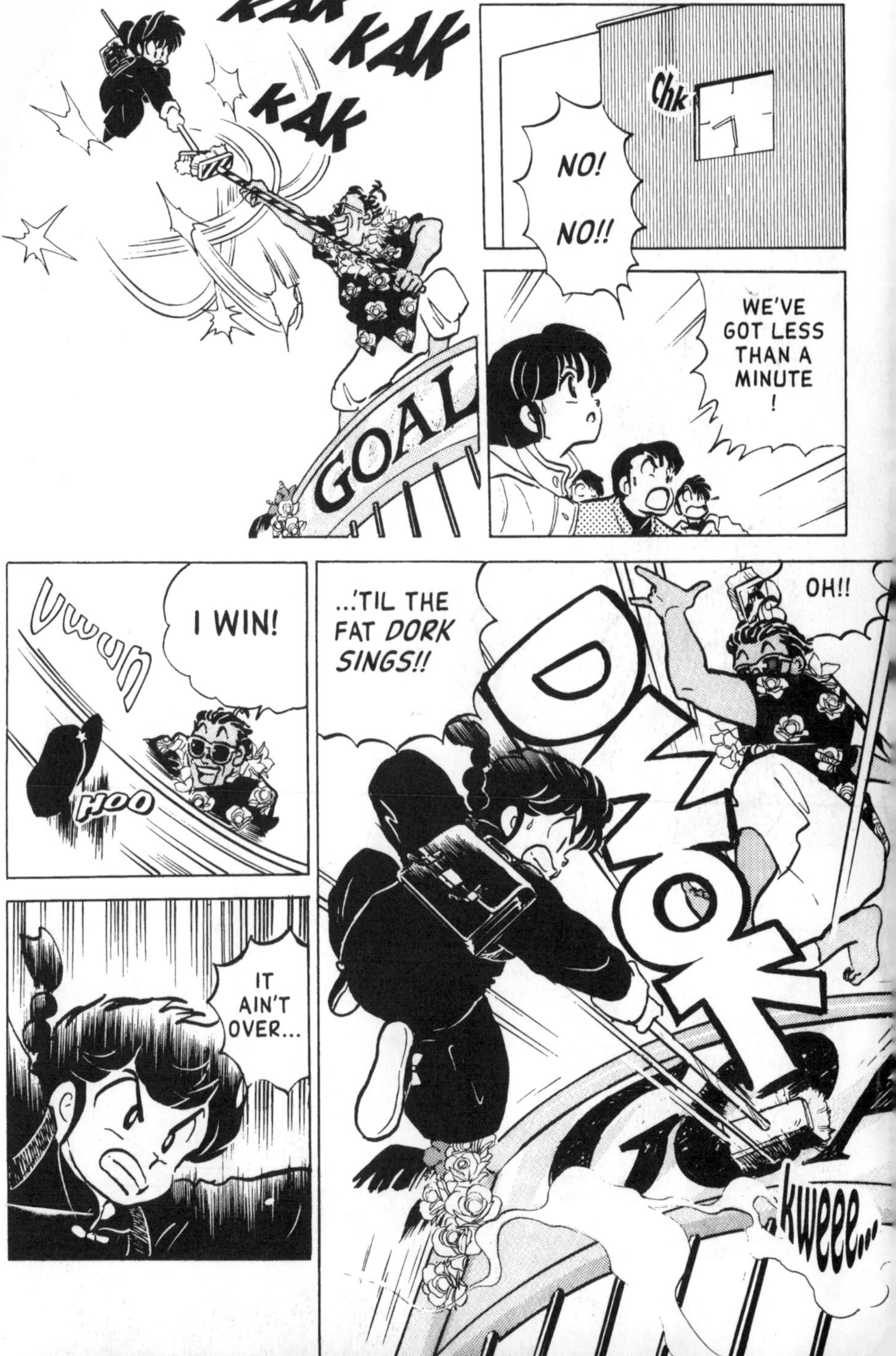
KAK KAK KAK
Chk
NO!
NO!!
WE'VE GOT LESS THAN A MINUTE!
I WIN!
HOO
IT AIN'T OVER...
...'TIL THE FAT DORK SINGS!!
OH!!
kweee...

END OF RANMA 1/2 VOL. 10.